Rumor had it that S
siastic supporter of either ~~Hitler~~
Well, Varner had his own doubts.

Casually, they walked farther from the building where the meeting was taking place. It was in the headquarters complex and command center near the Prussian city of Rastenberg. Hitler liked to come there to be away from Berlin, a city he heartily detested because of its perceived decadence.

Berliners returned the favor and did not appear to love Hitler as much as other parts of Germany did.

Sirens went off and antiaircraft guns began to fire.

Varner automatically looked skyward. "What the devil?"

A plane appeared, flying low and fast. *Dear God*, he thought. It was an American B17.

The two men ran to a slit trench and dived in just as the bombs began to explode. The earth shook with the power of the bombs and Varner felt he was back in Russia with Red Army artillery shells raining down on him. Dirt and debris rained down on them.

Finally, he sensed there was silence and lifted his head. Stauffenberg lay still in the bottom of the trench. His skull had been crushed by a falling piece of metal. Varner crawled out of the trench and gasped in horror at the desolation.

Then one thought occurred to him. What about Hitler?

BAEN BOOKS
by
ROBERT CONROY

Himmler's War

Rising Sun (forthcoming)

To purchase these and all Baen Book titles in
e-book format, please go to www.baen.com.

HIMMLER'S WAR

ROBERT CONROY

HIMMLER'S WAR

This is a work of fiction. All the characters and events portrayed in this book are fictional, and any resemblance to real people or incidents is purely coincidental.

A Baen Book

Baen Publishing Enterprises
P.O. Box 1403
Riverdale, NY 10471
www.baen.com

ISBN: 978-1-4516-3848-6

Cover art by Kurt Miller

First Baen paperback printing, November 2012

Library of Congress Control Number: 2011036877

Distributed by Simon & Schuster
1230 Avenue of the Americas
New York, NY 10020

Pages by Joy Freeman (www.pagesbyjoy.com)
Printed in the United States of America

AUTHOR'S NOTE

To humanity's dismay and grief, Adolf Hitler lived a charmed life. He could have died of wounds suffered in the First World War, yet lived on to establish the ghastly Third Reich, create the Holocaust, and initiate World War II, which then resulted in the Cold War and so much tragedy for the world. There were more than forty attempts on his life, some absurd and some very near misses, and yet he survived them all.

The most famous attempt was the conspiracy involving Claus von Stauffenberg on July 20, 1944, and this attempt arguably came closest to succeeding. However, a badly injured Hitler lived on, dragging out the war in an orgy of killing until committing suicide in a dank bunker in Berlin in April, 1945.

But what if Hitler had been killed not by an assassin but in an act of war? And what if that act was largely unexpected and accidental? It would have resulted in enormous unanticipated consequences. With Hitler gone, what would have happened to the Allies' policy of unconditional surrender? Without Hitler's nearly insane interference, would the German generals have fought a more intelligent war; thus causing massive and potentially unendurable Allied casualties?

This, of course, is the premise of *Himmler's War.* Instead of his committing suicide in the spring of 1945, my novel has Hitler dying a messy death in the summer of 1944, a full month before von Stauffenberg's conspirators would have been in place to effect a coup.

As chaos reigns, a new leader has to step forward in Germany and, in this novel, it is the murderous and sinister Heinrich Himmler. Also, with Hitler dead, this has the potential to devastate political alliances. The impact of Hitler's premature death would have had huge repercussions, and this is the story of that particular "what if."

★   ★   ★

To reduce any confusion, I have almost entirely used American equivalent ranks when discussing the German military. Aside from being difficult to spell and pronounce, the various military entities, the Waffen SS, the Volkssturm, and the regular army (the Heer), all had their own terminologies for the same ranks. The word *Wehrmacht* has been generally but incorrectly identified with the army. Wehrmacht is the umbrella term for all three services: the Luftwaffe (Air Force), the Kriegsmarine (Navy), and the Heer (Army). Also, to the best of my knowledge, no such unit as the Seventy-Fourth Armored Regiment existed in the U.S. Army during World War II.

—Robert Conroy, June 2011

HIMMLER'S WAR

★ CHAPTER 1 ★

THE B17G BOMBER WAS ALMOST UNIVERSALLY referred to as the "Flying Fortress," and for good reason. Painted olive drab on top to blend with the ground below, and with a sky blue belly for camouflage from enemies looking skyward, the bombers weighed more than thirty tons and bristled with .50 caliber machine guns. The designers at Boeing originally felt that each bomber would be able to defend itself against attacks by enemy fighters, and still deliver up to three tons of bombs far into Germany. She could speed over Europe at nearly three hundred miles an hour, had a range of nearly two thousand miles, and could fly at an altitude of more than thirty-five thousand feet. Everyone felt it was a helluva plane.

Like many well-laid plans, it didn't work out that way. Despite all her weapons, the bomber was vulnerable to attacks by German fighters, in particular the swift and deadly Messerschmitt 109G, a sleek single-engine fighter that savaged the formations when the bombers were required to fly without escorts. Since American fighters had much shorter ranges than the bombers, Nazi fighters often waited until escorts ran short of fuel and had to depart. The drop tank on the American P51 fighter was supposed to stop that and, in large part, it did. Range was extended and bombers were better protected.

But everything had gone wrong this otherwise bright and sunny day in mid-June 1944. The small flight of eighteen bombers was supposed to meet up with the escorting fighters, but the P51's never showed. Some snafu? Very likely, the angry bomber crews thought, but what the hell else was new. The flight's commander, an ambitious major who wanted to make colonel before the war ended, determined to soldier on. The fighters would either meet him or they would not. It didn't matter—he had a target to bomb and a promotion to earn. And, since the D-Day invasion at Normandy had been successful, it was thought that collapse of Nazi Germany was imminent, certainly by the end of 1944. Ergo, the major didn't have time to waste. His career was at stake.

Their target was not a high priority one. It was a factory complex near the city of Landsberg, which was north and east of Berlin. There were fewer and fewer German interceptors in the air and the major felt that this small group of bombers was unlikely to attract attention. Even though their attack would take them well into the Third Reich, it was considered little more than a training run.

Several of the eighteen bomber crews were on their first combat flight, and that included the men of the *Mother's Milk*. The name had been chosen while several of the crew had been drunk on English beer, and they compounded their mistake by hiring an artist of dubious talent who painted a farm girl on the fuselage. She wore a halter top, extremely short shorts that showed much of her cheeks, and a toothy smile. And she had grotesquely enormous boobs that other crews considered laughable, which pissed off the *Milk*'s rookie crew who were further teased by being called "Milkmen." They accepted the nickname and used it among themselves.

Twenty-four-year-old First Lieutenant Paul Phips was her commander and he was scared to death as well as freezing his ass off. He was not a warrior. Small of stature and slight of build, he reminded people of a Midwestern grocery clerk, not a bomber pilot. The truth was not that far off. He'd been in his first year as a high school teacher in Iowa when the draft grabbed him, and he still had no idea how he'd passed flight school.

This run had been their initial exposure to possible combat and that had caused more than enough stress. The more experienced crews had teased them, calling them Virgins or Cherries, and saying they'd shit their pants the first time they were shot at, all of which didn't help the crew's fragile morale.

As always, they were cold, despite the fact that they were wearing multiple layers of clothing. The wind whipped through the bomber, and their heavy flight suits, even though they were plugged into the plane like electric blankets, didn't do much. The fear and the cold sapped their resolve and the Milkmen wondered just why they had become bomber crewmen.

Before they dropped their bombs, disaster struck.

They'd been jumped by a dozen or more of the alleg-edly nonexistent ME109's that knifed down from above and shot down or damaged several bombers before anyone could even notice. So much for "Don't worry about German planes," Phips and his crew thought as they maneuvered wildly to evade their swift enemy.

Their flight commander's plane was one of the first destroyed, which rendered the remaining crews leader-less. As the fight became a mindless brawl, Phips had made a major mistake. He'd run. Instead of staying with the survivors and forming up defensively, Phips had sent his plane lower in altitude and flown to the west in the hope that he could escape the attacking German sharks.

Instead, two of the MEs had stayed with him, chasing the bomber and dogging it. Phips swore that they were taunting him as he gradually gained control over the bomber and his fears.

"What the hell do we do now, Skipper?" asked his copilot, Second Lieutenant Bill Stover. The sarcastic tone of voice was not lost on Phips, who was well aware that he'd panicked and screwed up royally.

Stover continued, "In case you haven't noticed, they're chasing us south and west. In a while we'll run out of gas and have to bail out even if they don't manage to shoot us down first."

"I know," Phips muttered. Despite the cold, he was sweating profusely.

The tail gunner, Sergeant Ballard, broke in. At thirty, he was the old man and his deep voice had a calming effect. "Skipper, it looks like one of them is pulling back. Maybe he's running out of fuel."

Phips prayed it was so. The ME only had a range

of about three hundred miles and must have used up a lot of gas chasing the bombers around the sky. Maybe the second one would have the same problem.

No such luck. As time dragged on, the lone ME stayed behind them, darting in and out, firing an occasional burst, and looking for an opportunity to make a kill. The German respected the bomber's many guns, which fired short bursts every time he got within range. It looked like an impasse but it wasn't. As long as he had fuel, the German held all the trump cards. At least they were low enough that the men of *Mother's Milk* didn't need oxygen to breathe.

"Skipper, will you take a suggestion from your beloved navigator?"

Phips managed a weak smile. "Yes, Mr. Kent."

"We are getting farther and farther away from Mother England. If you want me to find our way home, we've got to stop this running shit and head back."

Damn it, Phips thought. It was time to make up for his mistake. "Okay, we turn and attack the bastard."

The German must have thought that the plane's sudden and sharp banking to the right was an indication of damage and he dashed in for the kill with his machine guns and 20mm cannon blazing. Pieces flew off the bomber, and Phips heard shouting through his headset. Loose items caromed off the inside of the hull.

"Carson's hit!" someone yelled. Christ, Phips thought. One of the waist gunners was down. "Oh, Jesus, he's bleeding all over the place." The wounded man's screams carried up to Phips, who felt nauseated as the bomber continued its stately turn.

Suddenly, the German fighter pilot found himself facing an array of .50 caliber machine guns from the side, top, and belly that spewed torrents of bullets in his direction. Now it was the German's turn to panic and he tried to escape. As he did so, he exposed the belly of his plane for just an instant. A handful of bullets ripped through his engine. It started to smoke and the ME began to fall back.

"Christ almighty," yelled Stover. "We got us a kill."

The German pilot fell from the plane and a parachute opened. The ME was gone, but the pilot would live to fight another day. Now the *Mother's Milk* had to do the same damn thing—live to fight another day.

"How's Carson?" Phips asked.

"Dead, sir."

Phips sagged over the controls. His first mission and not only had he disobeyed orders to keep formation, but he'd gotten lost, and a crewman, one of the guys he'd been with for six months, had been killed. Now he had to make sure this miserable situation didn't get any worse.

"Navigator," said Phips. "Where are we?"

"Over Germany, Skipper."

Damn smart aleck, Phips thought. "Can you possibly narrow that down, Kent?"

"Seriously, Skipper, I'm trying, but we were all over the sky for a little while and I need a frame of reference. I think we're over East Prussia and now we are heading towards Russia. I suggest we turn north and west and hope to God we find something that makes sense, like the Baltic Sea. I also suggest we lighten our load. We've got a few tons of bombs doing nothing but weighing us down and using up our fuel."

Stover turned toward Phips, his expression still unforgiving. "We can go north to Sweden if we have to, bail out, and be interned. That assumes, of course, that we can even find Sweden."

"Yeah," Phips responded angrily, "and we'd be interned for the duration of the war and who knows how long that'll be. The experts say it'll be over in a few months, but with our luck it might just be decades. It also presumes that the Swedes won't turn us over to the Nazis. I hear the Swedes spend a lot of time kissing Hitler's ass since the krauts are right next door to them. And, oh yeah, we might just accidentally bail out over Nazi-occupied Norway or over those nice people in Stalin's Soviet Union."

It was common knowledge that Russia had interned some American and British fliers and wasn't keen on returning them. Winding up chopping frozen rocks in Siberia was not a pleasant option.

Kent chimed in. "Again, I suggest we turn north and west in hopes of finding the Baltic. At that point, I further suggest we stay over the water until we hit Denmark, and I mean that figuratively and not literally."

"Good." agreed Phips. "And then we can cut the angle by flying over Denmark. I don't think the krauts will waste sending fighters after one lousy lost bomber." Of course, he thought, nobody thought their little flight of eighteen bombers would have been attacked by so many German fighters.

"Sounds like a good plan to me," Kent said, and Stover sullenly nodded agreement. "But when are you going to dump the bombs? We will need that fuel if we're going to make it back."

"I don't have a target," Phips said.

Stover shook his head in disbelief. "Christ, Chief, we're only a couple of thousand feet over Germany.

The whole fucking country's a target. Just drop the damn things."

Phips thought for a second and decided he agreed. Finally he felt he was doing the right thing. Maybe he could recover from this nightmarish day. Back in England, he'd be criticized for his mistakes and the loss of Carson, but maybe, just maybe, he'd be allowed to learn from those mistakes and fly again. Regardless, his first job was to get his crew home.

"Just for the record," he said, "does anybody see anything that even remotely looks like it could use a good bombing?"

Stover's eyes were the sharpest. "Looks like a cluster of buildings coming up in the woods to our right front. And I don't see any red crosses or anything."

"Got it," said Cullen, the combination nose gunner and bombardier. "We'll use the Norden and drop bombs in their helmets."

It was a feeble attempt at a joke. The super-secret Norden bomb-sight was better than what anybody'd had before, but it was far from precise. Even at their low altitude, they'd be lucky to hit the compound.

"What the hell?" Phips said in surprise. Antiaircraft guns had opened up at the last second and black puffs of flak were exploding well above them. Whoever was down there was as surprised as he was. At least their shooting was off.

The bomb bay doors opened and more cold wind whipped through the plane. They might be closer to the ground and it might be the middle of summer, but it was still like being in a savage winter storm. A few seconds later, the bombs fell, and *Mother's Milk,* freed from their weight, lifted. Now Phips and the Milkmen really began to feel that they might just make it back to England.

"Anybody see if we hit anything?" Phips asked.

The only one with a view of the target was Ballard, the tail gunner. "Well, sir, we did hit the ground. Seriously, some of the bombs did fall in that cluster of buildings. Not a clue as to what kind of damage we might have caused. Looks like we've outrun the flak, though."

And we'll probably never know what we hit, Phips thought. An unwanted realization popped into his head. If they did make it back, he'd have to write a letter to Carson's family explaining how he'd died heroically and painlessly when the poor guy had really died screaming and bleeding all over the plane like a stuck pig.

A few hours later they had crossed Denmark and were again over water. They sighted a gray smudge on the horizon. Kent assured Phips it was England, Mother England, and they all breathed a sigh of relief. They were very low on fuel. A pair of British Hurricanes flew by and took up position on either side. They were used to nursing cripples and would guide *Mother's Milk* back to an airfield. They'd be on fumes when they landed, but they had made it. It was the middle of June 1944. Allies had landed in Normandy and the men of the *Mother's Milk* were still part of the war.

Finally, Phips could relax. He did wonder just what they had managed to bomb on their first and so far only run over Germany. He hoped to God it wasn't a girls' school or an orphanage. But then, how many girls' schools were protected by antiaircraft guns?

★   ★   ★

Colonel Ernst Varner walked away from the undistinguished one-story wood building that was jammed with the military hierarchy of the Third Reich. For the moment it was the site of the OKW, the Oberkommando der Wehrmacht, the headquarters of the German military. The Wehrmacht controlled the regular army, the Heer; the navy, the Kriegsmarine; and the air force, the Luftwaffe. A walk in the surrounding woods was what Varner needed to clear his head. The air within the building was stale in more ways than one.

Varner had been inside a few moments earlier and had actually heard Adolf Hitler speak emotionally and illogically about solutions to the military dilemma confronting Germany. And, the more he heard his Fuhrer pontificate, the more he realized the little man with the mustache was delusional at best.

Varner hadn't always felt that way about his Fuhrer. As a younger man he'd been an ardent supporter of Hitler and an early member of the Nazi Party, which had, in part, helped him reach his current rank at the age of thirty-eight. Of course, being a legitimate hero and combat veteran who'd seen action in both France and Russia hadn't hurt, either. His wounds suffered fighting the Russians were still healing and it was decided that he would serve better as a staff officer and aide to Field Marshal Wilhelm Keitel, the army's Chief of Staff and a man Varner had come to realize was little more than a spineless toady. Keitel would not question Hitler's orders no matter how preposterous they were. And many of them were well beyond preposterous. The chief of operations, General Alfred Jodl, was even worse. Both would simply nod and send men out to die.

Varner had been told he'd soon be promoted to general, but now wondered if it was worth it if he had to suffer working for fools like Keitel and Jodl.

Varner reached for a cigarette and recalled that he had given up smoking at the insistence of his wife, Magda, and his fourteen-year-old daughter, Margarete. They said it was a disgusting habit. Varner agreed, especially since the only cigarettes available in wartime Germany were absolute shit rolled in paper. He'd picked up the smoking habit to contain stress while fighting the Red Army outside Stalingrad. Now he needed to combat the stress of listening to Hitler.

"Here," said a voice from behind.

Varner laughed and took a cigarette from a fellow staffer, Colonel Claus von Stauffenberg. They had met in the hospital while being treated for their respective wounds. The darkly handsome Stauffenberg had lost his left eye, right hand, and two fingers on his left hand when his vehicle had been strafed in North Africa. Varner had been wounded in his upper left arm and shoulder, and doctors were still trying to remove shrapnel that moved and sometimes caused him great pain. Varner was shorter than the lean and aristocratic Stauffenberg. He was stocky, like a tank. This was serendipitous since Varner's specialty was armor. His dark hair was thinning and he was thankful that Margarete got her pixy looks from Magda, a woman he thought was far above him. Varner would never be mistaken for a blond and blue-eyed Aryan superman.

Between the two of them, they managed to light up. As always, the cigarettes were awful.

"Why aren't you in there with the others?" Varner asked.

Stauffenberg almost snorted. "Because it's too crowded and they don't need me to help them make their mistakes. I think it's incredible that there's still doubt as to whether the Allied landings in Normandy are the real thing or are just a feint. The Fuhrer does seem to be coming around, however, and no longer insists that Pas de Calais is the eventual main target instead of Normandy. However, the decision has come too late to throw the Allies out."

Varner was surprised at the other man's candor. Stauffenberg's comments were dangerously close to a criticism of Hitler, which was not a wise thing to do, especially for a relatively low-ranking staff officer, hero or not. Disagreements had a nasty habit of being interpreted as treason. Some very high-ranking generals had argued with the Fuhrer and were now languishing in obscurity.

He and Stauffenberg, while friendly and cordial, were not close enough to share intimate thoughts, and Varner wondered just what the other colonel was thinking. Was he being sounded out, and if so for what purpose? Rumor had it that Stauffenberg was not an enthusiastic supporter of either Hitler or the Nazi Party. Well, Varner now had his own doubts.

Varner decided to make light of it. "I left because it was obvious I wasn't important enough to stay."

Stauffenberg laughed. "Perhaps being unimportant is a good thing. If you're careful, you can become invisible."

Casually, they walked farther from the building where the meeting was taking place. It was in the headquarters complex and command center near the Prussian city of Rastenberg. Hitler liked to come there to be away from Berlin, a city he heartily detested because of its perceived decadence. Hitler had few vices. He rarely drank and ate sparingly. Varner thought Hitler had a mistress, a plump blonde named Eva, but no one was certain. Varner decided he didn't care.

Berliners returned the favor and did not appear to love Hitler as much as other parts of Germany did. Most of the field marshals and generals vastly preferred the luxuries and flesh pots of Berlin. Varner would have preferred being in Berlin, but only because his small family was there.

Sirens went off and antiaircraft guns began to fire. Varner automatically looked skyward. "What the devil?"

A plane appeared, flying low and fast. A bomber. *Dear God,* he thought. It was an American B17.

The two men ran to a slit trench and dived in just as the bombs began to explode. The earth shook with the power of the bombs and Varner felt he was back in Russia with Red Army artillery shells raining down on him. He tried to control his fear. Shock waves washed over him and he realized he couldn't hear. Dirt and debris rained down on them.

Finally, he sensed there was silence and lifted his head. Stauffenberg lay still in the bottom of the trench. His skull had been crushed by a falling piece of metal, and his one eye was dangling out of its socket. Varner crawled out of the trench and gasped in horror at the desolation. Then one thought occurred to him. What about Hitler?

He lurched to the building he'd just left. It was in ruins. There were great clouds of smoke, but little in the way of flames came from it. Survivors were staggering about and a handful of people were trying to pull others from the wreckage. It was utter chaos and he realized that some people were screaming as his hearing returned. Nobody was in charge. He realized that Germany might have just lost her leadership. Whatever doubts he might have about Hitler, he could not allow Germany's enemies to realize she was leaderless.

Varner took a deep breath. He would be the man in charge. He grabbed a dazed looking lieutenant and two confused enlisted men. His hearing had largely returned, although his voice sounded tinny to himself. "You. Go to the radio center and shut down all communications. Nothing comes in and nothing goes out. Do it on my authority on behalf of the Fuhrer and if anyone balks, kill them."

The three men saluted and ran off to do his bidding. He did the same with a handful of others, sending them to the gates of the compound. Again, his orders were that nobody comes in and nobody goes out.

Recovery efforts at the devastated building seemed to be progressing. Medics were crawling around through the mound of rubble. One of them was holding a dismembered leg, and there was a row of bodies on the ground. Several survivors walked around in a daze, their uniforms torn to shreds.

Varner forced himself to look at the dead. Keitel, the man he'd referred to as a toady, lay face up with a look of perpetual astonishment on his face. A medic informed him that Jodl was badly wounded, with both of his legs blown off, and would be dead within minutes.

He was about to ask about Hitler, when a desperate

shout and howl of emotional pain came from the men searching the rubble. They had found the Fuhrer.

Debris was removed and a doctor climbed down beside the pale and crumpled body of Adolf Hitler. Varner followed. Hitler's eyes were open and staring at the sky. He wasn't moving. "Is he alive?" Varner asked.

The doctor shook his head sadly. Again it was time for action and Varner realized what had to be done. "Doctor, you are quite wrong," he whispered. "You will announce that he is badly wounded and must be taken to the clinic. You will do it immediately and without anyone seeing his real condition."

The doctor, stunned, was about to argue when he realized what Varner was telling him. "Stretcher!" the doctor yelled. "We need a stretcher now! Get the Fuhrer to the clinic immediately. His life may depend on it."

Hitler's limp remains were put on a stretcher and covered with a blanket that exposed only part of his head, presenting the illusion that he still lived. The bearers almost ran to the clinic with the doctor alongside. Varner was now comfortable that only he and the doctor knew that Adolf Hitler was dead.

Jack Morgan, Captain, U.S. Army, wondered just what the hell was so important that the naval officer commanding the LST had summoned him. He also wondered just what the hell he was doing on an LST heading for France in the first place. He was an Army Air Force officer, even though he'd washed out as a bomber pilot, and American air bases were in England, not France. He'd assumed he'd be used by the air force in some capacity, but sent to France? Never. Even more important, why?

He had no idea what naval protocol was as he approached the bridge and, in the words of Rhett Butler in *Gone With the Wind,* he frankly didn't give a damn. The LST was supposed to take him from Dover to the beaches of Normandy where he would depart and find a military unit that wanted a washed-up bomber pilot. This was a complete shock. When he'd been first posted to England, he'd logically thought that he would be assigned as a staff officer at an air base. Now he had no idea what was going to happen to him.

The LST was more than three hundred feet long, and close to five hundred men were jammed in her along with tons of supplies for what was supposed to be a cruise of not more than a few hours from Dover to Normandy. Under those circumstances, the soldiers' discomfort meant nothing to those in charge. The LST was supposed to land the men after their short journey and that was it.

The LST's skipper was a short, plump, and very serious lieutenant commander named Stephens who was far from happy. "Captain Morgan, I'm certain you don't understand the navy's rules so I'll forgive you your transgressions."

"Thank you, sir," Morgan said with only a hint of sarcasm. Both men were standing and Morgan, at just under five-eleven, was several inches taller and much more slender at one hundred and sixty pounds. He also had a full head of short brown hair; Stephens was balding.

"In the future, when you come to the bridge you will ask permission before entering."

"I was under the impression you called for me, sir."

The naval officer was one rank higher than Morgan, which did not impress him. However, Jack did understand enough about the navy to know that the pompous little prick was considered God on his ship. He also decided that he would likely never again be on the damned bridge, so screw Stephens.

Stephens nodded solemnly. "I called for you because you are the senior officer among the mob the army stuffed in here. Therefore, you are the one who will maintain discipline among the passengers and get them organized and out of the way of the more than a hundred men who will be running this ship. I will not tolerate fights or drunkenness. Is that clear?"

"Perfectly," Jack said.

"Then get it done," Stephens said. Jack saluted and departed.

He had an hour before the LST was scheduled to depart. The first thing he did was to find any other officers and senior enlisted men. These he had organize the rest of the men into groups of a dozen or so. Some of the officers and NCO's were reluctant, even wondering why the hell the boys couldn't have a good time their last few hours before landing in hostile France, and Jack really didn't have a good answer. Rank, however, ultimately prevailed, and they did what Stephens ordered.

By the time he accomplished this and was satisfied that the mass of men in the hold of the LST were under at least a semblance of control, darkness had fallen and they were actually pulling away from Dover.

Stephens approached him on the upper deck by the railing. He had descended from Olympus to deal with mere mortals, Morgan thought.

"Good job organizing the men, Captain. I know

I was short with you, but we were running out of time and I needed things under control. The English Channel is not one hundred percent safe from the krauts. I've made a number of trips like this and I haven't lost a man yet and I don't want to start now."

"Understood, sir." Perhaps the little man wasn't such a jerk after all.

"You know what LST stands for, Captain?"

"No, sir."

"Large Slow Target," Stephens said with a hint of a smile. "It actually stood for Landing Ship Tank, its original purpose, and it's evolved into a very useful all purpose vessel, but it does make a hell of an inviting target."

He explained that the thirty-eight-hundred-ton LST had a top speed of a mere twelve knots, and Morgan doubted she was doing anywhere near that. Other ships, including more LST's, were making the trip and were visible as shadows in the night.

"Usually we carry supplies to the beaches. This is my third trip with unorganized replacement troops, Captain, and the first two were miserable experiences. The soldiers are going into war and they bitterly resent the fact that my sailors will head back to England and safety, hot meals, and maybe even girlfriends once they've dropped them off. This resulted in fights and vandalism. Two of my sailors were stabbed during the last trip and I am now trying to head that off by having you enforce discipline. A number of soldiers got into fights when they decided they'd been cheated at cards, and a larger number got drunk on booze they managed to smuggle in, and a lot of them got sick all over the place. Are you getting the picture?"

"I guess this isn't the *Queen Mary*," Morgan said with a smile of his own.

"Not even close. I have to put up with a normal degree of mess and the fact that half of the soldiers will be puking over the rail in a little while is considered normal, but the other stuff will cease."

To emphasize his point, a young soldier ran past them to the railing and heaved his guts over the side. Stephens actually laughed. "Another satisfied customer."

Morgan made his rounds and saw that all was reasonably well, or at least under a semblance of control. The drunks were quiet and the card players were working seriously at losing their money, but so far without fighting. He walked to the railing and looked over at the Channel and the other ships, which were little more than silhouettes in the night. He saw something in the water. What the hell? A line of white was racing through the water and towards the ship.

"Torpedo!" he screamed and threw himself onto the deck in an attempt to protect against the explosion. The torpedo struck and the LST shook violently from the impact. Jack was drenched with water and debris. Men screamed and were thrown about. Already prone, Morgan was spared much of it. Still, his head smashed against something and his shoulder was painfully wrenched.

He managed to get to his feet. Soldiers and sailors were already pulling wounded from below. Morgan grabbed a sailor who was about to protest until he saw Jack's captain's bars.

"What's going on down there?"

"Lotsa men trapped, sir, and water's coming in like a bandit. You could drive a truck through the hole."

Morgan fought his way down against a tide of men coming up. Water was filling the hold. Several bodies floated face down, mangled and clearly dead, but the dead weren't his concern. The trapped and wounded were. He grabbed some men and had them start passing wounded up top. Most of the men complied, although a few were too scared to do anything but scream. These were useless so he let them scramble up the ladder and out of the way.

Morgan found a pair of men trapped under debris. They were unconscious and hadn't been noticed in the darkness and confusion. Their heads were almost under water.

"Give me a hand," he yelled. A couple of men started pulling while Morgan held the unconscious men's heads above the rapidly rising water. One man was quickly freed and carried away. Smoke was coming from somewhere. He wondered if there was ammunition on board and whether it would explode.

The answer came seconds later and just when the second man had been freed. Small arms ammo began to pop off and fires began around him. Morgan suddenly realized he was alone. Everyone else had fled the fire and the rising water.

"Damn it to hell," he said to the unconscious man. He draped the soldier over his good shoulder and began to climb slowly and painfully up to the deck while bullets whizzed and clanged around him. Several struck him, but with not enough force to do much damage. Finally, hands grabbed him and relieved him of his burden. He fell to his knees on the deck. He recognized a very young sailor as one of the men who'd run away. "Sorry, I panicked, sir," the young man said sheepishly.

Jack nodded and patted the kid on the shoulder.
Being scared is one thing. Getting control and coming
back forgave a lot. He knew a helluva lot about that.

Captain Stephens helped him to a chair. "You're
wounded."

"I am?"

Morgan checked himself over and found a gash
on his forehead that was bleeding all over his face,
and a number of burns and bruises on his arms. His
shoulder hurt. It might have been dislocated but it
had popped back in.

"Hell, I never even noticed it."

"I'd say you were too busy to think much," said
Stephens, who handed him a cup. "Medicinal brandy.
I think you need it."

Morgan took a swallow and felt its warmth spread
through his stomach. Stephens was definitely not a
prick. "We going to sink, sir?"

"Nah. My men are plugging the hole and the pumps
are working. We'll be low in the water, but we'll make
it. Fire's being put out, too. That was never a major
threat. Bad news is that we've got more than a dozen
dead and three times that many wounded. So much
for my perfect record. Most of my crew were scared
shitless for a bit, and that includes yours truly, but
we'll make it to shore."

A medic slapped a bandage on Jack's forehead and
wiped the caking blood from his face. "That's good
to hear," Jack said.

Stephens grunted. "Oh yeah, welcome to France."

★ CHAPTER 2 ★

BEFORE HE COULD LEAVE THE DAMAGED VESSEL, Jack was questioned by an American rear admiral about the mine the LST had hit. When Jack insisted that he'd seen torpedo tracks, the admiral had sternly rebuked him. "It was a mine, Morgan. The krauts do not have subs in the English Channel. Do you understand that, Captain?"

When Jack persisted, Commander Stephens had grabbed him by the arm and pulled him away. "Captain, do you recall the story of the emperor's new clothes, the invisible ones?"

"Of course."

"Well, you are under navy jurisdiction now and the official line is that there are no U-boats in the Channel. If you persist, the navy will send you to someplace north of Iceland for the duration of the war plus eternity while they pretend to sort this out."

Jack had a sudden epiphany. He informed the navy brass that, darn, maybe he wasn't certain it was a torpedo. After all, what did a bomber pilot know about torpedoes and mines?

The investigation quickly ended and Jack was free to go. Stephens again collared him. "If you're feeling bad about that little lie, don't. It's not like it's going to change anything and it might just help protect our guys if the Nazis don't know that their U-boat attack was successful. Regardless, the dead are still dead, and the wounded still hurting. Oh yeah, thanks for helping out."

Jack agreed. Except for the navy's ego, who the hell cared what the truth was?

The Americans had taken Cherbourg, but the Nazis had blown up everything and destroyed its usefulness as a port. Repairs would take months, which was why the LST had to land on the beach in the first place. Nor had the LST been able to get terribly close as it had taken on a lot of water and everyone who was able to had to wade. The wounded and the dead were taken off by small boats or by medics who waded out with stretchers, but the majority of the soldiers, Jack included, had to walk through cold water that sometimes came over their waists.

The residue of war littered the beaches of Normandy. Burned out tanks and trucks and crushed German emplacements were everywhere as mute testimony to the battle that raged only a few days prior.

As a soggy Morgan walked across the sandy beaches, he had the unpleasant thought that he was treading on dead soldiers who were lying just underneath his water-soaked boots. This, he decided, was hallowed ground, like Gettysburg. He felt inadequate walking there.

A little farther on, the sight of temporary graves did nothing to dispel this feeling and a growing sense of inadequacy. How had he gotten himself into this mess? He should be flying bombers, not walking in sandy muck.

He knew the answer, of course. He'd frozen at the controls of his plane and the copilot, a mere trainee, was forced to land it for him. This happened after seeing one of his friends blown to little pieces when his bomber had crashed and exploded on landing. Jack first thought he could handle it, but he'd been wrong. Thus, he no longer flew bombers and was sent from Kansas to England and now to France. Who needed a pilot who wouldn't fly? Who would ever trust a pilot who froze up? Funny, but he thought he was over his collapse and could take the controls again, but it didn't look like he'd get the opportunity anytime soon.

Man-made thunder rumbled in the background as a constant reminder that the Germans were still very close to the beaches at Normandy. Even though the perimeter had expanded eastward, German artillery could still hit many targets inside the perimeter.

He trudged on. His clothing and boots were soggy and he was shivering from the cold, even though it was summer. Soon, he found the tent city that was the replacement depot. It was a confused sea of humanity, all dressed in olive drab. Literally thousands of men were arriving and departing to new units. Morgan was first sent to a clinic where he received some stitches in his forehead along with a fresh bandage. The medic assured him it made him look heroic. Jack told the medic to go screw himself, which the medic thought was hilarious. His bruises and scratches were treated and he was assured that his shoulder was fine but would pain him for a while, which was something he'd already figured out.

He'd recovered his duffle bag, but much of the contents had been ruined by salt water. This meant standing in long lines to get replacement uniforms and equipment. Fortunately, all his personal and official papers, along with his orders, had been in a waterproof envelope. A GI in England had made that suggestion and it turned out to be a damned good one.

The replacement depot was outside the ruined town of Trevieres, a place that would have been unlovely even if it hadn't been shelled to pieces during the invasion. Jack found a cot in a tent assigned to officers and settled in to wait. He was told not to unpack. He would be out and on his way the next morning. He lay down and wondered if he'd be able to sleep. It proved to be no problem.

Early the next day and after a shower and a bland breakfast, he found himself waiting with a bunch of other officers, most of whom were young and fresh-faced second lieutenants. They looked at him with a degree of wonder.

"Morgan, John C., Captain," came the call.

Jack walked over to the table where a staff sergeant named Sweeney awaited. "Here are your orders, Captain. You will report ASAP to the Seventy-Fourth Armored Regiment. Grab your gear and a Jeep will take you to them."

"Armor? You sure, Sergeant? I'm a pilot, not a tanker."

The sergeant shrugged. "This came directly from the major running this place. He said the Seventy-Fourth requested a captain and you're the only captain here right now. Congratulations."

"I don't know a thing about tanks," Jack said and realized he was sounding whiny and foolish.

Sergeant Sweeney shrugged eloquently. He didn't care. "If you know what a tank looks like, you're way ahead of those adolescent virgin second lieutenants who are standing there and wondering what we're talking about. And welcome to the real army, sir."

Sergeant Sweeney was right. Borderline insubordinate, but right. But what the devil would he do in an armored unit? Supply? Probably. Jesus, he didn't want to spend the war handing out underwear and pillowcases.

"Thank you, Sergeant Sweeney, and may you someday get reassigned to submarines as a deck hand." Sweeney laughed.

Varner had never met Heinrich Himmler and had never wanted to. The man's name was synonymous with terror and death.

In person he appeared pasty faced, even worse than his pictures. Himmler's fishy eyes looked coldly at him. Varner willed himself to be calm. This man was even more dangerous than the Soviets had been at Stalingrad. Heinrich Himmler controlled the SS and the Gestapo, and might now be the heir to the late Adolf Hitler. Himmler held the power of life and death in the Third Reich. Many thousands of people, perhaps hundreds of thousands, had disappeared, were tortured, and died without trial at his whim.

Himmler's detractors liked to claim that the forty-five-year-old Reichsfuhrer was nothing more than an ignorant chicken farmer, an opportunist, a murderer, and a man who'd ridden Hitler's coattails to prominence. They were correct, but Heinrich Himmler was now one of the most important men in Germany, if not its most important man thanks to the events at Rastenberg.

Varner was glad that he wasn't alone in Himmler's conference room in the basement of the Reich Chancellery located in the heart of Berlin. Field Marshal Gerd von Rundstedt represented the army and was now its de facto head because of the deaths of Jodl and Keitel. He was the man Varner had immediately notified by radio from Rastenberg. Varner had served under him in Russia and the sixty-nine-year-old field marshal had left his current position in France to fly back to Berlin and take control of the military aspects of the developing situation. The field marshal was terse and unlikeable, but thoroughly professional. He was bringing order back from the chaos that was the decapitated OKW.

Himmler bit his lower lip and glared at Varner. "You did extraordinarily well, Colonel Varner. The world still thinks Hitler is recovering from his wounds instead of lying in an ice-filled coffin in his train en route to Berlin. It might have been better if you had notified me first, but you are a soldier and contacting von Rundstedt must have made sense."

"It did, sir, and I apologize if I should have done differently."

"I'm quite certain he had no way of contacting you, Reichsfuhrer," von Rundstedt said.

Himmler blinked and waved his hand dismissively. "No matter. Everything is going well and you are to be commended for your presence of mind in both sealing off the compound and convincing those around that the Fuhrer was alive. Everything is under control and Goebbels is going to end the rumors and formally announce that Hitler is injured. We will announce his demise in the very near future when the time is appropriate. There remains some fear that dissident elements, traitors, remnant Jews, and communists will attempt to take advantage of any chaos and confusion.

"However, that is not my main concern. Tell me, Colonel, do you have any idea just how the Americans came to know that the Fuhrer was going to be at that particular place and at that particular time?"

The question stunned Varner. He had thought the bombing a tragic accident of war, but could it be that it was assassination, and not an accident? "Sir, I have no idea."

"You were with von Stauffenberg. Did he say anything suspicious?"

"No, sir. We had just managed lighting our cigarettes, no small feat when our wounds are considered, when the bomber suddenly appeared quite low overhead. We both jumped into a slit trench and tried to make ourselves very small. Otherwise, we had not spoken."

Himmler leaned back in his chair. "And how did you know each other?"

Varner felt himself beginning to sweat. He caught von Rundstedt out of the corner of his eye. The old general was expressionless, a flinty statue.

"We first met at the hospital. We were both there for therapy on our wounds. Prior to that I did not know him personally, although I had heard of him. Most people in the army had, of course."

Himmler nodded and Varner forced himself to exhale. Was it possible that von Stauffenberg had been part of a plot to assassinate Hitler, and, if so, had he somehow managed to carry it out?

There was a pause as Joseph Goebbels, the club-footed and diminutive Minister of Information and Propaganda, limped in and took a seat. The most important people in the Nazi hierarchy were now together, with the exception of Hermann Goering and Martin Bormann. Varner thought Goering's absence was particularly curious. It was commonly suspected that the obese air marshal was the heir to Hitler's Germany, and not Himmler. It was also rumored that he spent most of his time in a narcotic haze.

Himmler nodded to Goebbels to speak. "Thank you, Reichsfuhrer Himmler," he said formally. "We are just now announcing confirmation of the rumors that Adolf Hitler was wounded in an air raid. We shall issue medical updates as needed until the Fuhrer recovers enough to be interviewed."

Himmler turned towards Varner. "Tell him, Colonel."

Varner took a deep breath. "Adolf Hitler is dead. I helped pull his body from the rubble in Rastenberg and planted the tale that he was merely wounded."

Goebbels reacted as if he'd been punched in the gut. He paled and hunched over. "God in heaven, no."

"There is no God and there is no heaven." Himmler sneered. "Colonel Varner acted heroically by hiding the fact of Hitler's death, and may have saved the Reich from forces that wish to destroy it."

"I understand," Goebbels said. Grief was etched on his face. "Thank you, Colonel."

Himmler continued. He was clearly in charge. "Along with that announcement, there are other steps to be taken. First, all of Stauffenberg's friends and family will be rounded up and interrogated. Gently, at first, until and if we find a conspiracy, and then more harshly. Tell me, General von Rundstedt, is possible that the Allies have radio controlled weapons like we do?"

Field Marshal von Rundstedt was a proud man and he bristled at being referred to as a mere general. However, he did not correct Himmler. "Indeed it is possible. We sank a ship in Naples harbor with one and there is no reason to assume the Allies don't have them either."

Himmler nodded. "Which might explain the fact that Stauffenberg's briefcase was empty. Perhaps he had a signaling device in it which he used to guide the bomber."

Or, Varner thought, had the contents of the briefcase merely blown away, or had he left whatever papers he'd brought with Jodl or Keitel?

"Is that possible, Colonel Varner?" Himmler asked.

Rundstedt responded for a very perplexed Varner. "It is, Reichsfuhrer, but it also implies that von Stauffenberg either knew very little about the accuracy of bombs or that he was suicidal. While it might be possible to guide a robot plane fairly precisely, accurately dropping a bomb load on a small target is not. In my opinion, hitting the building where the Fuhrer was, was blind luck, and that leads me to think that a conspiracy is most unlikely.

"I might also add, Reichsfuhrer, that Hitler's decision to go to Rastenberg was made at the last minute and in great secrecy. He left by train the night before, arrived in the morning and had planned to return that evening. Therefore, I do not think there was enough time to plan and execute such a complicated assassination as you describe."

Himmler shook his head, accepting Rundstedt's analysis with obvious reluctance. "This is all speculation. We will have more knowledge when we are through with our investigations."

"And announcements," Goebbels said. "I will personally prepare to announce that Adolf Hitler died a martyr's death after heroically fighting terrible wounds inflicted on him by our cowardly enemies. The announcement will be made at your discretion, of course."

Himmler nodded. "And you will further announce that he was assassinated by murdering Americans conspiring with Wall Street Jews," said Himmler. "That will inflame the public on our behalf."

Goebbels made a note. "Excellent. And what about his funeral? It should be one fit for a god, with thousands of marching soldiers and the leaders of the Reich assembled to honor our fallen leader."

Rundstedt laughed harshly. "And won't that make a wonderful target for the Ami bombers? They could finish what they started at Rastenberg and end the war in an afternoon." Goebbels flushed at the criticism and hunched down in his chair.

Himmler stood. "Enough. We will meet again and soon."

"It cannot be soon enough," said Rundstedt as he rose. "Germany has been badly hurt, but we have also been handed potential opportunities. I wonder how the Allies will take the news and how it might affect their plans for the war? And how will this affect our own plans?"

Opportunities indeed, thought Himmler.

★　　　★　　　★

The ride from the replacement depot to the 74th Armored was short, only a few miles, but it took almost two hours because of all the traffic, most of it also heading for the front lines. Several times his lonely Jeep was shunted aside by MP's in favor of columns of trucks and tanks that had greater priority even though they were all headed in the same direction. This gave Jack an opportunity to look around and be shocked by the level of destruction. Except for the attack on the LST, he'd never seen war before and, in particular, a pilot was usually insulated from its effects.

Although the heavily cratered roads had been patched, there were still enough holes and bumps to shake his spine as the Jeep, driven by a thoroughly disinterested private named Snyder, lurched its way forward. Pushed off the road were the carcasses of numerous charred vehicles, almost all of them German. From the stench emanating from a number of them, their occupants, now thoroughly cooked, remained inside. Graves Registration gave American dead a high priority. Nazis could wait until hell froze over, and Jack was okay with that.

The road was dirt and narrow, hemmed in by dense hedgerows that Snyder said were called *bocages* by the locals. Along with Snyder and Morgan, the Jeep carried mail and Jack had a sack of it on his lap. Snyder'd hinted that the mail was more important than Jack was.

Morgan had picked up enough to know that the hedgerows had been a most unpleasant surprise for the Americans. Centuries old, some said they even dated to Roman times, the hedgerows were upwards of fifteen feet thick at the base and half a dozen feet high. They were topped by trees and hedges that added to the problem. They originally defined each farmer's generally small piece of property and were often separated by narrow roads. Vehicles simply couldn't bull their way through the hedgerows and men had to squeeze through extremely narrow openings in the foliage; thus, a handful of Germans could and often did hold up large numbers of Americans. Snyder mentioned that some tanks had been fitted with bulldozerlike contraptions that enabled the tank to slice a path through the hedgerow. He added that the 74th was a cherry regiment, virgins who had never seen much combat. Wonderful, Jack thought. He was one more virgin.

As they neared their destination, they passed numbers of parked American tanks and other vehicles. Morgan knew enough to recognize the squat and stubby M4 Sherman, and the smaller Stuart. Their crews were working on them in obvious anticipation of moving into battle, and the sounds of artillery were now quite distinct. This did not bode well, Morgan thought.

They also passed a number of antiaircraft batteries, their guns pointed toward the sky and their crews lounging about on the ground. Either U.S. radar was that good or it was testimony to the fact that the Luftwaffe was pretty well wiped out. He hoped it was both.

Finally, the Jeep pulled up in front of a nondescript tent. Jack took his gear, thanked Snyder, who simply grunted, and entered. Inside was a desk and a couple of chairs. A lieutenant colonel sat behind the desk.

"Sit down, Captain. I'm Lieutenant Colonel Jim

Whiteside and you can call me either colonel or sir, and I'm the executive officer of this regiment."

Morgan sat as directed. Whiteside seemed affable enough, but he also looked a little strained. He was a short, stocky man in his mid-thirties and had thinning red hair.

Jack had only been with the 74th for a few minutes and already the culture shock was huge. Obviously, instead of planes and bombers there were large numbers of tanks, half-tracks, artillery, trucks, and Jeeps. And, where there was a degree of cleanliness kept in the air corps because of the need to keep plane engines clean, such was lacking in the 74th. Men were covered with dirt and grease, and Jack felt hugely out of place in his new fatigues.

Whiteside leaned back in his folding chair. "I'll be blunt. You are not what we expected or wanted. We need an officer familiar with armor and they sent me you."

Jack was about to comment but the colonel shushed him with a wave. "I know it's not your fault. Somebody at the depot saw we had a captain killed and thought we needed a captain to replace him, when what we really need is an officer of any rank with a solid knowledge of tanks and armored warfare. Just a typical snafu, right?"

"Yes, sir."

"At any rate, you're here and we're gonna make the best of the situation. Now tell me candidly, why did you leave bombers?"

Jack told him what had happened, how he had frozen, and how he felt he was over it. "I'd seen a lot of trainees die, someone said ten percent are killed in training, but this time it finally got to me."

Whiteside was shocked. "Ten percent dead before they even make it to the war?"

"Yes, sir."

The colonel shook his head. This was news to him. "Well, I guess there are no minor accidents in an airplane. Not like a tank bumping into a tree. Hell, the tree would likely lose. We've lost men killed and injured in training, but nothing like ten percent."

"Of course, sir, there's also the thought that we have more than enough bomber pilots and planes?"

"What?" Whiteside said incredulously. "That better be somebody's idea of a joke."

"Sorry, sir, but it isn't. There's a feeling among air force brass that the Nazis are on their last legs and that victory is just around the corner, so a lot of pilots and trainees are being declared superfluous and transferred to other branches. Obviously, top brass doesn't talk to me, but there are rumors and nobody's disputing them."

"Shit."

"It gets worse. The air force thinks they're running out of targets."

"Bull-fuck and double shit," Whiteside said, his face reddening. "Why don't they come and ask the guys who are trying to clear Nazis out of the way? They want targets? Hell, I'll give them a dozen just a few miles away."

Whiteside again shook his head. "Jesus, what a war. Well, here we are, and, even though you don't know diddly about tanks, I have no choice but to put you in charge of Headquarters Company B, the position held by your predecessor. You'll be in charge of setting up the regimental headquarters when we move and for security at all times. The CO is Colonel Stoddard. He's at division getting orders and you'll meet him soon enough."

Whiteside looked through some more papers. "You a college graduate?"

"Not quite, sir. I made it through three years at Michigan State College in East Lansing, Michigan, before I got drafted."

"Life's a bitch," the major muttered. "I ran a hardware store in Cleveland."

"May I ask what happened to the guy I'm replacing?"

"What happened shouldn't have. I wrote a letter to his family saying that his Jeep struck a mine and he'd been killed instantly. Of course it didn't happen that way. He saw a dead kraut officer and tried to take the dead guy's Luger as a souvenir. Unfortunately, the body was booby-trapped and your predecessor lost his arms and his face. And he didn't die instantly. He screamed for two hours before medics got enough morphine in him to shut him up. Permanently. Rule number one for rookie officers is don't go souvenir hunting. I'll have someone take you to your quarters and you can meet Captain Levin. He's in charge of Headquarters A Company."

Morgan was dismissed but had a point to add. "By the way, Colonel. Maybe you don't want to wish for close-in bomber support."

"Why not?"

"It doesn't matter what propaganda they've been feeding you, but bombers can't hit anything accurately from high up. If you're within a couple of miles of the target, you're in more danger than the krauts."

"Shit."

"Frankly, sir," Morgan said wickedly, "the safest place to be when bombs drop is right at the target."

First Lieutenant Phips did what he was told. In the middle of a clammy and rainy night, he gathered the crew of *Mother's Milk* and they were taken away in two trucks while he rode in the back seat of an army sedan. The trucks were buttoned up and there were shades on the side windows of the sedan. If he didn't know better, he might have thought that the army didn't want anybody to see him.

And why not? He was a pariah. On finally making it back to base, he'd had his ass chewed up, down and sideways for having broken formation; thus putting both himself and others at risk. He'd endured it because he knew his superiors and peers were right and that he'd committed a major wrong.

Even worse, one of his men had been killed and likely as a result of his stupidity. Phips had been told in no uncertain terms that it might just be a cold day in hell before he ever saw the inside of a plane from the pilot's seat again. It was further implied that his crew would be broken up and that saddened him. They would pay for his fuckup and that wasn't right.

Thus, he wasn't really surprised when the trucks containing his crew went one way and he the other. He'd tried discussing matters with the sergeant driving him, but the sergeant tersely said he was not allowed to talk to him, which further depressed Phips.

After several hours of slow driving through the English countryside, they pulled up in front of a guard post where their papers were scrutinized and the car searched before being sent on. There was a splendid looking country manor house that might have been several hundred years old and it was surrounded by a several dozen large army tents and Quonset huts. To his surprise, they went to the main old building where Phips was hustled down an ornately furnished corridor lined with portraits of distinguished looking people in historic costumes, and finally into a room containing only a couple of chairs. His duffle bag arrived a few moments later and was deposited with a thud by his feet.

A little while later, a full colonel entered and glared at him. Phips snapped to attention and was told to sit down. The colonel was maybe forty and was powerfully built. Phips quickly noted combat ribbons on his chest.

"I'm Colonel Tom Granville with army intelligence and I've got a few questions for you. For the record, confirm that three days ago you flew a B17 named the *Mother's Milk* over Germany, East Prussia to be precise. Is that correct?"

"Yes, sir."

"Was your plane alone?"

"To the best of my knowledge, yes, sir. At least after we shot down that ME that'd been chasing us all over the place."

"Good job doing that, by the way. And after killing the ME, you knowingly and intentionally dropped a load of bombs on some buildings you spotted at the last second?"

Oh Jesus, Phips thought. Despite the antiaircraft fire they had hit a school, or a convent. He visualized dead and maimed children. He swallowed. "Yes, sir. We dropped the bombs to save on fuel and the buildings were the first things we saw."

"Any idea just what the hell you hit, Lieutenant?"

"No, sir. One of my crew said it was Germany so it didn't much matter and I agreed. We just had to lighten our load so we could get home."

The colonel's grim-set mouth flickered. Was that a smile? Maybe he hadn't hit a school. Granville continued. "Well you certainly did hit Germany and you did make your way back, and you did shoot down that ME, and now we don't quite know what to do with you."

"Sir?"

"Without divulging our sources, let me say that we now know that Adolf Hitler was at one of his secret headquarters in Rastenberg, Prussia, when a lone American B17 bomber flew low over the compound and dropped a load of bombs on his ugly fucking head."

Phips' jaw dropped. "Oh my God."

"Yeah, Lieutenant, oh my God. Germany has just announced that he was injured in a one-plane bombing attack. However, we are getting subtle hints that his Fuhrer ass is dead and that his unlamented demise will be announced in a few days. This delay will give the new Nazi regime a chance to get settled. The krauts are saying it was a Jewish-American conspiracy to murder Hitler. However, we know better, don't we? It was just one dumb, lucky son of a bitch in a lost B17 who dumped a load of bombs to save fuel and hit the jackpot."

"And you're sure I did it?"

"Yes we are, and until this all gets sorted out, you and your crew are going to be kept incommunicado. We don't know whether to give you a medal for maybe killing *der Fuhrer* or court-martial your ass for breaking formation and maybe for losing a crewman. Maybe we'll do both. A medal would look good on prison fatigues, don't you think?"

Granville rose and Phips did as well. "In the meantime, you will stay here in utter squalor in this sixteenth-century building that might have housed Queen Elizabeth at some time. Try not to break anything. Sleep in, eat all you want, drink all you can find, and keep your mouth shut."

"And my crew, sir?"

"I will be debriefing them shortly and you will all be reunited, hopefully to live happily ever after."

★ CHAPTER 3 ★

HEINRICH HIMMLER HAD ALWAYS BEEN A LOYAL
supporter of Adolf Hitler. He had joined the Nazi
party in its early days and had worshipped. The
Fuhrer had given the former fertilizer salesman and
chicken farmer's life a sense of meaning. Himmler
had flourished as head of the SS and the Gestapo
and now he was one of the most important men in
the Nazi hierarchy.

But Adolf Hitler was dead and there was much
for Himmler to do if he wished to live to a ripe old
age in a Nazi cult that didn't mind killing off rivals.
First, the Fuhrer's legacy must be sustained, even
improved on, despite the difficult times ahead, and
that called for strong leadership. Hermann Goering
was not capable of such strength. The First World
War fighter ace and one-time confidante of Hitler
was in virtual disgrace as a result of his incompetence
as commander of the Luftwaffe, his ineptitude as an
administrator, and his looting of museums to provide

41

artwork for his disgusting and decadent pleasure palace at Carinhall. Goering was addicted to drugs and alcohol, further impairing his limited abilities. Still, the obese fool considered himself a major participant in the Reich and the heir to Hitler.

Himmler had sent SS troops to Carinhall ostensibly to protect Goering from a possible coup. Instead, they'd taken him prisoner and had him sent to a small private hospital outside Berlin where he was under heavy guard. Goering, of course, was too far gone in a narcotic fog to realize what was happening to him. He would stay in the hospital and in a drugged stupor until a decision was made regarding his future.

Martin Bormann, Hitler's secretary and party chancellor, held power only while Hitler lived. Himmler had taken steps to isolate Bormann. He was held in protective custody by another SS detachment. Himmler was exacting sweet revenge against the man who'd plotted against him and tried to humiliate him in front of Adolf Hitler. Sadly for Bormann, Bormann had forgotten that while he had great influence with Hitler, it was Heinrich Himmler who had a private army.

As further security, Himmler had brought in one of his favorites, SS General Sepp Dietrich, who had raced to Berlin with several thousand SS soldiers. Berlin was secure. Whether Hitler's death was an accident of war or an assassination from within, no one but he would take advantage of the situation.

His secretary tapped on his door and informed him that Field Marshal von Rundstedt and Foreign Secretary Joachim von Ribbentrop were ready. Himmler preferred small meetings. Large groups, in particular during these uncertain times, drew attention and could lead to panic among the people.

The field marshal and the diplomat seated themselves and stared at Himmler with differing degrees of expectation and deference. Von Rundstedt was an aristocrat, while Ribbentrop presumed to be one. Like most aristocrats they looked down on Himmler and ignored the fact that Himmler's godfather had been the prince of Bavaria, a fact that was important only to Himmler.

Himmler began. "Gentlemen, let me begin with the obvious. Our beloved Fuhrer has been brutally murdered by an American-British-Jewish conspiracy. Steps are being taken to track down and destroy the perpetrators and they will succeed. Several diplomats and even some generals are involved and will be dealt with severely. However, we have a tremendous duty ahead of us. We must win the war."

Rundstedt nodded. "It is also an opportunity."

"How so?"

Himmler could see the older man choosing his words with care. Hitler might be dead but it was still dangerous, possibly even fatal, to criticize him. Many generals, Rundstedt included, had been critical in the past. Rundstedt had criticized Hitler openly, mocking him as a "Little Corporal" in reference to Hitler's First World War rank, but had carefully not crossed the line into treason.

Rundstedt smiled slightly. "Hitler is dead; thus, we will no longer have his brilliant intuition and inspiration to guide and inspire us. Instead, we must depend on our more pedestrian intellects to get us through the growing crises."

Well said, Himmler thought, even if it was a bald-faced lie. "I am aware that the professional military disagreed with the Fuhrer on many occasions," Himmler responded, "but had always acquiesced in the end. And look what it got us—France, Poland, and much of the Soviet Union."

Rundstedt laughed harshly, more confident that his comments hadn't been rebuffed. "It got us lands that the Soviets and the Americans are rapidly taking back from us. If we are not careful and if we do not act quickly, the Third Reich will become a footnote in history, and we will all be dead or prisoners."

Himmler flinched, but he could not disagree. It was exactly what was preying on his mind and the field marshal was correct. On the other hand, Ribbentrop's face showed shock.

"Then what should we do, Field Marshal?" Himmler asked. "How can we attain victory?"

"It may depend on how you define victory, Reichsfuhrer. If you mean forcing Russia, the United States, and Britain to the surrender table, such is not likely. If you define victory as the survival of Germany, the Nazi Party, and we here, then yes, that definition of victory is attainable. However, in order to do that, I am afraid that we will have to take some steps that are repugnant and even go against what our late Fuhrer has directed."

Ribbentrop, attempting to be the diplomat, regained control of himself and kept his face expressionless. This was what Himmler expected. "Go on," Himmler said.

"In order to defend Germany, I need men and supplies. It is that simple. Right now, many tens of thousands of trained German soldiers are languishing

away, far from the field of battle because the Fuhrer
declined to give up any ground we'd taken, especially
against the Soviets. I suggest that the circumstances
have changed and that we must act with decisiveness
and haste while there is still time. Our scattered
armies must be retrieved and our extended defensive
lines shortened."

Finally Ribbentrop spoke. "You would have us give
up our conquered territories?"

"Quite frankly, yes."

"Other than that, do you have a plan?" Himmler
asked.

"In theory and development, yes. However, I am
not ready to divulge it without input from Speer."

Himmler concurred. The young Albert Speer was the
Minister for Armaments and Munitions. The capabilities and limitations of the economy were paramount
to their plans. "He will attend here tomorrow."

"And what about me?" Ribbentrop asked, almost
plaintively.

"With Hitler dead," Himmler said, "you might find
it easier to negotiate with our enemies. Sound them
out. See who really wants this war to end and what
their true terms are."

In Himmler's opinion, Ribbentrop was useless and
his attempts to bring peace would prove futile. He'd
failed miserably as a negotiator in the past, often
insulting those with whom he was supposed to be
negotiating. Would anyone ever forget the time the
man greeted the king of England with the Nazi salute?
And in London no less. He'd become the laughingstock
of England and the diplomatic community. For the
time being, however, Ribbentrop was the best he had.

★   ★   ★

Franklin Delano Roosevelt looked up from his stamp collection and smiled genially. "Well, is the fucking little paper hanger dead or not?"

Chairman of the Joint Chiefs of Staff General George Catlett Marshall no longer winced at his President's obscenities. He sometimes wondered whether FDR swore to be one of the boys, or to aggravate his senior general, or because that was just the way he talked. Marshall thought the latter. Many people had canonized the President as the perfect man, but the truth was that he was a cripple who couldn't walk a step, and a man who drank and swore. And womanized. Jokesters in the know laughed about his womanizing and some wondered who wouldn't stray if a cold and stern Eleanor Roosevelt was all he had to come home to?

"Sadly, sir, we aren't sure what his condition is," Marshall said. "The Germans have admitted that he's badly wounded, although they're saying he's recovering. They're also saying it was nothing more than as a despicable assassination attempt and a Jewish-American conspiracy. They are again cracking down on dissidents, although I wonder how many are left after all these years. Whoever they are, I feel sorry for them."

"And what do you think, General?"

"I think he's dead."

Roosevelt leaned over the desk in the Oval Office and stared through his glasses at the array of brightly colored stamps, some of which were quite rare. "And why?"

"A very ambitious Heinrich Himmler is in charge and several of those associated with Hitler have, well, disappeared from the scene and perhaps forever. I believe Himmler and Goebbels are setting the stage for an announcement of Hitler's heroic demise, after which, Himmler will be proclaimed the new Fuhrer."

"And if Hitler really is dead, how will that affect the war?" Roosevelt asked.

Marshall was surprised. "I believe that's your call, sir."

"Indeed," FDR said softly. "I am afraid there will be pressures from many quarters to work with the new German government to end the war. If nothing else, so that we can focus on destroying the little yellow bastards who bombed Pearl Harbor."

Marshall nodded. Many senior military men, including Admiral Ernie King and General Douglas MacArthur, felt that America's war efforts should have been focused on the despicable Japs and not Germany. Many in Congress, particularly those from western states, also wanted America's focus on defeating Japan. Instead, Roosevelt had insisted on adherence to pre-war plans that called for defeating Germany first while containing Japanese aggression. Allied plans also called for Germany's unconditional surrender and, if Hitler was indeed dead, would that affect it?

"Enough speculating over that," Roosevelt said. "Now, what about this Phips person. A medal or what?"

"A medal at least, but I suggest waiting until Hitler's death is confirmed."

"And Ultra says nothing?"

Marshall instinctively looked around. Ultra was the name of the super-secret British code-reading activity at Bletchley Park in England. The Germans were unaware that England had broken their most secret and sacred codes and were now sharing the information, albeit reluctantly, with their American cousins. Very few Americans were in on the secret, and most key members of Roosevelt's staff were unaware of it. They were also unaware of what was being developed in New Mexico under the name of the Manhattan Project.

FDR sighed. "And this Phips person is such a nebbish, a fucking clerk. Why couldn't it have been the copilot who'd been in charge? He looks a helluva lot more heroic than Phips."

Marshall permitted himself a small smile. "That might work in our favor. The German supermen would be humiliated to find that Hitler'd been killed by a scrawny little nothing like Phips."

Roosevelt chuckled. "Perhaps it might. At any rate, do something about the plane. *Mother's Milk*, my ass. That name and the caricature have got to go. The tits on that farm girl are larger than several states and are an insult to every woman voter."

"Roy Levin's my name and yes, I'm Jewish, why would you even ask?"

Morgan grinned. "I didn't ask and you don't look Jewish."

Captain Roy Levin was short and stocky, and had an olive complexion topped by short curly hair. He looked more Sicilian than anything else. Morgan decided he was an easy man to like. Levin sat on the bunk opposite Morgan's in their four-man tent.

"Welcome to Stockade Stoddard's rolling armored circus. And by the way, don't let the colonel ever hear you refer to him by that name. He knows we all do, but not to his face. Could be fatal. You might bleed to death after getting your ass chewed."

"Understood, but how did he get the name?"

Levin sat on his bunk and lit a cigarette. Jack declined his offer. "The good colonel's regimental headquarters was overrun by the Germans in North Africa and he was nearly captured at a lovely place called the Kasserine Pass. His battalion was out of touch for several days until relief columns arrived, and he sincerely believes that a lot of his men died because his regiment's HQ was gone. He decided then and there that his HQ would always be fortified. Thus, he moves men and equipment around and sets up with each new move. Kind of like the Roman legions did. And, yes, that's your job now."

"Wonderful."

"To give Stoddard his due, the man is neither a coward nor stupid, just cautious. He's got legitimate medals from North Africa and he's also a decent guy as long as you don't piss him off, like screwing up the defenses around his HQ, for instance. He's also one of the handful of guys in the Seventy-Fourth who's actually been in combat. Even though we've been in Normandy for a couple of days, there's been no real fighting for us. Some shelling and sniping, but nothing major."

"I'll do my best to keep him happy. Now, you're supposed to tell me about the regiment."

Levin pulled a bottle of wine from his duffle bag, opened it, and poured some into their canteen cups. "Crystal would be better," he said after taking a swallow, "it enhances the bouquet, but beggars can't be choosers. Besides, the wine ain't all that good. One of my men got it from some guys in the First Infantry Division who liberated a bar or something."

Levin explained that there were three thousand men in the 74th, clustered around the seventy tanks that made up its strike force. He added that the regiment was an independent unit, currently assigned to General Leonard Gerow's V Corps, which was part of Courtney Hodges' First Army. "All of which belongs to Omar Bradley's Twenty-First Army Group," he added.

"If you're curious, and there's no reason you should be, there are other independent armored regiments and even a slew of independent armored battalions floating around. As to our strength, we have fifty M4 Shermans and twenty Stuarts. The Stuarts are light tanks and aren't worth a shit. Worse, all they've got is a piddly thirty-seven-millimeter gun, which won't hurt a Panzer Mark IV or a Panther. Might scrape its paint, but that's all. They're supposed to be phased out this winter and replaced by something called a Chaffee which also isn't worth squat against kraut armor. The Sherman is bigger than the Stuart, but isn't much better."

Levin went on to explain that the Sherman had a 75mm gun and could beat the Panzer Mark III with its 37mm gun and hold its own with the Panzer Mark IV and its 75mm gun, but the introduction of the Panzer V, the Panther, and the less numerous Tiger and King Tiger varieties had disrupted all that.

"The Panzer III is still around and the Germans' main tank is the Panzer IV, which is what the Sherman was allegedly designed to fight. The Panther has come as a terrible and unpleasant surprise that we've so far been able to avoid. It can't last, however."

Jack took another sip of the wine. "What's the difference between a Panzer and a Panther?"

"Contrary to popular belief among the willfully ignorant, Panzer is not German for Panther. Panzer is derived from something else, maybe a French term. Technically speaking, the Panther is the Panzer V. Others, like the Tiger—which actually is the Panzer VI—the King Tiger, and the Leopard are different breeds of cat." He chortled, "Damn, I am witty."

"Not really," Jack said, "but you are confusing the hell out of me. However, please continue."

"Screw you too," Levin said amiably, clearly pleased with his lousy joke. "Simply put, the seventy-five-millimeter gun on the Sherman can't penetrate the Panther's front armor and the Panther's gun goes through a Sherman's thinner armor like a hot knife through butter. Since we haven't seen any real combat it hasn't happened to us yet, but I've been told that, statistically, one Panther can knock out as much as a dozen Shermans before ultimately taking a damaging hit and a Tiger can do even better, which I hope is an exaggeration. The only saving virtue is that the krauts don't have all that many Panthers or Tigers."

"How the hell did it happen that we got the crappy tanks and the Germans the good ones?" Jack asked. "We make millions of great cars, so why not tanks?"

Levin shrugged and added some more wine. "Ask the politicians and the manufacturers who convinced the army that the Germans wouldn't be leap-frogging ahead of us with their designs. I've also heard that the Pentagon wanted the Sherman kept small so more of them could be shipped overseas without taking up precious space in ships. Oh yeah, it's got too high a silhouette so the krauts can see us long before we see them. There was also the idea that tanks wouldn't be fighting other tanks. Instead, tank destroyers would kill the German tanks while Shermans aided the infantry. That hasn't worked out that way either. Another perfectly good plan shot to hell."

Levin took a swallow and grimaced. The wine truly was pretty bad, but it was alcohol and they were beginning to feel comfortable. Levin continued, "And along with the tanks, there are a number of semi-armored half-tracks and a dozen M10 tank destroyers, which are also under-gunned against the Germans and don't have any tops on them in order to save weight, which is supposed to increase speed. Dumb.

"We have our own artillery, consisting of a number of one-oh-five-millimeter howitzers on open tank chassis. We also have a large number of trucks, gas tanker trucks, and Jeeps, but it's common knowledge that we don't have enough of them."

Jack added more wine to his cup. "What a fuckup."

Levin laughed. "Yeah, and we're supposed to be winning this war."

Colonel Ernst Varner was well on his way home when the sirens began to wail. He felt his stomach churn as he moved quickly to the nearest bomb shelter in the basement of an office building. It was the middle of the day and that meant it was the Americans who were going to rain destruction down on Berlin. Again, just as they did almost every day. The British bombed at night.

Varner was as brave as the next man, but he felt helpless as he cowered in the shelter. He could only wonder as he did each time—what the devil had happened to Germany's air defenses? Where were the fighters? Why weren't German bombers hitting enemy airfields? When the war started, Hermann Goering had boasted that if an Allied bomb fell on Berlin he would change his name to Meyer, a Jewish name. Well, the bombs fell constantly now on a relatively helpless Berlin and the disgraced Goering rarely made an appearance. To the people of Berlin he was a buffoon. Varner agreed, although only to himself.

The crump-crump of the bombs could be heard. Some nearby area was getting pasted. Varner could only hope and pray the bombs weren't falling anywhere near the apartment building where Magda and Margarete awaited his return.

The bombs were falling closer. The shelter began to vibrate and dust filtered down onto the scores of people who huddled in terror. People were moaning and a woman screamed. Children cried. Varner fought the urge to piss. A direct hit on the building above could bury them alive. No matter how many times he'd been in combat, there was always that feeling of unreasonable fear when the firing began. *Show me someone without fear,* he'd always thought, *and I'll show you either a fool or a lunatic.*

Like a thunderstorm in the summer, the bombs reached a violent and ear-shattering crescendo. The walls of the shelter shook with their violence, and still more dust fell from the ceiling, covering everyone jammed inside. Varner smelled smoke and prayed that the exit wasn't blocked by flames or falling debris. He'd seen instances where that had happened and the people inside were fried to a crisp, their bodies stacked by a blocked exit.

The woman screamed again, yelling for the bombing

to stop and then cursing Hitler and Goering for letting it happen. Someone stifled her and prevented her from crying out again. Varner could understand her fear and frustration, but not her outburst. While the Gestapo might not be everywhere, the Gestapo's informants were, and such hysterical comments could be construed as treasonous.

As the dust settled, he saw the woman, now standing alone. Nobody wanted to be associated with her. She was wide-eyed and terrified, but now from a new sense of panic.

The sounds of bombing faded. But were the Americans through or was this just the first of many waves of attackers? The Yanks seemed to have an inexhaustible supply of planes. Berlin wasn't totally helpless as hundreds, perhaps thousands, of antiaircraft guns fired at the distant bombers. They would hit some of them, but nowhere near enough to change matters. The British would come tonight and the Americans again tomorrow during the day. And so it would go on.

The all clear sounded and Varner led the group out of the shelter into a changed world. Walls were down and buildings were on fire. Choking black smoke filled the air and torn bodies lay in the street. Ambulances and fire engines were trying valiantly to stem the tide of blood, fire, and damage. He looked for the screaming woman, but she was nowhere to be seen. A policeman with a bandage on his face walked up to him.

"Excuse me, Colonel, but do you know anything about a woman saying treasonous things while in the shelter?"

Well, Varner thought, *that didn't take long*. "I

heard a hysterical woman howling, but that was all. I really couldn't make out what she was saying. I was really more concerned about two children who were crying nearby."

"Do you think you could recognize her?"

"No."

The policeman nodded knowingly. "Nor can anybody else. What a surprise."

"Officer, I really don't think a terrified woman's outbursts qualify as treason, even if she said them."

"Nor do I, Colonel, nor do I," the policeman said and walked away.

A child began screaming. Varner and others went to where a boy was pinned by debris. They pulled him out but not before his eyes rolled back and he lost consciousness. A quick check showed he was still breathing. The boy was about ten and his left arm was smashed and would doubtless have to be amputated.

A medic appeared beside Varner. "At least this one won't have to go in your army, Colonel."

"Careful," Varner snapped.

"Of what?" the medic retorted. "Sooner or later we'll all be dead and you know it, Colonel."

Varner found he could not respond. He left the medic and began the long walk back to his apartment.

Morgan sat in the front passenger seat of his Jeep and pondered. It was just like any other traffic jam except he was on a hedgerow-lined dirt road in northern France, and he had an M3 "grease gun" across his lap. He'd chosen that weapon because others recommended it. The M3 fired full automatic, and was smaller than the M1 Garand. Size was a factor

Robert Conroy

for tankers since room inside one was at a premium. He hadn't had a chance to fire it yet, so he felt just a little foolish carrying it. He also had a .45 automatic in a holster on his belt. He'd never fired that either. Nor had he yet been inside a tank.

Somewhere he recalled reading that armored columns were supposed to move quickly and charge dramatically into battle. Well, it wasn't happening this day. The tanks and tank destroyers were in the front of the column, while half-tracks and trucks followed. Literally hundreds of armored and support vehicles were lined up in the narrow dirt road, and all were heading into combat for the first time as a unit. That is, if they ever got there.

The hedgerows in this area weren't as bad as those closer to the Normandy coast, but they were difficult enough. They constricted vision and forced the regiment into one long single-file column.

Morgan had drawn PFC Snyder again as his driver. Jack yawned and glared at the half-track in front of them. A dozen men were stuffed into it and they all looked bored as hell. His radioman dozed in the back seat. His chief NCO, Sergeant Major Rolfe, and his two lieutenants, Hazen and Vance, rode in vehicles behind him.

Morgan decided to make light of it. "At this rate, Snyder, the war'll be over before we get to it."

Snyder grinned. With Morgan his commanding officer, he was no longer the taciturn and bored driver who'd brought him to the regiment. "Fine by me, sir."

There was a loud crack and the half-track in front exploded. Bodies flew through the track's open top and into the air. "What the hell?" Morgan said.

Flames erupted from the stricken vehicle as it slowly fell onto its side. A handful of survivors crawled out. One was on fire. Others screamed and tried to crawl away. Snyder floored the accelerator and pulled off the road to their left just as a second crack sounded and the vehicle in front of the dying half-track also exploded. Their Jeep slid onto its side and all three men jumped out.

It was a German ambush. "Everybody out of the trucks," Morgan yelled. The order was unnecessary as everyone was doing just that. He jumped up and ran down the line to repeat the order to a handful of men who remained frozen in place, grabbing a couple by the collar and hurling them to the ground. Sergeant Major Rolfe was already doing the same thing, but Morgan's young lieutenants, Vance and Hazen, seemed dazed and confused, and remained in their vehicles. Jack grabbed Hazen and threw him on the ground. Vance shook off his shock and climbed down. All up and down the line trucks were emptying of men.

Crack!

Rolfe dropped down beside Morgan, who was hugging the ground. "It's a German eighty-eight, Captain. I remember the sound of the fuckers from North Africa and Sicily."

The squat bow-legged sergeant was one of his few veterans. Properly identifying their enemy was one thing, but doing something about it was something else.

Crack, and another truck exploded. "It's a turkey shoot," Rolfe said. "You're in charge, Captain. I suggest we do something."

A Sherman tank roared down the line of trucks, its

stubby seventy-five looking for a target. It was on the Germans' side of the road and the stalled vehicles, and its run exposed the tank's less heavily armored side.

Crack, and the tank lurched to a halt. Black smoke began to pour from its hatches as the crew stumbled out. Only two of the five made it before the ammunition in the tank began to explode.

"God help the poor bastards," said Rolfe.

"Can you see where the kraut gun is?" Morgan asked.

"Kinda. I thought I saw a flash in those trees to our left front, maybe a quarter mile away."

The area wasn't as thick with hedges and trees as the ancient farms around the Normandy invasion site, but the foliage was thick enough to hide an antitank gun.

"Then get everybody shooting in that general direction. If nothing else, it'll keep them pinned down a little. I'm going to take some volunteers and see if we can creep up on it before the son of a bitch destroys the whole regiment."

He started to run, but slipped, falling on his knees. He gagged as he realized he'd stepped in the intestines of a soldier who was gasping and flailing his arms. All around him men were yelling and screaming. A few were trying to help the wounded, but panic reigned. If the Germans had a machine gun on this side of the road, they would have slaughtered the men of the 74th like sheep. He shook off his shock and got up.

With Rolfe's sometimes aggressive assistance, Morgan grabbed a half dozen "volunteers" and headed out to their right. He ordered the men left behind to keep shooting in the general direction of the German gun. Maybe they'd hit something. Maybe they'd help keep the Germans' heads down. At least it would give them something to do. He hoped to keep out of sight until he was behind the German gun.

No such luck. They had just squeezed through a section of hedgerow and onto some farmer's field when a machine gun opened up and two of his men fell. One was clearly dead while the other grabbed his leg, then writhed and screamed as blood spurted out. Of course the Germans would be expecting a flank attack, Jack thought savagely. Of course they would have machine guns waiting to cut the attackers to pieces. Damn it. What was he thinking?

A second Sherman arrived, but this one's commander was smarter. He drove down the other side of the road, keeping the damaged and burning U.S. vehicles between him and the Germans. Then he turned to his left, presenting his more heavily armored front, and began spraying the trees with his machine guns while the seventy-five-millimeter gun chewed up the place where they thought they saw the gun flashes. Jack was dismayed that there was so little rifle fire coming from the men in the stalled column. Was he the only one who wanted to take on the Germans?

After firing a few rounds, the tank crossed the road and moved carefully towards the trees. There was no return fire. Jack gathered his remaining volunteers and, reinforced by more men and Sergeant Major Rolfe, they moved slowly towards the enemy position.

The Germans had departed, but two of their comrades lay sprawled on the ground as testimony to the fact that the fight hadn't been totally one-sided. However, the eighty-eight and the machine guns were gone. Tracks showed where the Germans had loaded up and moved out down another dirt road.

The Germans had done what they'd set out to do, a quick massacre of a helpless column at the cost of only a couple of dead krauts.

Morgan laid his weapon against a tree and tried to control the shaking that was affecting his hands. He hadn't fired a shot. "Nice try, Captain," said Rolfe. He offered his canteen to Morgan who gratefully accepted. "Your first battle, sir?"

"Is it that obvious?" he asked and Rolfe chuckled.

Behind them the dead and dying were being picked up while destroyed and damaged vehicles were pushed off the road. The column was moving again. Morgan wondered if this was how it was going to be all the way to the Rhine and beyond.

Hours later the column had lurched to a halt and Morgan did a quick job of setting up a security perimeter— no real fortifications, only barbed wire this time as it was understood they'd be on the move again tomorrow morning. They hadn't reached the actual front lines, although the sound of artillery had grown sharper and they'd passed through American 155mm batteries firing at something off in the distance. Along with the one-sided fighting earlier in the day, the effect was sobering.

Morgan wasn't surprised when Colonel Stoddard told him to report. Like Levin said, unless provoked or served incompetently, Stoddard was a fairly decent sort. A West Pointer in his mid-forties, he was short like most tankers, had thinning gray hair and eyes that pierced right through you.

Morgan reported and was told to sit down. "Captain, I just don't know whether to congratulate you or kick you in the head. Your stunt this afternoon showed initiative and courage under fire and for that you are to be commended. However, you took half a dozen men on a senseless foray and now one is dead and another badly wounded. What do you have to say?"

Jack took a deep breath. *What's the worst Stoddard can do,* he wondered, *send me home?* "Colonel, we were under fire and men were dying. I did what I thought was best. I hoped to distract the eighty-eight and maybe get them to withdraw. I didn't suspect a machine gun, just like we didn't expect the eighty-eight."

"It was about a quarter mile away and you told your men to start shooting at it while you tried to flank it. Did you really think they'd hit anything?"

"No, sir. I just hoped to confuse the Germans and give our boys something to shoot back at. Frankly, sir, I was a little disconcerted at how few of our guys actually did shoot."

"Why didn't you wait for the cavalry?"

"I saw the first tank come down and get killed. I didn't want to wait for another to come and die."

Lieutenant Colonel Whiteside came in and took a folding chair by Stoddard. "I have casualty figures, Colonel. Fifteen dead and eleven wounded, several seriously."

Stoddard winced in pain. He might be a gruff bastard but he obviously cared for his men as much as he cared about protecting his skin. And, Morgan thought sadly, one of the dead and one of the wounded were a result of his actions. He could still see the half-track in front of his Jeep blowing up and the Sherman being destroyed. That was why there were more dead than wounded. Nobody had a chance to get out.

"We learned a lot today," Stoddard said quietly.

"First, we will have flankers out whenever possible, although the damned hedgerows hinder that. Second, we will have heavy weapons mixed in among the helpless so they can fight back. In sum, Morgan, you did well. Perfect? No. But well. You actually did something while others were hiding in the grass and crying for their mommies."

"Colonel, I was scared shitless, too."

"But, like the colonel said, you actually did something," said Whiteside, "and you learned a dirty little secret today. In combat, many, many men will simply freeze and not fire their weapons." He handed Jack a small box. "This just came for you, Captain."

Puzzled, Morgan opened it. His jaw dropped. It was a Bronze Star. "What the hell is this for, sir?"

"Your actions on the LST," said Whiteside. "You saved a man while the ship was blowing up, or don't you remember? A Commander Stephens put you up for it. There was some bureaucratic disagreement as to who should give you the medal, the army or the navy, since you saved a GI but were on a navy ship. It was decided the army should do it since you're one of us. Congratulations. You're now an official hero. And oh yeah, you're getting a Purple Heart as well, or had you forgotten about your shoulder and that ugly cut on your face?"

"Frankly I had, sir."

Stoddard stood and they shook hands. "Yeah," said Stoddard, "you've proven to be a pleasant surprise. Now go back and have some of Levin's clandestine wine and tell him to bring me some, too. I need it after today."

★ CHAPTER 4 ★

VARNER ARRIVED AT HIS BERLIN APARTMENT DIRTY and late for dinner. He didn't bother to change. He sat and ate slowly and without enthusiasm. He endured their stares because Magda insisted that he needed to eat to keep up his strength. Margarete, little Magpie, gazed at him, wide-eyed. She had never seen him in a filthy uniform before. She was a bright little girl and both he and Magda loved her deeply. Although, at fourteen and with her figure ripening, perhaps she wasn't so little anymore. Regardless, she knew when to keep still. The only question she asked was whether Hitler was dead. Rumors, she said, were flying. He told her he didn't know. He hated lying to his daughter, but he couldn't take the chance that she might say something to a schoolmate that could get back to the damned Gestapo.

When she was done eating, Margarete kissed him on the forehead and announced that she had studying to do. Magda then informed her husband that he was filthy and it was time for him to clean up.

Varner grunted and went to the bathroom where he filled a tub with hot water, stripped, and lay down in it, letting its warmth cleanse him in more ways than one.

He toweled down and walked naked into the bedroom. He was mildly annoyed that Magda hadn't brought any underclothing to the bathroom. His annoyance ceased when he saw her lying naked on the bed, her long blond hair undone and strewn across her pillow. He grinned wickedly. "Is it Christmas?"

She smiled and beckoned to him. "No, but you can open your present anyhow."

They made love with an intensity that had been lacking in the last few weeks as his job had overwhelmed and exhausted him. Magda was no longer the slender student he'd married almost two decades ago, but he thought the slight plumpness she'd gained in certain areas of her body was highly desirable. He proved the point by caressing her intimately, in preparation for a second time. She moaned and sighed. "Magpie will hear us," he said.

"I think she understands." They caressed each other with their lips, fingers, and tongues until he again entered her and they climaxed, totally spent.

Later, they lay side by side, sweaty and sated. Varner felt it was time to bring up an unpleasant decision he'd made. "You and Magpie must leave Berlin. When the bombs were falling and I was cowering in some filthy stinking basement and trying not to shit myself, all I could think of was the two of you and what danger you were in. And when I helped pull that boy out of the rubble, I thought I would weep in despair. We have no defense against the Allied bombers, and the next raid, or the one after that, could easily kill you."

Magda was not surprised. In fact, part of her welcomed it. She wanted to be by Ernst's side in Berlin, but she also wanted to protect their daughter. And she was not too proud to admit that the bombings, an almost daily ritual now, terrified and horrified her. She counted it a blessing that, so far, the sirens hadn't sounded this night.

"Now that I'm assigned to von Rundstedt's staff, I can get authorization for you to go to your sister's place."

Magda's sister Bertha and her husband Eric Muller lived in a village near Hachenburg, many miles farther west and near the Rhine. To her knowledge no bombs had fallen there, although Hachenburg itself had been hit.

"Agreed," she said, "and there is another problem that would be solved. Do you remember Volkmar Detloff?"

"Of course. Pure Aryan from a totally Nazi family, he's a fanatically Nazi Youth, and thinks he's a new god even though he's only, what? Sixteen?"

"Well, he told Margarete that if she wanted to be a good young Nazi, she should let him fuck her. For the glory of the Reich, of course."

Varner lit a forbidden cigarette. He'd borrowed a couple at the Chancellery. "Did he actually use those words?"

"Yes, but don't think our precious Margarete hasn't heard them before."

"I don't care. Young Volkmar certainly has a way with words. A shame he is going to die violently at such a young age."

Magda giggled. "She told me she told him she'd rather lose her virginity to a frog."

Varner's anger faded. He knew he would do nothing about Detloff. The boy's father was a fairly high ranking member of the Nazi Party and the SS, and a minor aide to Himmler. "I think an immediate move to your sister's at Hachenburg would be good. How do you think Magpie will feel about this?"

"She'll go. She'll miss some of her schoolmates, but she comprehends quite a lot. She even asked me too if Hitler was dead."

"What did you tell her?" He had told Magda the truth, knowing she could and would keep the secret.

"Just like you said, I told her I didn't know. She told me that meant he was dead. She said that if I knew he was alive, I would have said so. She's very smart, don't you think?"

Colonel Ernst Varner declined to respond. He was sound asleep.

Military, political, and economic were the three problems confronting Reichsfuhrer Heinrich Himmler as he assumed control of what remained of Hitler's empire. The political situation was somewhat stable, so that left military and economic. Albert Speer had proven himself to be as knowledgeable about the economy as anyone in the Reich and, at the tender age of forty, was Minister for Armaments and Production. If the Reich was to survive, it was imperative that Speer provide the sinews of war.

Himmler had just concluded a predictably unsatisfactory discussion with von Ribbentrop in which the very undiplomatic foreign secretary stated the obvious. The neutral nations most sympathetic to Germany—Sweden, Spain, and Switzerland—were confused. Just who was in charge in the Third Reich, was Hitler gone for good or just for a little while? Who gave Heinrich Himmler the right to appoint von Ribbentrop as a go-between, or to even think of commencing negotiations that would end the war? The Americans, British, and Russians had all previously issued statements stating that they would fight on until Germany surrendered unconditionally, which was totally unacceptable to the Nazi hierarchy. They understood fully that their heads would roll.

So what was going on, the neutrals wondered, and why did Germany think the Allies would change their stance on negotiations?

Ribbentrop had argued that an announcement regarding Hitler's death must be made soon, almost immediately. Rumors of his demise were already swirling. Some of the people who had seen his broken body couldn't resist blabbing.

Himmler agreed and said that steps were underway by Goebbels to prepare Germany for the terrible announcement that would shock all of Germany and the world. Himmler was also taking other steps which he kept to himself. Ribbentrop would be pushed aside as chief negotiator and Franz von Papen, the sixty-six-year-old relic of the First World War's failed diplomacy, would be recalled from his ambassadorial post in Turkey. The Turks were also neutral and Himmler wondered if they might function as a conduit to the Allies. At any rate, von Papen was a more subtle diplomat and not rough edged like Ribbentrop, who had gotten his position because of his slavish devotion to the late Fuhrer.

His secretary announced that Rundstedt and Speer

had arrived. He told her to send them in and they seated themselves. The young Speer looked uncomfortable, and why not? However competent, and he was indeed that, he was Hitler's creature and he'd just been told that there was a new regime.

"Let me be blunt," Himmler said to von Rundstedt. "I asked you how we could win the war, and you said we could not in the traditional sense. You said we must shorten our lines and give up many of our conquered territories. Is this still your plan?"

"Indeed, and to do that I need at least a million more men, Reichsfuhrer, and I need them as quickly as possible. However, they do exist. Four hundred thousand men are languishing in the Courland peninsula in Latvia. Hitler refused to withdraw them as such retreats were unacceptable to him. He consistently refused to give up conquered territory. Hitler is dead and I need those men. If I don't get those and others, we are doomed. Right now there is a corridor available for them to use and they must take it before the Soviets cut them off. Even though many of them are far from the best men, they will do well in the defensive. Kindly recall that too many of our very best soldiers are dead."

Himmler nodded. "Do it." Again he had the nightmare vision of himself as a prisoner of the British or the Americans, or even the French with their damned guillotine.

"Then, I want every available man from Norway. Another four hundred thousand men are doing nothing there but wait for an Allied invasion we now know will never come. Hold onto Oslo if we must, but send me at least another two hundred thousand men from a country that isn't fighting."

Again Himmler agreed, albeit with more reluctance. If the Allies realized that German forces were exiting Norway, they would invade and Norway was next to "neutral" Sweden which supplied so much of Germany's war-fighting materiel. The army would have to figure out a way to pull its troops out secretly.

"And as to Italy," Rundstedt continued, "several hundred thousand of our best and most seasoned combat troops are tied up fighting the Allies in the mountains north of Rome. I propose that we withdraw most of those men to Germany and leave a rear guard to defend the mountain passes. I've heard it said that Churchill feels it is the soft underbelly of Europe and that the Allies should attack up that route." He laughed harshly. "Let them try. Even a small force defending a mountain pass can ruin Churchill's hopes."

"Anything else?" asked Himmler. He was clearly unhappy but not arguing.

"Yes, Reichsfuhrer. Yugoslavia, Hungary, Bulgaria, and Rumania must also be stripped of German soldiers. Let the Croats and the Serbs kill each other like they've been doing for centuries. I don't care."

Himmler chuckled. "I don't either. What more do you want?"

"I want control of your SS forces. They are not very good as an army but they can be used to slow down the Reds."

Himmler glared but did not respond. He had a higher rating of the fighting qualities of the SS divisions than did the regular army's generals. Also, the thought of giving up his personal army was repugnant.

Rundstedt continued. "If you are concerned that I will make myself the new Fuhrer, don't be. I am nearly seventy years old and a soldier, not a politician or a governor. I want to save Germany, not rule her."

Himmler nodded weakly. It would be done as the field marshal wanted. "Are you finally through?"

Rundstedt laughed. "In a way I'm just beginning. In both France and Russia our armies must be allowed to fight a defensive war, and a fluid war at that. There must be no proclamation of fortresses that must be held to the last man when armies can be saved and used again. In other words, no last stands as at Stalingrad, and no North Africas. Those debacles cost a half million of our best men. I would like to have them today, wouldn't you, Reichsfuhrer?"

Himmler writhed internally. Everything the hateful old general was saying was true.

"In addition," Rundstedt continued, "I want at least two million men culled from the workforce and drafted into the army. How they will be replaced in the factories is Herr Speer's dilemma. The men drafted will construct and man defensive positions. We will also use civilians from occupied lands along with prisoners of war we hold. Can you do that, Herr Speer?"

Speer spoke for the first time and to Himmler. "If you will permit me to draft women, boys, and older men to work in factories and in other war efforts, yes." Using women had been anathema to Hitler. They were supposed to stay home and produce new little Nazis.

"And if you will also permit it," added Speer, "I recommend increasing the food rations of foreign workers so they don't die in such numbers that they always need to be replaced. And that includes the Jews."

"But only for a while," snapped Himmler. Ultimately the Jews would have to be disposed of. Their inevitable fate could be deferred, but not cancelled. He wondered just where Speer would get the additional food since almost everyone in Germany was on short rations. He didn't enquire further. If Speer said he could get more rations, then he could get more rations.

"Two last things," said Rundstedt. He was clearly pleased at the concessions made by Himmler.

"Only two?" Himmler responded with resigned humor. The steps so far proposed were vile, but he could see their necessity.

"First, there are U-boats in the Mediterranean and elsewhere that are doing absolutely nothing. They should be attacking shipping in the Atlantic and even in the Channel." Himmler nodded agreement. It had been Hitler's decision to maintain submarines in the Mediterranean where they had been effectively neutralized.

"And lastly, the Jews. The shipments of Jews to Auschwitz and elsewhere is tying up many scores of trains that are and will be needed to transfer armies to defend the Reich. I wish you to suspend the collection of Jews until the crisis is over."

Himmler nodded again. "But not a moment longer."

Lieutenant General Walter Bedell Smith, called Beetle by his friends and general by everyone else, was Dwight Eisenhower's chief of staff at SHAEF, Supreme Headquarters Allied Expeditionary Force; it was a position he'd ably held for several years. He was brusque and a taskmaster, and he was poring over reports when Colonel Tom Granville knocked and entered.

Smith glared at him. "I am too goddamned busy

to give you even a second, Colonel, so get the hell out of here."

"Hitler's dead," Granville said, stifling a grin.

Smith blinked and looked up; a smile split his face. "Sit down and take a load off, Tom. Let's talk for a spell, perhaps have some tea. Now what the hell's your source, and I sincerely hope it's good?"

"Berlin radio has commenced playing dirges and funeral marches."

"That's it? From sad music you extrapolate that the fucking little paper-hanger is dead?"

"That's enough, General. The Nazis only do that when something sad and significant has happened. I believe the last time they played dirges was for their surrender at Stalingrad. And, since nothing in the way of military disasters is occurring, it can only be that someone important is dead."

Smith was not convinced. "What about Goering? He's been out of the picture for a while. And how about Himmler? Goebbels?"

"Possible but not likely. We've picked up nothing being wrong with Goering other than the usual drugs and booze and, barring assassination, we've heard nothing about his health. Himmler, of course, is just fine and so is Goebbels. Ergo, it's Hitler who has just died from his injuries."

Smith grinned wickedly. "Damn, it would be a terrible shame if Hitler died. Did any of this come from our British friends?"

"No, sir."

"What music are the Germans playing?"

"Mainly recorded symphonies of Wagner's more somber music. He is, was, Hitler's favorite composer.

If the Nazis limited behavioral pattern holds, in about an hour or so, a deep voice will say that a major announcement will follow shortly. The whole process is designed by Goebbels to warn the German people that something bad has happened."

"But the Brits know about this too, right?"

"They have to, sir. They've got their own people monitoring German radio stations and they have doubtless reached the same conclusion. I wouldn't doubt that Churchill's already been informed."

Smith stood. Information about Hitler's death would go to Washington and FDR, but would come from Ike and not Churchill. "Okay, that's enough to interrupt Ike. The plans to move SHAEF to France and kick Montgomery out of his command chair will have to wait for a few minutes. If Ike concurs, and I think he will, we will be informing General Marshall pronto. He can take the info to Roosevelt." He laughed wryly. "At least FDR won't hear it first from Churchill if I can help it."

Granville decided to take it one step farther. "Maybe it'll help us decide what to do about Phips, the little man who killed him."

Smith rolled his eyes. "If only all our problems were that simple."

Fourteen-year-old Margarete Varner sat on her favorite chair in her bedroom. Her knees were tucked under her chin as she listened intently to what the man on the radio was saying. It was impossible. It could not be so. Adolf Hitler could not be dead. Yet, the strident voice of Joseph Goebbels cried out that it was indeed so.

Goebbels said that the Fuhrer had died of his massive wounds after fighting heroically for his life and for the Reich. Germany, he said, would mourn privately. There was a war to be won. The Fuhrer would be interred in secret so that Allied bombers could not desecrate either the ceremony or his final resting place. When the war was over and the enemies of the Reich had been defeated, then would be the time for a public ceremony and a mausoleum of epic proportions, a shrine to the life and dreams of Adolf Hitler.

According to Hitler's will, Heinrich Himmler was the new Fuhrer and Gerd von Rundstedt now commanded the armed forces of the Reich. Nothing was said about Hermann Goering, which puzzled Margarete. Nor was anything said about Martin Bormann, a shadowy figure her father had mentioned was becoming the *éminence grise* behind Hitler.

She could not quite shake the feeling of profound shock. She was fourteen and Adolf Hitler had been the Fuhrer for twelve of those years. All her conscious life was wrapped around Hitler. His picture was everywhere and his salute was a normal way of greeting friends and associates. Her teachers in school praised him just as they condemned the Jews who conspired against Germany.

She imagined an American girl's feelings if Roosevelt had died, or an English girl's if either Churchill or King George was dead. She sometimes wished she didn't imagine so much.

And Goebbels had said that it had been the Jews who had killed him. He said that Roosevelt, the Jew, had conspired with Morgenthau, the Jew who was in charge of America's money, to kill him, murder him.

Yet, Margarete was puzzled. She was a very bright girl and understood that the war was going against Germany. After all, weren't the Russians pushing into Poland and weren't the Americans, assisted by the British, crossing France? Italy's fascist government had surrendered and that pompous fool, Mussolini, was on the run. German soldiers were fighting the Americans and British in Italy and not the Italians who, her father said, were surrendering in droves to the Allies, and that was just so wrong.

She also knew that Roosevelt wasn't a Jew. Her father had let that slip one night.

She understood that her parents said things they didn't want her to hear and she understood they involved the conduct of the war and Germany's future. They didn't want her blurting out something to her schoolmates that might result in questioning by the Gestapo. She shuddered. People were arrested and turned over to the Gestapo and, so many times, were never heard from again. Or if they did somehow surface, they were never the same, either physically or emotionally. She knew better than to ask what had happened to them. A friend whose cousin had been arrested had whispered to her that the beatings were the easy part. It was terrible to contemplate, but what else should be done to enemies of the Reich? But if the Reich was so perfect, she asked herself, why did it have enemies?

So what would be her family's future? She had positive emotions about moving to a farm near Hachenburg, even though it would mean leaving her friends. It would be a great adventure, and it would be safer for her and her mother. Her father wouldn't have to worry about them during the bombings. No more cringing and hiding when the sirens went off and no more crying when the bombs fell. And better, no more staring sadly at empty desks at school the morning after the bombings.

That she would also escape the odious Volkmar Detloff was another benefit. She had first been flattered by his attentions. After all, she was a plump adolescent who considered herself far from being a beauty, and he was an older boy and a Hitler Youth to boot. She had ignored his pimples and his loud and pompous manner. He had brought to the surface her first stirring of womanhood.

She deeply regretted letting him kiss her since the first thing he'd done after that was to jam his hand inside her blouse, ripping off a button, and painfully squeezing her small breast. When she demanded that he stop, he'd called her a tease and a bitch. Then he'd told all his friends that he'd stopped since she was a fat little thing and didn't really have any tits yet.

Her mother entered the room. "Finished packing, Magpie?"

"Mother, I am just a little too old to be referred to as an annoying little bird."

Magda sighed. Her daughter was growing up far too fast. "I know. I just can't help it."

Magda hoped that Ernst's logic in sending them to a place near Hachenburg and nearer to the western front would render them safe. Hachenburg itself had nearly been obliterated by Allied bombers; thus it was presumed that there was little or no interest in further bombings. Besides, they would be at least twenty miles south of Hachenburg proper, and living in a large and even luxurious farmhouse. They would actually be eating real food and not the ersatz nonsense that was available in Berlin. Perhaps with good food Magpie—no, Margarete—would actually begin to develop properly. Certainly, walks in the countryside and work on the farm would help her.

A tear rolled down Margarete's cheek. "Crying for Hitler?" her mother asked cautiously.

"No. I'm crying because I can't take all my clothes."

Who was the consummate idiot who thought it would be a good idea for Jack Morgan to learn all about a Sherman tank? Oh yeah, Jack remembered, it was Jack Morgan. Damn.

Whiteside had also thought it an excellent idea. Thus, Jack had badgered one of his new friends, First Lieutenant Jeb Carter, into teaching him all about the giant metal beast. Since the campaign had entered another lull with the regiment again behind the lines, the timing was good. The U.S. Army had broken out of the Normandy perimeter and was slowly approaching Paris on a broad front. The British under Montgomery were in the north and against the coast, while Omar Bradley's Twelfth Army Group was south of the British. Patton's Third Army, which was part of Bradley's Twelfth, had originally broken out to the east, but then had turned east and was also approaching the south of Paris.

The entire enterprise was now under the direction of Eisenhower, who had established his headquarters in France, replacing Montgomery as ground forces commander.

Jeb Carter was a southerner through and through, and he mockingly referred to the U.S. Army as the

Union army and called the Civil War the War of Northern Aggression. He commanded a company of tanks and was delighted at the thought of training Jack. Nor did Carter concern himself about the small difference in rank. He'd confidently announced that he was going to be promoted to captain momentarily; ergo there was no rank issue.

"The Sherman," Carter explained, "weighs in at thirty-four and a half tons and has a crew of five. The main weapon is a seventy-five-millimeter gun. This is a short barreled version and it's going to be upgraded to a longer barreled seventy-six-millimeter one sometime down the road. That'll increase velocity and hitting power, which is a problem. In addition, she carries two machine guns. The tank'll go twenty-five miles an hour on a road and seventeen off road, although a good mechanic, and we have a lot of them, can goose that up five or ten miles an hour more."

There was neither the time nor the intention to make Jack an expert. He found the tank to be cramped and stifling hot. Carter explained it was always that way except when it was cold. Then you froze your ass off. Jack decided that bombers had been absolutely spacious in comparison. Carter had laughed at his complaint, telling Jack that the Sherman had a lot more room than other tanks.

Jack spent several hours learning all five jobs, even driving the tank a few miles and not damaging anything more significant than a few small trees. To Jack's mock dismay, he was not permitted to fire the seventy-five. Carter's tank was named the *Rebel Yell*, an inevitability, Jack thought.

Later, they discussed basic tactics as they sampled

some cognac one of Levin's French-speaking men had scrounged up. Another virtue of static warfare was that they also had a hot meal instead of C and D rations. Of course, Colonel Stoddard wanted the fortifications around his headquarters improved. More barb wire was strung and more sandbags piled strategically.

"If attacking, you should always keep your tank facing the enemy," Carter said. "That's where the Sherman's armor is thickest, just a hair over four inches. Other spots are a lot less, so the beast is vulnerable from the flanks and rear, as are most tanks."

"Why not add armor?" Levin asked.

Carter smiled knowingly. "Then, my friend, the tank would be too heavy to move, which would mean adding a bigger engine, which would require a larger tank, and the cycle goes on. Don't worry, the krauts have the same problem with weight and armor. Also, a Sherman's seventy-five won't penetrate many parts of the hull of a Panther. Apparently not enough velocity, which we all hope will be fixed with the new gun. But the flanks and rear of a Panther are vulnerable. The Panther is about fifteen tons heavier than a Sherman and is designated a 'heavy' tank, while our tee-tiny little Sherman is considered a 'medium.' We don't have any heavies in this man's army. I guess the Pentagon said it was too expensive."

"And when you're on the defensive?" Jack asked.

"Hopefully, Bomber, that doesn't mean the Panthers are attacking."

Jack interrupted him. "Bomber?"

Carter laughed. "Hell, man, didn't you know your nickname? Jesus, Levin, tell the man what he needs to know."

Levin poured some more brandy into Jack's glass. "I was waiting until he was ready. Seriously, Jack, Bomber is a helluva lot better than Stockade Stoddard and you don't want to know what the men call me except that it is an insult to my beloved Jewish faith. Has something to do with being circumcised. Carter, big surprise, is called Rebel. Don't worry, nicknames change more often than the men change their socks. Next week it'll be something else."

"Getting back to the defensive," Carter went on, "always try to dig in. Use the tank to swivel and do a lot of the earth-moving work for you. Fire a few rounds at the enemy, then pull back to another prepared position if you can. If you don't, their artillery and the German tanks will target you and hit you, dug in or not."

Jack had had enough. The cognac was working. "Carter, you really as rich and important as rumors say?"

"Probably not, but I ain't poor and my family does have a lot of connections. We lived in Virginia two hundred years before the Civil War and had a lot of property before you northerners stole it in 1865. But we recovered until the Depression came and we lost it all again, and we're now getting back on our feet. I've got relatives married to important people in business and some others in government. And you, did you really play football for Michigan State?"

"Third string quarterback. Despite my splendid efforts, our 1942 record was 4-3-2, and my big day came against Wayne University in Detroit. We won 47–7, and I carried the ball four times. Our coach, Charley Bachman, said I had potential. Unfortunately that was the second game of the season and I got drafted right after."

Levin grinned wickedly. "Didn't quarterbacks get to screw the cheerleaders?"

Carter shook his head. He'd played halfback for the University of Virginia. "Only the first stringers get the cheerleaders. Third stringers had to settle for fucking the ordinary students. And what did New York University accounting majors do for action?"

"We managed," Levin said. "There were a lot of young Jewish girls at NYU who thought I was going to grow up rich and I encouraged that belief. First, of course, I have to survive this war."

They heard the sound of cheering. "What the hell?" Jack said.

Sergeant Major Rolfe came up, grinning hugely. "Gentlemen, they just announced that the little fucker Hitler is dead."

President Roosevelt wheeled around the Oval Office. He was perturbed and it showed. The pronouncement that Hitler was well and truly dead was wonderful, but it had potentially thrown a monkey wrench into plans to win the war in Europe first, and then concentrate on Japan.

"Our strategy will not change," he said firmly.

General Marshall nodded his agreement while Admiral Ernie King showed his displeasure. King felt that America's focus should be on the Pacific where much fighting remained to be done. In particular, the Philippines were still in Japanese hands, although plans for its liberation by MacArthur were well underway. In the meantime, the Philippine people were being brutalized and American POWs treated even worse. Reports said they were dying in large numbers from beatings, overwork, and starvation. Despite his personal feelings, King would do his best to support the policies of his President. Still, he could not help but feel that more men and more resources in the Pacific would make the task of defeating Japan that much easier and save American lives.

FDR continued. "With that monster Himmler in charge, we can assume that the atrocities in those lands under German control will continue. We can also assume that there will be peace overtures that must be dealt with. Secretary Hull has already informed me that representatives of Sweden and Switzerland wish to talk with us. About what is obvious. Herr Himmler wants a separate peace. Well, he shan't have one."

"Will the British hold firm, sir?" asked Marshall. "And what about the Soviets?"

Roosevelt took a deep breath. "I've been on the phone with Winston and he is in agreement with me. There will be opposition in his Parliament to his refusal to negotiate, but he feels he can bring it under control."

"Are you certain, sir?" Marshall prodded. "England has suffered terribly. Food rationing has left her people malnourished and her cities have been bombed, and now they are under an ongoing barrage of V1 and V2 missiles. Her people are exhausted and her army is only a shadow of what it has been in the past, while her navy is now a distant second to ours. How long do you really think England can last?"

FDR winced. He respected General Marshall's opinions. Would Churchill be able to hold his country together, or would there be peace negotiations with the new German regime? And if Churchill resisted too hard, might he lose his position as prime minister? Another thought chilled him. Presidential elections were coming up. What if angry and frustrated American voters decided to elect a Republican who promised to end the war? Tom Dewey, governor of New York, was the likely Republican candidate and nobody knew what his thoughts on the matter were. Or maybe Eisenhower would run? Or even MacArthur? Anything but MacArthur, Roosevelt thought and shuddered.

"And if you don't mind my saying, sir," Marshall persisted, "Stalin's Russia is in even worse shape than England. The Russians are beyond exhaustion. They've lost millions of people and millions more may be dying of exposure and starvation. We don't really know how many since it is such a closed society, but things have to be truly awful in the Soviet Union. They might just like a breathing space."

Admiral King jumped in. "A breathing space would give us a chance to squash the Japs."

"Are you aware what the Nazis are doing to the Jews and others?" Roosevelt asked quietly.

"We've all heard the rumors and accusations, but they are very hard to believe," King said. "Concentration camps and prisons and people unjustly held, yes, but death camps, death factories? Assembly line mass murder of a people simply because they exist? It is beyond comprehension. We all know there are camps throughout Germany and a large complex near the town of Auschwitz, but to send people to the camps for the sole and entire purpose of killing them is both monstrous and illogical."

Roosevelt shook his head sadly. "But I'm afraid we

must believe. More and more information is arriving and a few brave souls have actually escaped from those places. We must put a stop to these exterminations."

King shook his head angrily. "Sir, are you saying we should give priority to rescuing a few thousand European Jews who might or might not be in mortal danger, while American soldiers are languishing and being brutalized in Japanese prison camps? Sir, our first duty is to our boys, not other people. The Jews and other inmates must wait, especially if the British and the Russians decide to leave us to fight this war alone."

"In that regard, the admiral is correct," said Marshall. "If England and Russia leave the alliance, we cannot go it alone and, if that occurs, we must give our own people first priority."

"It's well more than a few thousand Jews in peril," FDR said sadly. "The death toll will easily reach the hundreds of thousands, if not the millions."

Both men were shaken, stunned. King found his voice first. "It's impossible, sir, absolutely impossible. No man, no government, no civilized nation would ever even contemplate such a thing."

Roosevelt continued. "Admiral King, I am afraid we must contemplate the fact that the Nazis are barbarians, perhaps worse. The word civilized does not apply to them."

It was clear to the President that his logic and his decision were not totally accepted by his two senior military leaders. The idea of trading in American blood was repugnant and FDR accepted that there was no right decision, only a series of bad ones forced on them by Japan and Germany.

King and Marshall stood, gathered their papers, and departed solemnly. Roosevelt understood their logic, even agreed with a lot of it. More than ten thousand American soldiers, sailors, and marines were starving as prisoners of Japan, while millions of Philippine people, America's responsibility, were held in brutal slavery. The Japanese also held thousands of American civilians in prison camps in the Philippines and elsewhere.

Yet, to negotiate a peace with Hitler's heirs was repugnant. Himmler was a monster, the head of the SS and the Gestapo and the architect of the concentration camps. He was in charge of the mass killing of the Jews and other people deemed undesirable by the Nazis. Negotiating with him would leave the German people and much of Nazi-occupied Europe still in his control. But the idea of a breathing space was tempting. A lull in Europe would permit a fairly quick and decisive victory over the Japanese. However, breathing spaces had a way of ending, and that meant the fighting would begin anew, perhaps not a month later, or even a year. Maybe it would be more like the twenty-year lull between the First and Second World Wars, but fighting would begin again and with renewed savagery.

So what to do? Negotiations with America's allies was a paramount need. A shame that Secretary of State Cordell Hull was such a sick and weak reed. A fine man, but, Roosevelt thought wryly, Hull was in worse health than he.

Perhaps a weapon like the one the scientists were trying to develop in New Mexico would be the answer.

★ CHAPTER 5 ★

WERNER HEISENBERG WAS FORTY-FOUR BUT HE looked much older. Exhaustion had taken its toll and he appeared gaunt and strained. He was a Nobel Laureate, having won the prize for physics in 1932. He now headed the Physics Department at the Kaiser Wilhelm Institute in Berlin. He was exasperated at having to spend his valuable time meeting with a mere colonel, even though he'd received directions to do so from his superior, Albert Speer, and the new head of the OKW, Field Marshal Gerd von Rundstedt.

As a result of Allied bomber attacks, much of the institute's work had been scattered about the Berlin area, a fact that further aggravated Heisenberg. However necessary, coordinating efforts from multiple locations was extremely difficult and inefficient.

"Have a seat, Colonel, and please tell me how I can satisfy you and your leaders and then get back to my work."

Varner smiled with what he hoped was a degree of

geniality. There was no reason to aggravate the obviously exhausted little man. He'd dealt with scientists and academicians before and they'd all thought that whatever they were doing was the most important thing in the history of humanity. He'd been told that, this time, Heisenberg might be right.

"Field Marshal von Rundstedt wishes an assessment of the Reich's true military potential. I emphasize the word true, since much of what has been disseminated or reported in the past has been absolute fiction and fairy tales involving weapons that don't work and production levels that never happened. I need the plain, unvarnished truth, Dr. Heisenberg, and I don't care who is insulted or made uncomfortable. I have been told that you are working on a wonder weapon and need to know if this is true and if the weapon is feasible." He smiled tightly. "Does my candor bother you, Doctor?"

"We'll see," Heisenberg said. There was a hint of mischief in his eyes. "What do you know about the science of physics?"

"I believe I can spell it if I had to, but not much more, Doctor."

Heisenberg blinked and then laughed. "Good God, you're not a typical all-knowing OKW staff officer, are you?"

"Hardly. I much prefer commanding tanks and overrunning large countries like Poland or Russia. Now, please, what are you working on? I was told it was a very large bomb."

"Colonel Varner, I will keep it very simple. Do you know what an atom is?"

"Somewhat. The smallest thing in the world, I believe."

"What I am working on has the potential to be far more than that large bomb you referred to. My staff and I, along with a number of others in other countries, are working on the possibility that the energy inherent in the atom can be channeled and used as a bomb. And not just a large bomb, but a device with enormous explosive potential."

"How enormous?"

"An estimated twenty-thousand tons of dynamite per bomb."

Varner's mind reeled. One bomb would be enough to effectively destroy most large cities, and cause extensive damage to the largest ones. On the battlefield, it would destroy at least one enemy division, perhaps a corps.

"Is that possible?"

"Theoretically, yes. Right now, if you wanted a twenty-thousand-ton bomb, you would have to accumulate twenty-thousand tons of dynamite, somehow transport it to the target, and then figure out how to detonate it all simultaneously. Our efforts will, hopefully, correct that and result in a bomb of that strength, but only weighing a couple of tons, not twenty-thousand."

"You've used the word theoretical, Doctor, what are the difficulties?"

Heisenberg sighed. "Almost too numerous to mention, Colonel. First, I need scientists. Please recall that physics has often been referred to as a 'Jewish science.' Ergo, the brightest of the Jewish scientists fled Germany and other countries when Hitler either came to power or took over their countries. The people who remained behind are far too few and, in large part, second-rate. I need first-rate people and many more of them.

"Also, I need the equipment and resources. We need a substance called uranium and we don't have enough of it, along with other materials, such as heavy water. Do you understand this, Colonel?"

"I understand that you need help from a number of sources. Would you like me to invite Einstein to return? We could declare him an honorary Aryan."

Heisenberg chortled. "Him and a hundred others, yes. There are other issues. Are you aware of something called radiation?"

Varner shrugged. "It causes watch dials to glow in the dark and it killed Marie Curie. I understand it can cause cancer in large doses if exposed to it over a period of time."

"Excellent, Colonel. Extraordinary large doses will be instantly released when a uranium bomb explodes, and with what long- and short-term effects we do not know. And, of course, I have absolutely no idea just how such a large bomb could ever be transported to an enemy."

Varner thought quickly. The Luftwaffe had a handful of bombers with multiton capacity, but how to get them through Allied air defenses was a problem. "Could you make a number of smaller bombs, instead of one large one?"

Heisenberg was surprised and intrigued. "Quite possibly. Why?"

Varner grinned. "They would be far easier to transport. I can even visualize a uranium bomb as the warhead of a V1 or V2 rocket. Each one now carries a warhead of approximately one ton. And the FX1400 radio-controlled bomb that was used so successfully against Allied shipping off Italy weighs approximately half that."

"Indeed," Heisenberg said thoughtfully, "but I have to build the first bomb before worrying about the second and third."

Varner stood. He was making mental plans to visit Werner von Braun at the V1 and V2 launching sites. "I will report this to von Rundstedt, although I question what he will be able to do about solving your difficulties."

They shook hands. "Then tell your field marshal this, Colonel. Einstein and all those brilliant emigré scientists are in the United States, are they not? Well then, just what the devil do you think they are all doing?"

The little village was named St. Theresa of Something and was just a speck on the inadequate maps provided to the 74th Armored. It consisted of a dozen stone buildings, and included one church and a tavern. Jeb Carter said that 'bout evened things out.

Everything looked centuries old and all the stone buildings had thick walls and each could easily be its own fortress.

A patrol consisting of two Jeeps and one Stuart tank had circled behind the village and been fired on. Two GI's in the Jeeps had been wounded, one seriously. A subsequent probe had drawn heavier fire from the village, although no casualties, and Colonel Stoddard had come to the inescapable conclusion that the German garrison had to be removed before they could proceed.

The dirt road the 74th was on ran west through the village and on to Paris somewhere in the distance.

The road curved sharply as it wound through the village. Jack commented that there were no straight lines in France. Everything seemed to wander all over the place. Levin thought that all French engineers were drunks. St. Theresa could not be bypassed. Even though most of the bocage area was behind them, traveling cross-country was not an option. While the tanks and half-tracks might make it through the boggy ground, the wheeled vehicles were road-bound.

Levin handed the binoculars to Jack. "Everything's stone and six feet thick. Don't these people ever build with plywood or even straw?"

"That would be nice," Jack said. "We could huff and puff and blow the walls down."

He had never seen an armored assault and was intrigued. They were in the loft of a barn, also of stone, on a slight rise that gave a good view of the village. It was a mile away from the tree line and surrounded by neat farm plots all fenced solidly with stone. Another stand of woods lay a mile or so beyond the village.

Colonel Stoddard had assigned ten Shermans and two Stuarts to the attack. A company of infantry mounted in half-tracks would accompany the tanks. Jack had been close enough to the colonel to hear him say that a dozen tanks would be enough to handle any resistance from what appeared to be a small force seeking merely to delay the American advance. The German force had to be small. St. Theresa of Something just wasn't that large a village.

Delaying the American advance was something the Germans were proving to be quite skilled at. Bridges were blown, roads cratered, and mines were strewn everywhere. Some were hidden, but others just lay there, daring the Americans to advance. Houses, corpses, and anything that could be booby-trapped were tied to explosives. Everything, therefore, had to be cleared, painfully and with exquisite slowness.

The regiment's advance was less than a crawl. Jokesters said they'd be in Paris by the end of 1980. Others said they'd be collecting Social Security before they reached the Rhine.

The entire American army was barely moving as the Germans fought a masterful defensive withdrawal. Intelligence said that the krauts had successfully withdrawn their Seventh and Fifteenth Field Armies from vulnerable positions in southern and western France and were moving east towards the Seine where they would dig in and make a major stand. Nobody liked the idea of crossing a major river under fire.

With Hitler dead, there was grumbling among the troops, both enlisted and officers, about why they were still fighting. Hitler was dead, they said, then weren't the Nazis dead as well? Let's get the hell out of Europe and stick it to the little yellow bastards who'd bombed Pearl Harbor. And then let's all go home where we can drink ourselves silly and make babies.

Jack supported the idea of going home, although, like everyone, deep down he knew that nobody was going to leave until the German government had been toppled and that didn't look like it was going to happen anytime soon. Also, as the advance slowed, some of the older officers and NCOs had a horror of refighting the murderous trench warfare of World War I. Therefore, they had to keep moving before the krauts established a new line of trenches.

Major Tolbert would command the assault. Jeb Carter's tank company was in reserve. It felt funny to Jack to watch people he knew go into combat and know some would not return. It was a most unpleasant feeling and unlike anything he'd known before. He also felt strange being so useless. The overwhelming majority of the regiment was not going to be involved in the attack. He and Levin were merely spectators.

An artillery shell landed in the village and exploded, sending up a cloud of smoke and debris. "Ranging shot," Levin said.

Seconds later, shells from a half dozen 105mm howitzers began to paste the village. Roofs collapsed and great plumes of smoke and dust rose skyward, although most of the thick stone walls remained intact. The sound waves rolled over them. Colonel Stoddard might have had a reputation of being paranoid about security, but he was very careful with the lives of his men. He was not one for sending men charging hell for leather into enemy fire, which was greatly appreciated.

Colonel Whiteside crawled beside them. A secondary explosion ripped the village. The shelling had hit either ammunition or fuel, and some men cheered.

The tanks started to roll out and the barrage, on schedule, stopped. "Now they'll crawl out of their hidey-holes," Whiteside muttered, "and either fight or run to Berlin." Jack was incredulous. People were still alive in that smoking hell?

The armor fanned out and began their own firing. At about a hundred yards from the ruined stone buildings, a projectile streaked out and just barely missed a tank.

"Panzerfaust," snarled Whiteside. The German Panzerfaust was a self-propelled rocket, their equivalent to the American bazooka and, some said, far more lethal.

More Panzerfaust rockets streamed from Germans dug into the rubble. One hit a Sherman, stopping it dead. A second tank was hit, ripping its tracks off. The remaining tanks began to flank the village. They would attack it from the rear. Jack had a sense of foreboding as he watched the drama play out before him. Half a dozen tanks and ten half-tracks rolled behind the village, turned, and began to move towards it. Then it hit him.

"Colonel, it's another ambush."

Whiteside looked up, startled. "What are you talking about?"

"Our tanks are showing their fannies to that line of woods. If you look carefully, you can see tracks leading up to those trees and not beyond. There have to be more krauts in there, Colonel."

Jack was about to say some more when the woods on the other side of the village erupted in fire. German armor became visible as camouflage fell off. Three Panzer IV tanks began blasting at the American armor and tanks began to explode. German machine guns ripped through the thin armor of the rear of the half-tracks and Jack could only imagine the carnage inside.

Another Sherman erupted in a plume of exploding gasoline, reminding him of their sardonic nickname Ronsons, named after the popular cigarette lighter because they lit up so easily.

The American units hastily retreated, leaving four more burning tanks and three dead half-tracks. A number of dead and wounded littered the ground.

As the mauled American force returned in disarray to the American lines, German vehicles hidden in the village began racing out, carrying the survivors of the German garrison away to fight another day.

They were all in shock. It had happened so quickly. Only Whiteside was in control as he barked orders to have the artillery hit the wood line. It took a couple of moments to coordinate, and, by that time, the Germans were pulling back beyond it and the shells landed on empty dirt. Jack had never seen German armor in action and, even from a distance, their tanks looked formidable. Hell, they were obviously formidable. The Panzer IV was supposed to be inferior to the German Panther or Tiger, but a trio of them had just kicked the shit out of an American column of Shermans and Stuarts.

"Walk with me," Whiteside said. The regiment had taken up position just past the trees where the Germans had devastated American armor. Stoddard's headquarters was secure and the demoralized regiment had settled down for the night. There were no thoughts about pushing on. They had wounded to treat, dead to bury, and a number of vehicles to either repair or scrap. Tomorrow they would move out and again try to bring their elusive enemy to bay.

Whiteside led Jack through the ruined village. The stench of burned wood and flesh filled the air. They walked by the collapsed church where the smell was the worst.

"Villagers were inside here, maybe a score of them," the colonel said. "At first we thought we'd killed them with our barrage and maybe we did kill some of them, but a survivor in the village said the Germans went in just before our attack and hosed them down with submachine guns and then poured gasoline on them. I guess they were in the way."

"It's hard to believe there were any survivors, sir."

To everyone's surprise a dozen people had emerged from their vaulted and ancient basements, shaken and stunned, but alive. None, however, had come from the church. The villagers were also united in their hatred for the Boche who had brought such horror to their quiet homes.

A short row of German military dead had been laid out in the street. There were only eleven dead Germans in return for all the hell that had been visited on the French village and the American regiment. The villagers had looked on the corpses with contempt. Some of the dead Germans had been horribly torn and mutilated and were missing limbs, even a head. One had been charred to a crisp and appeared to be grinning through white teeth surrounded by blackened skin, while a couple looked unhurt, just surprised. The villagers had spat on them and one old man had exposed his ancient penis and urinated on them, cackling hysterically as he did.

"Do bomber crews realize this is what occurs when they drop their eggs, Morgan?"

Jack swallowed rising bile. "I doubt it, sir. I know I never did. I never bombed anyone, but, no, any thoughts were abstract."

The colonel chuckled. "Abstract? Wars are not abstract. Did you notice the dead krauts all have their belt buckles missing? That's because they were embossed with 'Gott Mit Uns,' which means they make great souvenirs. The phrase roughly means God is on our side, which is funny since we thought he was on ours, and not the Nazis'."

"Maybe God's neutral, sir."

"Maybe there's no God," said Whiteside. "Forget I said that."

The Germans were from the 21st Panzer Division. Intelligence had said that the division had been decimated by earlier fighting and was no longer an effective unit. Intelligence, Jack decided, wasn't worth a good shit.

"Jack, when you first came here we all thought you'd prove useless. In the short time since then, you've changed our minds and we think we can use you better than having you set up Stoddard's headquarters. Stoddard agrees, by the way. And don't worry, we won't put you in charge of an armored company. That'd be suicidal for all concerned."

"Thank you, sir, I think."

"Trust me, it's a compliment."

They'd walked through the village and past the dead tanks and half-tracks. Again their nostrils were assailed by the stench of burned flesh. These vehicles were scrap and would be replaced. One good thing about American wartime production—there would never be a shortage of vehicles. Just a shame, Jack thought, that they weren't all that good, and more than a shame that good men died in them.

At that moment, a flight of American P47 fighter bombers flew low and over them. "Where the hell were they a few hours ago?" Whiteside snarled. "When we asked for help we were told they were too busy for small targets. That is, after we finally got through to them in the first place."

Morgan decided it would be inappropriate to comment. Relations between the army and the air force were even more strained than he'd thought, even though they were still part of the same service branch. The air force wasn't independent yet and maybe never would be. A few seconds later, there was the rumble of thunder, and smoke billowed in the distance.

"Can you fly a Grasshopper, Morgan, or was the B17 the only thing you were trained on?"

"Not that it matters, sir, but I flew the B24, not the 17, and yes, I can fly a Grasshopper." The Grasshopper was the military variant of the Piper Cub. "I flew the Piper a couple of times before pilot training and a handful of times after."

"Excellent. We were caught with our pants down both this last skirmish as well as the one where the eighty-eight ambushed our column. We don't want that to happen again if it's humanly possible. The regiment is authorized reconnaissance aircraft; however, neither planes nor pilots were available. Now, thanks to you we have a pilot and a plane has suddenly appeared. Just don't ask how we got it, except that a division north of here is wondering why they're a plane short. You will command a detachment to fly it and any others we can dredge up. Levin will take over your duties. Take maybe five minutes to figure out what you'll need and get back to me."

Poor Levin, Jack thought. But at least he'd be back in the air, even though in an innocuous little plane. And, he laughed, no more tucking Stoddard into bed each night in a den surrounded by barb wire.

"Have you told Levin, sir?"

"Yeah, and now he's telling your former lieutenants

just what a joy it will be for them to have a Jewish commanding officer. He's also telling them they'll have to be circumcised."

When Phips woke up, he wasn't certain where he was. He'd been partying just like he'd been almost every night since it'd become public knowledge that his plane had bombed Hitler into Valhalla, or wherever dead Nazis thought they'd go. At least he wasn't too badly hung over. God, there had been some memorable celebrations with him as the guest of honor. Finally, he remembered that he was in a very large bed in an expensive suite in Claridge's Hotel in the center of London.

He rolled over and felt warm flesh beside him. He was naked, and so was the woman beside him. Who the hell was she? Oh yeah, her name was Margie and she was an English civilian working at SHAEF. Last night she told him she was thrilled to meet the man who killed Hitler, and then proceeded to prove it.

Phips thought he was becoming quite the man of the world. He'd met Ike, who showed steel behind his affable exterior; Churchill, who was shorter than he thought; King George, pleasant but even shorter than Churchill; Montgomery, who seemed a conceited twit; and a horde of generals and admirals.

And, for the first time in his life, he'd gotten laid. Margie wasn't the first, however. That encounter had been more than a week ago and there had been several since then, including a couple with "Lady" in front of their names and, he thought wickedly, ladies they weren't. All England, it seemed, wanted to honor him one way or another. He wondered if the rest of the crew of the *Mother's Milk* were doing as well. Probably, he thought. Somebody'd commented that his copilot, Stover, had movie star looks. He was probably sleeping with chicks who made Margie look ugly, and Margie was far from ugly. In fact, she was the best looking woman he'd ever been with. She hated Hitler and the Nazis. She'd been engaged and her fiancé had been killed in North Africa.

Then he recalled that his bomber's new name was *American Girl*, and that she'd been repainted, dismantled for shipment, and was on her way to the U.S. where she'd be on display. So would he, Phips remembered. He had a train to catch.

There was a knock on the door and it opened to admit Colonel Granville. "Rise and shine, Phips. Or you'll be late for your trip back home."

Margie sat up abruptly and smiled. She made no effort to cover herself. "Good morning, Colonel."

Granville rolled his eyes in an effort not to stare at her exquisite breasts. "And a hearty English good morning to you, Margie. You're looking exceptionally lovely."

Margie giggled, got out of bed and walked slowly to the bathroom, treating them both to a marvelous view of her voluptuous body and dimpled bottom. "I'll leave you two alone," she said, "while I take care of some personal things."

Phips looked at his watch. "Am I that late?"

"If you move your ass, you'll make it. We go to Victoria Station and you catch the train to Liverpool where another officer will take over as tour guide. You'll meet the rest of your crew in Liverpool and take the *Queen Mary* to New York. Don't get too excited about the accommodations, she's been made over into a troop ship."

Phips grinned. "Doesn't matter. It'll be good to get home, although England's beginning to grow on me."

Margie emerged from the bathroom. She'd managed to get clothed in only a few seconds, which probably meant she wasn't wearing anything under her dress. She grinned wickedly. "What's growing on you, Phipsie?"

Two hours later Granville was standing in Piccadilly Square. Phips was well on his way to Liverpool and he hoped Margie made it back to the office in time to do some real work. He also hoped she had managed to put on some underwear.

He checked his watch and looked around nervously. Jessica wasn't really late. How could anyone be late when civilian schedules meant nothing and military ones were changed all the time?

The square was filled with people. Most of the men and quite a few of the women were in uniform, and, even though it was early afternoon, a large number of them were drunk. When he got home, he'd have a lot of stories to tell his wife and kids. He wondered if he'd tell about Phips and Margie and decided he would. His wife would love it and his kids would be old enough to appreciate it. Hell, at the rate the war was going, they would all be retired before he got home.

He also decided that London had the potential to be a lovely city if only someone would clean it up. He didn't mean the sandbags piled many feet high around buildings to provide a little protection against German bombs and rockets. So far these had generally fallen on the West End and not that much on the center of London. They said that the Battle of Britain was over and that Nazi bombers were a thing of the past. He wasn't so sure. The Nazis had begun launching their rockets at anything in or near London with utter disregard to where they landed. Regardless, when the war was over the sandbags would disappear quickly.

No, by cleaning up the city, he meant getting rid of the many centuries worth of soot caused by the hundreds of thousands of coal fires used to heat London's homes and businesses. The city's buildings were almost all a uniform gray-black and cried out for a good scrubbing.

"Uncle!"

He grinned and turned. The young woman ran into his arms and they hugged fiercely. He kissed her on the cheek. "My favorite niece in London. I don't believe it."

Jessica Granville laughed. She was his only niece. She was twenty-one, almost as tall as he and slender. Her brown hair was cut almost boyishly short and she wore an American dress that style-starved British women passing by stared at enviously. She was well-fed and ruddily healthy, which also bothered British women and caused the men to stare. So many Brits were pale and drab thanks to clothing and food shortages.

At first glance, many people thought Jessica was plain, but when she talked or laughed, they found her vivacious. "I see you got rid of Phips," she said. He'd written her of life with the accidental hero. "Too bad, I wanted to meet him."

He told her how so many British women had managed to meet him and she laughed again. "Phipsie?

Good lord. At least his departure means I have a room for the short while."

Tom had shamelessly used his influence and managed to change Phips' room at the Claridge to Jessica's name. She would be able to pay for it. Her allowance from her family was more than adequate. Must be nice to have money, he mused.

"So tell me again, what are you going to be doing here in London?"

She took his arm and they strolled down Haymarket in the general direction of the Thames. "I'm with the Red Cross. When we get to France, I'll be working with refugees and those broadly being referred to as displaced persons. My job will be to try to unite them with their families."

"Good luck. There are hordes of them already and I don't think the real refugee crisis has even begun."

They paused as a column of American trucks drove by. "And you didn't want to join the WACs? With two years of college under your belt, I could have pulled some strings and gotten you into women's OCS, or whatever they call it. At least you'd have a commission."

She shook her head vehemently. "And then I'd be supervising either a bunch of typists or a gaggle of women drivers, all of whom would be working for lecherous colonels, present company excluded, of course."

He laughed. "Certainly."

She was absolutely correct. Regardless of her skills, she would wind up in some clerical capacity where her intellect and potential talents would be wasted. The Red Cross would use her far more effectively.

"Will you be going to France with Ike?"

"It's supposed to be a military secret, Jessica, but

yes. Ike isn't there yet." Not true. He'd crossed the Channel for good a couple of days earlier and set up a small headquarters in Normandy.

"I hope to see dear Cousin Jeb when I get there."

Granville sighed. "Highly unlikely. He's in an armored regiment and, well, close to the front. Please don't tell me you're still infatuated with him."

"Oh God, no. We're cousins, remember, and that infatuation occurred when we were kids."

"You're third cousins and much is permitted at that level."

"But not by me, Uncle."

However, she did recall a couple of times when Dear Cousin Jeb tried to get in her pants and one time when he very nearly succeeded. If he hadn't been so drunk that he'd passed out, who knew what might have happened. She'd been under the influence as well, but had managed to stay awake and reasonably alert. Still, he was a genial rogue and she was very fond of him.

They heard an odd and ominous sound and looked up. It sounded like a cross between a roar and a whine. They stared as a strange craft flew overhead. It looked like two large pipes connected to each other, and it was making the noise. The roaring stopped and the craft began to plunge to the ground.

"Down!" yelled Tom and he grabbed her, slamming her to the sidewalk. Around them, others were doing the same thing, while a bemused few looked around to see what was happening. The explosion was deafening and debris flew down the streets, funneled by the buildings. Screams of pain and fear followed.

Jessica and her uncle got up, shaken. Many people

were running away from the explosion, while others ran towards the source to help out if they could. Bloody walking wounded staggered from the bomb site.

"Uncle, what the hell was that?" She was badly shaken and gasping.

Tom Granville dusted himself off and tried to act nonchalant. "It's one of the late Adolf Hitler's V-1 rockets, Jessica. They've been falling indiscriminately for a few weeks now. Just like the Nazis. They kill innocent people, although they I don't think they've ever hit anything of military significance."

Jessica's knee was bleeding from where she'd fallen and a trickle of blood was running down her leg and into her shoe. She wiped at it with a handkerchief. Ambulances raced by, their sirens making that funny squealing sound. The city of London had plenty of experience with tragedies like this. The two of them would be·in the way at the bomb site.

She took his arm and squeezed it as they walked. She was shaken by her first experience with violence. She knew it wouldn't be her last. This time they would go directly to her hotel. "I thought the Battle of Britain was over, Uncle?"

"So did everyone else."

★ CHAPTER 6 ★

THE PIPER CUB, NOBODY CALLED IT A GRASSHOPPER, showed a lot of wear and tear. There were a number of patches to the wings and body that covered bullet holes. This did not sit well with Morgan as he flew two thousand feet above the ground looking for German activity below while simultaneously keeping an eye out for the Luftwaffe. The Germans weren't supposed to have many planes left, but all he needed was to run into one of them in his helpless little plane.

He tried not to wonder what had happened to the man, or men, inside the tattered craft when it had been shot up, and whether or not the plane had been intended for the junk heap before it was borrowed by Levin and some others on Stoddard's staff.

Still, with Corporal Leach seated behind him, and providing a second pair of eyes, he felt comfortable, even happy to be up in the air once again even if it was in a plane that was so ridiculously easy to fly. Someone had said if you could ride a bike, you could fly a Piper Cub.

Of course it wasn't anywhere near that simple, and a mistake at several thousand feet in the air was likely to be deadly and not simply result in bruises.

The Cub was a durable tool. She had a service ceiling of more than eleven thousand feet, although Jack had no intention of coming even close to that height. First, it was already cold at two thousand and would be freezing at eleven. Second, the thin air would require oxygen and the plane wasn't configured for it.

Her top speed was eighty-seven miles per hour and her cruising speed was a mere seventy-five. Under many circumstances, she couldn't outrun a car. He grinned as he looked down. Several vehicles were on the two-lane road below him. He presumed they were German and he really wasn't blowing past them. On the other hand, they weren't shooting at him. He thought about calling in some artillery, but the targets were moving and would be difficult, if not impossible, to hit. This time the krauts were safe.

Nor had any other Germans really shot at him. He knew they were down there someplace and had to be watching him carefully. After his nosing around low to the ground in previous flights had resulted in tracer fire arcing up to him, he'd moved his show to a higher altitude and tried not to give the idea that he'd seen something.

Leach tapped him on the shoulder. "Looks like armor in that clump of woods." A survey of the regiment had turned up several men who'd worked on airplanes and a couple, like Leach, who'd either taken lessons or actually flown one. Jack now had a dozen men led by Sergeant Major Rolfe who, it turned out, had worked on planes in his spare time as a hobby.

Jack took his Zeiss binoculars, a fine German pair taken from a prisoner, and looked where Leach directed. Yes, indeed, there were several tanks hidden in the woods. He called in the coordinates and pulled away. It was highly unlikely that he'd be hit by his own incoming artillery, but never take a chance.

A few moments later, the first shells hit near the hidden tanks, and Leach called in corrections.

Finally, shells hit the woods and shredded it. Trees and branches flew through the air as 105mm shells devastated the target. A few moments later, Jack got word that the barrage was over. He banked the plane and flew low to see the results, and what he saw puzzled him. Where were the burning hulks? What about ammunition exploding? What the hell? All he saw was splintered wood. And then it dawned on him, just as a line of tracers from a hidden machine gun leaped towards him.

"Shit," both he and Leach said. It was another German ambush. Morgan put the plane in a series of maneuvers designed to either evade the enemy fire or tear the wings off the plane. Somebody down there was sick and tired of his snooping and had built some dummy tanks to lure him in, and damned if he hadn't fallen for it. The plane shuddered and rocked. Morgan fought the controls and finally got them to obey him.

"You okay, Leach?"

"No," came the muffled reply. "Jesus, it hurts, Captain."

Jack flew low and fast towards American lines, trying to ignore Leach's moaning. When he was over them, his next task was to find a place to land. The Piper didn't need much room, or even the flattest ground, but he couldn't land the thing on a dime or even on a tree-lined narrow French country road that was little more than a path. Her thirty-five-foot wingspan precluded that.

Finally, he spotted a landing site and put her down. A half dozen curious American soldiers looked at him, wondering why he'd landed in their field.

"Get me a medic!" he hollered and they were suddenly alert. Hands helped him get Leach, groaning and barely conscious, out of the plane. He'd been shot in the thigh and was bleeding profusely. His face was pale and his eyes were unfocused. A tourniquet was applied and the bleeding slowed to almost nothing. Jack jabbed him with some morphine from a first aid kit and marked the fact on Leach's forehead. Leach smiled and quickly went into dreamland. A few moments later, a medic arrived and took over. Another few minutes and an ambulance pulled up and took Leach away.

Jack walked back to the little Piper. She now had another line of holes in her. And there were puddles of coagulating blood inside. "More patches," Jack muttered grimly.

Stoddard walked over and put his hand on Jack's shoulder.

"Colonel, I screwed up royally. There weren't any tanks. What I saw were wooden dummies, mock-ups. We wasted a lot of ammunition and nearly got Leach and me killed in the process."

Stoddard grimaced. "We learn something about the krauts, and then they try something new. All we can do is continue to learn from it, Morgan. This is going to be a helluva long war."

★   ★   ★

General Dwight Eisenhower stared glumly at the mass of documents on his desk. He'd crossed the Channel with a small group of several hundred men who would be the core of his headquarters, while several thousand more SHAEF personnel awaited their turn in London. Most were visibly annoyed that they weren't deemed important enough to go with the vanguard into the liberated portion of France.

Ike and the others were temporarily situated in the French town of Bayeux, the home of the Bayeux Tapestry. The tapestry was almost nine hundred years old and commemorated the Norman invasion and conquest of England in 1066. The irony was not lost on Ike. He'd just led a reverse invasion from England to Normandy.

He hadn't planned on taking direct command so early, but he felt that his so-called Allies were acting like complete shits. It had seemed logical and politically correct to give early command of the invasion force to British Field Marshal Bernard Law Montgomery. However, the arrogant and insulting Monty had delusions of grandeur and wanted to continue as ground commander forever, even though that question had already been decided by FDR and Churchill. The Americans were providing the overwhelming majority of the men and the equipment; therefore, the Americans would command and the hell with Bernard Law Montgomery.

Worse, Monty suffered from what some Americans referred to as a case of the slows. He was a good enough general, but methodical to a fault. Ike and many American, even some British, generals were convinced that Monty had frittered away too many opportunities to grab the Germans by the throat because he wasn't quite prepared to move. Hell, Ike thought, Monty would never be fully prepared and he was incapable of being flexible. Everything had to be just right before he'd move.

Even as he thought it, Ike knew the comment was unfair. Monty was trying to avoid the horrific losses suffered by England in the First World War by avoiding undue risks. England had lost nearly a full generation of her youth and the English people wanted nothing to do with bloodbaths and wars of attrition. America's losses in that war had been minuscule by comparison. There was the real fear that the British people might force their government to settle for a negotiated peace if the blood price got too high.

And, when given the opportunity, Monty truly was the master of the well-planned set-piece battle. He'd proven it at El Alamein in North Africa, the battle that had stopped the Nazi advance to Alexandria, saved the Suez Canal, and sent Rommel packing.

But now the situation called for Monty to move rapidly and decisively, and he simply wasn't doing it. This meant that Bradley, to Montgomery's south, had to slow down so as to not expose his flanks to potential German counterattacks. Bradley was meticulous enough himself, but Monty was ten times more so.

Worse, Montgomery considered himself to be the resident military genius and thought that the Americans were little more than well-intended but inept trainees, and he didn't mind telling this to anyone who would listen. His British public was charmed while the Americans wanted to strangle him. Ike had thought about firing Monty, but he was a hero to the

British people and would have to be tolerated for the sake of the alliance.

The flamboyant but brilliant Lieutenant General George Patton commanded the Third Army under Bradley and was screaming to anyone who would listen that he should be turned loose to chase the Germans instead of waiting for Montgomery and the rest of Bradley's army group to do something. Patton's ego was as great as Montgomery's and they despised each other. And these, Ike thought grimly, were supposed to be his friends. Once upon a time, he and Patton had indeed been friends, but Ike now realized Patton's serious flaws as a leader, and their relationship was strained.

The Germans were retreating slowly and devastating a helpless France as they did. Fortifications were being built for the Nazis by hundreds of thousands of French slave laborers, which created a dilemma for Ike. He could request the Eighth Air Force bomb the works under construction, which would result in tens of thousands of French casualties, or he could let them build and suffer untold American casualties when the attacks began.

"Beetle," Ike called. "What's the word from de Gaulle?"

Charles de Gaulle, the self-appointed head of France, had given reluctant permission for the Americans to bomb strategic sites before the Normandy invasion. As a result, thousands of French civilians working and living near the tracks, bridges, and marshaling yards had been killed or wounded. Even de Gaulle considered it a necessary cost of war. But would he agree to bomb much larger targets, and at another huge cost in French lives?

Smith entered, glowered, and took a seat. "Le Grand Charles gives his permission, but only if we let the French Second Armored strike towards Paris and be the first to liberate it."

"Wonderful," Ike said.

"According to de Gaulle," Smith said, "only the French can liberate Paris. And, oh yeah, he wants the Germans out of Paris as soon as possible. Yesterday, if we can do it."

"With allies like these, who needs enemies?" Ike muttered, paraphrasing himself. He was becoming convinced that the French didn't really want to totally defeat Germany. They wanted the Germans out of France and, above all else, they wanted to liberate Paris. After that, their corner of the world would be in order. Paris was their goal. All French efforts and thoughts were focused on Paris and not necessarily on eliminating the Nazis.

French losses in the First World War had been even greater than Great Britain's. If pushing Germany into unconditional surrender meant excessive French casualties, who could blame them for wanting to stop?

Ike lit a cigarette. He smoked too much, but who the hell cared? Mamie might chastise him, but Mamie was back in the States. Kay Summersby, his vivacious thirty-eight-year-old British driver, however, would soon be joining him in France. She was more than a driver, she was his confidante and to hell with those who saw more in it than friendship. Kay would never tell him to stop smoking.

What really concerned him was the fact that the German withdrawal to the east was working so well for them. The Germans always had good soldiers and even better leaders, and were dragging out their retreat to the Seine. Even with overwhelming superiority in the air and despite the Allies outnumbering the Germans in infantry, armor, artillery, and supplies, the Germans wouldn't quit and wouldn't break. Christ, they were good. He reluctantly admitted to himself that the average German soldier and NCO was better than his American or British counterpart. And their equipment was better as well. Their tanks were a damn sight better than the Sherman, America's best. Thank God they didn't have all that many of them.

Worse, the krauts were on the move everywhere. Intelligence reported massive relocations of German infantry and armor as whole armies shifted between his forces and those opposing the Russians. It seemed the Germans were doing a good job adjusting to life after Hitler and that did not bode well.

Field Marshal Walter Model now had overall command of the forces confronting Ike. He replaced von Rundstedt, who now ran the entire German military from Berlin. Von Manteuffel and Kesselring, the latter recently brought from Italy, were Model's subordinate army group commanders in France, and both were getting everything they could and then some from their troops. The days of Hitler's erratic and sometimes stupidly incompetent behavior were over. Hitler, the bitter joke now ran, was no longer on the Allies' side. At least Rommel was out of the picture. He'd been badly wounded in a strafing incident.

On the American side, Ike's army was also divided into two army groups. In the north, the Twenty-first was commanded by Montgomery, while the Twelfth, farther south, was commanded by Bradley. The Sixth, under Devers, was scheduled to land in southern France in a couple of weeks. That invasion, however, now looked redundant. The Germans were doing a masterful job of pulling their troops out of that area of southern France as well. Devers might well land in a military vacuum. At least, Ike thought, it would liberate the much needed port of Marseilles.

If the Nazis weren't so goddamned evil, Ike thought, it wouldn't be difficult at all to admire the way the German Army fought. But they were evil, he reminded himself. And however long it took, the Allies would continue to press them and wear them down. That is, if he could ever get Montgomery off his ass and back into the war.

Magda and Margarete Varner had first assumed that they would go west by train towards Hachenburg. However, cold reality changed that. The trains were subject to attacks from American fighter-bombers that couldn't, or wouldn't, differentiate between a civilian train and one carrying military supplies. The women grudgingly accepted the fact that any train had the potential for military use and was a legitimate military target. There was also the fact that multitudes of troop and other military trains had taken over the German rail system. Passenger trains carrying useless civilians would have to wait.

Thus, they went by car. Magda frequently let a delighted Margarete get some experience behind the wheel, which Magda found occasionally traumatic as her daughter tried to break land speed records. Even though they were clearly civilians, they had papers signed by von Rundstedt himself authorizing their move west. The

Gestapo's supporters and informers had been very active stopping those whose apparent flight from Berlin they considered disloyal. After what some still believed was Hitler's assassination, the Gestapo's diligence, along with overzealous local administrators, sometimes crossed the line into belligerence and abuse. There'd been summary executions of those who couldn't satisfy the Gestapo.

Magda had mixed emotions about these efforts. It was one thing, she thought, for the Gestapo to attack Jews and other enemies of the Reich, but there was no reason to assault German civilians for simply wanting to get away from the Allied bombers. She'd commented to Ernst that Berlin would be a better place with fewer useless civilians and he'd laughingly concurred.

Along their route, there was ample evidence of bombings. Even though they avoided the badly cratered Autobahn, they found the roads west were damaged in many places. Their vehicle was a large 1939 Maybach sedan. There was enough room for the two women and a half dozen trunks and suitcases carrying the essentials for life on a farm.

All went reasonably well until they were about ten miles from their destination. They'd been stopped several times by local police and the Gestapo, but, after only a few moments, they'd been allowed to go on their way. Only once was it intimated by a local Hitler Youth acting as a traffic cop that perhaps they were cowards for abandoning Berlin. As befits the wife of a colonel in the OKW, Magda had then given the boy a severe dressing down. Margarete thought his arrogance reminded her of Volkmar Detloff, the boy who'd fondled her and then slandered her.

The road they were on roughly paralleled the rail

lines and they were puzzled to see a crowd of people by a row of boxcars sitting on a siding. Magda thought it might be an accident and stopped the car. She'd had nurse's training and thought she might be useful. As the two women approached the boxcars, they were assailed by an almost intolerable stench. Civilians from a nearby village, their mouths covered by cloths, were pulling bodies out of the train and laying them into neat macabre rows. Dear God, Magda thought, the poor souls had been strafed by the Yanks, but when? The corpses were clearly in a state of decomposition. But then she realized that the train was undamaged.

She walked up to a policeman, a local officer and not the SS or Gestapo. Margarete walked behind; her face was pale and her mouth open in an expression of dismay while her eyes took in everything. She'd seen some carnage in Berlin, but here were several hundred bodies, all civilians, including women and small children, and all dressed in rags. Small and pathetic suitcases littered the ground. Some were open and clothing fluttered and blew about in the wind.

"What has happened?" Magda asked civilly but firmly. She showed her travel papers endorsed by von Rundstedt and the officer was dutifully impressed.

"They are dead and we are removing the bodies for cremation. The stench has become unbearable and we could not get any guidance regarding what to do with the train once the locomotive was driven away."

"How long has it been sitting here?"

"A week."

Magda shook her head and she heard Margarete gasp. "Weren't some of them alive a week ago?" her daughter asked.

The policeman nodded briskly. "Yes, we all heard them moaning and crying, but we could do nothing. They were the SS's problem and we were told to stay away from the Jew trains. The noise stopped a few days ago, thank God, but we still had no orders." He laughed harshly, "However, we could finally get some sleep."

Sadly, Magda recalled Ernst telling her that von Rundstedt had convinced Himmler to stop using trains to resettle Jews in Poland because the trains were needed for military purposes. But what sort of fool would have simply taken the locomotive and driven away, abandoning his human cargo? And what sort of fools in the area would have left a train full of Jews to die and rot just a few yards from German homes, simply because no one had given them orders to follow?

Magda looked at the number of bodies and the number of cars and concluded that the Jews must have been jammed inside. She walked to a boxcar and looked in. The floor was covered with urine, vomit, and feces. She saw what looked like a doll and realized it was an infant who'd been crushed in the press of bodies.

She gagged, vomiting on the ground beside the death car while Margarete wept. Like all Germans, she understood that Jews were being treated harshly and being forced to emigrate to resettlement camps in Poland and elsewhere, but this told a different story. It strongly hinted that the terrible rumors swirling around the ultimate fate of the Jews were true. They weren't being sent to new homes. They were being murdered. Even if the horror train hadn't been stalled, how many would have survived the summer's heat in boxcars designed for freight and not for human cargo? Not many, she surmised, and concluded that having so many Jews arrive dead solved much of the resettlement problem.

The policeman stood beside her. "Stinking, filthy people these Jews, aren't they?"

Behind her, Margarete was still half sobbing, half gagging. "Does that justify leaving them to die?" Magda snapped.

The policeman stiffened. "I would think, madam, that the wife of a senior officer in the army would fully understand that Jews are the mortal enemy of the Reich and that they must be removed from here so their cancer cannot spread. And if a few of them die in the process, what is that when so many of our young men are dying fighting the Russians and the Americans? You are a woman, and I understand women are instinctively maternal and therefore more foolishly sympathetic than men, so I will not press the point. I suggest you and the girl leave here now before I have to make a report."

Himmler glared at von Rundstedt who, as usual, was unimpressed. "Tell me, Field Marshal, will we stop the Allies at the Seine?"

"No, Reichsfuhrer, we will not. We will delay them, but nothing more."

"Then we have surrendered France for nothing?"

"Hardly," he answered bluntly.

They were in a small room in the basement of the Chancellery in the heart of Berlin. It was stark and grimy and there were puddles of water on the floor. It was nothing like the opulence that once existed in the upper floors before the Allies started bombing. However, it was safe, although it was presumed that key personnel might have to move to the bunkers that had been built for Hitler behind and beneath the Chancellery.

A few yards away from them rested the ornate and sealed coffin containing the mortal remains of Adolf Hitler. It lay on a stark concrete pedestal and a selected few loyal Nazis were permitted to visit the site, some seeming to worship as it if was a medieval Catholic shrine. Many reached out to touch it, as if they could draw life from a box containing a dead man. Rundstedt wondered if there would be a future market for Hitler relics, just as there had been for splinters of the true cross or vials of the Virgin's milk in the Middle Ages. The world was full of fools, he thought. How about hairs from Hitler's mustache or fingernail clippings in a crystal reliquary, he wondered?

The meeting included the members of what Himmler now referred to as his War Committee. Along with von Rundstedt, were Admiral Doenitz, Production Minister Speer, Admiral Canaris representing the intelligence world, the Abwehr, and General Adolf Galland, representing Goering and the Luftwaffe. Himmler thought it was deeply ironic that Rundstedt and Galland had been outspoken critics of Hitler's strategies, with Canaris and Doenitz less than wholeheartedly supportive. The world had truly changed since Hitler's death. But was it for the better or worse? Time would tell.

Rundstedt continued. "What we have managed to do is salvage an army in France that otherwise might have been encircled and destroyed. We have pulled our troops out of all French coastal enclaves, and those troops along with those of Rommel's old command—now under Kesselring—are now stiffening our much shorter and rational defensive lines. But stop the Amis at the Seine? No."

"And why not?" Himmler asked.

"Because the Seine isn't that much of a river; therefore, not that much of a barrier. Worse, it twists and turns north of Paris; which means it's almost impossible to create a coherent defensive line. Add to that the fact that our army has been badly mauled. and stopping the Americans is quite impossible. Our army's job is to delay the Allies until we can complete construction of the West Wall and, of course, the final defensive line which will be the valley of the Rhine itself. The steep valleys and the wide, deep, and swiftly flowing Rhine will be an impenetrable moat and there we will stop them."

Himmler was dismayed but not surprised. Von Rundstedt's draconian strategy meant abandoning the part of Germany west of the Rhine. Cities such as Aachen, where Charlemagne had ruled the Holy Roman Empire a thousand years earlier, would fall to the Allies, as would Koln and Koblenz. Strasbourg, recently recovered and returned to the Reich, would also be lost. The Rhineland, also recently recovered and which included the Saar Basin, would be lost again.

Rundstedt read his mind. "What we give up today, Herr Himmler, we will regain tomorrow. We must accept the fact that we bit off more than we could chew in fighting so many enemies, and must pay now with a difficult case of indigestion."

Himmler shook his head. He wondered how Goebbels would sell this catastrophe to the German people.

"That is a disgusting metaphor. Are you through with your reorganization of the army?"

"At least on paper," he responded. "Commands and commanders have been named, and armies are in the process of being moved to their proper positions."

Field Marshal Model was in overall command in France, with Field Marshals Kesselring and Manteuffel commanding army groups under him. Manstein was in overall command against the Soviets with three army groups reporting to him commanded by Guderian, von Kluge, and Vietinghoff. Senger commanded the army remaining in Italy guarding the Alpine passes, and smaller army groups still existed in the Balkans, Norway, Denmark, and elsewhere. They would be moved to Germany as soon as possible. Himmler admitted the command choices were good ones but had a question.

"Where the devil is Rommel? Do you think he won't recover from his wounds? Or do you plan on sending him back to North Africa?" Himmler chuckled at his own joke. Only Speer responded with a nervous grin.

Rundstedt answered. "He has a fractured skull and other injuries, but he will recover. For the time being, it does not make sense to include him in our plans since it might be months before he is able to take to the field and be his old dashing self."

Himmler nodded and smiled to himself. Rommel and Rundstedt couldn't stand each other. Perhaps this was the older general's way of banishing the brilliant but abrasive younger one, somewhat like he had isolated Bormann and Goering. Someday soon he would have to do something more definitive than isolation regarding his enemies.

Rundstedt continued. "On a positive note, Albert Speer reports that the emphasis on production of antitank weapons is beginning to pay off. More and more eighty-eight-millimeter guns are coming out, also large quantities of ammunition and vast numbers of Panzerfausts. We may not be able to make as many tanks as we would like, but we will soon have a pro-verbial forest of antitank weapons, and Speer further says we will be able to lay blankets of land mines to protect our armies."

"Good." Himmler silently thanked Rundstedt for not making the point that the army had earlier begged for an increase in the production of those and other weapons. But no, the late Fuhrer had insisted on other priorities, like the V1 and V2 rockets.

Reports indicated that, while literally hundreds of V1 rockets had rained down on England, their impact had been relatively insignificant. Werner Von Braun, the young genius in charge of the rocket program, had reported that the RAF had developed tactics to shoot them down. It was quite a disappointment. The soon to be introduced V2 would solve that little problem; it traveled far too fast to be caught. But would it be enough, Himmler wondered.

Admiral Doenitz added that the U-boats sent from the Mediterranean to the Baltic were not performing up to expectations. "American and British convoys are escorted by powerful naval forces. In too many instances our submarines simply cannot get close enough to launch torpedoes, and, when aggressive captains tried, their boats were sunk."

The shifting of armies had been largely successful, Rundstedt added. Much had been done under cover of night when the Allies were blind. Speer's engineers had built temporary sidings in a number of places where trains could be pulled off and hidden during the day.

Like the navy, the Luftwaffe had accomplished little. German planes were being swept from the sky by hordes of American fighters. Galland said that the Luftwaffe's only hope was the ME262, a jet that was vastly superior to anything the Allies had.

"Unfortunately," Galland said, "There are far too few of them and we don't have enough jet fuel to keep them in the air for very long."

"Which brings me to an uncomfortable point," Rundstedt said and Himmler noticed that Galland and Doenitz were looking at each other in dismay. "Both the Luftwaffe and the Kriegsmarine have large numbers of personnel doing very little since they have neither planes nor ships. I propose that our few remaining surface ships be stripped of men, guns, armor, and anything else useful and put to work elsewhere.

"The same with the Luftwaffe," he continued. "We have literally dozens of bases with no planes. At worst, those personnel currently loitering at them can be utilized as infantry, although that would be as a last resort. They will be more useful as antiarmor and antiaircraft defenders. Of course, those Luftwaffe personnel needed for existing planes and the new jets will be retained."

To Himmler's surprise, there were no objections from Doenitz or Galland. Had he been there, Goering would have had a tantrum at the partial dismantling of his precious and now almost irrelevant Luftwaffe.

Yes, he thought, something must be done about Goering. And Bormann.

★   ★   ★

The morning drizzle had turned to a steady, driving rain. Nazi weather, the men of the 74th called it. The rain meant that the dirt roads had turned to deep mud that even the tracked vehicles found difficult, and the far more numerous wheeled vehicles found impassable. As a result, the regiment was effectively stalled.

Rain also meant that nothing was in the air, including American fighter-bombers and, of course, Morgan's patched up Piper Cub. Leach was in a hospital and would recover; however, his return to the regiment was problematic at best. Rear echelon duty looked to be in his future. It was almost as good as a wound requiring a medical discharge, the proverbial "million dollar" wound.

PFC Snyder was now Jack's copilot but only after a very serious discussion. When initially tapped for the job, Snyder had flatly refused, even though disobeying a direct order might mean a court-martial and even jail time.

"At least I'd be alive, sir. With nothing but the highest respects for you as an officer and a pilot, what you have there is a flying coffin for the back seat driver. Think about it, Captain. If it'd been you who was hit, Leach would have been helpless. All he could have done was ride the thing down to the ground, screaming and praying and calling for his mother. No, sir, and again with profoundest respects, what that plane requires is a set of dual controls so the back seat guy stands at least some chance of landing that thing. You get those built and I'll gladly volunteer. If not, no thank you, sir."

Since it had only been the two of them talking,

Snyder was on fairly safe ground with his near insub-ordination. More important, he'd been right. While Sergeant Major Rolfe and the mechanics were fixing and cleaning the plane, Jack had them rig a set of controls for what Morgan now referred to as his copi-lot. He also had a pair of .30 caliber machine guns mounted on the wings with a crude trigger in the cabin.

"You know these things can jam, sir," Rolfe said. "in which case they'd be useless as tits on a boar."

Morgan smiled. "You know that and I know that, but I'd just feel better having them and knowing that I might just stand a chance of firing back at somebody shooting at me. I never realized how helpless we were up there until the krauts opened fire and I could do nothing but jerk and twist and run like hell."

Rolfe laughed. "Sometimes running's the best pos-sible move, if you ask me."

The plane was ready and Snyder was ready. It was time to go back up, but the weather wasn't going to cooperate. Damn.

With nothing much better to do, Jack drove his Jeep around traffic and towards the head of the col-umn. Jeb Carter's company had point this miserable and slow-moving day.

The column was stalled. Again. Trees had been felled across the road and there were clear indications that the road had been mined. If so, it was likely that the shoulders and the fields on either side were also mined. The Germans had a helluva lot of mines.

Soldiers were hunched over and moving cautiously towards the rude barricade. A couple of men had mine detectors and they swung them slowly over suspected areas like magic wands, while others waited the okay to start clearing the road. The mine detectors could pick up buried metal, but some German mines were made out of plastic, or even wood.

Jeb Carter, now Captain Jeb Carter, was in the turret of his Sherman and standing up with the hatch open. When he saw Jack, he grinned. "Hey, come on up here where real men hang out."

Several of Carter's men laughed at the jibe. "Good. Maybe I can get combat pay," Jack retorted as he climbed onto the tank's hull. It was slippery and he was wearing a poncho. He prayed he wouldn't slip and fall into the mud. Carter would never let him hear the end of it.

"Aren't you afraid you'll get rain in your tank?"

Carter laughed. "It'll help rinse all the crud out of it. Damn thing stinks of piss, oil, and sweat."

Bang!

One of the men at the roadblock jerked and fell. "Sniper!" someone yelled and the others scattered and one poor soul stepped on a mine. It exploded and Morgan watched in horror as the man's torso went in one direction and his legs in another.

Bang! Another GI fell, writhing and screaming. One of his buddies grabbed him and dragged him under cover. Jack slid off the tank and into a ditch. Carter had ducked into the turret and closed the hatch. The tank's engine roared and the tank lurched forward. Carter stopped his tank just before the roadblock. A mine could rip the treads off his vehicle and leave him stranded and helpless.

Levin plopped down in the dirt beside Jack. "Where the hell is Carter going? Does he even know where the sniper is?"

"If the sniper has any brains, he's halfway to Berlin by now," Jack said.

Another tank joined Carter's and the two of them sprayed likely areas with their machine guns. There was no response. An infantry patrol moved forward and disappeared into the rain, which had decided to fall in torrents. After what seemed an eternity, the patrol returned. Two men half-carried, half-dragged a wounded German soldier, while another carried a Mauser rifle with a telescopic sight. A Luger was stuck in a GI's belt. The German grimaced with pain as he was ungently dumped beside Morgan and Levin.

Carter reversed his tank, stopped beside them, and clambered down.

"The dumb shit didn't run away in time," Carter snarled, his face contorted with fury. Men in his company had been among those killed and wounded. The German had been shot in the thigh, but didn't seem in any life-threatening danger. They searched his pockets and found he was from the 89th Infantry Division, a unit neither had heard was in the area. Jack thought that intelligence would like to talk to this guy.

"The son of a bitch just stood up and surrendered," one of the soldiers said. "He was even grinning at us."

The sergeant in charge of the men clearing the roadblock walked up, took the prisoner's Luger from a suddenly grinning corporal, held it to the prisoner's forehead and pulled the trigger, splattering the German's brains on the ground. Morgan and Levin were stunned.

"Those were my guys the fucker killed, Captain," the sergeant snarled to Carter as if daring him to do something about it. Morgan had heard that a lot of prisoners never made it back to the prison pens. Surrendering in combat was very chancy, especially for someone who'd just killed several Americans. Too bad nobody would get a chance to interrogate this one, although his papers would tell a great deal.

Carter nodded. "Don't ever do that again, Sergeant. And, oh yeah, give me the fucking Luger. Shooting a prisoner does not qualify you for a souvenir."

★ CHAPTER 7 ★

HERMANN GOERING HALF DOZED IN HIS OVERSIZED hospital bed and thought of Carinhall, his magnificent estate northeast of Berlin. Named for his first wife, Carin, it had also been the site of his wedding to his second wife, Emmy. His dreamy drug-induced thoughts included his happily observing the magnificent and historic artworks taken from museums and private owners. Most of the latter were, of course, Jews. Much of it had been bought from the previous owners and not stolen, as some alleged, and so what if he paid only a minuscule fraction of the real worth? The owners were permitted to live, weren't they? At least for a while, he thought and giggled softly, unless they had somehow managed to get out of Nazi Germany, in which case they could live all they wanted.

He managed to realize that he desperately needed to get out of this damned hospital bed and go home to Carinhall. He wanted to know what was happening in Germany, but no one would talk to him even during those brief times when he was lucid. He was alone in the large, even luxurious room. Even though he knew better, he felt it could be a prison. But who would imprison the heir to Hitler?

His mind was fogged, but he'd been told that Hitler was dead. In that case, he, Hermann Goering, should be leading Germany in her fight against her many enemies. But if he wasn't leading Germany, who was? Bormann was an obvious choice, since Bormann was an odious snake who'd connived himself into a position of power, but the equally disgusting Himmler was another possibility. If only he could think clearly, he could work this out.

Goering thought the doctors were trying to wean him away from his drug addiction, but they were going about it in a very strange way since he was not suffering from any withdrawal symptoms. He chuckled to himself, making a sound like a gurgle. At least he was finally losing some weight. Perhaps some of his older uniforms would fit him. That would be nice. He'd look well at social events.

A new doctor in a white coat came in and looked at his chart. He was very tall, well over six feet, and he had dueling scars on his cheek. His eyes were cold as ice and Goering suddenly knew that something was terribly wrong. It wasn't a doctor! It was Hitler's personal commando, Otto Skorzeny. *So why is he in my room?* Goering thought, and then smiled. *He is going to take me from this wretched place and put me in charge of Germany as Hitler's rightful heir. So why is he fiddling with the intravenous solution?*

Skorzeny looked down on Goering and twisted his face in something resembling a smile. It made him look evil and Goering shivered. He tried to move his arms but they wouldn't respond. Then his tongue wouldn't either.

"It won't be long now, Fat Hermann," Skorzeny said.

It wasn't. In only a few seconds, eternal darkness enveloped Hermann Goering.

The city of Rennes in western France had fallen to the Allies. Located along the Ille and Villaine rivers, Rennes had been a major city since before Roman times and, along with medieval buildings, the city boasted a section of the third-century city wall.

It was also a major rail hub, which accounted for the fact that it had been bombed a number of times. It was now the latest temporary headquarters for Eisenhower and the rest of SHAEF, which had moved from Bayeux.

For Jessica Granville, it meant that she could finally begin the work for which she'd volunteered—reuniting refugee families. She and a score of other Red Cross workers from England and France, as well as the U.S., had set up shop in a warehouse near the center of town. At first people who saw the Red Cross flag thought they'd receive handouts of food and clothing and were disappointed to find that the intense and eager young men and women were simply gathering information on missing people.

But they soon caught on and now Jessica and the others were inundated with French men and women looking for family members who'd disappeared into the bloody maw of Hitler's Germany. Not only were many hundreds of thousands of French male POWs from the 1940 German assault somewhere in the Third Reich, but so too were many others who'd been swept up by the Nazis to work as slaves on various projects or in German controlled factories. Saddest were those who were looking for loved ones arrested by the Gestapo. Even they knew it was likely a futile search.

To her surprise, a number of Jews had escaped Himmler's dragnets and emerged from hiding, and they too desperately wanted information on loved ones who'd disappeared. The Jews were fatalistic. They did not think they'd ever see their loved ones alive. They only wanted confirmation of death.

This was information she could not yet give them.

Data gathering was only in its formative stage. Jessica interviewed them and would take down all the pertinent information she could gather on handwritten forms. These would then be sent to people who used data gathering and retrieval machines like those used in the U.S. Census. Information would be punched into heavy paper forms by IBM. She didn't quite understand it, but, apparently, it would enable someone to locate a name.

Assuming, of course, that the person's name was spelled correctly. For many of the undereducated French, spelling was an art rather than a science. When she'd mentioned it, one of her co-workers laughed and said it was how names of immigrants to America were recorded at Ellis Island, phonetically and not accurately.

Nor was her French up to the task. Three years of high school classes and two of college did not prepare her for the job. Her teachers had told her that French was the language of the world and diplomacy. The people she dealt with were not diplomats and spoke in often confusing local idiom along with heavy regional accents.

Nor were many of them very patient. With the arrogance of some French people, more than a few expected her to do something about their missing loved ones immediately and became irate when she told them it could take months, if ever.

At least she had her uncle to talk to. Tom Granville had arrived and was on Ike's staff. One afternoon, he showed up at the warehouse and took her by the arm. "Come on, Jessica, I'll treat you to some bad wine and stale bread."

They sat on the grass by the river. The wine was bad, vinegary, but the bread was delicious, particularly when slathered with local butter.

"Uncle, are there any good Nazis?"

"In a word, no. There are a few devout and fanatic believers, and a very large number who are just along for the ride, but they are all guilty to some degree, which is going to cause a mess when this war is over and we try to find some Germans we can work with. Along with the invasions and the slavery, I'm sure you've heard about the death camps."

She took a sip of her wine and tried not to grimace. It was described as a table wine and she wondered which table it'd been made from. "Death camps? Murder factories? It's just too fantastic. I find the stories about them just too hard to believe."

"Believe. And we are finding more and more about places like Auschwitz. They are nothing more than assembly line mass murder on an incomprehensible scale. We may find out that millions have been murdered."

The numbers were too much for Jessica to contemplate. "Is that why we can never negotiate with Nazis and why there must be unconditional surrender no matter how long and how many lives it takes? If so, the world truly has gone mad."

"That's the current plan, Jessica, and yes, the world truly has gone mad thanks to Hitler and the Nazis. Of course, the politicians who plan the wars but never have to fight them can always change our minds for us. But tell me, which would you prefer to deal with—Hitler who ordered the atrocities committed, or Himmler who enforced them?"

"Neither."

"Then let me ask you another question. What will you do when you have to coordinate the refugee efforts of Germans?"

Jessica paused and thought. "I hope I will do the best I can for them."

Tom stood and brushed crumbs off his uniform. "And that's all I or anyone else can do. I have to go back to my duties, but let's end on a happy note. Your cousin Jeb is with the Seventy-Fourth Armored Regiment and not all that far from here. If something works out right, maybe I can get you to see him."

"That would be wonderful."

Jeb was a couple of years older, and had always been the big brother she never had. Distant cousins, they had spent numerous summers together when her family vacationed in the south and his in the north. She even forgave him those few times when he'd gotten just a little horny and rambunctious. She would indeed like to see Jeb. Along with her uncle, he would bring a level of sanity into her new life.

★   ★   ★

"Welcome to Festung Seine, Colonel Varner," Colonel Hans Schurmer said with a wry smile.

Ernst Varner laughed and they shook hands warmly. They'd been friends for many years, starting with their early days as eager young officers in the army. Schurmer was short and plump, a no-nonsense engineer who was in charge of developing the defenses north of Paris along the Seine. He was also an intelligent and sophisticated man with a wicked sense of humor.

All around there was evidence of hurried activity. Hurried, not yet frantic, as the Americans were still more than a hundred miles away. German guards armed with submachine guns oversaw gaunt and half-starved French prisoners of war and freshly drafted civilians who worked with shovels, while German and French engineers worked with heavy machinery. The prisoners were unenthusiastic, to put it mildly, and had to be prodded by guards and prisoner overseers whose efforts often constituted beatings. The newly drafted French civilians looked in horror at the human wrecks who once had been French soldiers and then with hatred at their Nazi captors.

Varner looked on the scars the construction work had made in the earth. The bunkers and trenches would be visible to Allied planes as well as eyes on the ground once the Americans and British got close enough. Camouflage would be too little too late.

The work being done was impressive, but Varner still had his doubts. He took a puff of his cigar. It was a Cuban and thoughtfully provided by Schurmer who had gotten it and others from a Spanish diplomat in Paris. "Hans, do you really think this will stop them?"

"Of course not. The Seine is a miserable place to plan a defensive line. It twists and turns all over France and the embankments are no threat whatsoever. We will, however, attempt to correct nature's deficiencies."

"What I see is impressive," Varner said. "But you will be attacked from the air as well as by artillery."

As if to punctuate the statement, sirens began to wail. Workers laid down their tools and moved quickly to the shelters. Bombs did not discriminate between prisoners and guards.

Schurmer steered Varner to a slit trench as anti-aircraft batteries opened up, attempting to set up a wall of flak. "We'll be safe enough here. I have this deathly fear of being buried alive; ergo, I will take my chances on being obliterated by a lucky bomb. If that kind of death was good enough for Hitler, it's good enough for me."

"Why do the workers leave their tools behind?"

"So my soldiers don't get their heads split open by a French prisoner's shovel while they're in the shelter. They don't like us." He grinned wickedly. "Surely even those in Berlin understand how unloved we are."

Bombers were now clearly visible overhead, B17's by their silhouette. Varner saw something flickering in the air and realized bombs were dropping.

Schurmer laughed harshly. "Don't worry, Ernst, we are safe here. As usual the Yanks dropped their bombs too late when coming in from the west, which means they will pass over us. And if they fly north to south, their accuracy's even worse. They have a devil of a time hitting a long, thin target like this. A large sprawling city like Berlin they can find and bomb, but not defensive works like these. After a number of terrible incidents in Normandy, the Allied bomber pilots are desperately afraid of dropping too soon and killing their own men. They are now doing a marvelous job of plowing various farmers' fields for them."

The bombs impacted. Explosions rippled and sent artificial winds over them. But Schurmer was right. The bombs fell harmlessly well to the east.

Schurmer took a happy puff on his cigar. "Oh, sometimes they get it right and we lose some men and we have to rebuild something, but the normal day's bombing is of no consequence. Generally, they fly too high for precision bombing. They depend on their so-called secret Norden bomb sight, which is fine by me. Also, I don't feel that their pilots have their hearts in the effort to bomb us."

The all-clear sounded and the guards prodded the workers out of the shelters and back to work.

"As you can tell," Schurmer said, continuing the tour, "our primary ground defenses consist of tank traps, large ditches, and bunkers made of sandbags and concrete. The whole area is or will be saturated with numerous antitank guns along with soldiers armed with machine guns and Panzerfausts. In front of the bunkers, we've sown tens of thousands of antipersonnel and antitank mines. When the Allies do break through, there are several hundred Panzer IV and about fifty of our precious and carefully rationed Panther tanks waiting to counterattack and nip the Allies in the bud while the bulk of our army withdraws to the next line."

"So what should I tell von Rundstedt so he can tell Himmler?"

Schurmer chuckled. "I suggest you tell Rundstedt the truth and let him decide what to tell Himmler.

In the meantime, I suggest we go to my quarters for some dinner and brandy. There is no reason for war to be altogether hell, now is there?"

"They're fattening us up, you know," Levin announced as he stood in his clean and creased new boxer shorts and undershirt. "From here it's on to the Seine and God knows what else."

Carter grinned. He was similarly attired along with the rest of the officers in the 74th. "You're probably right, but, in the meantime, put a sock in it. Preferably a clean sock."

Officially the 74th had been pulled back to get some rest and new equipment. Unofficially, the regiment had suffered badly and needed to get over the shock of their losses. Of the seventy tanks, twenty-one had either been destroyed or were so seriously damaged that they were not repairable by the regiment's mechanics. Nor were other categories of equipment immune. Many Jeeps, trucks, and half-tracks had been damaged or destroyed.

Nor had they yet run into heavy German armor. While other units had fought the Panthers and the Tigers, the 74th had not.

Most significant was the human toll. Of the three thousand who'd landed in Normandy only a few weeks earlier, more than two hundred were dead and another three hundred wounded. Six men were reported missing and at least two of them had likely deserted. Nobody wanted to talk about desertion, but rumor said that thousands of GI's were wandering around France looking for a safe place to wait out the war. Morgan wondered what they'd do when it did end, and concluded that many probably hadn't thought that far ahead. They just wanted to get out of the horrors of the fighting no matter what the future price.

Thus, Jack and the others had the chance to have a long, hot shower and wear clean fresh clothing for the first time in more than a month. Even the mess hall food wasn't as bad as remembered. After all, it was hot and had been prepared by actual human beings. The time off was a major morale builder even though the coming advance to the Seine and beyond was on everybody's mind. The Germans were fortifying the east bank of the river and what once had been a romantic tourist destination now seemed like it would be a voyage to hell.

"I never thought I'd praise shit on a shingle," said Carter after they made it to the mess hall in their new uniforms. Nobody ever called it chipped beef on toast and it was almost always universally despised.

"And here I thought everyone else smelled terrible, or it was the stench from all the dead bodies around," added Levin, "but now I realize it was me. How did you ever stand me?"

"We didn't," gibed Morgan. "We attributed it to gas from all the kosher food you eat and tried to be tolerant of your religion."

"How thoughtful," Levin said. "And by the way, Jeb, did you notice that all the equipment was distributed by colored soldiers? Any thoughts on that?"

Carter scowled. "Actually, I have many thoughts. I have no problem with Negroes in the army so long as they aren't officers and so long as they aren't in combat."

"Why not?" asked Jack. "Wouldn't putting them in the fighting actually save white guys' lives?"

"Yeah, but it's not that easy," Jeb said. "Put a gun in colored boys' hands and rank on their shoulders and they'll begin to think they're equal to white men, and nothing good can ever come from that. Then they'll come home and want to go to school with us, be our bosses, and then maybe marry my sister. Now my sister may be truly ugly and desperate to get laid, but I still don't want her marrying a nigger.

"On the other hand," Jeb continued, "I sure as hell don't want them sitting on their asses at home while I run the risk of getting shot at. I admit it's a dilemma."

"Blacks served in the Union army way back in that misunderstanding we call the Civil War," Jack said, "and in combat. And we've had colored units in wars since then."

"That's right," Jeb said, "and did you know that several thousand free blacks volunteered to serve the Confederate army?"

They'd never heard of that. "Why?" Jack asked.

"Beats the hell out of me," Jeb answered. "If any are still alive go ask them. But let's quit talking serious stuff and get some of that bottled dog piss they call beer."

Levin concurred. The beer was low-alcohol, but it was better than no alcohol and, besides, Levin's contacts for booze had dried up, temporarily they all hoped. "Might as well enjoy ourselves before we get tossed to the Nazi wolves."

When the Nazis first invaded the Soviet Union, rumors flew that Josef Stalin had collapsed from the unexpected shock of Hitler's betrayal of their nonaggression pact and had suffered a nervous breakdown.

If they were once true, and no one knew for certain, they no longer applied. Stalin was in complete command of the Soviet war effort. His military title was Supreme Commander in Chief, and in theory there was a military hierarchy under him called the Stavka, but in reality Stalin controlled it. He also headed the Communist Party and was the Soviet Union's prime minister. In effect, the massive Soviet Union was a one person empire. Stalin ruled alone and with an iron fist. The blood of millions of his own people was on his hands. He didn't care. He cared only for the worldwide expansion of communism, and the Soviet Union was the tool that would do it.

It galled him that converting the world's oppressed working people to communism had to take a back seat to defeating the vile fascists who were now led by the odious Himmler. The Nazis had broken the treaty with the USSR, invaded, slaughtered, raped, and plundered. They had nearly brought communism and the Soviet Union to ruin.

Both Field Marshal Georgi Zhukov and Foreign Minister Vacheslav Molotov sat in scarcely disguised terror as Stalin's cold eyes fixed on them. They were in a large and ornate office in the Kremlin, one that had once served the Czar Nicholas II and other Romanov nobility. If anyone thought their presence in the home of the czars was incongruous, they didn't mention it. Zhukov and Molotov had begun to sweat. Stalin had murdered thousands of military officers and politicians. Two more wouldn't matter.

Physically, Stalin was a small man with a peasant's habit of smoking cheap cigarette tobacco in his pipe, resulting in a noxious cloud of smoke around him. He was crude and undereducated despite having spent time in a Russian Orthodox seminary.

"Comrade Molotov," Stalin said flatly and coldly, "is it true that the Hitlerites have initiated contact with Sweden regarding the Swedes functioning as a broker for peace?" He smiled without warmth. "Or should we now call the Germans Himmlerites?"

Molotov smiled wanly at Stalin's small joke. "It is true, Comrade Stalin, although nothing appears to be forthcoming regarding either England or the United States. They seem fixed on their policy of Unconditional Surrender."

"Have the Germans asked to contact us?"

"Not yet," Molotov replied. "It appears the Nazis are waiting for the current campaign for Poland to play itself out."

Stalin nodded. The thought of negotiating with the hated Germans was worse than repugnant. Still, he knew just how much the mighty Red Army had deteriorated. There were many fine units left, but second and third rate divisions were also being used in key areas, which meant that the poorly trained and inadequately equipped infantry were simply cannon fodder.

The same was true of his once proud armored forces. The tanks, in particular the T34, were magnificent, and the larger Stalin series were at least a match for the German Tiger and King Tiger, but their crews were raw and inexperienced. The Germans had their own problems with manpower, but theirs were easier to hide when fighting a defensive war, and the Germans were masters of defense.

The Soviet air forces were large in numbers and steadily improving, but they too lacked the skills necessary to fight the Germans in the air. The Nazis didn't have the numbers of planes they'd had in the past and their pilots were of a lower quality. On a qualitative basis, the Luftwaffe remained hugely better.

He accepted the simple truth that Russian peasants who'd never even been in a car would take forever to become mechanics, tank commanders, and pilots, while it came as almost second nature to German youths who had a long term familiarity with things mechanical. He knew that millions of Soviet soldiers had never seen a toilet, much less the engine of an airplane.

"Comrade Zhukov, your armies are now well into Poland and approaching East Prussia. The German defense is stiffening. When will you break them?"

Zhukov suppressed a shiver. He decided to answer truthfully. Why not, he thought, since Stalin had his spies everywhere and doubtless knew as much as he did. Zhukov was one of several leaders of what the Red Army referred to as "Fronts," Konev and Rokossovski being two of the more senior ones and both were Zhukov's rivals. He and Konev had a particularly bitter relationship based on personal ambition. Stalin understood that and played them against each other to keep them off balance. Neither Konev nor Rokossovski was at this meeting and each was doubtless seething and wondering what was transpiring behind their backs.

Zhukov answered. "Comrade Stalin, the days of breaking through and surrounding whole German armies like we did at Stalingrad, or hammering them to destruction at Kursk are over. The Germans fight much more rationally and logically without Hitler to lead them and make his senseless demands that each piece of ground be held to the last German soldier. We will push them back, but it will be a slow and tedious process and we will suffer enormous casualties."

Stalin barely nodded. Casualties were nothing to him as long as communism was safe. So many of his enemies misread him. They thought of him as a bloody and vicious dictator who used communism as a front for his iron-fisted and sadistic rule. They were wrong. Josef Stalin was a confirmed and dedicated communist committed to expanding his version of Marxism to the world, no matter what it cost. He was more than a dictator. He was a fanatic communist dictator.

He was also a realist. In the heady days after the fall of the Romanovs and the subsequent Bolshevik takeover, he and his mentor, Lenin, had been stunned when the proletariat of the world hadn't risen in support of Russian communism. Now he understood that much of the world wasn't ready, and that included many people in his own Soviet Union. In particular, the people of the Ukraine had welcomed the Nazis as liberators before they found out the truth. Therefore, he had to tread lightly, at least for now.

He was also concerned about the so-called communists who were fighting the Nationalists in China. They were peasants, not workers, and he doubted the depths of their commitment to true communism. He sometimes thought it would be good to side with the corrupt and incompetent Nationalists and purge China of her ersatz communists. After that purging, of course, he could easily turn on the Nationalists and impose true communism. That would have to wait. His first priority was the destruction of Germany.

"How much more can the army take?"

Zhukov understood the question. It was not a matter of dead and wounded, it was a question of possible mutiny by the masses when confronted with the likelihood of slaughter. The Russian peasant had fought desperately to save Mother Russia, but now Russia was safe and the Germans were slowly falling back through Poland, killing large numbers of Russians as they retreated. It was not a question of if the army would shatter, but when. If victory was unlikely and the primal urge to live perceived as hopeless, the army might revolt and communism go the way of the Romanovs.

"Unless something dramatic and unexpected happens, Comrade Stalin," Zhukov continued, "I would estimate a couple of months at best before the army either cannot or will not move forward."

"What do we need?"

Zhukov exhaled. Stalin was listening to him. He might make it through the afternoon without a bullet in the back of his head.

"A rest. A pause. A very long pause to build up our strength and train our armies. We must also weed out the defeatists who would poison our new recruits."

"How long?"

"At least a year, Comrade Stalin, preferably two."

Another purge, Stalin thought, with more people sent to the gulags. So be it. "Continue to push the Germans," he said and turned to Molotov. "While you, comrade, contact the Swedes. We will see what Himmler has to offer."

Life on the farm agreed with Margarete. After only a few days, she realized that she was eating better, losing weight, and gaining muscle. Of course, her mother said it might just be the natural shedding of baby plumpness, but it didn't matter to her. She only knew that she was well on her way to becoming a woman.

Aunt Bertha's farm was south and west of Hachenburg, which put it only a few miles east of the Rhine. The farm was prosperous. Bertha and her husband Hans grew wheat, raised cattle and pigs, and made a modest attempt to grow grapes to turn into the white wine that was grown so successfully elsewhere. Their pigs and cows prospered; the wine was ordinary at best. Magda whispered to her that some of the poorer versions could be used as paint remover. Hans and Bertha were stout and looked the part of wealthy farmers with more than enough to eat. As in contrast to the people in Berlin where fresh food was always short.

Margarete had taken with pleasure to milking the cows and feeding the pigs. There were cats and dogs everywhere demanding to be petted. It was almost possible to forget there was a war going on someplace and that people were being bombed to pieces. She could breathe deeply and think clearly. There was no smell of smoke and burned things in the air to choke and nauseate her.

No sirens went off when the American planes flew overhead, which they did quite frequently. Sometimes, she would just look up and watch the precise bomber formations and their fighter escorts as they headed eastward towards Berlin and other major cities. Sometimes she would say a short prayer.

Only two things bothered her. The first was petty— Bertha insisted on calling her Magpie despite Margarete's protests. The second was far more serious—the depressing presence of foreign laborers at the farm. Large numbers of prisoners of war had been pulled from the POW camps to help out on farms, freeing up German men to fight the enemies of the Reich, and the Mullers had three of them.

It was clear from their sullen expressions and the hatred in their eyes that they despised their situation and everything German. One prisoner in particular, a man she knew as Victor, gazed at her family with barely concealed loathing. Bertha noticed it too and simply told Magda and Margarete to stay away from him. They could send him back to the prison camp, but what if anything would they get instead? They needed him to do the work, so they would endure his silent insolence.

Bertha shook her head. "I cannot understand why the prisoners don't realize that they are so much better off with us than back in the prison camp. Here they get good food and decent living conditions. Why are they so hateful?"

Because they are nothing more than slaves, Margarete thought. They might as well be Negroes working on the southern plantations in America that she'd read about. Since seeing the death train and the dead Jews, Margarete had become more attuned to what was happening around her. Adolf Hitler's Third Reich had more than a few warts, she'd concluded, and Himmler was doing little to change matters. When she'd mentioned it to her mother, Magda had simply told her to be still. Hans and Bertha were devout Nazis and still mourned Hitler's death. According to them, he was the greatest man in Germany's history.

Everyone glanced up as a dozen American fighters

flew low overhead. They were so low they could see the outline of the pilots' heads in their cockpits.

"The arrogant yanks are doing that to annoy us," Bertha sniffed.

"I think they are looking for trains to attack," Margarete said, again thankful that they'd come by the automobile that was now locked away in a small barn.

Bertha agreed. "As long as we don't do anything to annoy them, they will leave us alone. Someday soon we will launch our super weapons at them and then they will learn humility."

Germany was a very large country and there were still whole sections where the war had scarcely touched them. Most of the major cities had been savagely bombed, but not little farms or villages like theirs south of Hachenburg. The war, however, was far from abstract. The enemy planes flying overhead prevented that, as did the feeling of dread when the mail came for those families with loved ones in the military. Far too many announcements had arrived saying that young Johan or Fritz had been killed, wounded, or was missing in such places as North Africa, Italy, Russia, and now in France. The war was an omnipresent dark and brooding background.

That evening, Magda showed Margarete a piece of paper that had just arrived by mail. Magda was clearly unhappy.

"We have been drafted," she said.

Margarete at first thought it was a joke. "Where?" she laughed. "Into the Luftwaffe? I've always wanted to be a pilot."

"No, you silly child, into one of the labor battalions that are being organized to develop defenses along the

Rhine. All eligible German civilians between fourteen and sixty, male and female, are to participate, according to Himmler and Speer. Since we are not the farm's owners or laborers, we are eligible. We will be trucked to the appropriate areas on Friday mornings and be returned on Saturday night so we can spend the Sabbath either praying for Germany's success or salving our sore muscles."

Bertha huffed. "You'd think that having a husband as a high-ranking officer in the OKW would be enough to exempt you."

Magda declined to tell her sister that Ernst wasn't all that high ranking and that he most likely wouldn't permit special favors even if he had the power Bertha thought he had. She did wonder if the policeman who'd scolded her for protesting the deaths of the Jews had found out who she was and had been behind the conscription notice. No matter. She would serve the Reich.

Margarete understood Aunt Bertha's dismay and shared it, but only to a point. Working to defend Germany would be an adventure and might help erase the lingering memory of those dead and rotting Jews. She stepped outside, away from bickering adults, and into a clear refreshing night filled with stars. She stiffened. Victor was slouching against a fence and staring at her. His hand reached down and briefly touched his crotch. She gasped and he walked away. She thought about telling Bertha, but what had she actually seen? Perhaps it was nothing more than a middle-aged man scratching himself.

Besides, she told herself, the farm needed men like Victor to work it. She would ignore the vulgar creature.

★ CHAPTER 8 ★

LOOKING DOWN, MORGAN THOUGHT THE SEINE resembled a twisting, winding blue-gray ribbon. It began in the Alps, flowed to Paris, and from there north past Rouen and on to Le Havre, where it entered the English Channel. Even from a distance, the gouges in the earth on the eastern side betrayed the location of enemy positions.

"They just don't give a shit if we see them or not," Jeb Carter said. At Jack's suggestion, several other officers had begun riding as copilot with him. It gave them an opportunity to see what he and his little plane could see and do and, equally important, not see and do. Several officers had found the Piper's capabilities and limitations to be real eye openers. Snyder, his normal copilot, didn't mind at all staying on the ground where it was safer.

"You gonna get closer, Jack?"

"Nope. Just 'cause I look crazy doesn't mean I am. We already know that a ton of antitank and antiaircraft guns are dug in there, so there's no reason to push our luck just to prove it."

To emphasize the statement, a few black puffs of flak erupted to their front. Jack turned the Piper to the north. They would turn back to base in a moment. "Warning shot," he said. "They're saying don't piss us off by getting nosy and we won't shoot at you either."

"Sounds fair," said Carter. He pulled a pack of letters from his jacket pocket, glanced at them and put them back.

"Your girlfriend?"

"She's my cousin, and more important, a really good friend. So don't give me any crappy comments about being surprised that I have relatives who can write. Literacy is not all that unusual in Georgia."

"It ever crossed my mind. Is she married?"

"Naw, she's single, cute, and actually she's from up north in Pennsylvania. I've forgiven her for being a northerner. She's here in France working on some Red Cross project trying to reunite refugee families."

"Christ, that'll keep her busy for centuries. Did you say she was cute and here in France?"

"Yes to both, although she's always putting herself down about her looks. Doesn't think she's as pretty as she is. We've been friends since we were little kids."

Jeb recalled a time when he'd thought she was both beautiful and desirable. After they'd both had a few illegal drinks, he'd managed to get her blouse and bra off before she'd stopped him and he'd never done anything like that to her again. Nor had they ever spoken of it, although he had a hard time forgetting just how lovely her breasts were. She had been seventeen and he'd just turned twenty.

Jeb pulled a couple of pictures from the envelopes and handed them to Jack. A young lady smiled at the camera. She was sitting on the ground and wearing shorts. Her legs were tucked underneath her and she had a bottle of Coke in her hand. Other people were in the area. It looked like a family picnic. A second picture showed the same woman playing tennis. Jack thought she had a great figure and outstanding legs. She was laughing and he wanted to laugh with her.

"Perhaps you can introduce me? Maybe you can arrange a blind date?"

Jeb Carter roared with laughter. "Sure thing, Jack-off. There's nothing easier than arranging a blind date in the middle of a continent at war. I'll call Ike and have him set up dinner and a movie. Maybe you can get Ike's girlfriend as a chauffeur."

Actually Jack thought the idea sounded great. But when did people start calling him Jack-off? Wasn't Bomber Morgan bad enough? Damn Carter. And who the hell was Ike's girlfriend?

Monique Fleury was a local Rennes woman in her mid-thirties. Plump, wide-eyed and still pretty, and, most important, she spoke fluent English. She'd found work with the Red Cross where her ability to translate the patois of the area into something Jessica could understand was helpful beyond words.

Monique said her husband was somewhere under German control. That is, if he was alive at all. When he'd first been taken prisoner in 1940, she said she'd gotten a terse postcard allegedly signed by him saying that all was well. The prearranged signal that all was not well was contained in the fact that he'd misspelled his own first name. He was an officer, which meant that the Nazis would be even more loath to release him as they had done with some enlisted men. Rumors said that the Nazis had massacred all the French officers. Monique thought it was likely, and said that this left her with a small child who had never seen his father. He was being cared for by an elderly aunt while Monique went to work.

At the sound of shouts and screams, the two women rushed outside. A local gendarme was herding six distraught young women in their late teens and early twenties, and only half protecting them from a larger group of outraged and mainly older village women. The six younger women had been stripped to their underwear, were bruised about the head and shoulders, and their hair had been roughly hacked or shaved off. Blood from cuts and slashes was beginning to scab on their scalps. Their faces were bruised, apparently from being punched. The young women might have been pretty once, but the looks of terror, the bruises, and the blood denied that.

"Whores!" women in the crowd screamed and chanted, shoving and jostling the six. The gendarme pushed one villager aside when it looked like she was going to hit one of the prisoners with an umbrella. Slaps and kicks were all right, but no umbrellas. A hand reached out and tore at a woman's slip, exposing her breasts to the jeers of the crowd. The gendarme shrugged and grinned.

"Collaborators, aren't they?" Jessica asked.

"They slept with the German soldiers and now they pay for it. The losers always pay, don't they?"

Jessica hadn't quite thought of it that way. "Why would they ever want to sleep with the Germans?"

Monique shrugged. "For the young ones, perhaps it was for love and adventure. There were very few young men left here thanks to the war, so a German soldier might have seemed attractive to a lonely young woman. After all, hadn't the Germans won? And weren't they going to be in charge here for a thousand years? For others, perhaps they screwed for the food that the German soldier had access to. There was never enough food provided by the Vichy government. Who knows? Maybe they really are whores and they did it for the money. Regardless, their side lost and they must now pay for being on the wrong side."

Monique spat on the ground to emphasize her point. One of the young women had fallen and the crowd began kicking and jabbing at her while she crawled on bloody knees. It reminded Jessica of a scene from the Crucifixion. But these were French women condemned of whoring with the enemy, not Jesus.

"But this is awful."

"Don't judge. What do you think will happen to me if the Boche come back and the villagers suddenly decide that the Germans are their saviors?"

Jessica blinked in surprise. "What do you mean?"

"Jessica, I have a little boy and what I make working with you isn't enough. Meanwhile there are vast mountains of supplies that well-meaning and helpful American soldiers can get to those willing to pay the old-fashioned price."

Jessica was shocked. "What are you telling me, Monique?"

"I have an American master sergeant who takes care of me and my son. I found him a couple of days after the Americans arrived. His name is Boyle and he has a wife and two children back in Oklahoma, wherever that is, but I'm here and she's not."

"And when your husband comes back?"

"Don't you mean if? I haven't heard from him in three years. I don't think he's alive and, if he is and does return, we will work it out. I will do what I need to for my child, and my husband will understand that or he will move on."

"Did you ever sleep with a German for food?" Jessica asked, not quite wanting to hear the answer.

"I was never that hungry, although I came close on a few occasions." She shook her head sadly. "I did have sex with the grocer a few times, though. He's an old man and, except for him, it wasn't very satisfying, but my son and I did have food."

The mob had pushed the six women towards the city limits. "Now what will happen to them?" Jessica asked.

"They will be turned loose outside the city to fend for themselves."

"How?"

Monique laughed. "Well, they are whores, aren't they?"

Below the slow-flying Piper Cub, a German rear guard detachment was pulling out after once more stalling and mauling the 74th's advance. The key position had been a two-story stone farmhouse. Artillery called in by Morgan had eventually obliterated it. The French had built well, and it had taken numerous hits before the burning roof had collapsed on the defenders.

A small column of German vehicles, several towing antitank guns, had then quickly limbered up and moved down the dirt road towards the west and the safety of another prepared position. They left behind two more burning Sherman tanks, along with dead and wounded crewmen. The continuing insolence and the success of the Germans infuriated the Americans and there had been a couple more incidents where Nazi prisoners had been shot. Morgan couldn't blame the men on the ground. Like the sniper, it was hard to let a man who'd just shot and killed your friends get away with it by saying, "I surrender and would like now to go to a camp where I'll be fed and warm while you go and try not to get killed by my buddies."

Prisoner shooting, he concluded, was an ugly but understandable fact of war, and one of those things nobody ever talked about.

Jack had called in artillery fire that had, as usual, missed the fleeing column by a wide margin. He'd then been informed that, as usual, no fighter-bombers were in the area. He'd sworn at the Germans' good luck, and been willing to let the krauts depart until a machine gun in the tail-end truck opened fire on him, spitting a column of tracers in the air.

"Captain, that silly bastard's shooting at us."

"I can tell, Snyder." He banked and twisted the Cub until the German gave up.

Enough of this shit, he thought. The tail vehicle was a Horch heavy all-terrain standard personnel vehicle. This one looked like it carried half a dozen German soldiers and was towing an antitank gun, although not one of the hated 88's.

As he drew closer, the machine gun erupted again, but the Cub's agility enabled Jack to evade the stream of bullets.

"Sir, what the hell are you doing?" Snyder yelled as Jack dropped even lower and lined up behind the Horch.

"I'm pissed off, Snyder."

"Aw shit, Captain."

"I had this little plane armed for a reason and this is it. Hang on."

He dropped the plane to mere feet above the road, closing at more than twenty miles an hour faster than the big truck. Again, he juked and jigged while the gunner, in the front of the truck, futilely tried to swivel and find him.

At two hundred yards, he pulled the trigger and the twin thirties erupted, hitting the ground behind the Horch. He walked the bullets up to the truck and raked it. The truck swerved off the road and rolled down a ditch. Several men tumbled out and ran off. Jack was elated to see that not all the Germans had left the truck. He was about to make a second pass when the truck's gas tank exploded. The other German vehicles had halted to protect their comrade and began to shoot at him. Jack decided it was time to go home.

"Jesus, sir, that was one helluva trick. Do me a favor though, and please don't do it again. Mama Snyder wants me back home again."

"Don't worry, I think I've got it all out of my system. I like to think I'm brave, not suicidal. When we land, you've got one job to do."

Snyder grinned. "Let me guess, sir. You want a silhouette of a truck painted on the side of the plane, don't you?"

That evening, Levin and Carter went looking for Morgan and found him sitting against a tree. The expression on his face told them everything.

"So now you know what it's like," Carter said quietly. "You just went and killed your first man and it's eating at you."

"It could have been worse," said Levin. "What if you were close enough to see their faces? I haven't done either and I'm not looking forward to the experience. I just hope to hell I don't flinch."

"But I didn't have to do it," Jack protested. "I could've turned and flown away. I just got pissed off because they'd killed more of our people and they were shooting at me."

Carter handed him a canteen. It contained a cheap cognac. "That's right. They were shooting at you and they had killed some of our buddies. And don't forget we're in the army of a nation that's at war with the most monstrous regime in the history of mankind. This isn't a game, Jack. It ain't football like you played at Michigan State. We were brought here to kill them, and that's the plain and simple truth. If you had let them go, they would've set up shop and done it again and again. Look on the bright side, Bomber Morgan, Captain Jack-Off, you may have saved some lives in the future."

"Doesn't make it any easier to face, and I wish to hell you'd stop calling me 'Bomber' or that other thing. If anybody was alive in that truck, they burned to death. I can't think of anything worse than burning to death."

Carter sat beside him and lit a cigarette while Jack took another pull of the cognac. "Somebody once said that it isn't that killing's so awful, rather it's so easy. I like to think it was Robert E. Lee because it's such a worthwhile statement, but I don't know."

"Ain't that the truth," said Levin. "I've seen enough dead bodies to qualify as a wholesale funeral director. But Jack's right, it's different when you're responsible for making them that way."

Carter took a swallow. "Know what I did back at that last farmhouse? I stuck the barrel of my main gun into a basement window and fired. Anything in that house was obliterated, Jack, and I don't give a shit who or what it was. I didn't care if they were soldiers trying to kill me, wounded waiting to surrender, or civilians, or some nuns drinking beer and playing poker. There were Nazis in there and they were trying to kill me. Kill or be killed and fuck the rules of war, the Geneva Convention, and anybody else who thinks you can teach soldiers to play nice-nice in a game when the loser gets a decent funeral if they can find enough of him to bury."

Jack looked at Carter and smiled. "Where's your southern accent? You lost it again."

"I'm bilingual," Carter said and burped. "I like to turn it on for the home folks and those officers here who think I'm just a dumb-ass cracker. When this war is over, I'm going into politics, and sounding like a down home boy is just a good idea."

"You're deeper than I thought," Jack said.

"Indeed I am that. And, by the way, I thought you

might be lonely, so I took the liberty of giving my cousin your name and how to contact you. If you're luckier than you deserve, she might write you a letter."

Jack thought he'd like to hear from Jeb's cousin. "Thanks."

Levin grinned wickedly. "Jeb, you don't have any Jewish cracker cousins, do you?"

Varner was exhausted. He fell asleep in the staff car that took him to the outskirts of Berlin and the laboratory of the physicist, Werner Heisenberg. He had barely landed in Berlin after flying from the Seine in a ridiculous little plane called a Fieseler Storch.

The Storch's pilot, a complete lunatic, was in his sixties and said he'd flown with von Richthofen in the First World War. He'd insisted on flying at treetop level to avoid being seen by American planes. When Varner wondered out loud if the Americans didn't have better things to do than attack a plane as small as the Storch, the pilot had cackled and said planes like the Storch were the only German planes flying; therefore, they were a likely target. Varner thought that the comment did not bode well for the status of the Luftwaffe.

The Storch had a rearward facing machine gun which the pilot said would be used if they were attacked from the rear. If they were attacked from the front or side, the pilot said they were fucked. He also said it was Varner's job to fire the machine gun if an American plane tried to climb up their tail.

When he'd finally gotten to the OKW, he was informed that Werner Heisenberg wished to see him and that Rundstedt also wished him to see Heisenberg. Immediately.

Before falling asleep, Varner had a chance to read the short letters sent him by Magda, detailing their journey and safe arrival at the farm. He was distressed at her telling of the death train, not only because Margarete had to see it, but because it was happening at all. Such stupidities should not be occurring in Germany.

He was appalled to find that the two women had been conscripted to help build the Rhine fortifications. Soon, those construction sites would be bombed by the Allies, if they weren't already. He didn't like to do it, but he would see if he could pull some strings and get his family out of danger.

Then he had dozed off while his driver dodged fallen buildings and bomb craters. It was just another afternoon drive in Berlin.

Heisenberg greeted him effusively in his cluttered office. "I've heard about your journeys to the west. I trust you found our defenses capable of stopping the Americans."

"Just barely possible," Varner said. "However, you did not bring me here to discuss Festung Seine or the Rhine Wall. Do you have more information regarding your nuclear bomb? Is it possible?"

Heisenberg smiled tentatively. "Indeed it is possible. However there are other practical matters you must discuss with Reichsfuhrer Himmler and others."

"Understood, but why is it now possible when a few days ago it wasn't?"

"Because one of my brilliant assistants suggested that I had made a significant miscalculation in my estimate of the amount of uranium that would be needed. Whereas I thought we would require tons, a revisit of the research indicates we will only need a few pounds. We could never have produced tons, but several pounds is well within our capabilities."

"Excellent, but when will the bomb be ready?"

"If all goes well, a year. Can the Reich hold out that long?"

Varner laughed harshly. "We'll know in a year, won't we? Now, what are the other practical matters?"

"The sheer size of the bomb that must be built. It will weigh at least several tons, which precludes it from being part of a warhead on a V2 rocket even if we wanted it to be. A V2 is an unstable platform and many have exploded while being launched. Should that happen with an armed nuclear bomb on board, the results would be catastrophic to the Reich."

Varner winced. He'd seen films of rockets exploding while launching.

"A bomber could possibly carry it, but, again, how likely is it that a German bomber would be able to penetrate Allied airspace and drop it on an important target, like London? More likely it would be shot from the sky and then the bomb would disappear in a relatively harmless poof. Perhaps I did not mention, but the bomb must be armed before it can detonate, and that should occur only when quite near the target and it is time to be used. For the same reasons, U-boats are not practicable and neither are the few surface ships we have remaining. There is a very high probability that they all would be caught and sunk."

"What about the idea of building small bombs, Doctor?"

"Alas, it is for the future. The mechanism needed to detonate a nuclear bomb cannot be shrunk at this time."

"Then we must build the bomb, plant it, and wait for the enemy to come to it," Varner said thoughtfully. "And that means it will have to be detonated in Germany. Dear God," he said.

Varner had a thought. "Tell me, Doctor, could the bomb be moved at all?"

Heisenberg was puzzled. "Of course, Colonel. Push hard enough and anything can be moved."

Colonel Hans Schurmer arrived at the headquarters of General Courtney Hodges blindfolded, a tradition when crossing enemy lines under a flag of truce. Both men thought it was a ridiculous custom and Hodges thought it would be nice if the German actually saw the firepower arrayed against him and the vast quantities of supplies available to the American army. However, he was overruled.

Omar Bradley's Twelfth Army Group consisted of Hodges' First Army, which was north of Paris, and Patton's Third, which was to the south. How and if the Germans would defend Paris had been a source of speculation for some time as the American advance inexorably drew closer. What would the Nazis do about defending the City of Lights, the home of Notre Dame, the Eiffel Tower, the Louvre, Montmartre, and so much else that the cultured world held dear? There was the more prosaic fact that the U.S. Army did not want a bloody fight in a major city, forcing them to take the place street by street and building by building. Ike, Bradley, and Hodges had all read about the horrific fighting in Stalingrad and Leningrad and did not wish to waste American lives on a gutted and burned trophy. Their choice would be to bypass the city.

Charles de Gaulle agreed up to a point. Paris would be liberated sooner or later and he preferred both sooner and that French troops be the liberators. However, if the Germans fought for the city, the French didn't have enough men in the one undersized armored division they had in the area. Other French units were well to the south and out of reach.

Nor did de Gaulle want the city destroyed as part of its liberation. Thus, the Americans were eager to hear what Schurmer wanted to say.

Hodges spoke first. "May I presume you represent the commander of the German forces in Paris?"

"I represent Field Marshal von Manteuffel and General von Choltitz, yes."

"And you are here to negotiate terms for the surrender of the city?"

"Ah, not quite, General. I am here to discuss the possibility of Paris not being a part of the conflict."

Hodges leaned back in his chair. "Are you proposing that Paris be declared an open city?"

"If that is the phrase you wish, then yes. Field Marshal Von Monteuffel desires that the city be spared the ravages of war. A bloody and destructive street fight for the city would serve no one. We propose that boundaries be laid out and that neither side initiate hostilities within those boundaries. We do not want a repeat of the mistake that occurred at Chartres."

Hodges winced. The magnificent cathedral of Chartres had been shelled by American artillery when it was believed that a German unit was fortifying it, when only a handful of wounded had taken refuge. Damage had been extensive, but it was thought the cathedral could be repaired. Fortunately, the historic and magnificent stained glass windows had already been removed for safekeeping.

"But the German army now garrisons Paris. What of them?"

"Under General von Choltitz, the garrison will remain to maintain order. As you are aware, the population of Paris is ready to rise up once your armies approach. Therefore, you must make it clear to all concerned that you will not be entering the city and that the citizens of Paris must remain calm. Von Choltitz is a reasonable and even humane man, but he will not allow his men to be attacked and killed. The French resistance movement must be held in check."

Hodges nodded thoughtfully. He could see much merit in Schurmer's suggestion. He could also see where any delay in liberating Paris would raise holy hell in SHAEF and with de Gaulle.

"And when will you actually evacuate Paris, Colonel?"

Schurmer smiled wryly. "In the unlikely event that your army does cross the Seine and appears to be capable of outflanking or surrounding Paris, you have my word that von Choltitz will evacuate the garrison and not harm the city."

When Hodges said nothing, Schurmer continued. "I assume that you will have to discuss this sensitive matter with your superiors. In that case, I suggest that you either return me to my people or hold me here as a guest until decisions are made."

Hodges agreed that Schurmer should stay. He would be fed and made comfortable and allowed to glimpse American might. Hodges liked the idea of Paris being an open city and not fought over as much as the German did. Hodges thanked Schurmer for his proposal and they parted company. The German was informed that some officers from SHAEF would like to talk with him and would he mind? Schurmer allowed that he really didn't have a choice if he was going to accept American hospitality. Hodges nodded and left Schurmer alone.

They did not shake hands.

★ CHAPTER 9 ★

THE SEINE, THE SEINE, THOUGHT MORGAN, THE beautiful Seine. Only now it was wreathed in smoke and fire and punctuated by explosions as artillery and bombs took turns trying to destroy what the Nazis had made.

The men of the 74th now took these things in stride. They'd seen how the Germans could dig in and how useless bombardments sometimes were. Still, this didn't stop the brass from making confident announcements that the attack would be a walkover. One visiting general had said that there wouldn't be a kraut left alive when the shelling was done. Carter had then asked the man if he would like to go in with him when the troops crossed, perhaps in Jeb's own tank? The general had snarled and walked away. Colonel Whiteside had merely rolled his eyes and pretended he hadn't heard the exchange.

Others were also not so sure it would be a walkover. Colonel Stoddard, for example, was not impressed by the shelling although he kept up a brave front. He couldn't have the men see that their commanding officer was worried. By this time, Jack had seen Stoddard and Whiteside often enough to know their moods and he was certain the two men were faking their enthusiasm for the battle that was coming.

In the First World War, intense and prolonged shelling hadn't penetrated the German bunkers and the result had been the slaughter of soldiers at the Somme, Ypres, and a host of other places close to where they were going to fight.

Nor had the intense naval bombardment destroyed the German defenses at Normandy on D-Day. Even worse, the fourteen- and fifteen-inch guns of the American and Royal navies' battleships wouldn't be a factor since they couldn't make it up the Seine in the first place. Nor would they make it up the Rhine, if it came to that.

In a moment of sanity, Jack had received a warm and chatty letter from Jeb's cousin Jessica. In response he'd dashed off and mailed a letter he now wondered might have been too much too soon. He'd found himself opening up about his fears to someone he'd never seen or met. But why not? For some reason he felt totally at home talking with her even though it was by mail. Jessica had told him of her frustrations with the refugees. He jokingly invited her for dinner at Ike's headquarters.

It was now mid-September and the advance to Germany was far behind schedule. The Germans were fighting tenaciously and it was looking increasingly like a winter campaign was going to happen and that the war would not end in 1944. They'd know for certain when winter gear was handed out. The weather was still warm, even comfortable now that the sometimes intense heat of summer was behind them.

There had been briefings regarding overall strategy and the 74th's part in it. The Seine crossings would take place on the same day and at several places. The Germans would be overwhelmed and unable to maneuver men and armor to reinforce threatened areas. Jack thought it sounded nice, but then, plans always did.

To the north, near Le Havre and the mouth of the Seine, Montgomery was going to attack the wide mouth of the river as it flowed into the ocean. His force would include the British First Airborne Division, which would parachute behind enemy lines near the town of Bolbec, which the Brits promptly renamed Ballbuster. It was rumored that the overall attack had been delayed while Monty made his usual methodical preparations. It was also rumored that Patton wanted to strangle him. Because of the Seine's greater width at Monty's point of attack, he had gotten what few of the landing craft, DUKW's, that were available, which further annoyed the Americans who would have to make do with inflatable rafts or whatever they could find.

South of Paris, Patton's Third Army was going to cross near the town of Melun, while north of the city Hodges' First Army would attack just above the city of Poissy, called Pussy by the troops, at a point where the river looped and the Germans could be enfiladed on three sides of American gunners. Paris had been declared an open city and the troops had been warned that great care needed to be taken to not break the fragile truce. So far, the French government had managed to keep their resistance fighters in check.

The day of battle began with the usual chaos. At dawn, American bombers flew in from the west, crossed over the river and dropped their loads. Almost predictably, the lead planes bombed their targets fairly accurately, while the following planes dropped short of the explosions created by the first. This resulted in the bombings creeping back to the river and then over to the American side of it. Fortunately, First Army's commander, Courtney Hodges, and V Corps commander, Major General Leonard Gerow, had prudently held their men several miles behind the lines fearing just this thing; thus, only a handful of Americans were killed or wounded by so-called friendly fire. However, it took more time than planned for the engineers and assault elements to reach the river after the bombers left. The resulting congestion on the narrow and miserable French roads meant that the attack was delayed from dawn until noon. This gave time for the Germans to dig themselves out of the rubble created by the bombers.

As Morgan watched from his perch in the sky, scores of small boats, launches, and barges containing men of the 116th Infantry Division surged across while American artillery rained down on the German bunkers. The 74th Armored Regiment would follow the infantry as soon as a beachhead was established and a pontoon bridge was laid down.

Morgan's small plane was buffeted by the shock waves caused by the artillery, and both he and Snyder tried to squash the fear that they might be hit by an incoming shell. American armor was arrayed on the west side and fired to keep the Germans' heads down.

As the infantry's improvised armada started to cross, engineers began to lay down a pontoon bridge strong enough to support the weight of tanks.

German fire discipline was excellent. They waited until the vulnerable small craft were in the water before scores of hidden pieces of artillery and hundreds of machine guns scythed the boats and the men huddled in them.

Boat after boat was hit and Jack heard moaning and realized it was coming from him. Some boats were burning while a few were blown apart, all sending men into the deep and cold river where he could see their heads bobbing as they were swept north towards the sea. Some managed to head towards the German side. The 116th was not an experienced unit and Jack could only imagine the horrors the men were enduring.

Despite the carnage, a number of boats made shore and unloaded their men, who were promptly pinned down by German fire. Worse, many of the boats that were supposed to return and get more men for the assault had been damaged or destroyed and could not be used as planned. The second wave was pitifully small in comparison with the first and the third wave never happened. The men who'd crossed were effectively trapped.

The German gunners turned their attention to the American armor arrayed on the western side and began to chew them up. Jack checked his fuel. They were almost out of gas and he flew the plane back to the landing strip where Stoddard grabbed him.

"Damn it, did you see anything good down there?"

Jack leaned on the fuselage. "I saw a lot of brave men dying, sir. Some of the guys who landed are trying to inch their way in, and they are using flamethrowers and bangalore torpedoes," he said. Bangalore torpedoes were tubelike contraptions that very brave men put either under or into enemy defenses and then exploded. "But there are so few of them. When will the bridge be built?"

The colonel sagged. "Our armor is pulling back. The engineers are going to give it up for the time being. We've been whipped," he muttered, then shook his head. "Maybe stalemated is the right word. Go get something to eat."

Darkness was falling and Jack watched as shadows moved down the road leading to the rear. These were the defeated and the walking wounded, although how some of them could walk, Jack couldn't imagine. As he drew closer to them, he saw that many had their faces bandaged, or were limping badly. Somehow, a couple of men who were missing arms were managing to head to the rear without assistance.

"Where the hell are the medics?" he asked out loud. They were overwhelmed treating the truly badly wounded, he realized.

He managed to walk to where he could see the riverbank and the sporadic fighting on the other side. Gunfire flickered like fireflies, only fireflies didn't crackle and snarl. Occasional tongues of flame showed where a GI with a flamethrower had gotten close enough to the enemy. Curiously, it didn't look like the Germans wanted to come out of their fortifications and fight the Americans who'd landed in their midst. Nor did the Germans have the firepower to wipe them out from the safety of their bunkers.

It occurred to Jack that there weren't as many

Germans as there ought to be or could be. He mentioned it to Whiteside, who concurred. "This is not their main line of defense; in fact, this loop of ground is pretty indefensible. We'll attack again in the morning, except this time we'll be smarter, and we'll push them back. Besides, we just found out that Patton is across south of us and his presence will force them to abandon these lines as well as evacuate Paris. Maybe they don't want to die any more than we do."

That night the Germans did pull back and left only a handful of men to harass the Americans and call down artillery fire. The Germans had built a second defensive line where the river's loop made a narrow approach the only alternative.

By mid-morning, two pontoon bridges were completed and both men and armor poured over. Again Jack was in the air watching the panorama unfold. The Germans had dug a dry moat across the neck of ground. They blew up the ends, sending torrents of water from the Seine gushing in and filling it. The moat, however, wasn't deep enough and the regiment's Sherman tanks plowed through and up to the new defenses, which they fired at point blank. Again, flamethrowers devastated the bunkers. A flamethrower operator was hit and his tank exploded, engulfing him in a pillar of flames. Jack hoped he died quickly. The guys with flamethrowers had to be insane, he concluded.

"My friends and comrades, it is time to leave," Colonel Schurmer said to the handful of his men who remained in Paris. General von Choltitz and his staff and the bulk of the garrison in Paris had already departed. The city was still quiet but who knew how long that would last. The Americans had crossed the Seine both to the south and the north and, as soon as they gathered enough strength, they'd be racing to cut off Paris and capture any Germans still inside the city. French troops were reported to be advancing from the west. The designation of an open city would not last forever.

They piled into the handful of vehicles remaining to them. These included three Panzer Mk1 tanks, which were lightly armored vehicles carrying a pair of machine guns each. Obsolete for a modern battlefield, they were intimidating to the semi-trained mobs of French resistance fighters in the city, even though they would slow down the rest of the column. Or at least Schurmer hoped they would intimidate the French. Large numbers of Frenchmen armed with a miscellany of weapons freely roamed the city as de Gaulle's supporters fought the communists and both began to fight the Germans.

The column attracted rifle and machine gun fire as they drove westward out of the city, but it did them no harm. Schurmer was in one of six Type 82 Kubelwagens, a rough equivalent to the American Jeep. They had been assembled by Volkswagen and were built on a Kafer chassis. Outside of Germany, the Kafer was known as the Beetle.

The vehicles seated four but were not armored and Schurmer felt vulnerable as they drove out of Paris. It was time to leave the fabled city of lights far, far behind and acknowledge that the Third Reich had lost yet another battle.

A surprising number of French civilians were also heading east. These were people who'd worked with

Germany and didn't want to face the wrath and vicious justice of their countrymen. It would be hell to be on the losing side, he thought, which would be his fate if Himmler couldn't pull something out of the mess Germany was in.

He tried not to cringe as badly aimed gunfire rattled off the street and the vehicles around him. Thankfully, the FFI, the resistance, were such poor shots. Most Frenchmen were. He did not think highly of French martial abilities after their utter and shameful defeat in the debacle of 1940. Thankfully also, they aimed at the tanks and the bullets that did strike armor simply bounced off. The two men in the back seat of his vehicle aimed submachine guns in the general direction of the buildings they were passing, but did not fire. Few French civilians were in view although he felt that thousands of eyes were watching him.

Schurmer was disappointed that the Seine Line had fallen so quickly, but had learned much that would serve him well on the Rhine defensive works and the other fortifications being built before that great river. He was not confident that the Allies would be stopped before the Rhine.

A young Frenchman carrying a lighted Molotov cocktail raced towards the lead tank, his mouth contorted in anger as he screamed something unintelligible. A gunner from the second tank fired a burst that nearly cut the Frenchman in half. The incendiary cocktail ignited in his hand, covering him in flames. The dying man writhed and screamed before falling still. So much for de Gaulle being able to control his countrymen, Schurmer thought. But then, who could control a Frenchman? It would be easier to herd cats.

A rude roadblock suddenly came into view, made up of overturned cars and piled debris. A score or so Parisians, men and women, were on it and in the buildings alongside. They opened fire with rifles and shotguns as the column approached. Two of Schurmer's little tanks paired up and blazed away with their machine guns. Several resistance fighters fell and the others melted away, dragging their dead and wounded. The two small tanks bulled their way through the flimsy barricade and the other vehicles followed through the opening.

Another partisan with a deathwish and a Molotov cocktail rushed up. This one was more successful, hitting the lead tank and inundating it with flames before the guns of the second tank killed him. Schurmer cursed. The damned French would proclaim him a martyr and name a road after him. How about Rue de Fool, he thought. Before the war there had been nearly three million people in Paris, many of whom even admired Germany, and now they all hated the Reich.

The burning tank's two-man crew jumped out and climbed onto the remaining tanks, and the column drove on. The men appeared unhurt and Schurmer was thankful. He laughed as one of them waved at him.

Safe, Schurmer thought as they reached the country-side, was a relative term. Being alive for the moment did not constitute safety. He did wonder just how far out of the city the truce extended and for how much time now that the damned Americans were across in two places. Thank God the little prick Montgomery had gotten his arrogant little nose bloodied to the north.

Schurmer got his answers a few moments later. They had just cleared the city proper on a road he thought was called Sebastopol Boulevard when he heard the sound of airplane engines over the motors of his vehicles. He turned and stared in horror as a pair of American P47's turned to strafe the column.

"Out," he yelled, as if anybody needed any urging. His men were already tumbling out of their vulnerable vehicles.

The remaining tanks were lightly armored and were ripped by the planes' machine guns. They wheeled and commenced to destroy the Kubels while Schurmer and his men hid in a ditch.

Fortunately, the Americans got tired of their fun when the tanks and Kubels were burning, and flew off. Perhaps they didn't see the score of German soldiers cowering in fear. Or maybe they were out of ammunition. He was thankful the Americans hadn't carried bombs.

Schurmer stood up and dusted off the dirt from his uniform. He checked his men. Several were wounded, but, thankfully and miraculously, none had been killed. Even the men in the tanks had moved quickly enough to survive. These were all good men and the Reich was going to have great need of good men to confront the coming ordeal.

He turned to his aide and said very loudly, "Willy, didn't we used to have an air force, too?"

The young lieutenant shrugged and the men grinned. "I think it was just a rumor, Colonel."

Schurmer formed his men up. "Since we have no choice unless you wish to stay here and become prisoners of war, or, more likely, be hanged by the French after they castrate you with a dull spoon, we will begin to walk back to Germany."

He had no illusions. Some of his men would doubtless not at all mind spending the remainder of the war doing farm work in Kansas, but the thought of the viciousness of the vengeful French was sobering. Any captured German soldier would be fortunate indeed to make it to a prison pen.

Schurmer waved with forced jauntiness. "Come on, my brave warriors. Germany can't be all that far away." He laughed genuinely as his men hooted at him. With men like these, Germany could have conquered the world. Why in God's name had Hitler fucked up so thoroughly?

Victor Mastny counted his blessings each day but they were more than offset by his hatreds. By forging some papers and stealing others from the body of another prisoner, he was able to pass him himself off as a French prisoner of war.

In reality, Mastny was a Czech and a thief, not a POW, although he had lived for years in France. He was also a drug dealer and had been convicted of both crimes, along with a count of sexual assault. The woman had been the wife of a shop owner. Her husband wouldn't pay Victor for drugs he'd bought and used, and Victor had used her to punish the man. Victor never dreamed that the fool would go to the police for him screwing his wife, although she did scream all the while he did it.

He was convicted and sent to a small German-run work camp where he was put in charge of a group of other prisoners who hated him with a vengeance. When an Allied air raid hit the camp, he took his phony papers and walked away in the confusion. The

decision to work on the Mullers' farm was based on
the sobering fact that he could not wander Germany
forever. The local police would stop him and turn him
over to the Gestapo. It did not escape him that he
was only marginally safer as an alleged French POW.

The farm at least provided shelter and an abundance
of food and they needed workers. It wasn't difficult
to convince the Mullers that he'd been assigned to
work for them.

Still, he hated the Mullers. He hated all Germans,
but not because he was a patriot. No, he hated the
Germans because they had interrupted his life and sent
him away to prison for several years. He also hated the
French for initially catching him and convicting him.

Victor had plans. When the war ended, he would
return to France and begin anew plundering the
people of that country. For that, however, he needed
money and he currently had nothing. But perhaps
the Mullers did?

He slept in the barn with a couple of illiterate oafs
from Latvia, twins named Janis and Juris. He and the
twins barely understood each other, but the Latvians
fully comprehended that Victor would kill them in an
instant if they crossed him. He could see the terror
on their faces when he looked at them and he liked
that. It further helped that, even though they were
large, they were stupid, even for Latvians.

As usual, they were not locked in the barn. After
all, where would they go? He felt that the Mullers
had deluded themselves into thinking that their slaves
were happy with their lot. Victor would be happy
when he could piss on their smiling faces.

He slipped quietly to the house. The dogs recognized

him and ignored him. He patted them to ensure their silence and they wagged their tails. Sometimes he gave them pieces of meat to cement their friendship.

Victor was intrigued by the fact that two more women had joined the Mullers. One was older, about Victor's age, and the other just out of childhood. Both of them aroused him. He had been a very long time without a woman. The last had been one of the workers he was supervising and she'd been old and ugly, although she had worked hard to satisfy him in return for extra food.

The two new women had been out working for the Germans and had returned earlier in the evening. He heard the sound of water running and visualized them naked and scrubbing down. On a couple of occasions he'd managed to get to the bathroom window and watch the beefy and very unattractive Bertha at her ablutions. If he had to, he would fuck her, but he wanted either of the two others. He laughed. Why not take both of them? Of course, he would do that after they told them where their money was. They'd come from Berlin, after all, and that meant they had money.

Margarete felt that all of her muscles ached, including some she didn't know she had. The work on the Rhine Wall was backbreaking. Many of the women, boys, and old men who'd been drafted to do the heavy work weren't very strong and some had collapsed. Their foremen weren't cruel men, and the worst of the weak were allowed to rest and some were even sent home. It was Magda's and Margarete's bad fortune to be healthy and thus able to pick up the pails of dirt that had been excavated and carry them away.

She had experienced a feeling of camaraderie while working with a crew of young girls her own age. They had sung songs and told jokes, some of them shockingly bawdy, while they worked and tried to ignore the growing stiffness in their joints and muscles. They were under the nominal control of a local schoolteacher whose name she couldn't remember. The next time she went, it would be with a different crew and another leader, so it didn't matter.

What impressed Margarete was the massiveness of the construction. Along with hundreds of people like her, she was told there were dozens of other sites each with its own labor force. She thought of herself as an Israelite working on the pyramids until she recalled the Reich's hatred of Jews in any form.

When she and her mother got home, Margarete let her mother soak in the hot-water-filled tub first. She'd teased Magda that older people took longer to recover from hard work and her mother had stuck out her tongue and made a vulgar noise that made both of them laugh.

Finally, she slipped into her own tub and let the hot water comfort her. When she finally stepped out, she paused for a moment in front of the full length mirror on the door. She scarcely recognized herself. Her body was leaner and longer and her breasts and hips more pronounced. She smiled. Now let an adolescent idiot like Volkmar Detloff try to paw her again. Not only would he find that she was a young woman and not a girl, but she would slap his pimply face silly.

She shuddered. She had the cold and sudden feeling that someone was watching her. The window to the bathroom was open only a crack, but she closed

it anyhow and latched it. Her fears were probably
groundless, but it paid to be prudent. What if one
of the workers had seen her? What if refugees were
wandering around the farm? She was worried about
the laborer called Victor. She decided to ask her uncle
where he kept his hunting rifles and shotguns.

Outside, Victor waited silently a few minutes after
the girl closed the window. Then he moved back to the
barn. He was more than pleased by what he saw. Both
women, the older and the younger, were magnificent.
The older was full bosomed, wide hipped and ripe,
while the younger was lean and taut.

He reached inside his pants and began to stroke
himself. He would take both of them.

Colonel Tom Granville waited as usual for General
Bedell Smith to notice him. Finally, he looked up.
"Okay, who's dead this time?"

"Now we think it's Martin Bormann, General."

Smith leaned back and laughed harshly. "First Hitler,
then Goering and now Bormann? Hell, somebody's
doing a lot of housecleaning in the new Reich. And how
do we know about Bormann? Did they announce it?"

A week earlier, German radio had informed its
listeners that Air Marshal and Reichsfuhrer Hermann
Goering had died of a massive heart attack and then
added that the grief of Hitler's passing had probably
played a part in causing it. The announcement had
been a eulogy, reminding listeners that Goering had
been a fighter ace in World War I and had been
one of the earliest of Hitler's devoted followers. The
announcer had glossed over the fact that the Luftwaffe's
performance in the current war had been spotty at

best and successes were due to regional commanders like Kesselring, rather than to the drug-soaked genius of Hermann Goering.

"General, Ultra picked up a message that Bormann was kaput. The sender appeared to be Skorzeny. It said that the Bormann problem had been, in his words, resolved. An hour later, a very terse announcement was made to key government officials that Bormann had been killed in an accident on the autobahn."

"Skorzeny's a busy boy," said Smith. "He keeps knocking off people like he's one of Al Capone's thugs and, even better for him, he doesn't have to worry at all about getting arrested. Capone's murderers had at least a theoretical chance of getting caught. But you're telling me that no one in Germany's too terribly upset about Bormann's demise?"

"Correct, sir. Aside from being a totally unlovable snake, he simply wasn't all that well known outside of government circles. He'll be cremated so no one will notice the bullet holes in his head and then be forgotten."

"But Skorzeny won't be. That son of a bitch is dangerous. He came really close to killing the Big Three and did kidnap Mussolini."

The attempt on the lives of Stalin, Churchill and Roosevelt had taken place at Teheran, Iran, in 1943 and Skorzeny had nearly pulled it off. At that time Skorzeny had been a fanatical follower of Hitler. Now he appeared to have transferred his allegiance to Heinrich Himmler.

"Tom, we're gonna have to keep an eye on Skorzeny. God only knows what he'll have up his sleeve with Himmler to prod him."

"And with our move to Paris, sir, we'll be that much closer to Germany, Himmler, and Skorzeny. Have you considered talking to Ike about staying someplace a little easier to guard?"

Smith rubbed his eyes. He would kill for a good night's sleep. "Like New Jersey? We talked. He agrees it's a good idea from a security standpoint, but, from a political point of view, SHAEF needs to be head-quartered in Paris, at least for the time being. After all," he said sarcastically, "it is the capital of our brave ally, France. Technically, we'll be just outside the city and Ike will at all times be in a protective cocoon, surrounded by MPs and other security types."

"Are you and Ike aware that Skorzeny speaks both excellent French and English?"

"Just what I needed, Colonel, more good news."

Granville grinned at the sarcasm. "At least there'll be some good restaurants in Paris."

★ CHAPTER 10 ★

MORGAN'S FLIGHT OVER LIBERATED PARIS WAS simply a joy ride. He'd informed Whiteside that he needed to check out the Piper's engine and then told Snyder he could stay home. Neither man believed for a second that there was anything wrong with the Piper Cub which now had the silhouette of a German truck painted on its side. Instead of a regular copilot, Levin sat in the back seat, enjoying the ride and the view.

The 74th was resting. For that matter, almost all the army was sitting on its hands, catching its breath and licking its wounds. The crossing of the Seine had not only resulted in heavy casualties, but had used up vast reserves of fuel and ammunition. Until replenished, it would be unwise, even dangerous, to place the army in a position where they'd have to fight a possibly better armed and well-supplied Nazi force.

Nor would resupply be quick. There were still no major ports close to the Allied armies. Cherbourg was still being rebuilt after demolition by the Nazis and

Marseilles was too far away. Stoddard had informed the regiment that the rumors were true—Montgomery's attempted landings to the north had been a disaster. Britain's First Airborne Division had finally fought its way to the sea and the remnants were being taken off by U.S. Navy warships, a further insult to the Brits. The British Airborne force had lost half its men and virtually all its equipment. Even those who disliked Monty and the British were appalled. It meant the Nazi tiger still had claws and teeth. Overall the Brits had suffered more than fifteen thousand casualties and there were echoes in Parliament for Churchill and Monty to explain themselves.

Patton's crossing south of Paris had been successful because he'd not used bomber attacks like Hodges had. The bombers in Jack's area had tipped off the Germans as to where the attacks would come. Instead, Patton had the bombers drop their load a full thirty miles south of his intended crossing point, which had thoroughly confused the Germans in the area.

Even though the American army had joined the Free French in Paris, a handful of fires still burned, which meant that fighting still continued as the Free French Forces wrested control of the city from Nazi collaborators and sympathizers, along with the communist-led labor movement. It looked more and more like leave time in Paris with a ration of wine, women, and song would have to wait a while.

For the sheer hell of it, he flew around the Eiffel Tower, doubtless exasperating gendarmes and American military police. A few moments later, a pair of American fighters flew by and checked him out. Jack decided buzzing the tower wasn't such a good idea, even though the fighters had wiggled their wings at him once they realized he was harmless.

"Now let's fly through Notre Dame and the Louvre and see how many other planes we can scare up," Levin suggested. "Who knows, if I like the place maybe I'll convert to Catholicism." He had been taking pictures. "By the way, I heard you got another letter from Carter's cousin. You and she are becoming regular pen pals, aren't you?"

Morgan felt himself flushing. "Yeah, and I kinda like it. It's nice having somebody fairly close by to write to. And it's an interesting way to get to know someone."

"So when are you going to marry her?"

Morgan laughed. "As soon as I can get her pregnant, which isn't very likely since I haven't even met her yet. She said her Red Cross unit will be moving to Paris soon, so just maybe I'll get some time off and get to meet her."

Jessica had sent him another picture and he'd decided she really was cute in a quiet sort of way. He'd sent her a snapshot taken by the regiment's photographer. It showed him leaning against the plane and, in his opinion, smiling foolishly. He'd also sent one of Carter and Levin.

"Of course, by the time she gets to Paris, we'll all likely be too far away."

"Not a chance," said Levin. "The way things are shaping up, we won't be in any condition to move for a couple of weeks."

"Okay, you know everything so what about the rumor that we're getting new tanks?"

"False," said Levin. "What they're trying to do

is upgrade the Sherman with a higher velocity gun that'll enable us to take on the Pk4 and the Panther on more even terms."

"That's not news, Roy."

"I know, but what is news is that they're actually doing it instead of talking the problem to death."

Jack checked the time and his fuel situation. He turned the plane back towards the regiment. One of the last things he wanted to do was run out of fuel and have to cadge some from another unit. That would be too embarrassing, especially since there would be no compelling reason for it to happen except pilot stupidity.

"Roy, so what does it matter if we get better guns? What kind of surprises will the Germans have for us?" Levin replied that he didn't want to think about it.

Much of the work on the weapons referred to by the Allies as the V1 and V2 rockets had taken place at Peenemunde, on the Baltic coast. In 1943, however, the facility had been heavily bombed, which resulted in the disbursing of its factory units to a number of other locations. This impaired efficiency, but the rocket program survived.

At only thirty-four, Dr. Wernher von Braun was technical director and effectively in charge of the program. He was almost childishly young for his position. Stocky, even plump, he smiled affably at Varner and the two men shook hands.

"So tell me, Colonel, Herr Himmler requires more information regarding the rocket program and wants to know why it isn't performing better and winning the war."

The so-called Vengeance weapons that had fascinated Hitler also had intrigued Himmler from the beginning, and he'd exercised considerable control and influence over the program.

"That's a pretty close estimate of the situation," Varner admitted.

Von Braun took a seat and gestured for Varner to do the same. "Sadly, Colonel, the V1 and V2 are merely high-tech toys. Someday when we are in outer space, history will say these were the first tiny steps towards taking man to the stars. They are capable of annoying the Allies, but not of winning the war. We can hurl them at England or even locations in France that have fallen to the Allies, but they cannot do enough damage to make a difference. As you know, both rockets carry a warhead of about one ton, while a single American or British bomber can exceed that by a wide margin. Better yet, a bomber stands a chance of actually hitting what it's aiming for, while our rockets are unaimed and simply fired in the general direction of a very large target, say London. Even with such a huge target, very many of them go astray or suffer mechanical failure, or, worse, are shot down as the British are doing to our V1's."

Varner already understood that. "But what about the rocket that can hit New York?"

Von Braun guffawed. "A pipe dream. Someday certainly, but not for a decade or more. What is possible, theoretically, is that a V1 or V2 rocket might be launched from a U-boat and thus strike New York or any other American port. However, the warhead will still be small and odds are that it will land in a pond on Long Island or a farm north of the city and never even be noticed."

"You don't paint an encouraging picture."

Von Braun smiled coldly. "I thought you wanted the truth, Colonel Varner. The wonder weapons will not change the course of the war. Ultimately and in another form, they might change the course of history, but that's for decades in the future."

Varner's opinion of von Braun diminished. The young scientist had just said that the missile program was a fraud. The expenditure of money and manpower had been for nothing. Scientists like von Braun were using the resources of the Reich to foster their dreams of spaceships and travel to outer space instead of winning the war.

The whole V-weapon enterprise had also used thousands of slave laborers for the construction of the facilities. The more Varner saw and thought of the plight of the Jews and others who were being mistreated by the government, the more he realized that Germany would have a lot to answer for if she lost the war. Therefore, she could not lose the war.

"I think," Monique said dryly, "that there are more American military police in Paris than there are Frenchmen."

Jessica agreed. Every block or so they were stopped by MP's who demanded their identification and orders and wondered why they were driving U.S. Army vehicles, even though they were clearly marked as belonging to the Red Cross. Jessica's American passport and ID got her through, even to the point of intriguing the MP's who hadn't talked to an American woman in a long while. Monique was just another French woman and they were sometimes curt with her.

Monique didn't mind. "They are the victors. The victors always set the rules."

"And write history," Jessica added. *Or rewrite it,* she thought.

She had been only mildly surprised when Monique decided to accompany her when the unit moved to Paris, leaving her son behind with relatives. It turned out that her master sergeant lover had also been transferred there as part of the massive American supply operation headquartered in Paris. He had used his influence to get them quarters they didn't deserve, close to the center of the city. Jessica had to pay an exorbitant rent for the apartment, but that was all right as rooms of any kind were at a premium. Jessica and Monique would have separate bedrooms with a shared bath and a stunning view of a rubbish-filled alley. It would be more than satisfactory in a city overflowing with refugees and military personnel from a multitude of nations.

Uncle Tom Granville was somewhere in the mass of humanity and Jessica was determined to look him up. Among other things, she wanted to swap news about relatives back home, and she wanted to know what he could tell her about Cousin Jeb's situation. She admitted to herself that she was more than a little intrigued by his friend, Jack Morgan. The photo he'd sent her made him look like a little boy alongside his flying toy, and the smile on his face looked genuine and not forced for the camera.

Dear God, she thought, *am I falling in love with someone I've never met?*

Monique had chided her frequently about dressing better and, therefore, looking better to men, especially American men who were starved for a familiar sounding voice. Jessica had laughingly informed her friend that she would not slink around the Red Cross offices in a low-cut red dress. Not only was it not appropriate, but all she had was very functional and relatively sexless clothing. She admitted that she'd never thought she'd wind up in Paris.

Along with a couple of letters from Jack Morgan, she'd gotten a batch from home. Most of the comments from her mother were complaints about the inequities of the ration system. There never was enough gas, they were supposed to do without meat on certain days, and, heavens to Betsy, nylons were nonexistent.

Jessica's father was more pragmatic. It didn't bother him that they were reduced to driving one car and that it was now almost five years old. Everyone was in the same boat and, he said, as long as the boat wasn't sinking, all was well. She sometimes wondered just what planet her mother came from. Ford, General Motors, and Chrysler hadn't made a new car since shortly after the attack on Pearl Harbor. Everything they now produced went to the military. Her father said there would be plenty of time for new cars, new houses, and, yes, nylons, when the war was won.

Jessica decided she'd write her father about the idiot pilot of a small plane she'd seen buzzing the Eiffel Tower. Hundreds on the ground had cheered and laughed while the military police glowered in impotent fury. There was no doubt that it was an American plane and she wondered if the pilot would get into trouble. Whimsically, she wondered if it had been Jack.

Finally, the small convoy arrived at their new offices. Sign painters were busy writing instructions to the people already waiting outside. To Jessica's dismay, there were hundreds of anxious French men and women, some clutching thoroughly confused and squalling small children. Once again, she would be telling hopeful people that she had no information at the moment, and that she could only hope to provide hope for the future.

Someone in the Red Cross had estimated that fully ninety-nine percent of those missing or displaced would find their own way home and to their families. The remaining one percent would be the cause of all the heartaches and grieving. With millions of displaced persons expected, it could still result in many tens of thousands needing their help.

Nor was Jessica comfortable with the ninety-nine percent figure not needing their help. Not when she saw the line of humanity waiting for them.

How was it possible, the Soviet Union's Foreign Minister, Vacheslav Molotov, wondered, that the senior representatives of two of the world's major powers were reduced to meeting in a seedy hotel room in Sweden? He had arrived that morning in a transport plane bearing Swiss markings, while his counterpart flew in from Germany in a plane also with Swiss markings. That neither was even remotely associated with neutral Switzerland was irrelevant. What was important was that nobody noticed and, most definitely, nobody at either the Soviet or German embassies was aware of his arrival or that of his counterpart. Embassy personnel were supposed to be trustworthy, but there was an old saying about secrets attributed to an American, Benjamin Franklin, that three could keep a secret only if two were dead. He sometimes wished a Russian had authored that wonderfully prescient quote.

Molotov was thankful that he would not be in discussions with that pompous and crude buffoon von Ribbentrop. Molotov hated the aristocracy with the true fervor of a dedicated communist. Aristocrats and capitalists were the cause of the world's ills and he wished he could exterminate them like the Nazis were exterminating the Jews. However, even he had been appalled by the reported numbers of dead coming out of Poland regarding the concentration camp complex near Auschwitz.

At least his counterpart, Franz von Papen, was a real aristo, and not a parvenu like Ribbentrop, who'd gotten the right to use the "von" mostly because he'd married well. Von Papen had history and ancestry on his side, while Ribbentrop had simply fucked his way into the nobility.

Von Papen entered the small room, and the two men bowed and nodded. They did not shake hands. Molotov got directly to the point. "You wished this meeting, why?"

Von Papen was not shaken by Molotov's bluntness. He'd expected it. "It is time to end this war, at least for a while. Our two countries have been tearing at each other like mad dogs, while the Americans and British do nothing. If we are not careful, when the war does end, as all wars do, they will be the winners and our two nations the losers."

Molotov silently agreed. The Americans had taken their own sweet time getting into the war. They had waited years while Mother Russia absorbed the best, and worst, that the Nazis could hand her. And in return for scores of millions dead and wounded, what did the Soviet Union get? A few thousand trucks and some useless tanks. He knew he was being unfair about American Lend Lease. It was brutally difficult to send supplies by sea around German-occupied Europe, and an incredibly long way to go overland from Iran and Iraq. Still, the American armies had waited until the heavy fighting at Stalingrad, Moscow, Leningrad, Sevastopol, and Kursk was over before finally sending a pathetically few divisions into France where a small German army had all but halted them. It did appear that the Americans and their lap dogs, the British, were more than willing to let Russia fight their war.

Molotov kept his expression cold. "May I remind you, von Papen, that your country violated a perfectly good treaty and invaded Mother Russia, thereby starting this ruinous war? May I further remind you that Germany is the cause of all the troubles and all the devastation in Russia that is now going to be repaid by Soviet armies as they invade your country?"

Papen nodded solemnly. "That tragedy was perpetrated by Hitler, Goering, and Bormann, none of whom are any longer with us, thank God. While there is nothing we can do to bring back the dead and remove the devastation, it is possible that we could consider some form of compensation in the future should the war be brought to an end."

Molotov noted that Himmler's name was absent from the list of those who'd perpetrated the surprise attack on the Soviet Union. Of course, Herr Himmler, inventor of Germany's concentration camp system, was as pure and innocent as the new fallen snow.

Regarding compensation, Molotov thought that the Soviet Union would like to take anything of value that Germany possessed, including the dubious virtue of the Reich's women. This would be in return for the countless rapes and other atrocities endured by the Soviet people. Russia wanted ten pounds of flesh for each pound earlier ripped from her. Still, what was von Papen proposing?

The German diplomat smiled. If Molotov didn't know better, he might have thought it was with warmth. "My dear Molotov, there is no reason for us to be enemies when our true foe is the United States. The Jewish capitalists will rule the world if we are not careful. If we destroy each other, the Wall Street barons will be in total control and will hold both our countries in bondage. You know that the Americans hate communism, and you must be aware that the Jew Roosevelt's government plans to turn Germany into a vast farmland devoid of manufacturing and incapable of defending itself. It is a tragedy that we went to war, and the Reich accepts the blame for it. Now, however, it is time to change the course of history."

Molotov eyed the German coldly. "Are you saying there is room to negotiate?"

"Comrade, there is always room to negotiate."

Jeb Carter whooped into his tank's microphone at the sight of the German vehicles on the road parallel to his and only a half mile away.

"So much for them being the master race. They screw up just like everybody else and we've got them dead to rights."

The German unit holding the crossroads had made a major blunder. Instead of heading east to safety, they'd taken a wrong turn on a road that looped west instead. By the time they'd figured it out and turned around, Morgan in his little plane had spotted them. Thirty German vehicles were all in a row. Most of them were lightly armored troop carriers like American half-tracks. Most happily, three trucks were towing what looked like 88mm antitank guns and they were accompanied by only a pair of Panzer IV tanks.

The Germans panicked, which was not a smart thing to do. Their vehicles scattered in all directions. Carter whooped again and ordered a general attack, a charge, with machine guns and cannon blazing from his dozen Shermans. The two German tanks gamely turned to protect their charges. Concentrated fire from the American tanks quickly knocked out one Mark IV and the other moved away in reverse, firing and keeping his more heavily armored front towards the Americans.

"They're getting away," Carter snarled.

He ordered three platoons to chase the other vehicles while the remaining platoon tangled with the surviving Panzer. A shot from the German blew the treads off one Sherman, but a pair of shells struck the Panzer, stopping him cold. Hatches opened and men jumped out while machine gun fire raked them. One man dropped and two others ran off. Carter recalled that the Panzer IV had a crew of five. Tongues of fire came from the hatches of the last tank, telling him that the other two men were cooked.

Carter's other tanks were catching up to the trucks, which couldn't move fast on rough terrain, nor did they have a chance to unlimber and man their guns. Again, men abandoned their vehicles and ran for their lives.

Overhead, Morgan watched the slaughter. There may have been people down there, but they were the enemy and the presence of the towed eighty-eights told him they'd been shooting and killing Americans. With a roar, a quartet of American fighter bombers, P47's, flew low and began to strafe the fleeing Germans. Morgan hoped to hell that the flyboys could tell which side was which. They could, and they chewed up the vehicles that Carter's tanks couldn't reach.

"You called for the cavalry?" Carter radioed. "If you did, we sure as hell didn't need them."

Jack wasn't so sure. It looked like several German half-tracks would have made it. Carter was a cocky bastard.

Prudently, Carter called a halt to his advance. He didn't want his men getting tangled with the Germans and a tragedy to occur.

"Hey, Bomber," he radioed to Jack.

"What, Rebel?"

"Looks like the good guys won one today."

"Yeah, Carter, but I'll bet you a dollar that the Air Force takes full credit for this little barroom brawl."

Molotov had given his report and sat nervously while Stalin contemplated the consequences of the German proposal. Josef Stalin ruled the Soviet Union with an iron and bloody fist. In his zeal to first consolidate communism in the newly formed country, and to export it to other countries, he had been ruthless. Millions of reasonably well-off peasants, the kulaks, had starved when he'd forced them to live in communal farms, and millions of others had died in the civil war that had resulted in him taking the reins of power from Lenin on that man's death. People had made the mistake of underestimating the small, rumpled, and often crude man with the thick mustache.

Above all, however, Josef Stalin was a realist. The Soviet air forces ruled the skies over the Germans, and Soviet armor and artillery outnumbered the enemy and were qualitatively better in many areas. Numerically, the vast Soviet horde was hugely dominant.

Realistically, however, the Red Army's march into Poland was slowing. The army continued to go forward, but now in small, painful steps instead of great sweeping advances. The reasons were several. The Germans had withdrawn isolated pockets of their soldiers to form new and stronger defenses. The Germans had retreated closer to their bases, which meant they could be supplied more easily while the Red Army's replacement equipment, manpower and ammunition had farther to go. Also, the Germans were now fighting behind a shorter defensive line.

Worse for Stalin's ambitions, the professional German generals were now running the war, and not the erratic and insanely stubborn Adolf Hitler. Not for the first time did Stalin wish that Hitler was still alive.

Zhukov's warning of several weeks earlier was coming true. The mighty Soviet war machine was running out of gas, and, in some ways, literally. There was little fuel, and the army was indeed exhausted. If it collapsed, so too might Josef Stalin and his dream of communist expansion.

So, he wondered, what might be the outcome of a truce?

Obviously, as Zhukov said, it would grant time for the army to rest and re-fit. But what about the political and long-term aspects of a truce?

Stalin agreed that communism's long-term enemy was the United States, and as the war was progressing,

America increasingly looked to be victorious and unscathed while Russia would be in tatters after having won a Pyrrhic victory. Worse, America would soon be in possession of the powerful nuclear weapons being developed in New Mexico and elsewhere, and would be in a position to impose a peace. His spies were keeping him reasonably well up-to-date on America's progress towards an atomic bomb. He shuddered at the thought of a victorious America having such a weapon. The Germans, too, were working on a bomb, and Soviet scientists were trying to apply the information stolen from the Americans toward building their own, but so far without success. He'd thought of executing a few of the Soviet Union's physicists, but thought better of it. Not even fear could improve the pace of acquiring knowledge. He'd purged the Red Army of thousands of officers prior to the war and suffered for it. He would not do the same with the few scientists he had.

The idea of Germany and the United States tearing each other's throats out appealed to him. Germany would buy time and quite possibly win a negotiated peace for itself, but Russia would be the stronger and could simply abrogate any truce at her convenience. Thus, Russia's new war with Germany would be against a seriously weakened opponent, and the United States would be in no position to intervene.

He was unconcerned about England and France. The French were in no position to affect anything militarily, while the British were far more concerned with conserving their manpower than they were in fighting and winning a war. His intelligence said that the English were growing disenchanted with Churchill's leadership and a war that seemed to drag on forever. Churchill might not survive the next election. It was incredible to him that England and the United States would permit political opposition, especially during a war. To Stalin, political opposition was synonymous with treason, and the reason the Gulags existed.

A respite would give him a chance to tidy up his own house. The self-titled Marshal Tito in Yugoslavia was showing signs of becoming independent of Moscow, which was intolerable. Granted, Yugoslavia and Tito were still fighting the Nazis from behind German lines, but, if the war paused, perhaps the Germans would do the Soviet Union a favor and crush Tito. Perhaps they would withdraw and let Russia do it.

Another benefit from a pause in the fighting would enable Stalin to resolve his relations with China's growing communist movement. He could join forces with Mao Zedong and throw the Japanese out of Manchuria and Korea; thus earning Mao's gratitude. Or he could ally with Chiang Kai-Shek, dominate that man and subsequently destroy him. Mao called himself a communist, but Stalin considered him a peasant and worse, a potential rival.

Regardless, the attack on the Japanese would also aid the Americans, whom he wished to destroy. It was an irony he understood and appreciated. The Americans would be grateful while two more countries would be added to the Soviet bloc. Three if China was counted.

If he did it correctly, Stalin thought, he could confuse the Americans and leave them wondering just what had happened to them.

Stalin smiled grimly and Molotov shuddered at the sight. "We will negotiate with the devil, Comrade

Molotov." Stalin wrote furiously on a sheet of lined paper while puffing equally furiously on his pipe. "And here are the terms we will settle for."

Molotov scanned the sheet and nodded approval. "The Allies will realize rather quickly that we have departed the war."

Stalin was unperturbed. "Then we will have to have a reason that is plausible enough to justify our defection."

"Do you have something in mind, Comrade Stalin?" The question was rhetorical. Stalin always had a plan.

Again Stalin smiled, this time with humor. "The French, of course. The French are always good for something. They think the world turns on them and the sun rises and sets on Paris. They cannot abide being second fiddle to the damned Americans and the British. The communist party in France is very strong and, since many of its members were in the Resistance, fairly well provided with light arms. I believe they would provide us with a most useful distraction."

★ CHAPTER 11 ★

THE DEAD AMERICAN SOLDIER MORE RESEMBLED
a pancake with flattened arms and legs than a human
being. He looked like a cartoon character that could
have been peeled off the ground like a coat of paint.
Being run over by a tank will do that. The pounding
rain made matters worse.

"What the hell happened?" Whiteside asked. The
half dozen wet infantrymen in ponchos from the 116th
Division looked stunned, while the driver of the tank
that had run over the GI stood a few yards away,
puking his guts out.

Finally, a corporal spoke. "Sir, we was hitching a
ride when it happened. For some reason the turret
turned and the barrel swept Hickey right off and under
the tracks of the tank behind. He didn't scream, he
just kind of squished. I don't think he knew what hit
him. Hell, I hope he never knew it."

Infantrymen were always hitching rides on the
hulls of tanks. It beat the hell out of walking, and

the infantry and armor were supposed to support each other, so riding on the tanks made sense.

Whiteside turned to the sergeant who commanded the tank that had thrown the man off. The man looked stunned and near tears. "I thought I saw something suspicious to my left and I instinctively swung the turret. I completely forgot about the guys riding topside."

Medics had arrived and were gawking at the flattened corpse. "Get him out of here. Now!" Whiteside barked.

Two medics lifted, almost slid, the distorted caricature of a corpse onto a stretcher. The ground was soft and an impression of his body remained. It began to fill with water like an obscene pool. Curiously, there was very little blood and it was being diluted and washed away by the rain. A moment later, the ambulance was heading down the road and in no great hurry.

Whiteside looked solemnly at the tankers and infantry gathered around him. "It was an accident, men, a damn tragic accident and nobody's responsible for it because everybody was doing what they were supposed to be doing. If you do want to find somebody to blame, try the Germans. If it wasn't for them, we wouldn't be here and none of this would have happened."

Whiteside turned and walked away quickly so no one would see the look of anguish on his face.

An infantry corporal looked at the tanker. "We're getting back on, you know."

The sergeant nodded sadly. "Yeah, I know." They climbed up and the column began to move again.

Levin looked at Jack and shook his head. "I got a letter from my mother today. She's complaining about the shortage of butter. Maybe I'll write her and tell her about what happens when a tank runs over you. I took a picture. Maybe I should send it to her."

Morgan managed a bitter laugh. The rain had grounded him. "It's fun to think about doing, but you know you won't write about anything like that. Censors don't like any of that nasty but accurate stuff in letters to the home folks. Might make them think that war is actually dangerous and we can't have that, now can we?"

Levin lit a cigarette. "Right. I'll save it for my memoirs. By the way, hear anything from your girlfriend?"

Morgan flushed. "Once more, how can she be my girlfriend if I've never met her in person?"

"Maybe it's better that way. If she met you and really got to know you, I'm certain she wouldn't like you."

"Screw you, Roy."

"You do know that obscenities are the refuge of the small-minded, intellectually shallow and illiterate people."

"Fuck you, Roy."

Jessica had sent a letter saying she'd received the photo of him beside the Piper Cub. She said she'd like to take a ride in it. It sounded like a great idea, but he somehow knew that Whiteside and Stoddard would put the kibosh on it. Still, it was great to think about.

Margarete was constantly amazed at the amount of equipment and manpower brought to the defensive construction sites. Heavy artillery, including enormous fifteen-inch naval cannon that she was told could hurl a shell weighing almost a ton for more than twenty miles, were being dug in. Men from Germany's navy, the Kriegsmarine, cheerfully told her that the guns had come from now useless warships and would be a nasty surprise for the Yanks. They said the casements housing the great guns and many others of smaller caliber would be impregnable and impervious to bombing.

Underground barracks for thousands of men were being constructed along with deep trenches and tunnels to enable reinforcements to be sent from one spot to another. It was a shortcoming that had led in part to the swift collapse of the Seine River defenses. No one wanted to say that the massive American assaults were the main reason.

Margarete no longer worked with a shovel. Both she and her mother had better jobs and she suspected her father's hand in it. Magda worked in an office trying to make sense out of the project's records while Margarete, to her delight, was assigned as a driver. Her learning to drive a car on the journey from Berlin and a tractor on the farm had paid dividends. The only downside of driving a staff car or a truck was that they were fair game for American fighters, while groups of civilians digging holes were generally left alone. Thus and regardless of the weather, she always drove with the windows open so she could listen for the sound of enemy planes. On a couple of occasions, she'd thought she'd heard fighters, stopped the car, and jumped into a ditch leaving whoever she was driving still in the car. She'd been scolded for doing that, but she didn't care.

Most disturbing to Margarete were the hordes of men coming to help work on and man the defenses. Some were the pathetically thin men who, she was told, came from the various prisoner of war camps.

She suspected that a number of them were really Jews and other undesirables taken from death camps. Since their alternative was to go to places like Auschwitz, whose existence she no longer doubted, she thought they were the lucky ones.

A second group was the "Volkssturm," literally the "people's storm," or the people's army. To her dismay, they consisted of the old and the very young. There were no uniforms and rank was designated by armbands. Their weapons were sparse. Some had old rifles that a few joked had seen service against France in 1871, while others carried captured weapons, and many had antitank Panzerfausts slung over their shoulders.

That a number of those men had seen service in the First World War was fairly obvious. Some men limped, many had scars, and a few were missing arms or hands. She suspected that a few had artificial legs. Was this what the Reich was coming to? Were these all that was left?

A few younger men were included in the ranks of the Volkssturm and she wondered why. Her mother told her they were men who had physical ailments that eliminated them from being in the regular army.

As a group of about fifty Volkssturm walked by—they didn't even pretend to march—she was startled by a familiar face. "Volkmar Detloff," she called out, and a young man turned awkwardly. He smiled tentatively.

"Is that you, Margarete, I didn't recognize you. You've changed."

Yes, she thought. *I'm no longer weak, plump and vulnerable.* "And you as well, and what are you doing in the Volkssturm? I thought you'd be an officer in the Waffen-SS by now."

He winced. "I hurt my knee in the training and now neither the army nor the SS wants me. I am still considered a lieutenant, but now I'm stuck commanding old men and misfits."

Several of the old men and misfits turned and glared at Detloff. "Don't you think you should be a little more tactful?" she said.

"Why? These so-called soldiers are scum and won't fight unless they are forced to," he said and patted the Luger on his hip. "This will remind them who's in charge and what happens to cowards."

Margarete smiled inwardly as she heard one of the misfits, an old man who might have fought in a dozen earlier battles, say "arrogant little shit" just loud enough to be heard. Detloff wheeled and stared at his platoon, all of whom were looking innocently at the sky.

"Good luck with your command and your knee," she said and left him. Volkmar hadn't grown up. He hadn't learned a thing. She waved at the old man who'd insulted Volkmar and he grinned.

Later that evening she was back at the farm and recounted the meeting to her mother. "Just think. Once upon a time I had a crush on that lout. God, how young and stupid I must have been."

Magda chuckled. "I believe it's called being young and growing up. I do wonder if young Lieutenant Volkmar will ever realize what a fool he is and grow up."

Margarete nodded. "I wonder if the war will let him grow up."

Alfie Swann had twice jumped into combat with England's First Airborne Division. First had been in

Normandy where things had worked out relatively well. They'd accomplished most of their D-Day objectives and had stayed together as a cohesive unit, unlike America's two airborne divisions, the 82nd and 101st, which had been scattered all over by a number of factors beyond their control, and had suffered enormous casualties. The paras of Britain's First were sad that it happened to the Yanks, but happy it hadn't happened to them.

However, their turn for disaster came when they jumped east of the mouth of the Seine. The krauts had been ready for them and antiaircraft tracers and machine guns had lit up the skies. Telephone poles and other obstructions had been planted in fields and connected by wires to impale and hang up paratroops or cause gliders to crash with appalling loss of life.

Alfie had been lucky. He'd made it to the ground unscathed. So many of his mates had been killed or wounded. He'd connected with some other lucky ones and fought on for days until they'd been forced to surrender. He'd heard that a few men had made it north to the sea and he hoped his fighting had helped their escape.

Except for some bruises, Alfie was unhurt. He was twenty-five and had enlisted when the war first started in 1939. Alfie'd been brought up in the slums of London's west end, now a funeral pyre thanks to Nazi bombers. He'd lost an uncle and a couple of cousins in the bombings and subsequent conflagrations, and wanted nothing more than to take out the Germans. He'd killed a few in the fighting but not enough to satisfy him.

Alfie and a half dozen other captured paras, accompanied by three SS guards, had been marching along a road heading towards a prison camp east of the Rhine when an American fighter mistook them for a squad of German infantry. Bullets had plowed through the group, shredding prisoner and guard alike. When the dust settled, he was the only man alive except for a badly injured guard whom he promptly stabbed with the guard's own bayonet.

"That's for my family," he'd muttered. The guards had been overweight garrison types, but they were Germans and SS, and the particular German he'd stabbed had taken delight in beating and harassing the prisoners.

After pushing the bodies of friend and foe into a ditch, Alfie had headed south, hoping to find a place to hide out until the Americans crossed the great river. He didn't go north, as that was where he'd been captured.

In his opinion, the British army was through, fought out, and there weren't any more young men left at home to flesh out the depleted ranks. He liked to think that the men in charge of Great Britain's war effort, Churchill and Montgomery, knew that. However, he did doubt and wonder.

He was able to pilfer enough food at night to stay fed, and he traveled only during the darkness. He also had a Mauser rifle and two Luger pistols for protection, along with one slightly used bayonet, courtesy of his guards. Alfie was a damned good shot and it felt good to have a rifle again, even if it was a German Mauser and not a proper Enfield.

This early evening he'd found a fairly large but dilapidated shed with its door unlocked, a clear signal that it was empty. That was fine by him. He just wanted a place to hide and sleep. He slipped in backwards and immediately felt there was something wrong. He wasn't alone.

"Shit," he muttered. No sense being still. Even though it was getting dark, anyone in the shed would have seen him silhouetted against the open door. He carefully turned around, the rifle pointed into the gloom. "Okay, who the hell's in here?"

There was a shuffling and two shapes stood up and held out their hands to show they were unarmed. They were men, thin beyond gaunt, and they were dressed in striped rags. He recognized the garb from pictures he'd seen. They'd been in a concentration camp and were less of a threat to him than two field mice. He lowered his rifle.

"Either of you speak English?" Alfie asked.

"We both do," the taller one said, "just not very well."

Alfie thought the man spoke well enough indeed.

"Do you have any food?" the second man asked. "We haven't eaten in days."

Alfie handed them some bread and vegetables he had in a sack. "Just eat slowly. Too fast and you'll cramp up and die."

Like dogs they did as told and ate with restraint. In between bites, they told him that their names were Aaron Rosenfeld and Saul Blum and that they'd escaped from a work camp a few miles away. "We were all going to be shipped to Auschwitz and nobody returns from there. It's a death camp."

Alfie wasn't certain what they were talking about, but accepted that they were afraid they'd be killed outright rather than simply beaten to death or starved. They further told him that they had once been university professors and had taught English literature. They had families but hadn't heard from them since being taken by the Gestapo a year earlier. They quite candidly told him they thought their loved ones were dead.

Shit, Alfie thought, what kind of a fucking war was this? He'd heard of Nazi atrocities of course, but this was his first direct experience with them. What the hell danger were two English literature teachers to Hitler and his fucking Reich?

Aaron spoke. "How far away is the rest of your army?"

Alfie laughed harshly. "Plenty far away. It might as well be on the moon. They're on the other side of the Rhine and nowhere near it for that matter. The krauts are getting real smart and holding us at bay."

Saul broke down and sobbed. "Then we're lost. We can't hide out forever."

"Why the hell not?" Alfie said angrily. "I don't plan on surrendering to the fucking SS or the Gestapo or any other fucking Nazi."

"Then you'll protect us?" asked Aaron.

Alfie took a deep breath. What the hell was he getting himself into? It was trouble enough for one man to stay alive, but to be saddled with a pair of useless Jews? Christ on a crutch.

"Yeah," he said.

Whiteside was livid. "Morgan, just who the hell do you think you are and just how the hell did you think you could get away with such a jackass stunt as buzzing the Eiffel Tower? Thousands of people saw you and your plane was easily identifiable. Somebody even took pictures for the French papers and your ugly face is clearly visible."

Jack stood at attention and took the butt-chewing he knew he deserved. At least Levin wasn't involved. Whiteside was only interested in the idiot pilot, and that was Jack.

"Sir, it was a dumb thing to do and I apologize for it."

"And let me guess, you think you can't get punished because you're already in combat. Well, you're wrong. I could drop your worthless ass down to second lieutenant in a heartbeat, or I could court-martial you down to buck private and put you in an infantry platoon. However, since you would likely last less than thirty seconds in the infantry, that would be tantamount to murder, so I am only going to seriously consider dropping your rank."

Whiteside took a sip of cold coffee, winced, and glared at Jack. "The French are pissed off because the touchy bastards think you insulted them, which you did. Would you have buzzed the Statue of Liberty or the Washington Monument? Or maybe St. Peter's in Rome?"

"No, sir."

"And Ike's joined the list of pissed off people because the French are spending a lot of time complaining to him about stupid, insensitive Americans, and now he has to spend valuable time solving the problem you created."

Oh Jesus, Jack thought. *It's gone all the way to Ike?* Jack swallowed. That was not what he'd had in mind. "Sir, it was a sophomoric prank. It won't happen again."

"Morgan, you are going to get one chance to survive and keep your rank. Do you have a class-A uniform?"

"No, sir," Jack answered, puzzled. "When the LST got sunk my stuff was ruined. They didn't give me anything other than fatigues as reissue."

"Damn. Okay, we'll scrounge up something for you, because you are going to SHAEF, where you'll grovel and whimper and kiss Ike's ass, and then you'll plant a big wet one on de Gaulle's ass if you have to, and then you'll ask him if he'd like you to kiss it again. If the weather clears up and permits flying, Snyder will take over as pilot while you're gone, and Rolfe will be his spotter, so we'll survive quite nicely without you.

"And don't think for one second that you're going to have a good time in Paris. Levin will be with you and he'll have strict orders to keep you under wraps."

"Yes, sir."

"Wonderful." He handed Jack an envelope. "Here are your orders. You are to meet a Captain Grayson at SHAEF who will tell you when and where to drop your shorts so you can get your ass kicked, not kissed. Now get the hell out of here."

Another day in Sweden and another dingy hotel, thought von Papen as he looked around at the tawdry room that said that the Swedes' penchant for neatness was vastly overrated. At least this one had a private bath and a toilet which he'd already used, however reluctantly because of the grime. It occurred to him that he was getting soft as he grew older.

This time both he and Molotov had flown in planes with Swedish markings. The Swedes were too cowed by the presence of both Russia and Germany to make any protest whatsoever. Sweden was terrified about the future. The opportunistic Swedes had allowed themselves to be bullied into supplying Germany with vast amounts of war materiel. Now they were far too concerned about what might befall them when the fighting inevitably ended to worry about two planes making unauthorized flights. Their fear was that Russia would overrun them and make Sweden another satellite country.

Von Papen had arrived first and checked the room for recording devices. He'd found them, of course, and his men had then planted their own, even though he suspected he'd found the bugs he'd been expected to find. Both sides would have a transcript of the discussions so neither could be blackmailed. Or perhaps both could, he thought.

Molotov entered, looked around the room in mild disgust, shrugged, and took a seat on the chair opposite von Papen. Their respective translators took up station.

Von Papen began. "My government is very interested in your proposal, but you already know that. We propose a one year truce, to be renewed annually if both sides concur."

Molotov nodded. "We would prefer two years."

The German shrugged. "Then two it is."

That both men managed to say it with a straight face was a tribute to their diplomatic skills. The two nations had and would disregard truces or treaties at will. The truce would last for as long as either or both wished it.

"How will you explain this to the Americans?" von Papen asked.

Molotov shrugged dismissively. "We will tell them much of the truth, which is that our armies are exhausted and need to rest and refit. I would suggest that our two forces periodically nibble at each other in order to maintain the fiction that we are still at war."

Von Papen managed to conceal the fact that he was shocked, even disgusted. Such "nibbling" would result in numerous dead and wounded, a fact that didn't dismay the Soviets in any way. A point to remember about Stalin was that he didn't care about the piles of dead and wounded.

Molotov smiled icily. "However, we must discuss spheres of influence so there are no, ah, misunderstandings during the truce."

"Indeed," said von Papen. "We are more than willing to cede Finland, Lithuania, Estonia, Latvia, and eastern Poland to you."

This time Molotov actually laughed. "These are lands we already hold, Comrade von Papen. You can and will do better than that."

Von Papen was too much of a professional to be disturbed by the blunt rebuff. "Then we will make no objection if you continue westward into Rumania, Bulgaria, and that part of Yugoslavia known as Serbia. That will unite the Soviet Union with Tito's partisans, which, I understand, is highly desired by Stalin."

Molotov nodded. Did the Germans know how concerned Stalin was about Tito's independence and lack of solidarity with the Soviet Union? "Albania must also be ours."

Von Papen laughed. "Who would want the miserable place?"

"And we must be permitted freedom in Greece and Turkey."

The German ambassador agreed to giving Turkey to Russia but said that the British and Americans would likely protect Greece, which was an ally. Turkey was another matter. She was nominally neutral.

The stony faced Russian blinked in pleased surprise. Molotov didn't give a damn about Greece and agreed to leave it alone. He had gotten what he really wanted. Seizing Turkey would give Russia what she'd desired for centuries—unimpeded access to the Mediterranean. No longer would she be dependent on the ice-choked passages of the north for her commerce and sustenance.

"Germany would keep East Prussia, West Poland, Hungary, Czechoslovakia, and, of course, Austria," von Papen said. "There is one other thing we desire."

Molotov sighed. "There always is."

"The American and British bombers have severely hampered our production of armor. We would like to trade for five thousand T34 tanks."

Molotov was incredulous. The T34 was the finest tank on the face of the earth. Other tanks, like the new Stalin models or the German Tiger and King Tiger, might be larger, but nothing compared with the T34's all around capabilities. His first instinct was to reject von Papen out of hand. Instead, the diplomat in him took over.

"Trade for what?" he inquired cautiously.

"Vlasov."

In order to make Paris by morning, Morgan and Levin had left by Jeep in the middle of the night.

They could have flown, following the roads below to Paris, but there was always the possibility that the miserable late September weather would break and the regiment, standing down again for supplies, would have a need for the plane.

Levin drove like a maniac. Even so, they were frequently stopped by eastbound convoys and MP's checking for orders and ID. After all, going AWOL in Paris, even for a short while, was hardly an original idea. They'd heard that numbers of American deserters were hiding in the town and managing to elude both the Paris gendarmes and the military police.

They arrived in the city in the early morning, just as Paris was waking up. Levin continued to drive and he obviously knew his way around.

Levin grinned. "Didn't I tell you I lived here once upon a time?"

"No, although nothing about you would surprise me. What were you doing here?"

Levin swerved to avoid a horse-drawn milk truck that had emerged from a narrow alley. "I lived here for a year after I graduated from high school. My parents thought it would be a great education and I'd learn all about art and stuff. What I really learned was how to get laid in so many different ways. God, what a place."

Jack shook his head. "After I graduated from high school, I got a job in a grocery store to earn some money before football started."

"Poor baby. I stayed here with relatives, which is why I volunteered to escort you and why I'm going to dump you and come back for you about five o'clock. I was very fond of those people I lived with, and I want to know how, or if, they made it through four years of living under the bullshit Nazis." He turned grim. "I somehow doubt that I'll find all of them. I just hope a few survived."

The things we take for granted, Jack thought.

They crossed the Seine. The address on Jack's orders was not for Ike's headquarters at the Trianon Palace, but for a support organization that had something to do with military intelligence. They found it and Levin wished Jack good luck before driving off.

Literally hundreds of American military personnel bustled about, all of them in freshly starched and pressed Class A uniforms that made Jack's look dingy. Some looked at him sideways until catching the Purple Heart and the Bronze star, which changed their expressions.

After a few questions, he found Captain Grayson's office. He knocked and entered. No point being too timid, especially since Grayson was a captain, too.

Grayson was short and pudgy and wore thick glasses. To Jack's surprise, he smiled warmly. "Good to see you, Captain. Have a seat. Like some coffee?"

"Love it, but aren't I here to be chewed out? Or is it traditional to give coffee to a condemned man?"

Grayson laughed. "Oh, that Eiffel Tower thing? Yeah, the froggies are all in a snit, but who gives a shit about them? Most everybody here thinks it was funnier than hell and you'll probably get your picture in Stars and Stripes. The French can go to hell as far as we're concerned. No, Captain, you were brought here for other purposes. Wait here."

Bemused and relieved, Jack did as he was told. He sipped his coffee, which was a lot better than what he drank in the field. The door opened behind him and he turned. His jaw dropped. It wasn't Grayson. It was a very lovely young woman who looked very familiar and much prettier in person than in a photograph.

She smiled timidly. "Good morning, Captain Jack. I'm Jessica Granville."

Jessica drove. She had her Red Cross car and knew where she was going. This gave Jack a chance to look at her more closely, hoping all the while he wasn't staring. Jeb had been right. Jessica wasn't a classic beauty. Instead, she was vivacious and bright and altogether enchanting. He might have been conned into coming to Paris thinking he was going to get his butt ripped, but he didn't care.

Neither'd had breakfast so she suggested a small restaurant that served good eggs and ham. On the way she told him that the meeting was her uncle's idea. Tom Granville was a full colonel and on Ike's staff.

"He and I had talked about the letters you and I exchanged and how we'd both like to meet and, when he saw the picture of you and the Eiffel Tower, he had the idea of bringing you here for a talking to. By the way, your Colonel Whiteside is a friend of my uncle and he thought the idea was great."

"And here I thought I was going to be skinned alive, court-martialed and executed, in that order."

They ate and talked, hesitantly at first, and then more comfortably. To their surprise, they found it had been easier to converse in writing than face to face. Soon, however, they worked through it and began to talk as if they'd known each other for years.

"My big fear," she admitted, "was that you'd be

angry at the trick and storm off. That's why I got a vehicle. It's a long walk to my apartment if this didn't work out."

After eating, they sat on a bench that overlooked the Seine along the Quai de Montebello, just across from the Ile de la Cite, which provided them a splendid view of Notre Dame Cathedral. He mentioned that Levin had suggested buzzing it as well, and Jessica broke up into most unladylike guffaws. Other benches were occupied with a variety of people, ranging from young couples to older men and women. Curiously, there were only a few men in American uniforms. Jessica mentioned how thin, gray and drab both the women and the city looked after four years of Nazi occupation. She added that many of the city's trees had been chopped down for firewood during the occupation. It would be a long time before Paris regained its premier place in the world of art and fashion. She said some previously glamorous spots looked dingier than what she'd seen in London. Someday, he told her, he would like to visit the cathedral of Notre Dame that was so tantalizingly close. They could go there right now, but neither wanted to be a tourist in the few hours they had. And someday he wanted to see the Louvre, Versailles, Montmartre, and a score of other places that Jessica had already visited. But today all Jack wanted was to spend as much time as he could with the incredibly charming Jessica Granville.

They spent the morning and afternoon talking and discovering each other. Jack had idle thoughts about suggesting they go to Jessica's apartment, but he decided any suggestion to that effect would be premature and might spoil the mood.

The only sour note was a group of several hundred protesters marching in loose order down the Rue de Montebello. They carried red flags emblazoned with the Soviet Union's hammer and sickle. Placards proclaimed the glory of Stalin and someone named Maurice Thorez. Jessica thought he was the head of the French communist party and a Stalinist.

"What do these people want?" Jack asked.

"Communist rule in France. The commies had been quiet and Thorez was pardoned by de Gaulle for whatever he did in the past, but they're getting active again. Everybody thinks there's going to be trouble."

A large detachment of gendarmes appeared and, with lead-weighted capes flying, halted the protesters and literally beat them back, arresting a number who now had bloody foreheads. Jack and Jessica stood and watched with Jack slightly in front. Jessica thought it was nice that he was symbolically at least trying to shield her. However neither Jack nor Jessica felt in any danger as the brawl receded. The two sides were fixated on each other and unconcerned by the presence of spectators.

All too soon, the day had to end. They arrived at Grayson's office about four-thirty. Jessica introduced him to her uncle and they spoke briefly. Tom Granville left them, saying he had a war to run. He'd unintentionally put a damper on the day. Yes, there was a war to run.

Only a few minutes after five, Levin pulled up. "Get in, Cinderella, the ball is over."

"Are you the wicked stepmother?" Jessica laughed.

"No, the ugly Jewish stepsister," he said and they were introduced.

Jessica kissed Jack on the cheek and told him to keep writing and try to figure a way to get back to Paris. He kissed her lightly on the lips and said he would. She grinned and squeezed his arm.

"Nice girl," Levin said as they drove off. "Far, far better than you deserve."

"Thanks for your ringing vote of confidence, and may your future wife at least come from one of the Twelve Tribes of Israel that walks upright. So how did your search go?"

"Not so good," he said sadly. "When the Germans took Paris, I had eleven cousins living here including the nice middle-aged couple I lived with. When the Germans left, there were five and not the couple who cared for me. The survivors spent four years hiding in closets and being fed by neighbors who ran great risks doing so. They should be considered heroes if not saints. Of course, Jews don't have saints."

His voice broke and he hit the steering wheel in anger. "They spent four fucking years hiding out, not talking loudly, not going outside, and fearing that any noise outside their cubbyhole would be the Gestapo or the French police come to take them away. Oh yeah, and don't get sick while you're hiding. How do you go to a doctor, or get a doctor to make a house call? Christ, can you believe the French police helped the Gestapo? What the hell kind of world is that?"

"Is that what happened to the others?"

"Yeah. They were swept up a few months ago and not heard from since then, and these included the wonderful people I stayed with. Oh, they sent postcards to neighbors saying that they'd arrived at their destination and were doing fine, but we all know that's a fucking bullshit lie. If their destination was Auschwitz, then they're likely dead and turned to ashes. If they were sent to some other camp, then it's just barely possible some might be alive."

Jack slumped in his seat. The enormity of what the Nazis had done and were continuing to do to Jews and others was just beginning to sink in. That he now actually knew someone directly affected by it was almost overwhelming. "I don't know what to say."

Levin shrugged. "Then don't try. There's nothing you can say. All I want to do right now is get back to the regiment and see how I can kill Germans."

★ CHAPTER 12 ★

BILL STOVER HAD GOTTEN HIS PROMOTION TO
first lieutenant, received a Distinguished Flying Cross
for his part in killing Hitler, and, best of all, now had
his own B17 and was now flying in formation with a
hundred other bombers over Germany.

At first he'd been annoyed that mousy little Phips
had gotten all the glory and the publicity while he,
his copilot, the man who'd actually urged him to drop
the bombs, was basically forgotten. When the crew
went on a bond tour, it was Phips who got the cheers
while the rest got polite applause. When women threw
themselves at the scrawny pilot, his faithful copilot got
the leftovers, which, he'd laughingly decided, wasn't all
that bad a fate. That life, however, quickly bored him.

Bill Stover, age 24, basically was not a jealous man
and, when logic took over, he sincerely wished Phips
good luck. All Stover wanted to do was get back in a
B17. He'd volunteered for the air force so he could
fly and fight, not hustle war bonds from civilians. He'd

pestered his superiors and finally gotten his wish. He was back with the Eighth Air Force and flying a B17, the sweetest bomber in the world.

This was his third mission over Germany and he'd laughingly told his new buddies that it was two and a half more than he'd had in the *Mother's Milk*'s historic one and only bombing run.

The morning's briefing had raised a concern. Intelligence had apparently picked up indications that the krauts were going to try something new. As a result, the number of P51 fighter escorts had been increased. Stover felt quite comfortable with that idea, and, regardless what happened, he'd vowed that he would never break formation like the incredibly lucky Phips had. Germany was below him and bombers were arrayed on all sides of his plane.

He stiffened. Something was happening. He focused his concentration on the increasingly strident radio chatter from the escorting fighters indicating that a small number of German fighters was headed for them. "Holy shit, look at them," a voice said in a not very military manner.

"Jets," another voice said and Stover's blood ran cold. He'd heard that jets existed and that they could fly at incredible speeds. His own plane's machine guns started chattering at something he couldn't see. And then he could, and then it was gone in a shrieking second. At the same time, his plane shuddered. It'd been hit. His outer left engine had been shredded, pieces were flying off as it and his left wing were disintegrating.

Slowly and with apparent dignity, the wing collapsed and the plane began a slow death spiral. Stover ordered everybody to jump, but it was almost impossible as centrifugal force pinned them to the hull. Finally, Stover clawed his way to a hatch and pushed two of his men out into the wind. He couldn't see the rest of his crew. He hoped they'd gone. He couldn't wait. The ground was coming up far too fast.

Stover jumped and felt the blast of cold air grab him and spin him. He missed the bomber's tail by a few feet. Seconds later, he opened his parachute and watched as his bomber sped downwards and corkscrewed itself into the ground. The bombs exploded with a mighty blast. He looked around as he descended. The rest of his formation was disappearing and the German jets, if that's what they were, had also vanished.

He landed awkwardly and he felt his right leg snap. He screamed and was dragged by his chute until he managed to overcome the agony from his leg and free himself. He lay there for a few minutes fighting off the waves of nauseating pain and trying to compose himself.

Stover heard voices and, a few moments later, several German civilians were gathered over him. "*Bitte,*" he said. He thought it meant please. "*Kamerad,*" he tried again.

The civilians glared at him with undisguised hatred. Here was one of the American murderers who was savaging their cities and massacring innocent family members.

One of the German men leaned over and spat in his face, and a woman kicked him in his obviously injured leg. Stover screamed and they laughed. A man with a pitchfork stuck it into his other thigh and twisted. Stover writhed and tried to evade further jabs. It was futile and the pain from repeated stabs nearly made him unconscious. He screamed some more and the German civilians cheered. "Now you suffer like we do," one of them said in English.

An authoritative voice stopped them. A man in a uniform, probably a cop, Stover thought, looked down on him with contempt. He barked some orders and the men picked him up without care for his injured legs and he screamed again. He continued to scream when they threw him in the back of a truck, and finally he passed out when they drove down the rutted road.

Miles away and thousands of feet in the sky, Lieutenant General Adolf Galland, "Dolfo" to his friends, flew alongside Major Walter Nowotny who commanded the ME262 squadron. It had been a most worthwhile test run. Of course, some would say that generals should not fly in combat, but Galland was sick and tired of desk duty and he'd flown the ME262 on test runs before.

This fine day, he'd bagged a P51 fighter and a B17 bomber without any damage to his plane and Nowotny had killed two fighters and damaged a bomber. The jet could go more than twice the speed of the Flying Fortress and a hundred miles an hour faster than the fighter escorts.

Sadly, it would be a while before the ME262 appeared over Germany in any great numbers. Aircraft manufacture of any kind had been slowed by the damned Allied bombers. The plane was designed to destroy the bombers and obviously could slaughter them in great numbers. There was a shortage of jet fuel, too, although there were more than enough qualified pilots to fly the few jets the Luftwaffe possessed.

Still, many of the best and brightest Luftwaffe pilots had been killed in the war and replacement pilots from service in other planes were scantily trained, little more than cannon fodder for the Americans who shot them down as fast as they went up.

Perhaps, Galland thought with a smile, the situation would require him to spend more time in a cockpit.

Beetle Smith was in his normal lousy mood. "Granville, please tell me you know what the hell is going on because nobody else around here does."

Colonel Tom Granville took a seat and adjusted the folders he'd brought. He knew everything in them, but their physical presence reassured him. Smith was a harsh and demanding leader on a good day, and this wasn't a good day.

"Regarding the jets, it's easy, General. The ME262 is something we've known about for a long time. It was inevitable that the krauts would introduce it, and they have a number of other new planes being developed, including a rocket plane that's a real pilot killer, the ME163 Comet, and another jet, the Heinkel 162, which they refer to as the Salamander. Of the group, the 262—it's called the Swallow, by the way—is by far the most formidable if only because they are beginning to make them in numbers that are large for German war production, although quite small in comparison with ours. We picked up a message that Galland himself flew one of the planes involved in that attack on our bombers, and that he referred to the jet as an 'angel.' He also said it was worth five ME109's. We should thank our lucky stars, or our air force pilots who have been bombing their factories, that the Germans are unable to produce them in any real quantity."

"Shit. Tell me again what we've got in the way of jets to counter the ME."

Granville sighed. "Not much. The British are introducing something called the Meteor, but it's nowhere near as fast as the 262, and we've got the P80 but it's a long ways away from entering the field. Apparently it's killing more of our pilots than anyone likes."

"Fantastic. So what is the air force going to do now?"

"They are going to saturate the skies with fighter escorts, mainly P51's. The air force believes we will win a battle of attrition if only because we outnumber them so vastly."

"And that will be a great comfort to the widows and other family members of those killed."

"General, the air force does have other tactical plans. The German jets guzzle fuel, so they have to land and gas up fairly frequently. The idea is to follow them and either shoot them down when they slow down to land, or hit them on the ground, or bomb the crap out of the airfields so they can't take off or land."

"I guess it's better than our boys lining up to be shot at," Smith said, again grumpily. "Now, what the hell is going on with the French and what the hell are the Russians up to? All I'm getting is word that the French commies are rioting and that the Soviet advance is slowing and we don't need either to happen, not for one damn minute."

"General, we're trying to pin things down, but nothing looks very good. In fact, it could wind up being real, real bad."

★　　★　　★

Jack flew the Piper in lazy circles around the barn a thousand feet below while Snyder called out information that was largely superfluous. The American tanks were pounding the building. For reasons known only to them, a handful of German soldiers had opened fire on the head of the 74th's column. A Jeep and a half-track had been damaged and two men lightly wounded, but now the barn, yet another old stone structure, was surrounded and being blasted to pieces by a platoon of tanks. Although he could not tell the difference from the sky, he knew that the American tanks were Jeb's and now had the higher velocity 76mm guns that could knock out most German tanks. Unfortunately, they still had inadequate armor and were vulnerable to both German tanks and antitank guns.

"Can't have everything," Jeb Carter had said. "And by the way, keep yourself out of my cousin's pants."

They'd had the conversation that morning. "Got nowhere near her pants, or any other part of her clothing or anatomy," Jack had responded in mock anger. "Even though she's related to you, she's got more class than to allow that."

Jack was well aware that the relationship was by marriage, not blood. "I've seen her naked," Jeb volunteered, shocking both Jack and Levin. "Of course she was two and I was about four. Still, she said she was impressed with the state of my manhood even at that young age. Sadly, I thought she was a little flatchested." He declined to add that he'd seen her half naked just a few years ago when she was much older.

Jack flew lower to see the damage being done to the barn. As he did, Snyder caught motion and suggested they reverse course and fly higher. "Good catch, Snyder," he said and keyed his radio to the ground. "Jeb, you've got a handful of German tanks coming right at you."

Carter chortled. "How many in a handful? Some of my cracker relatives got eight webbed fingers on a hand."

"Four tanks and one scout vehicle and, oh shit, I think they're Panthers." He flew low, almost at ground level and picked up the distinct slope to the hull and turret. "Confirmed, Jeb, they're Panthers."

Carter swallowed, or tried to. His mouth was suddenly dry. The five-man Panther weighed nearly forty-five tons, but, more importantly, carried a high velocity 75mm gun as its main weapon, and its sloping front was heavily armored and virtually impervious to many American weapons. Now it was time to find out what the Sherman's new 76mm gun could do. Many other U.S. units had fought the Panther with mixed results. In most cases, the German tanks had inflicted serious damage and withdrawn.

The Germans were in sight and Morgan again confirmed that they were the dreaded Panthers. Now they were just within range. "Open fire," Carter ordered.

All four of his tanks shot, but, at long range, only one hit, and that shell bounced off the glacis, or sloping frontal hull. *We're in trouble,* Carter thought. He'd also fired way too soon and cursed himself for the mistake.

The Panthers fired and one of Carter's tanks was hit. The shell penetrated the tank's armor and it began to burn almost immediately. Jeb heard the explosions but was too focused on his immediate front to care about the other tank and its crew. Carter's tank fired and again the shell bounced off the glacis.

"Damn it to hell," Carter swore. Even with improved

guns, the Panther's front armor was impervious to the Sherman. The reports were right, only a hit on the side or a damned good shot on the turret would stop a Panther.

A second Sherman was hit and damaged. Carter called for reinforcements and the remainder of his twelve-tank company responded rapidly. The Germans saw them and decided they'd had enough. They began to back away. Carter's tank fired again; this time the gunner's aim was true, hitting a Panther's turret. Smoke and fire billowed from it. Carter was about to cheer when his own tank was rocked by a hit, hurling him against the turret's wall. Smoke filled the compartment.

"Abandon ship," he yelled, coughing violently from the smoke. The order was probably unnecessary. Everyone knew to get the hell out once fire started. He tried to open the turret hatch but it was stuck. Jesus, he thought as he fought off panic, I am going to burn to death.

Carter slid down through the smoke to the belly of his tank. The bottom hatch was open and one of his crew was already escaping that way. Carter called out and heard no one else. He hoped they were all gone. If not, their life expectancy was now in seconds. He slid down and crawled out behind his immobile tank, hoping that he wasn't going to be machine-gunned. When he was far enough away and thought he might be safe, he stood up and watched the remainder of his force moving carefully in the direction of the Germans, who could no longer be seen.

"Anybody call for air support?" he yelled. His voice was hoarse from inhaling smoke.

"They're coming," was the answer.

"Yeah," he said. "Once again a day late and a dollar short." Worse, they'd just had their first real taste of fighting the best tank the Germans had, and it had just clobbered the best tank the U.S. had, the up-gunned Sherman.

"This is going to be a long fucking war," he said to no one in particular.

Colonel Otto Skorzeny stood at attention. Both Reichsfuhrer Heinrich Himmler and Field Marshal Gerd von Rundstedt waved him to a seat. Skorzeny smiled inwardly at the fact. Which of them, he wondered, was truly in charge? And who would still be standing when this damned war was over, Himmler the snake or Rundstedt the warrior? Never bet against the snake, he decided.

Himmler smiled. "Colonel, we have several important and discrete tasks for you. I've been told you speak both English and French, true?"

"Yes, but not as fluently as a native."

Himmler smiled. "No, we would not think of passing you off as one. Do you also speak Russian?"

"A very little," he admitted, "but I am certain I could improve on my skills."

"An excellent idea," said Rundstedt. "In the meantime, we wish you to develop separate detachments of men who can speak English, Russian, or French, or, perhaps, all of them. And in these cases, the men must be fluent enough to fool the natives, so to speak."

Skorzeny paused for a moment, thinking. "Finding large numbers of men who can, as you say, fool the natives, will be very difficult, if not impossible. Many of my men who have those language skills from living in other countries have now lived in the Reich so long that they've picked up accents or forgotten old idioms, or are unaware of current ones. The Americans, for instance, ask questions about current baseball standings if they are suspicious of someone, and most of my English speakers don't even know the rules of the game, or they learned their English in England where they know even less about it."

"As do I," Rundstedt said dryly, and even Himmler smiled.

"Although, there are times when an English accent is often a good excuse for not knowing about American trivia," Skorzeny said. "In fact, Americans are almost childishly impressed with an intelligent sounding British accent." His mind was racing with possibilities. What on earth did they want him to do?

"What would be feasible," Skorzeny continued, "is to establish certain levels of language skills, such as Class A for the handful of those who could pass as natives, Class B for those larger numbers who are fluent but have accents and lack knowledge of minutiae, and Class C for that largest group who are fluent enough to understand and be understood, and read newspapers, bulletins, menus, etc."

"Excellent," said Himmler.

"Since it is obvious that these people would be intended to operate behind enemy lines, the Class A types would be the ones who would actually come into contact with the enemy, while the others would avoid it as much as possible. It goes without saying that they would need appropriate clothing, uniforms, identification, and equipment."

Himmler beamed while von Rundstedt nodded.

"Colonel," said Himmler, "all that will be done. In the near future, we will have several assignments for you. First you are to deliver a package, human, to the Soviets. Second, you are to disrupt matters in France as much as possible, and last, think about how you would deliver an extremely large bomb or two into the heart of the enemy."

Skorzeny thought quickly. Disrupting the French would be no problem. They were in a state of near anarchy already. "I assume you want the French communists blamed for those disruptions, which would result in a heavy-handed response by de Gaulle and the fools around him."

"Indeed," said Himmler, again pleased by Skorzeny's intelligence.

"As to delivering a human package to the Reds, would the package have to be still living, or even intact? For instance, would just a head be satisfactory?"

The field marshal turned away in disgust while Himmler beamed. "We will check on that, now what about the bombs?"

"How large, Reichsfuhrer?"

"Assume five tons each."

Skorzeny whistled. What on earth could weigh that much? "When and where?"

"Several months, and let's assume Moscow and New York," Himmler said. Von Rundstedt looked surprised.

"It can be done," Skorzeny said. Nothing surprised him anymore. He was confident about delivering a bomb to Moscow, but New York? Despite what he'd just said, he would have to think about it.

"Then go and work on it," Himmler said and dismissed the scarred colonel, who saluted and left them.

"I wasn't aware that Heisenberg was that far along with his work," Rundstedt said when they were alone. He was thinking of Varner's last report on the matter.

"He isn't, but he will be. He is too much of a scientist with his checking and rechecking until everything is perfect. He will be informed that he must race to completion and if that means taking shortcuts, even dangerous ones, then so be it. If he loses some of his precious physicists in the process, then they will be casualties in our war. Heisenberg can no longer think of himself as working in a lab. He must begin to realize that he is a soldier in the trenches and the enemy is coming at him. He must stop them now, and not a year or two from now when everything is perfect and he can say 'eureka' and astound the scientific world, perhaps winning a second Nobel Prize. He will also understand that he and his family will be forced to pay the price of his failures should he not succeed."

Rundstedt nodded silently. He wondered if Heinrich Himmler had any idea just what the hell he was talking about.

Jessica heard the groans while she was still out in the hallway. She paused and was tempted to go somewhere else while Monique and Master Sergeant Charley Boyle completed their usual noisy mating ritual. Nuts, she thought. She was tired and, besides, her money was paying for the apartment.

She quietly entered the apartment and tiptoed past Monique's bedroom. The door was open and she stopped. Boyle was on top of Monique. He was a stocky man with reddish hair on his back. She wondered if Jack had a hairy back. Monique's legs were wrapped

around her lover's waist. He was thrusting inside her
while his hands grabbed her breasts. Monique's hands
were on Boyle's buttocks, pushing him ever deeper
inside her while they both groaned and sighed.

Jessica tore her eyes from the scene and quickly
went to her room, quietly closing the door behind her.
She took off her dress, and cleaned her face, arms,
and shoulders from a bowl of water. She thought about
what she'd just seen. Vive la France, she thought.
Jessica had never before seen people making love, if
that's what it really was. A few years back, she'd had
the chance to see a smutty movie that cousin Jeb had
gotten from his friends, but had passed on it. He'd
later admitted it involved some foreign people and
the film quality was really bad.

"And the people were ugly, too," he'd added.

My education is sadly lacking, Jessica concluded.
She wondered about Jack's and thought she knew
about Jeb's. He'd bedded several of her friends who
had told her what a wonderful experience it was.
These comments had led her to let Jeb take a few
liberties with her until they'd both called a halt to it.

Monique knocked and walked in. "My beloved
sergeant is gone, if you haven't noticed. Did you
enjoy the view?"

Jessica was not abashed. If Monique had wanted
privacy, she should have closed the door. "It was
intriguing."

Monique laughed. "Intriguing? Now you sound like
an Englishwoman. It would have been truly intriguing if you'd brought your Jack Morgan up here and
romped on your bed, with the both of you squealing
with pleasure like Charley and I did. You should have,

you know. Life is too short and sometimes people make it too damned complicated. There's a war going on and we'd all better enjoy it while we can."

Jessica and Monique had had this conversation before and Jessica had explained that, first, she wasn't ready to have sex with Jack or anyone else for that matter, and, second, American women didn't usually jump into the sack with someone they'd just met. Monique had said that was a shame because they were missing so much time and pleasure. She'd then gotten Jessica to admit she'd never gone all the way, and that some reasonably heavy petting had been about it. Monique again thought that was a terrible waste.

"You're lovely and you have a wonderful figure, why don't you use it?" she'd said. "Someday you'll be old and wrinkled and no one will want you. Use it now, while you can still enjoy it."

Why not indeed, Jessica had thought, although she figured she had more than a few years to go before she'd be old and withered. But Monique had a point. Jack could be dead at any time, and bombs were falling around Paris although, so far, its status as an open city had been sustained and kept it from damage even though the Allies now occupied it.

It was time to change the subject. "What do you mean about complications?" Jessica asked.

"I told my sergeant to go away and not come back," she said sadly. "That was a farewell lay."

"Good grief, Monique, why?"

"Because he is a thief and a crook and is going to get arrested. And that means anyone close to him might be arrested as well."

"Ah."

"Ah, indeed. Recall all the food and other things he got me, much of which I sold and sent back home to help with my son? Well, all of it was stolen. I thought as much, but I closed my eyes to it. My sergeant and a bunch of others are stealing from the U.S. Army and now the MP's are investigating it. He is debating turning in others in return for a light sentence and came to me to tell me to get rid of what I might still have and be ready to answer some questions. He will doubtless lose his stripes and probably have to go to jail. He may be dishonorably discharged, but he may also be sent to a combat unit as a private. Either way, he is dead to me. I will miss him. He was a competent lover and a great purveyor of luxury items."

Jessica had heard rumors from her uncle that some GI's in the supply units were pilfering large quantities of supplies and selling them on the black market. A little thievery was common enough when temptation presented itself and, as Tom had said, who counts paper clips and pencils? Still, stealing to provide one's self with creature comforts was one thing, but this level of thievery was much more ambitious. Jessica was glad that the apartment was in her name and that she could prove where the money came from.

"Monique, I'm sorry."

"So am I," she said with a mocking pout. "Now it will take me weeks to find a replacement for him."

Jim Byrnes' career in the United States government had been varied, even spectacular, although he'd been denied his nation's highest honor, the presidency. And, at age 65, he knew it would never happen. He'd been a congressman from his native state of South Carolina and then a justice of the U.S. Supreme Court. He had stepped down as a Justice in order to head the War Mobilization Board for his good friend, Franklin Delano Roosevelt. He'd also been born a Catholic, which offended many Protestants, and then converted to Episcopalian, which offended Catholics, thus making him unelectable to national office.

Still, the President trusted him and liked to use him for unofficial duties like the one he was pursuing today. Andrei Gromyko, the gloomy looking Soviet ambassador to the United States, awaited him in a conference room in the uninspiring red stone castle that was the Smithsonian Institute. Gromyko was much younger than Byrnes and was considered a rising star, a Red Star, Byrnes thought whimsically.

Typically, Gromyko came right to the point. "Why do you wish to speak to me, Mr. Byrnes?"

And a bright good morning to you too, James F. Byrnes thought. "We would like to know what is happening to your army. It seems to have disappeared," he said dryly.

"I don't understand," Gromyko said, either ignoring or not understanding the sarcasm. "We are fighting bravely and enduring casualties on your behalf." Gromyko was known to be a stubborn negotiator.

"Ambassador, your vaunted Red Army does not appear to be moving. What has happened to your great advances and even greater victories?"

"The Red Army continues to fight. As you are aware, the Germans are now fighting far more intelligently than in the past. I believe your own forces are discovering this unpleasant fact in France. The Red Army's senior commander, Marshal Zhukov, has informed our high command, the Stavka, that the army is exhausted. It requires far more in the way of supplies and manpower; thus, a period of relative rest is required. However, do not fear, the pace will increase once the situation improves."

Byrnes continued in his soft Southern drawl. "In the meantime, the American army bears the brunt of fighting the Nazis. We are seeing German units in France that had been in Russia until recently."

Ultra was providing disheartening information that numerous other German units were moving from the Soviet front to France. Aerial reconnaissance, along with captured enemy soldiers was confirming this.

Gromyko laughed unpleasantly. "Now you know what it is like to fight alone, even temporarily. From 1941 until now, Russia stood alone while your country dithered. My people bled. Our soldiers were killed and maimed, our cities ruined, our women raped, and all the while you Americans slept snug in your beds."

Byrnes bristled. The accusation, however truthful, was unfair. The American people weren't going to go to war against anybody until the Japanese had conveniently attacked Pearl Harbor and Germany subsequently and foolishly declared war on the United States. FDR had correctly identified Germany as the greater evil and had ordered the military focus to be against Hitler, even though there had been fierce opposition to that decision by those who felt that Japan should be defeated first. They both knew that an American focus on Japan would have meant defeat for Russia, and perhaps even Great Britain.

"It takes time to prepare an army," Byrnes said, "and we were separated from the war in Europe by an ocean, whereas you had the Nazis by the throat. In Teheran, less than a year ago, we promised a cross channel invasion this spring and we have done it. We expected to be marching in lockstep with you, and not have you giving the Germans a respite."

Gromyko nearly sneered. "I concede that, however late, your army has arrived. But it is nowhere near the size of ours or that of the Germans confronting us. Your invasion of France is, for all intents and purposes, a sideshow."

Byrnes nearly gasped at the insult. "Our army is large, getting larger, and will continue to grow, as will the amount of aid we are giving you. Our concern is that the Red Army isn't fighting."

Gromyko was clearly unimpressed. "I will relay your concerns. However, I will also remind you that General Winter was a Russian ally when the Hitlerites invaded, but is now a friend of the Germans. Winter in Poland might not be as severe as it is in Russia, but waging war in ice and snow and mud is still an extremely difficult enterprise."

Byrnes reluctantly but silently concurred. "Then please add this. We are working hard and our people are in great danger in order to send supply convoys to the Soviet Union. Those supplies could just as well be used by our own soldiers as yours."

Gromyko stood. His expression was one of controlled anger. "As I said, I will convey your concerns."

★ CHAPTER 13 ★

COLONEL ERNST VARNER THOUGHT HE COULD hear Margarete's cry of delight even before his Fieseler Storch landed in the dirt road by the farmhouse. He hopped out when it slowed and the pilot taxied towards some trees where the plane would be covered with a tarp and, hopefully, be out of sight of the damned Americans. He'd endured a couple of scares on the flight from Berlin to the farm.

Margarete jumped into his arms and hugged him while Magda approached a little more sedately. Her eyes, however, were warm with a promise of better things to come and he winked at her. Magda's response was to grin and lick her lips provocatively.

As they walked to the house, Varner noted with distaste the presence of foreign workers. He felt that using prisoners and drafted foreign civilians as little more than slaves was almost as distasteful as what was going on in the concentration camps. Once more it brought home the necessity for Germany to win the war, or at least negotiate an honorable peace. If not, the world would doubtless wreak a terrible vengeance on the Third Reich, regardless of who was in charge at the end. Eric and Bertha doubtless thought having slave workers was their due as Nazis and conquerors. After all, weren't the prisoners being well fed and cared for? What more could people who weren't quite human want?

Despite the gathering dark clouds of disaster outside, dinner was jovial and the food plentiful. Ernst had been on rationed food and ate too much. So too with the drinks and he made sure that his pilot, an eighteen-year-old lieutenant who appeared both too young for his rank and to be flying a plane, was well taken care of. They would not be flying tonight, so let the boy have a good meal and a couple of glasses of wine. Normally, he would have eaten with the pilot, a pleasant young man named Hans Hart, who seemed spellbound by Margarete, but Hart was intelligent and discretely excused himself and gave Varner the privacy to be with his family.

Afterwards, Varner was told many things, including the details of the death train and the fact that his wife and daughter were working on the Rhine Defenses.

He didn't know which disturbed him more. The fact that the two women—Margarete clearly was no longer a girl—had seen such horrors as that train, or that they were in danger from Allied bombings while working. He made a note to try again to have them totally excused from their current assignments.

Later, after he and Magda had made love, they lay together in their bed. "I hope we didn't wake anybody," Ernst said and Magda giggled.

"Don't worry. Eric and Bertha are at the other end of the house and they sleep like rocks. Margarete is no longer a little girl and I am reasonably confident she knows what goes on behind closed doors."

Ernst laughed softly. "Did you see the way my pilot looked at her? My God, is this what the next few years are going to be like?"

"I just hope we have a few years in front of us," Magda said wistfully.

He sighed. "I think I liked things they way they used to be. I still can't believe that the idiot Detloff boy is nearby. I think I shall hurt his other knee for insulting my daughter."

"*Our* daughter," she corrected. "And she's quite capable of taking care of herself. She can drive cars and small trucks, and Eric has taught her how to shoot his guns. The Ami's come and we'll be ready," she said only half-jokingly.

Varner visualized a line of women and old men defending the Reich against vast numbers of American tanks and planes. It would have been funny if it hadn't been so close to reality.

"So how is the war coming?" she asked with forced casualness. He had tried to hint at the truth in his letters, using code words and phrases, but he couldn't be too specific. Even though he was an OKW staff officer, the post office had the right to open his mail and turn anything suspicious over to the Gestapo, and candor could be defined as defeatist and suspicious.

"There may actually be a glimmer of light. With Herr Hitler no longer around to guide us with his catastrophic sense of brilliance, Himmler is letting the generals fight the war properly; thus, the Russian and American advances have been slowed dramatically. Winter will soon be upon us, which means that the Soviets will stop and the Americans will at best be slowed even more. All forecasts by the group of shamans who profess to understand the weather say that the winter will be colder and snowier than normal, and that will help us considerably since it will keep American planes on the ground and turn the roads into muck for their tanks."

Magda sighed. "Which only means that the war will go on and on. What if it never ends? What if this is only the beginning of a new Hundred Years' War?"

"I can't argue with anything you said. However, I keep hearing rumors of a political and diplomatic solution. Perhaps a negotiated peace is not out of the question if the two sides become exhausted. First, however, we must resolve the Jewish question, although not necessarily in the way Hitler originally planned."

He laughed harshly. "Perhaps we will ship them all to Palestine and let the British and the Arabs fight over them. At any rate, we have to get them out of the Reich for their own good and for the future of Germany. Hitler originally wanted to ship them to Madagascar. It's a shame it didn't occur."

"Peace," she sighed, "what a wonderful thought. And what is really happening about the Jews? Please tell me there aren't trainloads of corpses rotting all over Germany."

"I'm certain that utter bureaucratic stupidity caused that and other, similar situations. Unfortunately, nobody knew quite what to do with Jews already in transit when word came down to stop shipping them. They couldn't be returned to their homes or the camps they'd come from, and no trains were supposed to deliver them to their destination camps. Somehow it's been straightened out by the SS, although I'm certain I don't want to know the details."

She decided to change the subject. "When are you leaving?"

"Tomorrow morning."

Too soon, she thought. But she knew better than to argue with him. She reached down below his belly, found her target, and stroked him. He reacted and hardened immediately. "Then we'd better make sure we don't waste any more time," she said, "and no, I don't give a stinking damn if Margarete hears us or not."

Andrey Vlasov had once been considered a rising young general in the Red Army. Then, a series of unfortunate events had resulted in his own forces being left stranded and overwhelmed by the Germans. Requests for support, and then rescue, had gone unheeded. Vlasov's force had been destroyed and he'd been captured.

Furious, and realizing the callousness and ineptitude of the Soviet high command, he'd turned traitor and had gone over to the Germans. Now the former Soviet lieutenant general led an anti-Soviet force, called the Russian Liberation Army.

Vlasov understood Berlin's reluctance to use his forces, now at nearly sixty thousand men, in key areas. Simply put, if they'd changed sides once, what would stop them from doing it again? Time would vindicate them, he told his second in command, Sergei Buny-achenko, as they traded shots of vodka.

However, the actions of the Nazis against Russian

civilians had upset him deeply. The Germans could have been welcomed as liberators, not conquerors, and · their savagery had horrified him. It was one thing to be brutal to combatants, and he didn't much give a damn what happened to the Jews, but the manner in which the SS in particular was treating Russian civilians was appalling and he was beginning to wonder if he had indeed made the right decision. Rape and massacre seemed to be the code of the SS, especially the *Totenkopf* divisions who fought with incredible savagery on the Russian front. He wondered why almost all the Reich's SS divisions were now confronting the Soviets. Why had those divisions in France and elsewhere been moved to the Eastern Front? He felt that the answer was that the SS would fight with incredible savagery against Slavic peoples they didn't think were human.

He looked across the table. Bunyachenko was nearly asleep. Vlasov was puzzled. Sergei hadn't had all that much vodka and the man had the capacity of a bear. Perhaps it was because they had just eaten a good heavy meal, were tired, and that the room was warm? Yes, that must be it. They were in Berlin awaiting a meeting with von Rundstedt. The field marshal had said he wanted Vlasov's army sent to Yugoslavia and Vlasov thought that might be a good idea. They would earn the OKW's respect by putting down the civil war going on in that godforsaken country by squashing Tito's partisan armies. He would succeed where the regular German Army had failed, thereby earning the German high command's respect and gratitude.

Vlasov yawned. Damn, he was getting sleepy too. Bunyachenko's head came down and rested gently on the table. Vlasov couldn't keep awake. Dimly, he knew that something had gone terribly wrong, but what he couldn't say. Nor could he think. Nor could he fight the sleepiness.

His last coherent thought before he lapsed into unconsciousness was the horrible realization that he'd been drugged and that he was looking at the face of Satan.

Now it was Jack's turn to go looking for a missing friend. After his narrow scrape with the Panthers, Carter had simply walked away and hadn't been seen in a couple of hours. His crew, all of whom had almost miraculously survived, saw him walking off with a bottle in his hand.

"And I don't think it was Coca-Cola, sir," said Carter's driver. All but one of the crew would return to duty immediately, or as soon as they got another tank. One man had a broken arm and would be replaced, but the rest only suffered from bumps, bruises, and minor burns. The driver's eyebrows were singed black, which made him look like he'd been made up to look like a tramp.

Jack and Levin easily picked up Carter's trail. Other GI's simply pointed them in the right direction and, soon enough, they found him sitting behind a stone fence, the bottle of cognac, now half empty, cradled in his arms.

"Want to talk?" Jack asked as they plopped down on either side of him. Jeb's eyes were red and his face was flushed.

"I think I'm through," Carter said. "How many more tanks can I lose and how many more men can I get killed or maimed? Next time it might be me. I can handle that, but what I can't deal with is people dying on my behalf or because of my stupid mistakes."

"What mistakes?" asked Levin.

"We fired too soon. If we'd waited until they were closer, we might have hurt them."

Jack shook his head. He was hardly an expert on armored warfare, but he'd picked up a goodly amount of knowledge since joining the 74th. "It didn't matter. They saw you and would have shot just as soon as they could, which, please recall, was only seconds after you opened up. If anything, your firing first might have rattled them."

"Sure," Carter snarled. "Of my four tanks, only two were destroyed and one, mine, badly damaged. Four men are dead and five others wounded badly enough to be sent back. Let's face it. I fucked up."

Levin took the bottle. "If you're finished with this, I'll take a turn." He swallowed and passed the cognac to Jack, who took a healthy snort. Hell, Jack thought, if Jeb wasn't going to finish drinking it, somebody should.

"Jeb," said Levin, "the problem is very simple. The Germans have better tanks with better guns and better armor. Someday, the powers that be will realize that and get us weapons that will match up better with the krauts. In the meantime, we do the best we can with what we have. You know as well as I do that we outnumber them in tanks by a huge margin. Ergo, we've got to get on Whiteside and Stoddard's case to keep our Shermans together in large numbers so we can overwhelm the next batch of Panthers that comes down the pike."

Carter wasn't listening. His chin was down and his eyes were closed. "Nappy time," said Levin.

"We better get him inside before he freezes to death," said Jack. It was mid-October and they'd already seen brief flecks of snow.

They took him under the arms and gently propelled him into a medic's tent. "That doesn't look like a combat wound, sir," the medic, a corporal, said stiffly.

"He just lost three tanks and nine men, Corporal," Jack responded, just a little testily.

The corporal was unfazed but a little more sympathetic. He saw the bottle and smiled. "Self medication often works quite well, Captain. Put him on that cot and we'll take care of him."

Jack handed the corporal the bottle. It was still about a quarter full. "For services rendered?"

Jessica wearily walked up the three flights of stairs to her apartment. Even though she'd worked up a little sweat, she still clutched the thin overcoat tightly. Paris in the spring and summer might be lovely, but Paris in the fall and impending winter was cold, damp, and drab.

She stopped when she saw the door was ajar. She walked slowly, wondering if burglars were inside and she should start running down the stairs, when Monique popped her head out. "Your turn," she said, tears streaming down her face. "Tell them the truth. Tell them everything you know." With that, she turned and began walking down the stairs, sobbing loudly and dramatically.

Jessica entered her apartment. Two army majors stood and introduced themselves as members of the OPMG, the Office of the Provost Marshal General. In short, they were cops. The taller introduced himself

as Major Harmon and the shorter officer with dark
curly hair was Major Pierce. The OPMG had checked
her background before letting her join the Red Cross,
which she'd thought was a ridiculous waste of time
and effort.

Jessica sat down. After all, it was her apartment. "I
assume you're here about Monique's friend."

Harmon answered. He appeared to be the leader.
"Sergeant Doyle, yes."

She smiled. "It's Boyle, major."

Annoyed, the taller officer corrected something
on his notes. "What do you know about Boyle, Miss
Granville?"

"Very little. Monique met him when we were all
stationed at Rennes. He works in supply and that's
about all I know about him. I did not socialize with
him. He is, was, Monique's friend."

"Did he ever bring around any presents?" Pierce
asked.

She shrugged. "Flowers, food, chocolates, some
wine, and some cognac are all I can remember."

Pierce persisted. "I mean anything truly expensive?"

Jessica laughed. "Look around. Do you see anything
remotely expensive?"

Harmon smiled. "Good point. By the way, is Boyle
paying for this place?"

"No, I am. I'm also quite sure you're aware that my
father is a lawyer, and that my uncle is on Ike's staff."

"Actually, he's on Beetle Smith's staff," Harmon said,
"which may be a distinction without a difference, and
yes, we do know about your family. Our asking you
these questions is just a formality. But we do have
to cover all our bases."

"Gentlemen, what concerns me is the level of interest you're showing. Boyle told Monique that he was under suspicion of stealing something, but we both thought it was relatively petty. I'm beginning to think we were mistaken."

Harmon took a deep breath. "Look, just about everyone in supply takes something and it's generally used to make their lives more comfortable, rather than trying to make a huge profit."

"Yeah," Pierce said, "for instance, you'd be shocked, simply shocked, at how many bottles of liquor destined for officers' clubs go missing, or how many sides of beef run off like they still had hooves, but, you're right, this is different. Ever hear of penicillin?"

"A little. It's supposed to be a wonder drug that kills almost all infections. It's supposed to be saving a lot of lives of wounded soldiers." Realization dawned. "Oh God."

"That's right," Harmon said. "It's extremely valuable and extremely expensive. Significant quantities of it have disappeared and Boyle's involved. And a suitcase full of it could be worth many thousands of dollars, unlike a case of whisky or a side of beef."

"Even worse," Pierce added, "every little bit missing means some wounded GI isn't the getting help he needs to recover from his wounds."

Jessica shook her head sadly. Boyle had seemed like a nice guy. "What's Monique's involvement?"

Pierce answered. "We can't prove she knew anything and, like you, she doesn't appear to have profited. In short, she's in the clear until proven otherwise. So are you for that matter, although I sincerely doubted you were ever involved."

"Thank you, I guess. And Boyle?"

"He's disappeared," said Major Harmon, standing to go. "He's joined a growing number of deserters who feel they can hide out in the chaos surrounding the war."

Pierce glared. "And God have mercy on them when we find them, because we'll hang them."

General George Catlett Marshall fumed quietly. Had the late General Leslie McNair been the problem or the solution? They'd had heated arguments over the proper use of armor on the battlefield and what type of tanks should be built. There would be no more arguments. McNair was dead, the victim of friendly fire on the beaches of Normandy just a couple of months earlier. That Leslie McNair had been a good and honorable man was without question. But had he convinced the army to make a bad decision? Hindsight always provided a hell of a view and Marshall decided to leave it at that.

Pre-war army doctrine had said that tanks did not fight other tanks. That job was left to the so-called tank destroyers, which were light and quick and designed to wait for enemy armor to attack them. Tanks supported infantry, or smashed like cavalry into the rear of an opponent's army and destroyed their supplies and communications. That, of course, was dogma before the Germans and their blitzkrieg attacks and their rapidly moving and well-armored tank columns.

With significant influence from the late General McNair, the decision had been made to go with the M4 Sherman as America's main battle tank, and let M10 tank destroyers fight the Nazi armor. It hadn't

worked out that way, and now U.S. armor was being
cut to pieces by German tanks, while the open topped
and lightly armored tank destroyers accomplished relatively little. The men were brave, but their weapons
were inadequate, and that was intolerable to Marshall.

Marshall looked across the table at Eisenhower. He
had flown into Paris from Washington that morning.
Marshall was tired and looked it.

"Bradley feels the answer is the M26, the Pershing," Ike said and Bradley nodded. "Patton agrees to
a point but says it doesn't matter since we'll never
get the Pershing in sufficient numbers to make a
difference. Therefore, Patton wants more and more
Shermans and plans to overwhelm the Nazis with
numbers and speed."

The decision to go with the Sherman had come
because it could be built relatively cheaply and transported across the ocean both economically and in great
numbers. It also was better than anything either the
Germans, or the Russians for that matter, had at the
time. Now, the Sherman was outclassed by the main
battle tanks of either Germany or Russia. The Pershing,
with its 90mm gun, would solve a lot of those problems.

Bradley continued. "Patton discounts the fact that
we are taking large casualties with the Sherman. He
says that's a cost of war and, to a point, he's right. If
the Sherman is the best we have and the best we're
going to have, then there's little else we can do except
follow Patton's plans to overwhelm the Germans."

Patton wasn't present. His massive Third Army was
to the south and Marshall would visit him in person.
By the end of this year, forty-thousand Shermans would
have been built, with the vast majority of them coming

to Europe, and France in particular. With the war in Italy at the stalemate stage, and armor unsuited to the mountains, additional tanks were being shipped from that country to France.

However, the Germans appeared to be doing the same thing. According to Ultra estimates, only about five thousand Panthers had been built to date and most had been sent east to fight the Russians. But now, if the Russians were indeed pulling out of the war for however long, the German tanks would be moving west to aid German armies as they slowly retreated towards the Rhine. The same held true for the even larger German Tiger and King Tiger tanks, which dwarfed and outgunned the best the U.S. had or would have, even if the Pershing came into action. Thankfully, there were relatively few Tigers and even fewer King Tigers. Even the Russians, first with their T34 and then with their KV and Stalin tanks, had larger and better weapons systems than the U.S.

"Ike, I take it you don't agree with Patton."

"I don't like the idea of wasting lives. We have to have something better. The Sherman is now a second tier weapon," Ike answered. "We need the Pershings. They can stand up to just about anything the Germans have, or the Russians for that matter."

Marshall shook his head. "I agree with you, but I can't flip a switch and change over from one tank to another. We're already making some Pershings, just not a large number of them. I've been told there'll be a dozen or so by the end of the year."

Ike laughed harshly. "A dozen? Good God, that's not even a drop in the bucket. We'll need hundreds, thousands, if we're to take on the Germans." Ike lit another cigarette and grinned. "Kick some butt, General. Push the manufacturers hard. Winter's coming which should slow things down for a while, but when spring comes we'll need the Pershing's ninety-millimeter gun if our boys aren't going to get slaughtered. A Panther is worth at least five Shermans. If we maintain that ratio we'll wipe out the Panthers, but also our armored divisions."

"What does Patton say about that?" Marshall asked.

"He agrees with the casualty numbers. He just doesn't think there's an alternative. Like I said, he doesn't see enough Pershings arriving soon enough to make a difference, and a dozen sure as hell isn't going to make any difference at all."

Marshall stood and looked at Bradley. "Okay. Brad, I'll make you a deal. You will get no significant increases in the numbers of Shermans, only replacements for losses. Any increases will go to Patton. In the meantime, I will do my best to accelerate production of the new tank and every one of them will go to you."

"Agreed," said Bradley.

"Any questions?" Marshall asked.

"Just one," said Ike. "What the hell are the Russians up to?"

Half a world away, Franklin Delano Roosevelt angrily snuffed out his cigarette into an ashtray emblazoned with the symbol of the White House. The ashtrays had a habit of disappearing each time he had a first-time visitor. He wondered how many were proudly displayed in somebody's library or living room, even those of the handful of annoying nonsmokers.

FDR and the others were in the map room, a place

he loved to visit and take in the war's latest events. The walls were covered with maps of all the war's theaters, and colored tabs and pins showed him at a glance the makeup and location of all the combatants. Thanks to code-breaking successes, virtually all the German units were correctly placed. It caused some concern as it appeared that the Germans were repositioning their forces.

Not quite as much was known about the Japanese since what remained of their navy could pick up and move at any time while maintaining radio silence. Nor was it difficult to hide a fleet, as the United States had learned to its dismay on December 7, 1941, when the Japanese navy, thought to be safe in the Home Islands, emerged out of the cold Pacific and attacked Pearl Harbor. The Japanese army was fairly immobile with many of her garrisons bypassed and those scheduled to be attacked unable to be reinforced. The large Japanese army in China posed no threat and was of no immediate concern.

There was some information on the Soviet side thanks to breakthroughs by the army's Signals Intelligence Headquarters at the nearby former girls school called Arlington Hall. It was a point of concern for Secretary of State Cordell Hull who felt that spying on the Soviets was a violation of the U.S. agreement with them. It was noted by this day's attendees in the Map Room that Hull, ill and soon to be replaced, was not present. Dean Acheson represented State, while OSS head Bill Donovan and Secretary of War Henry Stimson rounded out the small group.

To a man, they wished General Marshall was present, but he was still in Europe.

FDR's righteous anger flared again. "Do not for one moment even think of telling me that Joe Stalin is going to renege on his agreements. I looked in the face of that man when we met at Tehran last year and he assured me that he would be in the fight to the finish and that he would not even consider a separate peace. I believed him then and I've seen no reason to change my mind. We can trust Joe Stalin and don't forget it."

Donovan stood his ground. "Then please consider what has happened. If we take Stalin's statement that his army needs a rest at face value, then why are the Germans moving large portions of their Eastern Front armies to France? A rest and refit might last a month or two, but this has all the earmarks of a major pullback; thus, a big change in overall strategy, which has to reflect a change in the relations between Germany and Russia. It's as if the Nazis know that the commies aren't going to attack for a very long time and not just for a month or two. Otherwise there's no reason for them to strip their armies of so much strength."

"He gave me his word," Roosevelt said stubbornly.

Acheson took his turn. "Stalin is a murdering monster. He's slaughtered millions of his own people and enslaved millions more. His word is as trustworthy as that of a gangster, an Al Capone."

"Stalin is an ally," added FDR as if that said it all. "But what then are the Soviets doing?" he asked, suddenly reasonable.

The others looked at each other. The army's code-breaking efforts were providing them with some diplomatic information, but they knew very little about the Russian military.

"We have no OSS agents in the Soviet Union," Donovan admitted.

"Our embassy in Moscow might as well be on the moon," Acheson said. "Our personnel are followed everywhere and only allowed to go to certain areas, and see what the Soviets wish us to see, and talk to people with whom they wish us to speak, all of whom are spies. Russia is as much a closed society as is Japan."

"Even so, there's nothing on the Russian side to indicate perfidy, is there?" FDR said smugly.

"Nothing concrete," Acheson admitted. "But the embassy is still picking up rumors of vast troop movements headed towards the Urals and Siberia."

Roosevelt laughed hugely and slapped his large hand on the table. "And that, gentlemen, makes no fucking sense whatsoever. They do not have an enemy in Siberia, and what would they do with an army in that frosted land in the winter?"

It was Stimson's turn. "German military intelligence also indicates that the Reds are pulling out."

"Rumors, counterrumors, and rumors of rumors," FDR said, practically sneering. "Gentlemen, please, do not bother me with bogeymen and monsters under the bed."

He lit another cigarette and took a long, slow drag. It seemed to calm him down. "Gentlemen, I respect your opinions and I even permit the possibility that you might be right, however much I doubt it. In fact, I doubt it so strongly that I want no further discussions of the possibility of Russian treachery to take place with me. Continue to gather data, of course, but do not bother me without concrete facts, which I am confident you will not find."

He coughed and laid the cigarette and its long holder in the ashtray. "There is, of course, another reason for keeping the lid on these wild rumors. In just under two weeks we will have the election and I will either be President for a fourth term or tossed out on my can and Tom Dewey will be voted in for his first term. Now, this Dewey person is an excellent governor of New York and might make a fine President under other circumstances, but not right now. We need continuity in the White House. A ship does not change captains in mid-course."

He looked around and they all nodded. FDR's decision to run for a third term in 1940 had provoked enormous controversy. No President had held the office for more than two terms, following an implied guideline established by George Washington. His decision to run for a fourth term, whatever the circumstances and the rationale, had upset a large part of the nation who were beginning to think that Roosevelt was establishing a dictatorship of his own. Many voters were thinking continuity be damned—it was time for a change. Similar winds were blowing in England where it was felt that Churchill's skills as a war leader were no longer needed, and that he should be replaced by someone who knew how to rebuild the shattered British Empire.

Republican Tom Dewey was a formidable opponent, which truly concerned Roosevelt. If it should get out that the alliance between the U.S. and the Soviet Union forged only a few years earlier was falling apart, it would strongly imply that FDR was no longer in control of the international situation. While photographs still did not show him in a wheelchair, no one who saw his picture in the newspapers or in newsreels could deny that he was a frail and sickly man. An openly discussed question was whether he would even be still living four years from now. Thus, failure with Russia would indicate a need for a new hand at the helm. The others nodded. They would keep the possibility of a problem with Stalin quiet for a couple of weeks.

Unsaid was the fact that Henry Wallace would no longer be Vice President after the elections. Politically, he leaned too far left for the comfort of the men in the room. If FDR won, the new Vice President would be the senator from Missouri, Harry Truman. Nobody knew much about him except that he'd served honorably in World War I and wasn't a communist.

Roosevelt smiled his famous smile. "Wonderful. Now, let's do something constructive about this. Mr. Acheson, you will have our Moscow people find out all they can without, of course, endangering themselves or their sources. Mr. Byrnes, you will meet with Mr. Gromyko again and push him to let us know a precise date when the Russian offensive will start up, while I will send a letter to 'Uncle Joe' essentially asking the same thing."

He leaned forward, more confident now. "And you, Mr. Donovan, will try to infiltrate the Soviet Union, or at least focus more on what they are doing."

"That would take years," Donovan said ruefully. "Realistically, Mr. President, we should be working with sympathetic Germans to find out what they are observing regarding Russian moves, and develop sources who might know of secret German-Russian agreements. What I can and will do regarding the Soviets is send teams into Poland to observe."

Roosevelt thought for a moment. "Very well," he said thoughtfully and then beamed. "Martinis?"

★ CHAPTER 14 ★

THE TROUBLE WITH LANDING A PLANE IN A GRASSY field was that you were never quite sure what you were landing on. Morgan had dropped his plane quite gently into tall grass and been taxiing comfortably when the left wheel hit a rock, dipping the nose of the Piper Cub into the ground and breaking the blades of the propeller. Save for mortal wounds to their pride, he and Snyder were unhurt. The plane, however, would be hors de combat until someone scrounged up a new propeller and the mechanics determined whether or not the structure had been damaged.

As a result, Morgan was now an unofficial aide to Whiteside. Now piloting a Jeep, he kept his ears on radio traffic while his eyes took in the countryside. The American army was moving even more slowly than before as the Germans grudgingly gave up the remnants of French territory that remained in their possession. If they were fighting like devils for occupied France, he wondered how they would fight when the army crossed the border into the Rhineland, that large portion of Germany that lay to the west of the Rhine. It had been occupied by Allied armies in 1918, when Germany had been forced to give up the Rhineland as part of the Treaty of Versailles. The Nazis had taken it back in 1936.

Worse, the closer they got to Germany, the more armor and artillery the Germans seemed to possess. It made a kind of sense since German supply lines were shortening, but there were rumors of German troop pullbacks from the Russian fronts and that made no sense to Morgan or anyone else in the 74th. Of course, what the hell did they know about grand strategy in the first place?

With the presidential election only days away, there was a lot of talk about whether Roosevelt would be reelected for the fourth time. He'd been President for twelve years and many younger soldiers really couldn't recall anybody else in the White House, while older ones recalled Hoover and the other idiots who preceded him and, in their opinion, caused not only the Great Depression but this fucking war.

For his part, Jack recalled the anxiety his parents felt during the Depression and remembered the sight of people waiting in long lines for free bread. At first people they knew seemed embarrassed to be seen getting handouts, but they soon got over it. Handouts beat the hell out of starving.

Jack's family had come through the Depression poorer and possibly wiser, but not economically destroyed like so many others had. Some meals had been sparse and he'd gone a long time wearing worn out and patched clothes, but they'd never been bankrupt and never had to stand in lines for handouts.

Another halt and they piled out of their vehicles. Levin walked up. "You voted, didn't you?" he asked.

"Yeah." Helluva strange question to ask while standing alongside a column of military vehicles, Jack thought.

"Didn't it feel funny, filling out a ballot in the middle of combat? It was almost like what the Union soldiers did during the Civil War with McClellan running against Lincoln."

"And the soldiers overwhelmingly voted for Lincoln even though it meant more war," Jack said thoughtfully.

Most of the guys who'd been willing to admit their preferences said they were voting in favor of FDR. If the 74th was an example, Roosevelt would carry the soldiers' vote and the war would go on. FDR had said there would have to be unconditional surrender on the part of the Germans and the Japanese, and Dewey hadn't said much that Jack could remember on the topic.

Stick with the devil you know, dance with the girl you brought, and ride the horse you rode in on were some of the sayings and they all made a kind of sense to Jack. It was not time to change direction. Replace the President, and you had to replace the Cabinet and many other people in leadership positions, which might cause chaos in the short run, and chaos could result in people dying unnecessarily.

Whiteside's voice came over the radio. "Morgan, Levin, get up here now. This is nasty."

★　　★　　★

"Jesus," Morgan said and covered his mouth so he wouldn't puke. The bodies had been dead for several days and, despite the cooling weather, the stench was bad. A couple of them looked like they'd been chewed on by birds and animals. Levin looked like he would throw up as well.

Men, women, and children, some just infants, had all been shot. Some of the men looked like they'd been bayoneted as well and he wondered if the knife work had been performed before or after the shootings.

Jack moved down the rows of bodies and counted a little more than a hundred, and they all looked like they were French.

"They weren't Jewish," Whiteside said. He used a stick to show where some wore religious medals around their necks. Many of the women were naked, clearly signaling that they'd been raped, and some were mutilated. Maybe they'd pleaded with the Germans for their lives? Maybe they'd offered sex to protect themselves, their children, or their men? If they had, it hadn't worked.

Colonel Stoddard had gone to the other side of the field of death and he looked as grim as they all did. "You're bright, Morgan, who did it?"

"My money's on the SS, sir."

"Mine too. Okay, now why?"

Jack shuddered. "Because they're a bunch of sadistic murdering mother-fucking lunatics who did it because Hitler told them they were a master race and then gave them guns to go and prove it."

In the distance, a machine gun chattered. Nobody moved. It was just too normal and too far away. "Your dispassionate scientific analysis sounds about right," Whiteside said.

"Over here!" a GI yelled, and they trotted over to an area obscured by bushes. A dozen more bodies were lying on the ground, only this time they were GI's. They'd been bound hand and foot and been shot in the back of the head. Jack remembered the time when the sniper POW at the roadblock had been shot by the friend of a man he'd killed. But that had been an immediate act of passion and anger. This was cold-blooded. Surrender was futile was the lesson.

The firing in the distance picked up in intensity. It sounded like someone had found another German strong point. The crack of an eighty-eight followed.

Levin shook his head, despair etched on his face. "If this is what they do to Christians, what the hell are they doing to my Jews?" He looked at Jack and at Whiteside. "Tell me, should we negotiate with these fucking animals?"

Jack couldn't find an answer and Whiteside turned away.

Otto Skorzeny drove the truck slowly on the wet and slippery dirt roads. A light snow had fallen and the last thing he needed was an accident, especially with this valuable and fragile cargo. As a colonel he could have let someone else drive, but this was too important to leave to another.

As agreed, a kubelwagen preceded the truck and it flew a white flag. He wondered if the Russians could see it and would they honor it if they did. It was strange to be driving towards the enemy without any sound of battle. Normally, artillery would be crashing even if the fighting was considered light. The truce was holding, but he wondered for how long.

A mile behind him a long column of trucks followed. These were filled with unarmed German soldiers who were doubtless fearful as they entered their enemy's territory. It occurred to Skorzeny that the Soviets could win a decent prize by breaking their word and snatching up him and his cargo.

A Russian soldier emerged from the darkness. He waved a white flag and Skorzeny slowed. An American-made Jeep came into view and the soldier made the obvious signal that Skorzeny and his column were to follow.

They drove on for a couple of miles and stopped by a large field. Skorzeny grinned when he saw the neat rows of T34 tanks. A Soviet colonel appeared. He was wearing the insignia of the NKVD, which was the Russian government's instrument of enforcement, state security, and terror. In Skorzeny's opinion, they were the equivalent of Himmler's Gestapo and SS.

The stone-faced colonel identified himself as Pyotr Orlofski. He looked in the back of the truck and grunted. Sergei Bunyachenko, Vlasov's second in command, glared at him in feral fury. The others jammed in the truck either moaned or wept when they saw the Russian who grinned at them. Orlofski had metal teeth that made him look monstrous. Skorzeny thought he smelled urine. Maybe one of the prisoners had pissed himself, or maybe it was just too long a drive to hold one's bladder. He didn't care.

"Ah, if it isn't Bunyachenko, my old comrade," the Russian colonel said and spat in the man's face. He pulled his Tokarev pistol from his holster and stuck it under Bunyachenko's nose. Skorzeny thought the Russian was going to kill the traitor right then and there.

"We have so much planned for you. The rest of your life will be quite dramatic, just not very long." The Russian laughed and brought the butt of the Tokarev down on Bunyahenko's nose, crunching it. Bunyachenko groaned and blood poured down his face.

Skorzeny understood what the colonel had said, but didn't let on. He'd been improving his Russian skills but preferred to keep that fact his little secret. He did, however, agree with what Orlofski had just done. He had no sympathy for traitors.

Orlofski switched to German. "We will identify them, if you don't mind."

"They're your toys now. Do whatever you want."

The colonel thought that calling them toys was hilarious. He signaled and a squad of NKVD troops emerged. They opened the back of the truck and dragged the captives out and onto the ground. The soldiers were armed with the virtually indestructible Shpagin machine pistol that was so popular with the Red Army.

The colonel made a fuss of identifying the prisoners, comparing each prisoner with a photo, sometimes kicking them when he felt like it. Finally, he was satisfied. "Your new toys are there in the field. When you hand over Vlasov and the other traitors, the rest of the tanks will be delivered to you."

Skorzeny nodded. He knew the terms of the agreement and didn't need to be reminded. His drivers would pick up five hundred tanks today, another five hundred in a week, and a thousand more when Vlasov was delivered a week after that. They were the older model T34/76 and not the newer version with the 85mm gun. No matter, the T34's would be upgraded by German technicians and driven by skilled drivers who would make mincemeat of the American army. It galled him that the German military machine could not any longer make tanks in sufficient quantities because the Yanks and Brits were so efficient at bombing the factories that made them. Still, two thousand T34 tanks would be a nasty surprise for the Allies. He'd been told that the original request for five thousand had been whittled down.

Germany had captured a number of T34's and had turned them against the Soviets with impressive results. Unfortunately, many had been destroyed by German soldiers who only saw the Soviet-made tank and ignored the German markings. Pitting these and the remaining earlier ones against the Americans would solve that little problem.

The trucks had arrived and German soldiers, all tank drivers, spilled out. They and the Russians glared at each other with mutual and undisguised hatred. Skorzeny was glad he'd insisted on their being unarmed. They formed up and moved out to the field where the tanks were parked. A few moments later the first of them rumbled down the road and soon a long column of what had been Soviet armor rolled down the dirt road towards Germany.

The Russian shook his head. "I still don't believe it, Skorzeny. Yesterday we were killing each other and today we do business."

"And tomorrow we'll be killing each other again."

Orlofski laughed savagely. "I look forward to it."

With the Piper still grounded, Jack was assigned scouting and flank support by Whiteside. He didn't mind. Even though it was much more dangerous, it was better than being a glorified clerk in Stoddard's headquarters. At least he'd think that way until somebody took a shot at him. Levin told him he was nuts for putting himself in harm's way.

Jack and the long-suffering Snyder led a small column of vehicles that, along with Morgan's Jeep, consisted of a pair of half-tracks each carrying a squad of infantry. There was concern that the fighting would intensify once they finally reached the German border, now only a couple of miles away. They drove slowly and kept their eyes open for anything unusual. The last thing they wanted was to run into a German ambush or a mine. The area was densely forested in spots, leading some to wonder if they were driving into more bocage territory. There was a lot of forest in this area and intelligence said it extended well into Germany.

The distinctive sound of German machine-gun fire erupted to their left and from behind a line of thick shrubs. There was a pause and they could hear screams, then more shooting. Snyder radioed in their situation. Jack paused. He had a terrible premonition.

"Snyder, drive towards the shooting."

Morgan stood and grabbed the .30 caliber machine gun mounted on the Jeep, cursing that they didn't have a separate gunner. The Jeep erupted onto a field. A score of German soldiers were methodically shooting at a crowd of civilians who were trapped by fences. The Germans were laughing as they used their machine pistols to casually slaughter their helpless victims, which, like the previous massacre they'd found, included women and children. The Germans turned in shock as the Jeep roared down on them from less than a hundred yards away at more than forty miles an hour.

Jack was nearly thrown from the Jeep as it crossed the uneven ground, but he held onto the machine gun and managed to open fire, raking the nearest Germans and hurling a couple of them to the ground in bloody heaps. Other Germans turned to fire at him, while a few started to run away. Bullets slammed against the unarmored Jeep. One hit the engine and the vehicle came to a sudden halt. Jack fought for control and somehow managed to spray bullets and drop a pair of Nazis who were running towards him. The half-tracks appeared behind him, their machine guns and the infantry inside shooting down more of the enemy.

It was enough. Most of the surviving Germans threw down their weapons and raised their hands, while a handful managed to run off into the bushes. Jack jumped off the Jeep and took control of the situation. There would be no repeat of the killing of the sniper if he could do anything about it, although executing these murderers seemed like a great idea.

Some of the survivors of the massacre ran up to the Americans, hugging and kissing them, while others moaned and wailed beside their dead and wounded. Medics quickly appeared and began to treat them as best they could. An old French woman picked up a German machine pistol and was about to kill a Nazi prisoner when she was stopped.

"Tell her we'll see the fucker hanged," Jack told one of his men who spoke fairly fluent French. "But not until after a trial."

The French woman began to weep. She said the

Nazis had killed her husband and daughter. "Maybe we can let her pull the rope," Snyder suggested.

"Not a bad idea." Jack noticed the Germans' insignia was different. They were SS, but not the usual ones. "Who the hell are these guys?"

"We are Germanic-SS," a stone-faced enemy sergeant replied in decent English. "We are volunteers come from the Netherlands who've come to France to protect the Reich."

Jack was incredulous. "You mean you guys are foreigners whose land was conquered by the krauts, and you actually volunteered to join the SS and kill innocent people?"

The Nazi stiffened. "They are enemies of the Reich and are racially impure. Their deaths are of no consequence."

"Then yours won't be either, you fucking prick," Jack said.

Margarete had become an expert on airplanes. From the sound alone, she could tell what country it came from, and what model fighter or bomber it might be. She could also tell whether it was in distress or running normally, and this one was in great distress.

It was also flying very low. She jumped out of bed and put a coat over her nightgown and some boots on her bare feet. Her mother and the others had heard the sound of the laboring, lumbering bomber as well. As they ran outside, Margarete told them it was an American B17.

It roared overhead, missing the house and the barns by what seemed like only a matter of feet. They could see that one engine was blown away and another was on fire. The plane fought for altitude or a place to land safely. She wondered why the crew hadn't bailed out. Perhaps they had. Perhaps the bomber was out of control and flying dead.

But then it lifted up and she knew there were living hands at the controls. The plane staggered one last time and dropped, tail first, into the ground at the end of their field and erupted in flames.

The explosion swept over them, staggering them. They covered their faces with their arms as the heat hit them. Small amounts of debris landed all around them.

"No bombs," her uncle said. "Thank God."

The explosion, however devastating, wasn't large enough to have included bombs. Probably the bombs had already been dropped and only fuel was burning. And maybe the crew, they thought. Aunt Bertha shrieked and said there was a hand on the ground near her. Uncle Otto pulled her away, sobbing. Margarete swallowed and looked. It was indeed a hand, a left hand, and there was a wedding ring.

They ran to the wreckage, or at least as close as the flames would permit. Uncle Eric muttered a prayer. He hated the Americans but watching someone possibly burn to death was too much.

"There is nothing we can do," he said. "Anyone in there is beyond help. We must let the fire burn itself out and then we will see about burying the dead."

Margarete hugged her mother. The smell of burning fuel and scorching flesh emanated from the plane. Why hadn't the pilot jumped? Perhaps he couldn't. Maybe he'd been injured and couldn't leave his post and was trying desperately to land it in the field? She wondered if it was the pilot's hand she'd seen. It brought back too many memories of bombings in Berlin, memories she'd just about blocked out of her mind. Somewhere there must be a land where fourteen-year-old girls didn't have to live with the sight of death and the stench of decaying corpses, but these were everyday occurrences in Germany. She wondered if this was what it was like in England or France. Somehow, she knew it was even worse in Russia.

"Mama, I want this to end."

Magda hugged her fiercely. "We all do, Magpie," she said using Margarete's now forbidden childhood name. This time her daughter didn't seem to mind. She just wanted to be a little girl again.

A few hundred yards away and back at the farm buildings, Victor Mastny prepared to slip back into the barn. He'd dashed out in the night afraid that the plane would come down on top of him and trap him inside. He was concerned that the Mullers and the two Varner women would see how easy it was for him to slip in and out of the barn, which might cause them to have second thoughts about confining him more securely.

The girl was looking in his direction, but he was certain that the shadows and the flickering flames would not betray him as long as he didn't move. When the women turned, he slid back into the barn.

The 74th entered Germany south of the ancient city of Aachen, Charlemagne's capital when he founded the Holy Roman Empire more than a thousand years earlier, and north of the rugged and wooded area called the Eifel. They estimated they had forty or fifty crow-fly miles before they hit the Rhine. If any of them cared, intelligence said they were up against the German Seventh Army under General Erich Brandenberger.

American troops entering the city of Aachen were meeting stiff resistance in this first major German city to be attacked. Troops were fighting street to street and even building to building, just like what they'd heard of Stalingrad and Leningrad. Street fighting in old stone cities was a lousy situation for tanks, and the men of the 74th were universally thankful to not be involved in it.

Even though there actually was a sign saying "Welcome to Germany," it was quickly apparent that they'd entered a different country. For one thing, they noted that it was cleaner in Germany than in France. They'd concluded that French idea of sanitation was minimal at best, what with people pissing in the streets, while everything was tidy and clean in the Reich. Even the ruins had been swept, apparently by old men and women since the men were away in the army. The roads were better as well, paved instead of dirt.

To their surprise, they'd met no immediate resistance when they crossed the border. They'd half expected the sign saying they were entering Germany to be booby-trapped, but it wasn't. Nor had they seen any discernible German defenses. The Nazis had fallen back to more defensible positions rather than fighting for every inch of homeland soil like Hitler would have insisted.

The first German village they entered was only a mile from the border, and many of the neat and well-maintained houses were festooned with white flags made from sheets.

"Apparently nobody thought surrender was a likelihood," Jack said. "Otherwise the proper Germans would have had regular white flags already made up."

Sergeant Major Rolfe chuckled. Snyder and a new lieutenant were up in the repaired plane with Snyder piloting. He had quickly developed into a qualified pilot. Snyder said it was because he was so smart, while Rolfe and Jack said it was because the plane was so easy. A second plane and another pilot were being prepped. Jack had written Jessica that he now commanded his own air force.

The white flags brought home the fact that they were conquering Germany, not liberating it, and that was reflected in the troop's attitude. If they "accidentally" broke something, well, tough shit. They had freed the French and were now going to punish the Nazis, assuming of course, that any Nazis could be found. When the villagers emerged, they told them the Nazis had all gone, which the Americans found laughable, especially since a number of civilians glared at them with unbridled hate in their eyes. Blank spaces on walls showed where pictures of either the late Hitler or his successor, Himmler, had once been displayed and had been prudently taken down. A handful of young men on crutches or missing limbs, or both, watched them stonily. These were former Wehrmacht and would be watched. They had been knocked out of the war because of their wounds, but they had not surrendered. Jack wondered how he'd feel seeing enemy soldiers in his home town, and decided he wouldn't be happy at all. He didn't sympathize with the krauts, but he thought he did understand them.

Still, some of the people looked happy to see the

Americans, admitting that they were exhausted by the war and wished the killing to end. They'd supported Hitler when he'd solved Germany's economic woes, but, when questioned, solemnly said that they'd never supported his conquests and couldn't believe what was said about the Jews.

"Bullshit," Levin said. "They're all Nazi motherfuckers. The Russians are doing it right, giving them back just what they did in the Soviet Union."

It was common knowledge that the Reds were retaliating for the atrocities committed by the Nazis when they'd conquered large sections of the Soviet Union. They were taking a savage vengeance—looting, killing and raping their way west. Or at least they had been. There were more and more rumors that the Soviets had slowed, if not stopped.

Denying their Nazi affiliations didn't save the German civilians from having their houses, foodstuffs, and liquor taken by the Americans as they bivouacked for the night. Stoddard wouldn't permit any heavy looting or the abuse of women, but chickens, eggs, and other delectables managed to make it to GI dinners. It amused them to see the displaced Germans carrying bags of extra clothes on their backs as they looked for a place to spend the night. For all Jack cared, the krauts could sleep in piles of barnyard shit. They'd get their houses back, and reasonably intact, when the regiment moved on, which he felt was more than they deserved.

That night and for the first time since he'd landed in Normandy, Jack actually slept in a bed. Ironically, it was so comfortable he tossed and turned for much of the night. Still, he loved the feeling. Even better, the house he and several other officers had taken over actually had indoor plumbing, and they'd taken turns wallowing in the tub adjacent to the toilet. Carter suggested weighing one's self before bathing and then right after to see how much the dirt on their skins weighed. Carter was told to go screw himself.

Not having to use a latrine tent or relieve oneself outdoors was another almost forgotten civilized pleasure. Snow had fallen and lightly covered the ground. Soon enough they'd have to tramp through it to squat over a disgusting latrine trench, but this night was a wonderful reprieve.

Morgan was enjoying a second cup of coffee when a PFC told him Colonel Stoddard wanted to see him ASAP. He took a couple of quick swallows and trotted to the mayor's house, now Stoddard's HQ.

"Jack, one of the townspeople in this little piece of heaven whispered to me that there's a work camp just outside of here, maybe a mile away."

"Jesus, is a work camp the same as a death camp, sir?"

Stoddard nodded grimly. "That's what you're going to find out. Take an infantry platoon and a couple of Carter's tanks and see."

Once again they smelled death before they reached it. As before, even the cold air couldn't mask it. A dozen decrepit wooden barracks were surrounded by barbed wire forming a rectangle. Watchtowers were at each corner and were manned by guards who looked astonished at the sight of the approaching American column. Apparently, the guards were unaware of the American presence down the road. So much for Teutonic efficiency, thought Morgan.

German guards in one of the towers opened up

with a machine gun and were blown to pieces by a shell from the lead Sherman. German soldiers spilled out of a barracks building and what looked like a headquarters. They saw the American column and ran towards the rear of the camp where another gate was quickly opened, allowing them to run through and away.

"Shoot them," Jack yelled. Cannon and machine gun fire cut down many of them, but a few managed to escape. Good riddance, Jack thought.

A handful of prisoners were taken and they wore the skull and crossbones insignia on their caps. Jack had heard that these the special units assigned to run concentration camps and were especially cruel. He found it satisfying that most of them looked frightened. Some of their Nazi prisoners were women guards, exceedingly hard looking and ugly women, but females nonetheless.

"Come here, Captain," yelled a sergeant as he exited a barracks building. He turned and threw up against the barracks wall.

Jack entered the barracks and walked into a hell dimly lit by light coming through holes in the walls. Scores of eyes stared at him from stark benches. They were shapeless and in rags and it took him a few moments to realize they were women. An emaciated hand reached out for him and touched his uniform. Without thinking, he recoiled and the woman cringed as if expecting to be beaten.

"Who are you?" came a voice, timid and weak.

"American," he said softly.

There was silence, then gasps and sobs. "You've come?"

"Yes." He didn't know what else to say.

There must have been a hundred women jammed into the small building. Some of them stirred and got up. They lurched hesitantly to the door. Jack let them pass and go out into the fresh air. It was too cold for their rags to be much use against the weather, but being able to step outside seemed worth it to them.

Several women remained on the benches. Jack checked them. A couple of them were dead and the others might be dying. More soldiers had entered the barracks and were looking around. He found a radio man who put him in contact with Stoddard.

"How is it, son?"

"Worse than you can begin to imagine, sir. We need medics, food, blankets, and, oh yeah, if you've got a correspondent or two hanging around send them here to take some pictures."

At that point, Jack went out and looked at the liberated women who were staring at the open gate and the empty watchtowers. Some of the GI's had found blankets and given them to the women to cover their nakedness and help warm them.

Sergeant Major Rolfe emerged from the headquarters building. "All gone, Captain, but you're not going to believe this."

"Try me."

"We're the Seventy-Fourth Armored, right? Well, this is work camp number seventy-four. Quite a coincidence, huh, sir?"

"Yeah," Jack admitted. "But it does make me wonder how the hell many of these snake pits there are."

★ CHAPTER 15 ★

FDR WAS LIVID. THE PHOTOGRAPHS ON HIS DESK were damning beyond belief. One showed emaciated dead bodies stacked like cordwood, while another displayed the decomposing bodies of inmates hung on barbed wire, shot while trying to escape. Others were equally horrible. He glanced at them all, overwhelmed by the agony and inhumanity they showed.

As the camps near the French border were overrun, the depth of the accumulated horror was becoming apparent, and no one had yet gotten near the most terrible places of all, a series of camps near the city of Auschwitz.

"First, I want these pictures released to the troops and the American public. We must show them what we're fighting for and what'll happen if we lose. Above all, show these to our so-called allies, Great Britain and France. They most definitely need their spines stiffened."

Churchill had lost a vote in Parliament, which would almost certainly require a new election. Winston might be a hero to much of the British public, but he was not well loved even by his own party. The English people were exhausted by the long and bloody war and wanted it to end. They had been fighting since 1939 and had endured bombings and catastrophic battles. As long as victory was achievable, they were on board, but the increasing German resistance was demoralizing them. It reminded so many of the stalemate of World War I. All that was needed to cause England's collapse was the sight of trench lines snaking along the Rhine.

A growing number of people in England were clamoring for a negotiated peace, and the same clamoring was beginning to be heard from America's citizens. So what if a Nazi stayed in power? was the increasingly strident cry. Hitler was the monster responsible for the war, and Hitler was dead. Wouldn't his successors be more reasonable? After all, wasn't the little dictator insane? They couldn't all be crazy, could they?

Yet how could he negotiate with the authors of these atrocities? But so many wanted him to, and they included congressional members of his own party. Supreme Court Justice Felix Frankfurter and Treasury Secretary Rosenthal as well as a number of Jewish-Americans had screamed their anguish at what was happening to their fellow Jews. Frankfurter, a man who at first disbelieved the atrocities, now wondered if many of his faith remained alive in Europe. It was a good question.

FDR and Churchill had had a number of disagreements and Churchill was fighting the fact that Great Britain was now a bit player in the global conflict. Still, Churchill was a cut above whoever would replace him, in particular the colorless—and, in FDR's opinion, spineless—socialist, Clement Atlee.

Ultra intercepts said that the Nazis were slowing or stopping the shipment of Jews to death camps, but would that truly save the remaining Jews and other concentration and death camp inmates? Or did it make sense to negotiate an end to the war that included getting the Jews and others out of the clutches of the likes of Himmler? FDR rubbed his forehead. He had a miserable headache. He had won his fourth term, and, God willing, another four years in office. But at what price? Christ, his head hurt and it felt like his heart was racing to get out of his chest. He needed a rest, but had no idea when he would get one.

Heinrich Himmler mentally worked on his list of people to be eliminated once he consolidated power and a working peace had been achieved. It was a pleasant diversion. Once he'd seen a Shakespeare play in which characters dressed as Romans decided who would live and who would die. He appreciated it now that he was in a position to do something.

Von Rundstedt headed the list. The arrogant field marshal was choice number one. He and a number of others in the military hierarchy were proclaiming themselves saviors of Germany for their efforts in slowing down the Americans and knocking Russia out of the war. For all intents and purposes, England was also no longer a factor, while France was on the verge of tearing herself in two.

Ribbentrop would go as well, although Himmler thought the fool might be allowed to retire. The same held with the aging von Papen. The navy's Admiral

Doenitz seemed loyal, but the Kriegsmarine had always followed an independent line. His case would be reviewed. Admiral Canaris, head of the Abwehr and the font of all military intelligence, was also considered a candidate for purging. As yet unverifiable rumors had him supporting those who would have murdered Hitler. The Gestapo was working hard to confirm those rumors. While Himmler now firmly believed the bombing that killed the Fuhrer was a tragic coincidence, he did wonder just when the plotters would have made their move. Canaris would be carefully watched.

And what to do about Rommel? The former golden boy from North Africa was still recovering from his wounds. Rommel had served as commander of Hitler's bodyguard and had appeared to worship him. However, there were rumors that his devotion had soured as defeats mounted. Rommel was a popular war hero and would not be touched as long as he behaved himself. Himmler thought it was strange that Rundstedt hadn't actually said that he would give a command to Rommel once he was better. Perhaps their personal animosity could be put to good use.

Joseph Goebbels still served a purpose. The club-footed propaganda minister had once been very ambitious, perhaps even coveting ultimate leadership as Hitler's heir, but the Fuhrer's unexpected death had taken the wind out of his sails. Maybe he would make Goebbels an ambassador to an irrelevant country.

Himmler was greatly concerned about what was happening to his SS army. Once it had consisted of thirty-nine divisions, but now it had been mauled to less than half its strength by the Russians. It would have to be rebuilt, which should not be a difficulty. Only finding the time to do it would be a problem. He had held back two divisions from being sent to the Eastern Front and they now constituted a personal security force in Berlin.

It occurred to him that the entire regular army, the Heer, should become part of the SS instead of the arrogant and far too independent force it was now. He thought that the same should happen with the Kriegsmarine and the Luftwaffe. Yes, make them all swear allegiance to the Nazi Party and Germany, but in that order.

But first he had to win the damn war. Or at least not lose it.

The intensity and fury of the rioting caught Jessica by surprise. There had been many disturbances in the previous few days as the French communists fought the police and some of the French troops who had been brought into Paris to maintain order, but nothing like this day's fighting. Other demonstrations had been fairly restrained while this one had quickly turned savage.

Several thousand communists had suddenly emerged from the side streets and taken over the area around the Arc de Triomphe, the sacred monument whose arches rose over the First World War's tomb of France's Unknown Soldier. Their banners and shouts proclaimed their goal to make Paris a communist-run soviet, and further said that de Gaulle was a fascist dictator. So far this was nothing new, except for the size of the crowd and the quickness with which they'd shown up. Jessica concluded that they'd been waiting in nearby buildings and alleys for a signal.

Noncommunist demonstrators showed up only a few minutes later, which led Jessica to conclude that much of this had been choreographed. These held signs that said that the communists were Moscow-inspired traitors deserving of death. Within seconds, the two groups were at each other's throats. Clubs and blackjacks cracked heads and men and women fell, screaming or unconscious, or even dead, Jessica thought grimly. She realized that she was getting used to sights like these. What had happened to the sheltered college girl, she wondered.

Whistles and sirens screamed as the police made a belated entry. Again, more brawling and more people were lying injured on the pavement. A horrified Jessica saw knives flashing and tearing at flesh. A young man ran past where she'd taken shelter in a store doorway. The skin of his cheek hung down like a piece of bloody meat. He howled in pain as the flesh of his cheek flapped.

Jessica had merely thought to take some time off and see the Arc and the tomb. She'd seen them before, but their quiet dignity always gave her a sense of purpose. But now her goal was to stay out of the fighting. Regular army troops began arriving by truck and forming into battle lines. They had rifles and bayonets. The communist rioters were badly outnumbered and outgunned. It would all end in a few minutes.

The communists fired first. They had pistols or small submachine guns hidden in their coats and they shot into the advancing soldiers and police or the de Gaulle supporters. More scores of people fell to the ground, lifeless or writhing. Blood poured from hundreds of wounds.

Jessica had thrown herself on her belly and was watching the slaughter. It was ghoulishly fascinating, horrifying. She couldn't turn away. The soldiers, enraged, opened fire and dropped a large number of the communists into bloody heaps. The communists broke and ran in a score of different directions while the police and soldiers chased them. A young French army private ran up to her and pointed his rifle at her. His face was contorted with anger. Some of his friends had just been killed or wounded and he wanted revenge. He saw her Red Cross uniform and nodded grimly, then he laughed and trotted away.

What was so funny, she thought? Then she realized that her skirt was up at her waist and she'd just given the soldier a look at her long legs and her panties. She got up, dusted herself off and looked around. Ambulances were already carting away the injured, while trucks took away the dead, and there were many of both, perhaps hundreds.

Women had come out from the alleys and were screaming at the soldiers, calling them murderers. It didn't matter that the rioters had opened fire first, the soldiers were the killers. Jessica realized that the whole massacre had indeed been staged. It didn't matter who'd fired first or who was right or wrong. The dead and injured communists had just become martyrs. France, she decided, was going to hell.

She also decided she would begin wearing slacks.

The sight of long columns of refugees coming east from the Rhineland delighted Victor Mastny and his two fellow slaves. It was good to see the supermen and women from Germany looking so bedraggled and forlorn. Even better, their presence was an opportunity for Victor to advance himself financially and have some measure of revenge on the people who'd caused him so much misery.

The two Latvians were a little slow to agree with him, but he bullied and threatened them into following his orders. He didn't think they'd protested overlong. The idea of striking back at their tormentors was just too pleasant.

The first couple of raids had been quite simple. Rush in during the middle of the night, take something they'd spotted as valuable, and rush out under the cover of darkness before either resistance or a chase could get organized. They'd gotten some loot, but nothing of real value. Mastny didn't care that little money, jewelry, or watches had made it into their pockets. As far as he was concerned, these were practice runs. He was convinced that something major would turn up and he wanted to be ready.

Mastny had the feeling that many of the refugees were so confused and bewildered by the turn of events that had destroyed their nice little German lives, that they were psychologically incapable of defending themselves. Also, most of the refugees were women, children, and older men. The army had taken all the young men and even many of the older ones. The long and bedraggled columns of pathetic people were indeed quite helpless.

It was the middle of the night and the three slave laborers were a couple of miles from the Mullers' farm, and there were several score refugees sleeping alongside the road. Many were huddled together for warmth as the nights got progressively colder. Mastny wondered just where they intended to go and how they would be housed once they got to their destinations. He concluded that he didn't care. Some of them, he noted, had moved a ways off the road. Perhaps losing your home, your status, and your possessions makes you antisocial, he thought.

One particular little group of neat little Germans had moved well into a stand of trees and had set up blankets for privacy. An older woman had actually dug a trench for a latrine, and a small fire burned. Victor didn't think burning a fire in a forest was a bright idea and concluded that these Germans must be city dwellers. The group consisted of two older men along with three women. One of the women was also old, but there was a younger one in her mid-twenties and a girl about twelve. Now Mastny thought he would really take revenge as well as initiating his companions into his world.

They reached the sleeping refugees at three in the morning. There would be plenty of time for them to do what they wanted and return to the barn before dawn. The ground was hard and no snow had fallen, which meant they would leave no tracks. It would be difficult, if not impossible, for others to follow them. The three men carried clubs and homemade knives made from scrap metal. They hadn't yet gotten their hands on any guns. They wore caps and their faces were blackened with soot.

The Germans slept soundly. At least two of them were snoring. Mastny gave the signal and they rushed in, clubs flailing. The two men and the older woman were hit and clubbed unconscious before they could even move. Victor jumped on the young woman and held a cloth to her mouth and a knife to her throat while the others grabbed the girl. The two were bound and gagged before they were even fully awake. So too were the three others, although Mastny wasn't certain they were still alive.

"Don't make a noise and you won't get hurt," he hissed at both of the women. "The others are only stunned. Cooperate and they'll be all right. Don't and we'll slice their throats and then yours. Understand?" The woman and the girl nodded, their eyes wide and frantic with terror.

It was cold and the idea of sex in that kind of weather would normally have been off-putting, but it had been so long and the idea of fucking the helpless Germans was just too exquisite. They stripped the two women and enjoyed the sight of their pale bodies shaking from both cold and fright. Both of them were stout, like good German frauleins, and they writhed in terror as Victor touched them. Victor took the youngest one first, while the Latvians took the older. Then they traded places. The Latvians had been brutal with the woman. She was bleeding heavily and unconscious. Victor laughed and rolled her over on her belly. Victor had just finished taking the woman anally while the Latvians did what they wanted to the girl when a sudden scream pierced the air.

"Help! Murderers!"

The old woman had not only regained consciousness, but had slipped out of her bonds while the three men had been violating her daughters. She ran towards the road, screaming and howling.

Sounds came from other refugees and the column was stirring itself. To further complicate matters, the young girl now managed to get up and get away from the astonished Latvians with her screams adding to the din.

Shit, Victor thought. "Get their bags." He had a thought and groped through the women's clothing. He laughed as he found a bulge sewn into a coat. He grabbed it and other coats and ran off with the Latvians.

They did not go directly to the Mullers' barn. Instead, they zigzagged. As far as they could see, the refugee column was awake, but no one was looking for them. When they were a mile or so away, they opened the luggage. There was money, lots of money, and not only Deutschmarks, but British pounds and even a few hundred dollars in American money. It seemed the family was hoarders and speculators who couldn't possibly complain to anyone about losing their illegal stash. Even better, there were several items of jewelry that Victor thought were gold. More money was found in the lining of the young woman's jacket, but these were all Deutschemarks which would be valueless if the Nazis lost.

They threw away the luggage and the clothing and headed to the barn where they would bury their valuables. They weren't rich, but it was a start, especially since Victor had no intention of sharing it with the stupid Latvian twins.

Colonel Whiteside grimaced as he looked at the score of officers and senior noncoms in front of him. They had a rough idea what he was going to say and weren't terribly happy. They'd heard plenty of rumors and, if they were correct, the world according to Eisenhower had gone nuts.

"Gentlemen," Whiteside began, "the word has come

down from Eisenhower that we are to treat the Germans as a conquered nation, and not a liberated people like the French. We are not to go easy on them and we are most certainly not to fraternize with them. You will doubtless hear protests from civilians that they weren't Nazis, or they quit when they found out what the Nazi swine were doing, or they were afraid not to be Nazis because of repercussions, but it is all bullshit. You are to disregard all protests as the lies they are and consider all Germans as the enemy."

There was shifting as the men didn't quite look at each other. "That means," Whiteside continued, "that you may not do any business of any kind with a kraut. You may not buy anything with our money because it's illegal for Germans to have American money, and you most certainly may not sell anything for kraut money with Hitler's picture on it."

Levin raised his hand. "How do we buy local stuff like food if we can't pay for it, or is looting now sanctioned by Ike?"

Whiteside glared at him. "Someday, Levin, I am going to kill you. If you have to requisition something, you give the ex-Nazis a receipt."

"Does that go for sex?" Carter asked impishly. "A lot of these hungry little ex-Nazi fraus and frauleins will happily fuck for food. Is that okay?"

Whiteside was normally a calm man, but his face was turning red. "The word for the policy is a long one, Carter, it's nonfraternization. It means that not only may you not buy or sell anything, you also may not have any sexual contact with the conquered Germans, or any other social contact with them, and that includes being invited to dinner by a bunch of ancient nuns. Now, I know that a lot of kraut women will go down for food, but it is against Ike's policy of nonfraternization and there will be punishments if someone is caught."

Twenty heads nodded. The word "if" was the key. As with anything else, if you don't get caught you can't get punished. Enforcing this was going to be fun, Morgan thought.

"Any idea how long this policy is going to be in effect, and what will happen to anyone who violates it?" Jack asked.

Whiteside managed a smile. "Got anybody in mind?"

Morgan laughed along with everyone else. "Probably half the regiment. Sir, it's common knowledge that we're going to halt for the winter on this side of the Rhine and that there'll be a lot of guys with a lot of time on their hands and a lot of women who'd do just about anything for a good meal, even if that includes C-rations. So what's going to happen to the poor klutz who gets caught?"

"First off," Whiteside answered, "we have to get to the Rhine before we can discuss a halt for the winter. As to the rest of it, I think we all recognize that we can't totally stop three thousand horny guys from taking advantage of many thousands of willing, hungry, and maybe equally horny German women. Use your discretion when something happens. Threaten to drop them in rank, give them extra duty, and, if that doesn't work, say you're going to write their wives and mothers if you have to. If all else fails, tell them if they catch the clap, they won't get penicillin and they'll have to suffer until their dicks fall off."

Jeb grabbed his crotch and moaned. "It hurts, it hurts."

Whiteside shook his head. "I have no idea why anybody thinks we are winning this war. Dismissed."

"Cigarettes will become money," Levin said as they walked back to their tents. "Each GI gets two packs a day. Just cut down on smoking, which is probably good for you, and you can use the money to buy happiness."

"Buy it?" Jack said.

"I believe he's talking about a short-term rent, not even a lease." Carter grinned. "I hear the going rate is two cigarettes for a suck and four for a genuine fuck. At twenty fags a pack, you do the math. Give up the smoking for fucking and you'll not only live longer but you'll be a lot happier."

"What's the German word for fuck?" Carter asked.

"Hitler," Levin answered. "And the German words for sucking cock is Himmler. So you tell a kraut broad you want a Himmler and she'll understand and start working your fly."

Jack chuckled and shook his head. "How the hell can we make fun of this and laugh when a war is going on?"

"Do we have a choice?" Levin responded. "If we don't laugh we'll all go nuts. Don't you recall something about the gods first making mad those they will destroy?"

Carter shook his head. "Levin, you are a cheerful fuck."

"I just wonder what I can get for only one cigarette?" Jack wondered. "Probably just a titty-grab."

Schurmer turned and waved proudly. "Ernst, my friend, we are now fifty or so feet underground in what will likely be Kesselring's Army Group B headquarters in the Rhine Wall. Unless, of course, the command lines change, in which case Monteuffel will be the first tenant."

Varner grinned. "And not Model himself?"

"No, no, we would be far too close to the front for that senior a commander."

It was indeed impressive. Thick reinforced concrete walls, floors, and ceilings surrounded them, while bare light bulbs provided stark illumination. Numerous phone lines and radios were set up, while wires carrying electricity were attached to the walls. It was a grim and utterly functional dungeon as well as a thoroughly modern communications hub capable of supporting the efforts of a very large army. Varner felt it was also extremely claustrophobic. The walls were drab and water stained from leakage, and there was the pervading smell of moisture. Even though there were food storage areas, kitchens, and lavatories, how long could large numbers of men exist like troglodytes before they went mad?

They had to laugh, however, over a bit of Teutonic thoroughness. Restrooms had been provided for both men and women. "Just what women would ever grace this pleasure palace?" Schurmer asked.

Varner shuddered. "The hell with toilets. Other than the main entrance, how many exits are there?"

"Two main ones that branch out into three exits each. They start shortly after leaving this area. I know what you're thinking and it's extremely unlikely that all six widely separated exit points could be blocked by artillery or bombs. We could also exit via ladders up the ventilation shafts if necessary, and not all of those are directly above the command bunker."

"Wonderful," Varner said. "Given a choice I'd still rather be in a tank. At least they can move away from danger rather than waiting out a bombardment. I had enough of that in Berlin when the bombs were falling."

They stepped into an elevator that took them to the surface and welcome winter sunshine. They breathed deeply of the fresh air. "There are a number of senior command bunkers like this and countless other bunkers for lesser commanders and literally thousands for the rank and file who will comprise the Rhine Wall's garrison. The Yanks and the Brits are in for an unpleasant surprise."

"My dear friend," said Varner, "I don't think what you're doing will be much of a surprise. Their planes have been overhead every day and they must have countless photographs of the construction of these structures in every stage of development. Seriously, I am most pleasantly surprised and gratified that they haven't been able to disrupt your works and stop them while in development."

"Oh they've tried, Ernst, they have indeed tried. We lost many good men along with a large number of foreign prisoners, mainly French and Poles, as the Ami bombers got better at their job. Still, they were only able to delay us a little."

"Are you impregnable?"

Schurmer snorted. "You know there's no such thing."

Varner laughed. "I just wanted to hear you admit it. Actually, I'm going to tell Himmler that the Rhine Wall is so strong that not even the combined forces of God and man could take it. And, should the Wall be breached, it's all the fault of one Colonel Hans Schurmer."

"It's good to have friends like you," Schurmer said, happily returning the sarcasm. "Now you can play devil's advocate. Tell me how you would breach the wall. I've been so wrapped up in building the damned thing I haven't been able to look at it objectively."

Varner thought for a moment. "Giant blockbuster bombs like the RAF uses would cause considerable damage if they hit on or close enough to surface bunkers, but I doubt they'd do more than shake the dust in the command bunker you just showed me."

Schurmer nodded. Blockbusters could weigh from four thousand pounds to more than eleven tons and, like the name indicated, could destroy an entire city block. However, their destructive strength had been factored into his calculations. There was only so much destructive capacity that a bomber could carry.

American artillery would be used to clear out the smaller bunkers and would ultimately cause great damage once the Americans figured out which works were real and which were dummies. Still, well-embedded and strongly constructed defenses would stand a great number of American shells.

"I would be concerned with fire," Varner added softly. "Flamethrowers shooting down the vents would incinerate or suffocate the inhabitants by drawing out the oxygen."

Schurmer sniffed. "That presumes the Amis would be on top of us, like we were when we took Eben Emael."

In the early days of the war, German gliders had landed fewer than a hundred men on the top of the massive Belgian fortress of Eben Emael. They had hurled explosives into the vents and forced the almost immediate surrender of a fort that was supposed to halt the German advance for weeks.

Schurmer dropped his voice to a whisper. "And what about the bomb Heisenberg is working on?"

"Are there no secrets in the Wehrmacht?"

Schurmer laughed. "All right, rumored to be working on."

"Since the bomb has not yet been built, much less dropped, I have no real idea what the impact will be, no pun intended. Nor does Heisenberg. However, if it is anywhere near as powerful as what the little physicist thinks, then I believe anyone in your command bunker will be in a terrible mess if the Yanks should have one of their own."

"And we will have the bomb before the Yanks make one?"

"Hans, who the devil knows what the Yanks will have."

Sporadic rifle and machine gun fire came from the German village. German guns had found a home in the rubble and it would be a tough nut to crack. The 74th's artillery and armor pounded away, making dust out of the ruins.

Morgan's air force was on the ground getting refueled from their limited supply. Word had it that V Corps was running out of gas and that future flights would be curtailed. It was frustrating. Carter had complained that the U.S. produced more oil than anyone in the world, so why couldn't they get it to the front lines? Of course, he knew his argument was irrelevant. Cherbourg and the other Channel ports were finally working, but the massive and growing American and

British armies sucked up immense quantities of supplies that all had to be sent to France by ship. It had become irrelevant where the tankers made port. The fuel had to be off-loaded onto trains and trucks and then driven to the front lines.

"White flags!"

Several white flags could be seen in the ruins. "Cease fire," Stoddard radioed his units, and the shooting slowly stopped. Not everyone heard the order and some didn't want to quit when there were Germans to kill. Finally, however, a strange calm prevailed.

A man emerged carrying a sheet attached to a pole. He moved forward cautiously, fully aware that hundreds of weapons were trained on him.

"I'll handle it," said Levin. He walked forward a few paces and waited for the German, who was clearly and professionally surveying the American men and weapons arrayed against him. Well, let him look, Levin thought. Hell, he probably already knew all about them.

The German was tall, lean and late middle-aged, and carried himself with a dignity that said he'd been in the army before. He needed a shave, wore dirty and ragged civilian clothes, and an armband said he was an officer. Volkssturm had their own ranks and Levin was unsure exactly what the man was. Regardless, he wasn't going to salute.

"Are you surrendering?" Levin asked in German.

"Yes. I am Major Otto Kuehn and I now command this Volkssturm regiment," the German responded in English.

Regiment? Holy shit, thought Levin. How many men were in that damned village? "Tell your men to

lay down their arms and march out with their hands
on their heads. I'm sure you know the routine."

Kuehn smiled tightly. "I remember issuing the
same orders to British Tommies in the early days of
the last war."

The German wheeled and returned to the village.
A short while later, the ruins began to disgorge large
numbers of his fellow Volkssturm. They obeyed orders
and were unarmed, some were even laughing. Their
hands were clasped neatly on their heads. Many were
wounded, but even they managed to smile at the
Americans. Their war was over and they appeared
damned glad to be out of it.

"Surrender becomes you," Levin said. "Your men
seem pleased."

Kuehn shrugged. "Better you than the Russians and
better surrendering than fighting to the death for no
reason whatsoever. It was the only sensible thing to
do. Other than old rifles and Panzerfausts, we had
nothing to fight you with. The swine who command
us also forgot food and water and medical facilities.
We are here as cannon fodder to try to delay you
and I will not have my men slaughtered. It may make
sense militarily, but the war is over and our deaths
would only delay the inevitable."

"Good to hear," said Morgan, who had reached
the two men.

The long column of German prisoners had begun to
wind its way to the rear. At least none of these would
be murdered. There were just too damn many of them.
There really is safety in numbers, Jack thought. The
farther they walked through the American lines, the
more relaxed the Germans became, smiling, nodding

and even trying out their English on their captors. Whiteside gave orders to collect their weapons, especially the panzerfausts. He thought they might just come in handy.

"Do other Volkssturm units feel as you do?" Jack asked the German major.

Kuehn happily lit a cigarette offered by Levin. "I would say so, although it might depend on each one's unique situation. Most of the soldiers you are facing here on the west of the Rhine are either miserably armed Volkssturm like us or fanatic SS assholes. The regular army has pretty well departed across the river to man the Rhine Wall."

Jack nodded. The Germans were gone? This information will go upwards real fast, he thought. "Were you a Nazi?"

Kuehn smiled. "Of course, and I still am. Did you expect me to be a lying hypocrite like so many of my countrymen have become? After the disaster of the First World War and the Weimar Republic, I thought Hitler was great man who would bring Germany back to life and her rightful place in the world. I never thought he would bring us so much death and so many murders. Had he stopped with Austria and Czechoslovakia, or even Norway and Poland, Germany and the world would be a better place."

"And what about the Jews?" Levin asked quietly.

"I truly thought they'd be deported, not murdered."

Was this an honest man, Morgan thought, or just another lying kraut trying to rationalize what he'd done? And did it matter? He'd just surrendered a regiment and saved a number of American lives by doing so. "And what did you do in civilian life?"

"For whatever it's worth, I was a baker. My shop was destroyed by bombers. My family was in it at the time. My wife and two children were killed. There's been enough killing, Captain, enough. I've had enough war. I surrender."

Stoddard heard the last part and asked Levin if Kuehn thought other Volkssturm units were as disgusted as his, and whether he could get them to surrender as well.

Kuehn blinked in surprise. "I suppose I could. My God, it would save lives, wouldn't it? Yes, tell your superiors I will do my best."

★ CHAPTER 16 ★

ALFIE SWANN THOUGHT IT WOULD BE HARD enough for one man to survive a German winter, especially if that one man wore a British uniform and didn't speak German. His only hope had been to find a place where he would be out of the wind and cold and then steal food from wherever he could. As plans went, it truly stank, but he couldn't think of another one.

But then he met the two Jews and his troubles had more than tripled. There was no way in hell he could simply turn them loose to be picked up by the Gestapo and sent to a death camp. After talking with the two men, he now firmly believed in the Reich's horrors. No, the two Jews were now his responsibility, and he would do his best for them.

The trick, he decided, was to look inconspicuous. Thus, he had to steal clothes to replace both their rags and his uniform. Then he had to acquire enough food so they didn't look like death warmed over. All right, he thought, it could all be done, but where would they stay and not freeze to death in the coming months? There was no reason to think that the Americans or his own savaged British army would be coming by to save them anytime soon. Nor was there any real likelihood of their getting to the west bank of the Rhine under the guns of both sides. Ergo, they would plan for the long haul. Bloody hell, he'd never had to plan anything before. He was in the army and the army did all the thinking and planning he'd ever needed. What was the saying? Yeah, if the army wanted you to think they would have issued you brains.

"A cave would be nice," Aaron said. "With enough insulation from trees, grass, and even rags, we can keep the place reasonably snug. With only a little luck, we'd survive."

"Are there caves in Germany?" Alfie asked.

Saul laughed. "The land here is hilly and sometimes rocky. I rather think we could find a niche in some escarpment and keep ourselves alive."

Alfie shook his head. What the hell was a niche and what the bloody hell was an escarpment, and who the hell said these two guys couldn't speak English very well? But maybe they could find something livable in a land that was surprisingly heavily forested.

"Can you find us something like that?"

Saul answered. "We used to explore caves for amusement and sometimes we actually found ones that nobody knew existed. It was great adventure. I know we don't look like much, Alfie, but we always liked to go camping and what some people called roughing it. We may even know more than you do about survival in the wilderness."

Indeed, Alfie thought. "Then let's go find ourselves

a fucking cave. Jesus Christ, does this make me a caveman?"

Eisenhower riffled through the stack of glossy photographs. He was impressed by their detail and clarity. They all pointed out that what they'd suspected was the dismal truth. The German army was indeed evacuating the Rhineland and moving into the massive fortifications they'd built in depth on the east bank of the Rhine. Lieutenant General James Doolittle, commanding the Eighth Air Force, was present as was Lieutenant General Omar Bradley. The Royal Air Force's bomber command was not represented, nor were the Allies' navies.

Any crossing of the Rhine would be made by Bradley's massive 12th Army Group and by either Hodges' First Army or Patton's Third Army. The demoralized British to the north would have the very wide Rhine delta to cross, while Devers' 6th Army was too small and, being south, was in rugged terrain that more resembled the Swiss Alps than anything German.

Ike turned to Doolittle and pointed to the pictures of the forts. "These things have to be destroyed. These fortifications are a hundred times more formidable then what we faced at Normandy."

Doolittle was clearly uncomfortable. "Sir, you know that both America's and England's bomber command's priorities are Germany's factories and war-making potential. It's the opinion of both commands that every bomber taken from attacking those targets will prolong the war. If we can stop their ability to produce weapons and fuel, the German military machine will grind to a halt."

"Indeed," Ike said dryly, "but it will grind to a halt with us on one side of the Rhine and the Germans safely on the other. Jimmy, the only way to do it is the old fashioned one—we have to dig them out because, no matter what, we will still have to cross that damned river in order to end this war. Unless your bombers pay greater attention to these defenses, our casualties will be horrendous."

"Ike, we've been bombing them off and on since we crossed the Seine. And before that we bombed the Seine works. We have a lot of planes and crews, but not enough to do both things."

"Then why is bomber command implying that they don't need as many pilots as they are getting and that they are running out of viable targets? If my bluntness offends anyone, so be it," said Ike, "but I don't think strategic bombing has been all that effective. The Germans have successfully repaired much of what has been bombed, and they've dispersed their factories to hidden and underground locations. They have been able to fix their railroads overnight. While we've certainly made life inconvenient for them, they are continuing to produce weapons, including their damned tanks and that jet fighter. In my opinion, continued massive bombing of factories and rail facilities would be redundant."

Ike lit another cigarette and puffed angrily. "We need to confuse Rundstedt and Himmler as to where we will finally cross. We need confusion like we did with Normandy. Everybody in the German high command was uncertain as to whether the real attack would come at Pas de Calais or Normandy. We need them confused as to whether Patton's or Hodges' boys will be in those landing craft, and that means two major areas east of the Rhine have to be isolated and bombed to hell and back."

Doolittle smiled wanly. "You don't want much, do you?"

Ike flashed his famous grin. Doolittle was one of his favorites and a past member of his staff. Ike was angry, but not with his old friend. "And I want it yesterday. Look, everybody's convinced that we're going into winter quarters and they are largely correct. When we clean out the west bank of the Rhine there really won't be much of anything for our forces to do until the spring and we do fight our way across."

"Forgive me for being an idiot, Ike," said Doolittle, "but why not cross in the winter?"

Bradley answered. "Because planes can't fly and bomb accurately in bad weather, because it's too cold and muddy for our vehicles to operate effectively, and because the Rhine will be so cold that our men won't be able to wade in like they did at Normandy. Even worse, any poor soldier spilled into the river will likely freeze to death before he makes shore or is rescued. At least the waters off Normandy and the Seine were reasonably warm. We can and will try to send isolated swimmers across, probably Navy Amphibious Scouts, for reconnaissance purposes, again like Normandy, but not in any numbers large enough to affect anything."

"In a very large way," added Ike, "this will be like D-Day all over again. We will rest and refit, and we will train, and train. Hopefully, we will get enough landing craft, the LCVI which carry a platoon and can be brought to the river by train, or even the DUKW that can carry a squad, or maybe something else. Our reconnaissance shows that the Germans are stripping the west bank of the Rhine of anything that floats, which will stop us from using local boats for the crossing."

"Nor can we bring ships up the Rhine," Bradley added, stating the obvious and enjoying Doolittle's discomfort. "First, any ships would be within point blank range of German guns, and, second, the Nazis will doubtless destroy all the Rhine bridges, which means that the resultant rubble will halt any river traffic."

Doolittle shook his head. "Jesus, anybody here got any good news?"

Ike smiled. "We do have a few surprises up our sleeves. The Germans are good, but we're pretty good, too, and we're getting better. Regardless, Jimmy, I need those bombers and I need them over targets soon and for a very long time."

"And if the air force balks?"

"If they balk, then tell them that Germany wins the war."

The forests of Germany to the west of the Rhine came as a shock to the men of the 74th. They were dense, the trees were tall, and the roads primitive to nonexistent. The American forces to the north of them were having an even tougher time navigating woodlands that reminded them more of the forests of Pennsylvania or northern Michigan than what they thought Germany would be.

The Germans were retreating as usual—slowly, tenaciously, and fighting hard to inflict as many casualties as they could on the advancing Americans. One of their new favorite tactics was to fire artillery timed to explode in the tree covering thus showering the exposed troops below with splinters that ripped into soft flesh. The men in the tanks were fairly safe, but those on foot or in Jeeps or trucks or those roofless tank destroyers or half-tracks were vulnerable.

Morgan's Jeep was covered by a couple of pieces of sheet metal patched together from wrecked trucks. It wasn't armor, but he hoped the metal would deflect the lion's share of the deadly debris that rained from the sky. So far he'd been lucky. Nothing major had tested their improvised defenses, although some shells exploding nearby had sent twigs clattering onto their roof. Many of the drivers of other exposed vehicles had make similar armor out of anything they thought might protect them, including wood. Still, casualties had been severe and bloody.

As usual, the 74th was crawling, slipping and sliding over the muddy and narrow roads, while a light snowfall made their lives even more miserable. Jake was on the ground while two other pilots took the planes on their excursions. Their reports were dismal. The forest hid much of what the Germans were up to. Enemy machine gun nests were well hidden and well sited, and their artillery was invisible. German big guns would fire a few rounds and then move. American mortars were ineffective because no one could see the fall of shot. It was galling to know that very small numbers of Nazis could cause such disproportionate casualties and halt the advance of a much larger and more powerful American force.

German machine gun fire ripped insanely a few hundred yards ahead of him. Morgan was too tired and too cold to wince. He almost agreed with the philosophy that if a bullet had your name on it, there wasn't much you could do about it.

Fortunately, the Germans were only fighting a series of delaying actions as they moved men and equipment east and over the Rhine, and not making a major stand. More and more Volkssturm outfits were surrendering, including several that seemed to have somehow "lost" their officers. The consensus was that the enlisted men had killed them because the officers wanted to continue suicidal resistance. The only units that were now really fighting were the SS. Jack assumed that was who they were now up against.

"Morgan, can your pilots pinpoint the krauts?"

It was Whiteside and he looked angry and frustrated. "In a general sense, sir," said Morgan.

"Could you give a fighter pilot a rough perimeter using smoke?"

Morgan said they could and Whiteside told him to have his pilots drop smoke and flares around the German strongpoint that was holding them up. Troops on the ground would do the same thing to identify their own lines. Whiteside informed them that the fighter bombers had a new weapon they wanted to test.

"And that means we pull out when the perimeter is outlined," Whiteside said. "No insult to your past calling, Captain, but I don't trust anybody else's aim."

"Sounds like a prudent idea to me, sir."

Half an hour later, an area several hundred yards in diameter had been outlined by a circle of smoke and, hopefully, was visible from the sky. Just as important, the 74th had pulled back nearly a mile. Jack was wondering just what the hell was going to happen when a pair of P47's flew over, turned, and began another run. This time, what looked like bombs dropped from them.

Jack was thinking that dropping bombs in a forest wouldn't accomplish much, when the bombs hit and erupted in billowing clouds of fire.

Two more planes came and dropped their deadly cargo, then two more. Within seconds the area in which the Germans were supposed to be entrenched was engulfed in greasy clouds of roiling fire. He couldn't see the base of the flames because of the trees blocking his view. He could tell, however, that the area in front was being consumed by raging flames.

"Smokey the Bear's gonna be angry," laughed Snyder. A bear in a hat and jeans was the hallmark of a new homefront plan to prevent forest fires back home because lumber was needed for the war effort.

They got the signal to move forward. Jack hoped the bombs hadn't started a real forest fire. "Be a helluva note," he muttered, "to be cremated by a forest fire started by our own planes."

The fire was not spreading. There was little wind and the wet snow was stopping it from expanding. As they approached the burn zone, they again smelled the stench of cooked human flesh. Coverings over enemy bunkers had been burned away and the machine gun crews inside turned into charred ruins.

Not all the Germans had died that way. They found a number of bodies sprawled on the ground. "Looks like they tried to run away," Jack said, and others nodded. "Tough shit," said one of the men near him.

The dead Germans were SS and that made Morgan and the others feel good. Popular wisdom said if it wasn't for the lunatics in the SS, maybe the war would be over. Jack didn't think it was that simple, but the SS were easy to hate for a variety of reasons, such as slaughtering American prisoners, civilians, and running concentration camps.

As they moved through, somebody counted bodies and came up with twenty-four dead Germans. "We were held up by less than a God damn platoon," Whiteside snarled.

"Were those fire bombs the something new you said the air force wanted to try, sir?" asked Jack. "If it is, I like the way it cleared a path for us."

Whiteside actually smiled. "It's called napalm, and the top brass have big hopes it'll clear a lot of paths for us before this war's done."

Tyree Wall was thirty years old, a sergeant in the United States Army and a Negro with skin as black as the night. He loved the army. It had given him food, clothing, and a sense of dignity, all of which were lacking from his childhood as the son of hardscrabble tenant farmers rooting in the red earth outside of Columbus, Georgia. He liked to joke that they were so poor they didn't even notice the Depression. How can you lose something when you never had anything in the first place?

When the war started he had enlisted and excelled. A big man at five-ten and two hundred pounds, he found he had leadership abilities he never thought existed. Almost of necessity, he'd improved his reading skills and gone from scarcely literate to the point where he actually read books both for pleasure and knowledge. He'd just finished *Gone With the Wind* by Margaret Mitchell, and thought the depiction of the

South around Atlanta was a hoot. Should've burned down all the damned white people's mansions since they'd been built on slave labor, he thought. In many cases the Union Army had tried real hard, but they'd missed quite a few.

He was giving serious thought to staying in the army if the army would have him once the war was over. He wondered about that. It was clear that whites in the army resented Negroes and kept them out of combat positions as much as possible. In a way this was fine with Tyree. If the idiot whiteys wanted to keep the honor of getting shot at and killed all to themselves, well let them. In the meantime, he'd learned to drive a truck and to lead men.

The army had also given him an M1 carbine, which lay on the passenger seat of the truck he was driving across France en route to the front lines. He doubted that the white men who ruled rural Georgia would approve of him having it. Back home, only white people had the guns. That was one way they kept the blacks in their place.

Tyree commanded a squad of other drivers, also black, whose trucks were strung out behind him. They were part of a long convoy of more than a hundred trucks and tankers, all part of the Red Ball Express. The vehicles carried a variety of supplies, ranging from guns and ammo to gas and oil and more mundane supplies like food and toilet paper.

Second Lieutenant Jimmy Johnson, a complete horse's ass even for a white man, commanded the convoy and was in the lead vehicle, a Jeep. He was from Alabama and rumor had it that the army liked to put Southern white men in charge of blacks because it was believed they "understood" black soldiers. Johnson didn't understand shit. Behind his back, the colored soldiers joked that Johnson didn't know how his asshole worked.

It was dark and they'd been driving for hours. Tyree didn't mind that. Men were dying at the front and he was not going to complain about fatigue. Being tired compared well with getting shot at.

They drove with their lights partly blacked out. German planes were rare, but they did exist and being strafed was on nobody's priority list. The way they were packed along the road, if a German plane did show up they were dead meat.

Tyree jammed on his brakes. The trucks in front were stopping hard. "What the hell!" he said and barely controlled the truck.

Men on foot appeared beside him, their faces blackened with soot. For a ridiculous instant, Tyree thought they were white men pretending to be Negroes, but realized the soot was a form of disguise. They opened the driver's door and someone stuck a pistol in his face and yelled at him to get out. It was in French but he got the message and got out, his hands up.

Other drivers bunched up beside him. "What the hell's going on, Sarge?" one of them asked. It was his friend, Leon. "These boys working for the black market?"

"Beats me," Tyree said and tried to smile at one of the gunmen who simply glared back at him. In front of him, Lieutenant Johnson was struggling but stopped abruptly when somebody struck him hard on the head with the butt of a shotgun. He fell to the ground and didn't move. Whoever these guys were, they weren't all that well armed, but they were dangerous.

When all the drivers had been rounded up, a small man wearing a beret and with a red scarf around his neck stood before them. "I am Professor Avant. Before this war I was an instructor at the Sorbonne," he said in heavily accented English. "Now I fight to free the oppressed people of France from the capitalist warmongers and their allies. If you do not resist, you will not be harmed. Unfortunately, your officer chose to fight and has paid the price. He was brave, but stupid."

Tyree gulped. Did that mean asshole Johnson was dead? It probably did. Tyree was aware that the Sorbonne was some kind of French school and this Avant obviously thought it was important.

Avant continued. "We are communists, French communists, and we are going to overthrow the fascist dictatorship of De Gaulle and those like him. Since you Americans are fighting with De Gaulle, you are our enemy. Your trucks and the supplies they carry will be destroyed."

Tyree and the others were puzzled. Weren't the French our allies? "Thought we were all fighting the Germans," he said.

Avant stood directly in front of him. Tyree thought he was an arrogant little shit, but a shit with a gun, which meant he would be respected. "There is a greater cause and that is the freedom of the worker. You are a Negro and I thought you would understand that. You, a Negro, are nothing more than a slave of the capitalists."

Tyree bristled. "I ain't nobody's fucking slave. My granddaddy was freed by Lincoln and we may be poor but we ain't slaves."

Avant laughed. "Really? Are you free to vote, to go to school, to work, or to marry a white woman?"

He had a point, but Tyree wouldn't admit it. "White women are ugly," he said and his companions snickered. "And they're afraid of black men because we all got such big cocks."

Avant was about to respond when one of the tanker trucks exploded, sending debris flying and all of them running for cover. Avant yelled for his men to destroy the rest of the trucks and Tyree watched as several score French communists threw grenades into their vehicles.

"Fuck this shit," Tyree yelled. He ran to the other side of his truck, opened the door and pulled out the carbine. He shot at the first Frenchman he saw and the man doubled over, his leg shattered.

Within seconds, the French were shooting at him and his comrades. Several other drivers had gotten their weapons and began shooting back. Tyree heard a scream and his friend Leon fell.

Tyree had only one extra clip. He forced himself to be calm, aimed carefully, and shot another communist. The American soldiers outnumbered the French and soon began to overwhelm them with fire.

Avant yelled something that must have meant retreat because the French began to pull back.

"No, you don't," muttered Tyree. He jumped from behind his truck and ran to Avant. "I ain't no fucking slave," he said and shot the Frenchman several times in the chest and head at point blank range.

Within minutes it was over and the surviving communists had departed into the shadows. Lieutenant Johnson wasn't dead, at least not yet, but it did look

like his skull was fractured since there was a big dent
in it. Tanker fires billowed and ammunition exploded
while other supplies simply burned. There was nothing
to do but care for their wounded, and watch and wait
for the next convoy to rescue them. It wouldn't be
long. The Red Ball Express ran an almost continuous
line of vehicles across France to Germany. Another
convoy would be along shortly and the fires must be
attracting attention.

Other than Leon who'd been shot in the chest and
was dead, no others in Tyree's squad had been killed,
although a couple had been wounded. Maybe twenty
in the entire column were casualties, and at least a
dozen dead French littered the area. Tyree walked
over and looked down on Avant's shattered body.

"Told you I weren't no fucking slave. Maybe now
you'll believe me, asshole."

Morgan kept a low profile as he breasted the hill
crawled down the other slope. He thought he was
an innocuous target even if anyone did see him, and
didn't think anyone would shoot at him from such a
distance, but why take a chance?

Levin crawled beside him. "Is that what I think
it is?"

Morgan laughed. "Unless somebody's moved the
Nile, Roy, yes, that is the Rhine."

"No pyramids and no Ay-rabs and no camels in
sight, so I guess you're right. Jesus, what a barrier
and what a mess getting over is going to be."

Their hill overlooked the German town of Remagen
and the Ludendorff railroad bridge, that until only a
few moments earlier spanned the Rhine. The bridge

had been blown by German engineers and now lay in ruins in the river. Not only was the bridge down, but the shattered remnants blocked the river. They had watched the explosions in horror as there were still people crossing it. Those unfortunates had been tossed into the air like toys. All that remained of the bridge were the twin medieval-like towers at each end, now nothing more than useless artifacts. The railroad tracks on the German side ran slightly upgrade and disappeared into a tunnel.

"Kind of hard to believe the Nile is even bigger and longer," Levin continued. "So too are the Mississippi and a whole bunch of other rivers. Statistically, the Rhine is small potatoes except for the fact that we're going to have to cross the damn thing with people shooting at us."

"Thanks for the redundant and irrelevant geography lesson," Jack said. "Even though I went to what you think is a cow college, I did learn basic geography, beginning with the fact that the world is round."

"Jews figured that out a long time ago during their wanderings," Levin said with mock solemnity. "They knew that because they always kept coming back to where they started."

The small town of Remagen was on the west bank of the Rhine and across from an even smaller town of Linz. Remagen was roughly halfway between the German cities of Cologne to the north and Koblenz to the south.

"Too bad we couldn't have taken the bridge intact," said Levin.

Jack sighed. "A pipe dream at best. And I'll bet every other bridge across the damned Rhine is blown too. Or will be in the next ten minutes."

It was downhill to the river and then steeply uphill

from the other side. Worse, the land on the German side was higher than the western side which meant the defending Germans had another slight advantage. The river banks were not straight up like the Grand Canyon, but they were steep enough and would be difficult for a crossing army to take and climb. Numerous gashes in the hillside were clearly visible and represented German defenses. The sheer number of them was daunting.

"They can't all be real," Jack said. "But it'll be hell figuring out which ones are and which aren't."

A gust of snow swirled and momentarily hid their view. Floes of soft ice bobbed northward towards the English Channel. It was a further reminder that the water was dangerously cold and that winter was just beginning.

"Think it could freeze solid?" Jack asked.

"I read that it has in the past," Levin said. "When it did, Germanic barbarians in Roman times were able to cross, but maybe it was just a bunch of krauts all liquored up so they didn't notice they were getting wet. But who the hell knows? All I do know is that I don't want to go swimming in that mess. I just can't see us trying anything until the weather is a lot warmer."

"I suppose that's good news," Jack said, "but all it really does is extend the war by however many months while we just sit here. Of course, just sitting here might extend our lives."

Artillery boomed behind them and shells exploded near the tunnel entrance. "Oh, that'll do a lot of good," Jack said. "I got a nickel says the krauts don't even respond."

Levin laughed. "Sucker bet. The Nazis won't expose their batteries for no good reason. All that shelling is doing is chewing up useless ground. God, I hope it isn't our guys wasting our ammunition getting their rocks off by shooting into Germany."

The bombardment stopped as quickly as it began, like somebody had told the gunners to stop. "Christmas is just a little ways off," Jack said. "Maybe we'll get some leave if things stay quiet. Of course, it won't involve you since you're Jewish."

"Screw you, Morgan. I'm entitled to free time, too. Besides, Hanukkah starts December 11, so I'll be celebrating just like you."

Sergeant Tyree Wall quickly came to the conclusion that First Lieutenant Stanley Bakowski was all right for a white guy. For one thing, he came from up north, Chicago, which meant he wasn't an ignorant redneck cracker, and second, he too wanted revenge on the French communists who had kept up their attacks on American truck convoys. More important, the stocky and blond-haired Bakowski seemed to treat Wall and the other Negroes with respect. Maybe he was lying about it, but he lied well. Regardless, it was appreciated.

The lieutenant wore a cloth badge that said he was a Ranger. Tyree was less than thrilled about being a human target, but if it helped get the French communists off his back and maybe save the lives of his men, so be it.

Thirty trucks made up the convoy of human decoys. Each driver rode alone as per usual. Bakowski tried to get the colored drivers to at least wear helmets but they said it made driving difficult, especially at night, and the Ranger lieutenant reluctantly concurred. "Keep them by you so you can put them on real fast," he'd said.

Instead of supplies, each truck's cargo consisted of four heavily armed men. Slits had been cut in the canvas to facilitate shooting, and the men were prepared to jump down quickly. They too wore Ranger insignia.

Tyree and Bakowski had gone over photos and maps of the route and decided there were only a couple good spots for an ambush. If there was no ambush tonight, they'd try again in a day or so. Bakowski didn't think the commies could resist the sweet fat target the column presented. Tyree said he half hoped the lieutenant was wrong.

"You boys are professional soldiers, Lieutenant. We're just truck drivers some fool gave guns to."

Bakowski laughed. "Bullshit. You gave a good account of yourselves that time."

Tyree felt strange. When was the last time a white man paid him a compliment? He decided to take a chance with the lieutenant. "I hear you Rangers eat human flesh for breakfast, sir," he teased.

"Lunch," Bakowski said and the men in the back of the truck roared. Damn, but Tyree thought it felt good. He had heard the word camaraderie and understood how it applied to his men, but to a bunch of white Rangers? My, my.

They were coming up on the first likely ambush site. They had to slow to make a turn and the woods were within a few yards of the road. Suddenly, men surged from the trees and began firing at them. Tyree's instructions were to hit the brakes hard and he did so with a vengeance. The truck lurched to a halt and he rolled to his right, grabbed his helmet and his carbine and slid to the ground.

The Rangers in the trucks had already commenced

firing on their attackers. For a few seconds it seemed like an even fight, but the firepower, numbers, and discipline of Bakowski's Rangers began to push the communists back. Tyree and the other drivers fired as well and soon there were a number of French bodies on the ground.

The lieutenant shouted commands and his men moved out to the left and right. Tyree wondered what the hell they were up to and then realized. They were going to flank the bastards and scoop them up.

The shooting petered out and stopped. At least a dozen French were dead in front of Tyree and at least that many wounded lay writhing on the ground or trying to crawl away. A couple of stunned Frenchies stood with their hands up. After a while, the Rangers herded another fifty out of the woods. Some of them were walking wounded and they all looked shocked. Tyree was surprised to see a couple of scruffy looking women in the group. These French people were all crazy, he thought.

Bakowski took a tally. His Rangers had suffered four wounded, and only one seriously. One driver was dead. He'd taken a shot in the skull when the attack first began. Tyree shuddered. That could have been him. Two others were wounded.

Bakowski walked over and slapped Tyree on the shoulder. "Damn fine work, Sergeant. You and your men did yourselves proud. And if you're ever in Chicago, look me up and I'll buy you dinner, all of you."

Tyree said thanks and looked at his men who looked rightfully pleased. And maybe not all white men were assholes after all.

★ CHAPTER 17 ★

THE POLICE OFFICER CAME FROM THE TOWN OF Hachenberg, just a few miles away from the Mullers' farm. The Mullers knew him and he was normally a very jovial man even though he had only one arm. He'd left the other one at Verdun a generation before, and had been living in a state of semi-retirement until so many young men had been drafted that he had been asked to take on some police duties.

"I have come to issue a warning," Officer Klaus Oberg stated grimly. "There have been a number of very brutal assaults on refugees passing through the area."

Bertha gasped. "How horrible."

"Indeed," Oberg continued. "There have been robberies, sexual assaults, and at least one murder. We believe the perpetrators are not German. Instead, we believe they are foreigners uprooted by the war and who are preying on good Germans to either gain revenge, or simply because they are criminals. Survivors have commented on what sounded like foreign accents."

"What can we do?" said Uncle Eric.

The others nodded in dismay. This could not be happening in Germany. The older ones recalled the chaos and near civil war of the twenties, but had assumed that to all be in the past. Anarchy was one problem Hitler had seemingly solved.

Margarete looked away. She had her own problems. She had just started her period and was suffering from cramps and bleeding. Her mother thought her slightly late start was due to the near malnutrition conditions in Berlin before they came to the farm, and that she was now catching up to life. Margarete didn't care for the interpretation. She was in pain and she wanted it to go away. The thought that this was going to happen every month was appalling.

Oberg continued. "May I assume you have weapons here?"

"Indeed," Bertha answered proudly, "We have several shotguns, two rifles, and a couple of pistols, souvenirs of the Great War."

"And ammunition," added Eric. "With all of it safely locked away."

"You might wish to unlock it," Officer Oberg said somberly. "If bandits do come, you will want the guns at hand and not in a vault. I suggest you carry a gun with you at all times, especially when outside this house. It will make work inconvenient, but much, much safer."

"Has it come to that?" asked Magda.

"I believe so," said Oberg. "While it is not yet happening here, there are rumors of troops from both sides perpetrating atrocities on each other and the civilian population. Some are even calling it revenge.

I cannot believe that German soldiers would have done anything that would call for revenge."

Margarete and Magda looked at each other. They both thought of the death train and Magda recalled stories Ernst had told her about campaigning in Russia. He'd been insistent that he'd never done anything criminal, but that others had. In particular, the SS units had been terribly savage and sadistic, so much so that the details had shocked Magda. Margarete was told only what they felt she needed to know.

Oberg continued. "There are those who feel the predators might be foreign workers. I understand you have three of them. May I assume that they are kept secured?"

"Indeed you may," Uncle Eric pronounced. "They are watched when in the field and they are locked up at night." ·

Magda and Margarete looked quickly at each other. Dear Uncle Eric was lying through his teeth. The workers were not locked up, although she assumed they would be from now on. Good, Margarete thought. It would keep that Victor person from wandering around and possibly spying on her. When she'd mentioned her concerns to Eric and Bertha, they'd laughed at her. Her mother had been more sympathetic.

Margarete glanced at the policeman and caught a hint of humor in his eyes. He seemed to understand that her aunt and uncle were pompous fools who would now scramble to keep themselves out of hot water regarding their workers. He had come to deliver a warning and it had been done.

With that, the policeman left. Eric unlocked the weapons cabinet. He gave the two adult women a shotgun each and kept an old Mauser rifle for himself. He looked sadly at Margarete.

"I do not like giving guns to children."

"I appreciate the thought, Uncle, but I am no longer a child. Even though I'm only fourteen, I've seen death and violence in so many forms. Do you really think there are any true children left in Germany?"

Bertha gasped at her effrontery. Eric was startled for a moment but regained his composure and smiled tightly. "You are right, young lady. There are no more children in Germany. They've all gone and the world is worse for it. This is not the way it was supposed to end."

He handed Margarete a 9mm Luger and two clips of ammunition. She examined it and put it in the waistband of her slacks, but did not load it. She would go out and let Victor see it. She had thought briefly of informing the policeman of her concerns and suspicions, but had dismissed it. She had no proof of any wrongdoing on Victor's part and if he was innocent, her claims might send him back to a concentration camp and probable death. She kept seeing the bodies by the train. She would never be a party to that.

"If you're curious as to where it came from," Eric said to Margarete, "it's a 1908 model from the previous war. My commanding officer, a good and decent man, carried it until he was killed in the last few weeks of the war. I kept it in memory of him. If you have any questions about how it works, I will show you tomorrow."

Margarete thanked her uncle and said, yes, she would like some lessons. Impulsively, she hugged him. He might be a pompous fool, but he loved her.

Aunt Bertha began to sob loudly. "This sort of thing never would have happened if Hitler was still alive."

Colonel Ernst Varner recoiled in horror at the sight of the skeletal creatures on the hospital beds. There were five of them and they were all naked except for small white cloths that covered their genitals, and were hooked up to machines and tubes. Their skins were blotched and covered with raw wounds. They were almost totally bald.

Varner was wearing a hospital gown and a mask. He had gloves on and had been told to touch nothing. He had no intention of coming in contact with anything in this chamber of horrors.

"These are the dead," Heisenberg said. "Even though they still breathe and can sometimes speak, they are as dead as if they had been buried a month ago. In a short while, days or weeks, they will stop breathing and be buried in very deep graves by people who, just like you, will be afraid to touch them. They were good men and women."

"Women?" Varner was momentarily incredulous. There was nothing that would indicate that any of the patients ever had a gender.

"Yes, women. Some of our best scientists are women."

"What happened?" Varner asked.

Heisenberg laughed bitterly. "Herr Himmler wants haste and this is the price we pay for it. These were not the first, nor will they be the last. We are now discovering the lingering effects of radiation. As discussed earlier, there was some hope that radiation burns could be treated just like any other burns, but we've found to our horror that radiation is terribly different. It is a sickness that eats at the body like a cancer or leprosy. Sometimes, the body is strong enough and the infection weak enough that a patient will live. However, the survivor will carry scars for the rest of his life, even though the scars might be invisible."

"What a terrible way to die," Varner said after they'd left the sealed-off clinic.

"Is there a good way?"

"And this is from careless handling of radioactive material?"

Heisenberg glared at him. "Colonel, I resent the use of the word careless. The Reichsfuhrer required haste above all and that meant the relaxing of safety standards that should have been kept because we were, and still are, ignorant of what we are dealing with. At least we are no longer in Berlin where these horrors might be unleashed on the city."

As a result of the possibility of a premature explosion, the scientific facilities had been moved well to the east and were now in the outskirts of Breslau, near the Polish border. Himmler felt that an accidental explosion destroying Breslau could be blamed on the Russians. Varner had been appalled by the callous attitude, but grudgingly agreed that Himmler was right. However, this situation with radiation put Heisenberg's bomb in a whole new perspective. Even though he was not a scientist, Varner could visualize a bomb exploding in a city and thousands, perhaps tens of thousands of civilians, condemned to a horrible lingering death like the five living corpses before him.

More logically, developing the bomb at Breslau meant that it would be several hundred miles closer to its target, Moscow.

"Does Himmler know about the radiation sickness dilemma?"

Heisenberg winced. "He has been informed and sees no dilemma. He had Skorzeny tell me that anything that kills the enemies of the Reich in any way and no matter how long it takes is a successful device."

"When will it be ready?" Varner asked. He wasn't certain he wanted to know the answer. Never would have satisfied him, but they knew that Heisenberg's life and the lives of the scientist's loved ones, along with his staff's, were hostage to Himmler. Perhaps the dying were martyrs and not victims.

"Spring should see it finished. When the thaw comes and the flowers bloom and the world becomes alive again, Skorzeny will be able to move the damned thing, although I really have no idea how he plans to do that. Perhaps it doesn't matter. Just get it over with."

Varner took his leave of the harassed physicist. He had been sent to Breslau by von Rundstedt to get a true picture of the situation regarding the atomic bomb. Rundstedt didn't entirely trust the reports he was getting from Himmler and Albert Speer.

Varner now wished the field marshal had sent someone else. This atomic bomb, if it worked, was the devil's brew and anyone associated with it would be damned. He would report about the lingering effects of radiation to von Rundstedt.

Perhaps Rundstedt could get Himmler to reconsider using it on the Russians, or anyone for that matter? Perhaps he could get the Reichsfuhrer to agree to a test or a demonstration to show to the Reds and the Americans just what power the Third Reich possessed?

He shook his head sadly. It was more likely that

Hitler would come back to life than that Himmler would show mercy to anyone, especially the Soviets. Dear God, he thought, visualizing the living cadavers, what a hell of a turn of events.

Private Wally Feeney stood at attention. Morgan was seated behind a table and Feeney was staring intently at an invisible spot on the canvas wall behind him. The soldier did not look in the slightest bit cowed or concerned. The man was twenty-six and had been drafted recently when standards had been relaxed. He said he had bad feet which had previously kept him out of the military. In Morgan's opinion, Feeney also had a bad attitude. However, the man decently did his job as a half-track driver under Jack's command.

"Private Feeney, you are accused of fraternization with the enemy. How do you plead and what do you have to say for yourself?"

This was Jack's first time as judge and jury and he wasn't quite sure what to do. Levin and Whiteside had briefed him, but it wasn't the same. Nor was the crime all that serious.

"What the hell can I say, sir? I got caught and that's that."

"You were having sex with a German woman."

"Yes, sir, she had just sucked my dick and I had paid her for it."

Morgan sighed. This was not going at all well. "That's against orders."

"The nonfraternization rule is dumb, sir. With all due respects, sir, what the hell is wrong with getting screwed or sucked by somebody who wants to do it?

And I didn't force her to do anything, even though the krauts are supposed to be conquered people."

Ah, an opening. "Last I checked, Feeney, Germany hadn't surrendered. What if she was one of those fanatical Werewolves we've been hearing about? You know, those people who want to go on killing and fighting? What if she had decided to clamp down on your Johnson and leave you singing soprano?"

Feeney laughed. "Then my buddies would have stomped the shit out of her, sir. We ain't that dumb. We were all looking out for each other."

This was getting worse and worse, Jack thought. "There were others?"

"Sir, there were four of us. The only reason I couldn't get away is that I was, well, occupied. Hell, sir, that's why she was sucking instead of fucking. She said there were too many of us for her to fuck. And, oh yeah, sir, I ain't gonna give you their names."

Jack tried not to smile at the mental picture that had emerged. "Feeney, I sense that you're not too concerned about all this."

"No, sir, I'm not. Look, you're supposed to be one of the good guys, so can I speak frankly?"

"I thought you already were," Jack said dryly. "But go ahead."

"I already said the rule is dumb, so I won't repeat myself. But let's get real. You're going to chew me out and then threaten me with punishment. But what can you do? You can't threaten to send me to combat because I'm already there. How about permanent KP? Hey, that'd get me out of combat, so that's a great idea. Loss of rank? I'm a private. Loss of money? I get paid shit and have no way to spend what I do have. Stockade time? The crime ain't serious enough and, besides, if you sent everybody you caught nailing German pussy to jail, we wouldn't have an army no more."

Jack mentally conceded the points. "How about if you get the clap and I deny you penicillin?"

"That might work, but I did use a condom. I ain't stupid, sir. And you won't cut off my condom supply because I use that to keep my weapon clean. My other weapon, that is, the one that goes bang."

This time Jack couldn't help but smile. The army issued condoms to the soldiers who had long ago realized that putting one over the barrel of a rifle helped keep the dirt out.

"How much did she charge you?"

"Ten cigarettes, sir."

"You overpaid. I heard it was a lot less."

"Maybe, sir. But she was there, damned cute, and I didn't feel like haggling."

Jack could understand. Just about every man in the regiment was horny. Ike's rule was nuts, but he couldn't say that to Feeney or any of the other men.

"Sir, this may be seriously out of line and maybe it's none of my business, but we understand you have a girl, an American girl, and she's here in Europe. Do you realize how fortunate you are? I don't know what the two of you are doing, and it ain't my business, but you actually have a female friend on the same continent and that's gotta be great."

"You're right, Feeney, it's none of your business."

"Sorry, sir."

"So, how was it?"

"Just great, sir. It sure as hell wasn't her first and it was a great early Christmas present."

Jack had a thought. "Feeney."

"Sir?"

"You still a Catholic?" Feeney nodded, curious as to where this was going. "You know Father Serra?" Jack added.

"Yes, sir. He's the chaplain nobody likes because he's such a hard-ass prick."

"Excellent. Your punishment is to go to Serra for Confession and do whatever penance he gives."

Feeney paled. "Sir, that's not fair. He'll give me a rosary a day for the rest of my life."

Morgan smiled. "Who cares? And for the record, I'm going to tell the good padre that you're going to see him, so if you don't show up he'll come looking for you. Now get the hell out of here."

William Donovan, head of the OSS, was the last to enter the Oval Office. General Marshal glared at him, but Donovan's friendship with FDR permitted him to take such liberties. FDR barely looked up. He was listless and gaunt, and his face was a deathly gray. "Sorry to be late, sir," Donovan said to Roosevelt, "but I just got the latest info from my men in Europe."

FDR brightened slightly. "And what do they say?"

Donovan took the opportunity to remind them that he'd been hurriedly inserting teams into Poland and Russia. There had been no shortage of volunteers from emigrés in England and elsewhere. Even better, these were Polish and Russian nationals who knew the customs and the language. The real problem was keeping them alive in such hostile environments and still able to report.

All of the spies were men. Both sides' casual brutality to the women of the other side was beyond belief.

Women were being gang-raped, tortured, mutilated, and murdered for the simple crime of existing, much less spying. Not even old women and small children were safe.

"Poland and Russia are vast lands, so the handful of teams can only give us a partial picture, but what they show is significant," said Donovan, "and very disturbing. It does appear to confirm information from other sources that the Germans are pulling out west towards the Rhine, while most of the Russians are simply disappearing into their vast country. What little we've been able to glean indicates that the Reds are sending some troops south and others west."

"South?" mused General Marshall. "That would indicate a sweep through the Balkans and into Yugoslavia, which makes a kind of sense. But why would they be going east and to what destination? And where would they be heading in the beginning of the winter?"

"Perhaps they're doing as they said—just pulling back to refit and rest?" Roosevelt said hopefully.

Donovan shook his head. "I doubt it. It would be simpler to keep the men in position rather than withdrawing them. I think the commies are up to something."

"Agreed," said Jim Byrnes and Marshall nodded, while FDR shook his head.

The information provided by Donovan's brave people was good, but it merely reinforced what the military's intelligence people were picking up and was being provided by Ultra. The army's own inserts, coupled with photographs taken from planes had also seen the withdrawing German army. Access to Russia was extremely limited; thus, information was even sketchier than what was coming from behind German lines. Code-breaking efforts were continuing despite resistance from the State Department who continued to feel that it was a betrayal of trust in Good Old Uncle Joe Stalin.

The army and the navy had mixed feelings about the OSS. Yes, they were brave, but too many were considered lightweight socialites out for an adventure. Marshall thought that was an unfair generalization, but Donovan and his people did play by their own rules and that irked the military.

"Either way," said Marshall, "it will be many months before the Reds are able to reconstitute their forces against Germany. They are effectively out of the war until at least spring as are we."

"At least we have won great victories," said Roosevelt in almost a whisper.

Almost on cue they glanced at the map on the wall. Antwerp had fallen to Montgomery's armies, but the port was useless. First, it had been thoroughly sabotaged and, second, the Germans still held Walcherin Island, a boggy mass on the Scheldt River north of Antwerp that enabled the Nazis to control access to the city. Montgomery had moved too slowly to prevent the Germans from digging in on the island. Now its capture would require a major effort by the British.

Moving south, Bradley's and Devers' army groups had reached the Rhine at a number of spots and were mopping up resistance on the western side of the river. More than half a million German soldiers had surrendered, although the great majority of them were the Volkssturm. What remained of the regular German army had escaped and was ensconced in the forts facing the Allies.

Edward Stettinius had recently replaced Cordell Hull as Secretary of State. He coughed now to get attention. "May we also discuss the situation with France and how it relates to Russia?"

Byrnes and Marshall eyed the man with some distaste. They considered the forty-four-year-old investor and banker "soft," even naive, particularly regarding Russian intentions. If Stettinius had his way, there would be no code-breaking efforts against the Russians.

"Of course," said Roosevelt.

"Gentlemen, the Soviets are complaining about what they refer to as our unwarranted attacks on French communists," Stettinius said solemnly.

"Bullshit," snapped Byrnes. "The communists attacked several of our supply columns and even killed a number of American soldiers. Our men defended themselves and did a damned fine job of it."

Marshall nodded. "And our boys will continue to fight off attacks."

"I'm telling you what the Reds are saying," Stettinius retorted. "I'm not saying I agree with them. The Russians want guarantees that there will be no more fighting and certainly no support of de Gaulle in his now near civil war with the communists. I've spoken with Ambassador Gromyko, obviously speaking for Stalin, and he strongly suggests that we stop using France as a base for operations and stop supporting the French army. Either that or we support the French communists and this Thorez person as France's legitimate government."

Marshall slapped the table in a rare show of emotion. "All of which represents a reason, or series of reasons, for the Russians to pull out of the war. The chaos in France is just another excuse."

Byrnes laughed bitterly. "And it doesn't matter what we do—it'll be wrong." He turned to Roosevelt. "Now do you see, sir, that the Russians are changing their role and can't be trusted?"

"There's one other thing," added Donovan. "One of my teams was able to confirm a tank park near the old Polish border with what they first thought were several hundred German tanks in it being painted and repaired."

"So what?" snapped Stettinius, in a most undiplomatic manner.

"All of the tanks were Russian T34's. What the hell are the Nazis doing with a large number of Russian tanks?"

Marshall drew a deep breath. "I can see them capturing some of them in the course of fighting, but hundreds?"

"Yes," said Donovan, "and my source said a maintenance worker proudly told him there were other parks just like that. He, the source, said that Germany had bought them. The information's been passed on to the air force and I presume Doolittle's bombers will plow the park."

"It doesn't make sense," said Stettinius. "Why the devil would Stalin sell tanks to Himmler? What did Himmler have that Stalin would have wanted so badly?"

There was silence until Marshall spoke. "Vlasov."

"Dear God," said Byrnes. The Soviets had recently proclaimed the capture of the turncoat Vlasov and his key lieutenants by a party of heroic Red Army commandos. There would be a show trial and then the executions.

Roosevelt looked around. Agony was etched on

his face as he finally absorbed what he'd been told. "They've played me for a fool, haven't they?"

Donovan tried to soothe him. "Sir, they've lied to everyone. At least now we know what they are capable of and can react to it."

Roosevelt's voice was barely a whisper, "Too late." His eyes rolled back in his head. He fell forward and hit his forehead on the desk with a terrible thud.

Vice President-Elect Harry Truman walked into the Executive Office building located across the street from the West Wing of the White House. He was puzzled by the nighttime summons. He only knew that Jim Byrnes, FDR's trusted advisor, had requested his presence to discuss some matters related to the transition between him and outgoing Vice President Henry Wallace. Truman had almost laughed at the caller. There was nothing Wallace did to justify a transition, and Truman had the terrible feeling that the vice-presidency would be the same for him. Wallace's predecessor, John Nance Garner, had accurately described the vice presidency as being as exciting as a bucket of warm piss. Truman could see no reason for any such transition meeting to take place at night.

He was met by a uniformed guard and taken to a meeting room. Henry Wallace had arrived and was sipping a cup of coffee. The two men asked each other about the summons and both pleaded ignorance. Truman asked for and got some coffee. He would have preferred some bourbon, but he sensed that this was neither the time nor the place.

Jim Brynes entered and took a seat. He looked like he hadn't slept in a while.

Truman caught on immediately. "My God, does this have anything to do with Roosevelt's flu?"

The press had been informed that FDR was suffering from a mild form of influenza and had been ordered to rest for a couple of days. That had been two days ago.

Byrnes' mouth quivered. "There was no flu. The President has suffered a stroke."

"How bad?" asked a shocked Wallace.

Byrnes swallowed. It was difficult for him to speak. "At the moment he is in a coma. He does not communicate and does not respond. Doctors are not hopeful of a full recovery and some feel he will never come out of the coma."

"Then who is running the country?" asked Truman. He had a sinking feeling he knew what the answer was going to be in a short while.

"Right now, it's a committee made up of Secretary of State Stettinius, General Marshall, Secretary of War Stimson, Secretary of the Navy Forrestal, Admiral King, Treasury Secretary Morgenthau, and myself. It is obviously a war cabinet and an expedient."

"And why wasn't I on it?" Wallace said angrily, his face turning red. "Or had you all forgotten that the office of vice president exists?"

Byrnes flushed. "Let me be blunt. FDR never included you in anything substantive for reasons best known to him. We thought—prayed?—that this crisis would pass quickly, but it appears that it isn't going to happen. Therefore it is indeed time to begin including both of you for reasons both constitutional and honorable."

"Good," said Truman. He'd harbored the fear that

he too would disappear like FDR's previous vice presidents.

Byrnes continued. He seemed relieved that the two men would now be informed. "I have discussed the matter with Chief Justice Stone and he confirms that, while the President yet lives, neither of you has any authority whatsoever. The President can die, or he can resign, but you cannot become President or assume the duties of President until one or the occurs. The Constitution makes no provision for an acting President, not even in the event the President is merely ill or, in this case, has suffered a stroke. Congress might be able to pass legislation to enact a succession, but that would take time we don't have."

"That should be changed," muttered Truman. "There's a God damn war on. At least Woodrow Wilson's stroke and incapacity occurred during a period of relative peace. What the devil do we do if something requires the President to act?"

Byrnes shrugged. "At best, the law is murky, and you're right, Mr. Truman, the law should be changed and doubtless will be. However, for the moment we are stuck with what we have."

"What about Tom Dewey?" Truman inquired. The New York governor had been the Republican candidate defeated by Roosevelt in November by a more than four to one margin in the Electoral College. "And what about the Democratic Party? Can there be changes in the candidates at this time?"

"I need a good night's sleep," Byrnes said as he rubbed his eyes. "First, Justice Stone says that the Democratic Party could have changed the names on the ballot before the election, but not after. Therefore,

FDR has been elected and you, Mr. Truman, will be at least the Vice President. If FDR is unable to take the oath on January twentieth, you will become President."

"Dear God," Truman said with deep emotion. That date was just a little more than a month away. "I feel like the roof is falling in on me."

"Much like we all do," Byrnes said. "And to answer your question about Dewey, Justice Stone said there can be no do-over election. What is done is done. General Marshall took an air force plane to Albany this morning to inform Governor Dewey about FDR's health. Governor Dewey is an honorable man and I doubt that he will do anything contrary to the best interests of the country."

"Other than those mentioned, who else knows about this, ah, dilemma?" Wallace asked.

"Eleanor, of course," said Byrnes, "and she is with the President in the White House. Also, a woman named Lucy Mercer who is not in the White House."

Truman suppressed a smile. So the rumors were correct. FDR had a mistress. "Will we be a part of this war committee?"

"Effective immediately, yes." He handed each man a binder. "This is a summary of our position vis-à-vis the war in Europe. The war against Japan is proceeding just as the newspapers are saying so there's little new in the binder about it; however, it is the situation in Germany and Russia that is most disturbing. With your permission, we will adjourn. You will doubtless have many questions to ask after you've read the reports. Tomorrow morning, I'll have cars pick you up and return you here where the committee will meet. It was considered unseemly to continue to meet in the White House."

"How long can we keep up this charade?" asked Wallace.

"God only knows," Byrnes answered.

They left and an exhausted Byrnes stared at the table. One or both of them would likely become President of the United States. If the worst happened, the U.S. could have three presidents in six weeks. Even if FDR was to die today, Wallace's term in office would be mercifully short. An inauguration would take place on January 20, 1945, come hell or high water, and if Roosevelt was unable to take the oath, it would be given to Truman. Which man was most qualified to be President, Byrnes wondered, and then realized it didn't matter. Justice Stone had confirmed it—if Roosevelt didn't recover, Harry Truman, the virtually unknown senator from Missouri, would be President.

Byrnes took a deep breath. As of now, neither Wallace nor Truman knew anything about the Manhattan Project and the plans for an atomic bomb. He would continue to keep it from them. Wallace would fade into well-deserved obscurity in a couple of weeks, while Truman might or might not become President. Roosevelt had intentionally not included him in the secret, so Byrnes would not add him, at least not yet. He made a mental note to tell those on the committee who knew about it to keep quiet in Truman's presence. Some day Truman might be pissed, but so be it.

★ CHAPTER 18 ★

A DAY IN THE SKY WAS A WELCOME ELIXIR FOR Morgan. on the ground, the world was snow-covered and cold, brilliant white except where it was bloodied and black-scarred from the intermittent fighting. Near blizzard conditions had prevailed in much of the area, blanketing the world in snow depths that made walking difficult and driving nearly impossible. Even tanks had a hard time plowing through the accumulated piles of snow and slush.

Finally, the army had begun to get winter uniforms, including boots, liners for field jackets, gloves, and hats with ear pieces. The result was a welcome reduction in incidents of frostbite.

At least as important were white coverings for the uniforms that helped the GI's blend into the ground and avoid drawing attention from the Germans across the river. It was a source of aggravation that the

Germans had their snow coverings long before the Americans. Tanks and other vehicles had been hastily white-washed. Tankers groused that when the thaw came, it would mean the tanks would have to be scrubbed clean. They were reminded that war was hell.

Morgan turned back to his copilot. "Snyder, what do you want for Christmas besides an honorable discharge?"

"That about covers it, sir."

"Sorry I can't get that for you. If I could, I'd get one for myself first."

"Then maybe getting laid would be nice, too, if they'd ever drop that damn rule."

"No comment, Snyder." The unrepentant Feeney was now the butt of many jokes. Non-Catholics who had no idea what a rosary was actually stopped and watched him pray, which thoroughly annoyed Feeney.

Below them, the Rhine was still snow-choked. On a different day, it might have been scenic. Now they looked below for a military advantage. Had anything changed since the last time they'd flown over? If so, what was it and why? They would both take notes while Snyder took pictures.

As always, their orders were to stay on the American side of the Rhine. Across the river on the German side, a German Storch flew on an almost parallel course. Jack fought the insane urge to fly over and see who the pilot was and ask him what he thought of the war. There was an informal truce between the two sides regarding the small observation planes—don't shoot at me and I won't shoot at you. Also, don't cross the damn river.

Suddenly, the German banked sharply away. "What

the hell," Jack said. Fingers of tracer fire erupted from a dozen hidden sites and streaked skyward. They looked up and saw a plane much higher in the sky. "Somebody's using a real plane and taking real pictures now that the weather's cleared."

For the past week, reconnaissance flying had been nearly impossible as the snow had socked in everything. Now that the weather was beginning to get better, everyone wanted to see what had happened while they were grounded.

"Y'know, sir, I don't think it was a smart idea for the Germans to shoot at that recon plane."

Morgan concurred. Never give away your hiding place unless there was a really good reason. To prove the point, a flight of six American P47 Thunderbolt fighter bombers swooped low and dropped their loads. Clouds of flame erupted where they landed, exploding in a horrible beauty.

"Napalm," Jack said, recalling the destruction of the SS position in the forest. Death by burning was a horrible fate, even for a Nazi, but if it ended the war or even got them across the Rhine by turning German forts into charnel houses, then napalm was a godsend. Nobody on the U.S. side could imagine a weapon they wouldn't use against the Germans, with the possible exception of poison gas. It was common knowledge that the krauts had stockpiles of gas and everybody wondered if the Germans would use it when the crossing came.

A dark shadow sped by and one of the Thunderbolts exploded, while the others scattered like sparrows attacked by a hawk. One of the American planes flew low overhead and was quickly followed by a shape that screamed by at incredible speed.

"Jesus, Captain, did you see that?"

"Yeah," Jack answered. He was a little stunned by the savage turn of events. One minute they were enjoying the view and the next people were burning to death on the ground and being shot out of the sky.

"That was a jet, wasn't it, sir?"

"Snyder, I've never seen one, but I'll bet that's exactly what it was. I think we've had enough excitement for today. Let's head for home."

Home, he thought. What the hell was home? He'd just been served napalm and a jet fighter for Christmas.

"Who in God's name gave you permission to piss on the floor of my shiny new bunker?" Schurmer raged at the hapless young officer standing and shaking before him.

Volkssturm Lieutenant Volkmar Detloff stood at attention and took the scolding. His lips were trembling but he swore he would not cry. Colonel Schurmer's face was livid. "Answer me, you little turd, why? And did you shit yourself as well as pissing on the floor and why did you find it necessary to perform such acts in front of your entire platoon?"

Volkmar flinched. He had shit and pissed himself, but not that much. He had never been so afraid in his young life and had completely lost control.

"Detloff, I hope you recall that, in your cowardly haste to leave the bunker, you trampled over two men who were seriously wounded and a lot braver than you."

"I'm sorry," Detloff stammered.

"I should have you shot," Schurmer snarled.

He wouldn't, of course. Schurmer had made a

quick call to Berlin and his friend, Ernst Varner, and confirmed that the odious little twit's equally odious father was still a senior aide to Heinrich Himmler. This was why he, and not Detloff's direct superior, was handling the incident. Not only would the boy not be shot, but Schurmer had to figure a way to hide this incident.

Nor did he think young Detloff was all that much of a coward. From everything he'd found, the situation in the bunkers when the American planes had dropped napalm had been terrible.

"How old are you?"

"Eighteen, sir."

"Don't lie to me! Your disgusting pimples say you're younger."

The boy gulped. "Sixteen, sir."

"Now tell me the truth. Wouldn't you rather be at home waiting for the Christ child to deliver presents on Christmas Eve, or do you believe Santa Claus does it at night like the Americans do?"

Prudently, the boy didn't answer. Schurmer thought it more likely he, like so many devout Nazis, didn't believe in anything except Hitler's dogmas. Perhaps the boy's family would just sit around the lighted and decorated Christmas tree and exchange presents and lift a glass of schnapps to Himmler and the memory of Hitler.

Schurmer knew what had happened to the boy. When planes had dropped napalm on a bunker beside Detloff's, the men inside had been incinerated. A cloud of flame had rushed over where Detloff and his men were justifiably cowering. Air had been sucked out of the bunker and men had collapsed, choking and gasping, but the napalm had been a near miss and blessed breathable air had returned quickly. Fingers of liquid fire leaking through embrasures were extinguished, but the air stank of scorched flesh and burned meat. In terror, a slightly singed Detloff had led a stampede out of the bunker. On their way, they passed a number of cremated German soldiers and it was then that young Detloff had lost what remained of his courage.

Detloff was almost in tears. "I was more afraid than I ever thought possible. I have never seen such horror in all my life, not even during the bombings in Berlin."

Schurmer had no sympathy. "Then you have never truly seen war." But why should a sixteen-year-old boy have to see war in the first place? Have we sunk that far?

"It wasn't only the fire, Colonel, it was the fact that the walls were closing in on me and I thought I would either suffocate or be crushed."

Wonderful, Schurmer thought. How many other claustrophobic soldiers were down in the bunkers and what would make them also break when the real attack came? Fire, not claustrophobia, was the true Achilles' heel of the fortresses of the Rhine Wall. They were almost impervious to shelling and bombing, but nothing could stand up to fire, and the liquid napalm used by the Americans could possibly unravel all his work.

"I even hurt my leg again."

Schurmer wondered if the wretch hadn't reinjured his knee on purpose. It wouldn't be the first time someone thought a self-inflicted wound would get him out of the military. Well, if that had been Detloff's plan, he was wrong.

"Please don't tell my father."

The look of terror on Volkmar's face said it all. His father was a petty tyrant who probably beat his children for the slightest transgression. Schurmer wondered if the elder Detloff had killed or beaten any helpless Jews. Schurmer had no love for Jews, but felt contempt for those who took advantage of the helpless.

"I will not tell your father about your cowardice, nor will I have you shot, or even court-martialed. However, you cannot go back to your unit. They had little confidence in you before and none now. You will keep your rank for your father's sake, but you will command no one. You will be assigned to a new unit being formed to counterattack the Americans if they do succeed in crossing the river."

Detloff brightened. "Werewolves?"

Schurmer sighed. "There is no such thing as were-wolves, Detloff. They are figments of the imagination just like bogeymen and witches. No, you will be part of General Dietrich's staff. Do you understand English?"

"A little. I learned it in school."

"Which means you don't understand a damn thing. However, you may still be useful."

Detloff snapped back to attention. "I will not fail."

Schurmer sighed. Better the little fool did fail. At least he would stand a chance of living.

"I will not fail," Detloff said again. A broken record, Schurmer thought.

Detloff saluted and left. Alone, Schurmer poured himself a couple of shots of good Scotch. Not much more of that left, he thought, but there was no reason to save it. Germany had reached the point where they were sending old men and totally ignorant boys like

Detloff out to fight the overwhelming might of the Americans. A Jew at Auschwitz had a better chance of surviving until summer than sixteen-year-old Volkmar Detloff. He took a swallow. Merry Christmas, Germany.

"So what was in your package?" Carter yelled.

"Some socks and some stale cookies," Jack answered. "Along with some paperback books that look interesting. I don't think my family knows just what to send."

"It's the thought that counts," Levin said with mock piety. "What did you send them, snow from Germany?"

"What a great thought." Jack laughed. He decided not to tell them he'd sent Jessica a vial of water from the Rhine.

He smiled at the thought of his parents trying to figure out what to send to a son who either has all he needs or nothing at all. They knew that there was no room at the front for luxuries. They also knew that really valuable stuff, like liquor and cigars, might not make it to him. The vast majority of personnel handling mail were honest, but it took only a few creeps to ruin things.

Jack was most pleased by a letter from Jessica and the fact that it began "Dearest Jack." Dearest? Wow, had he come up in the world. She also said that she missed him and hoped he would get some leave time. Leave time was another rumor. If the war really was on a winter hiatus, would the powers that be grant leave? Whiteside and Stoddard thought it was a good possibility. Maybe the regiment would be rotated out for a while, or maybe just individuals or units could go. It didn't matter. That Jessica wanted to see him was the important thing.

However, he'd been told that Paris was off limits, and not just because of the near civil war now engulfing France. Apparently the city was becoming a Mecca for deserters. It didn't matter. He'd find a place for them to be together.

Jack laughed softly. He was in love with a young lady he'd only seen once although, again, he felt their letters had brought them very close together. Hell, they hadn't even made out. He wondered what would happen if they did get time together. He started to visualize her naked and caressing each other and it began to get warm in the tent. He decided it was best not to dwell on those possibilities.

Life where they were bivouacked wasn't intolerable. The army had done its damndest to do what it could for the GI's. Since it was fairly obvious that they weren't going to move for a while, tents had been set up and wooden floors laid down. Mess halls actually served hot food, and there were showers and laundries working. Colonel Stoddard's headquarters buildings were solidly fortified and with good reason. There were reports that German infiltrators would try to attack vulnerable spots, so the men were constantly reminded that they were in hostile territory and should carry their weapons at all times.

Other rumors said that the nonfraternization rule would be relaxed to permit "essential" transactions. Levin wondered if that would permit Feeney to go back to the fraulein who'd serviced him. Probably not, was the consensus.

The penance given Feeney by Father Serra had been delicious. Not only did he have to say a rosary each day, but he had to serve as an altar boy whenever needed. Feeney still insisted it was worth it, and that people were jealous.

In the back of everyone's mind was the ugly reality that spring would inevitably come and with it the titanic battles that would claim so many of them. Jack couldn't help but look at his comrades and wonder who among them would be alive the next Christmas, and who would be maimed. He knew they were looking at him and wondering the same thing.

If it hadn't been for the war, he would have finished college and been well on his way with a good job and a career. Maybe he'd even be married and planning a family with a wife who, in his imagination, looked surprisingly like Jessica Granville.

Now he had no idea when any of this would occur, or even if it would occur.

Carter slapped him on the shoulder and passed him a bottle of Rhine wine. "Ain't it crazy? Christmas is supposed to be joyous but we can't shake the sadness. Bittersweet, isn't it?"

Jack took a drink. The wine was pretty decent for once. "Sure is. So what do we do about it?"

"You know as well as I do, my friend," Carter said. "All we can do is live for today, this moment, and ignore anything beyond that, which is why you should take advantage of every moment you can find to be with my lovely and virginal cousin. Hey, she is still a virgin, isn't she?"

Jack laughed. "If she isn't, I had nothing to do with it."

Levin sat down and smiled widely. He was drunk. "And to all a Merry Hannukah."

★　　★　　★

Across the Rhine, Ernst Varner had managed to get leave to spend Christmas with his family. Von Rundstedt had laughingly said that since Varner had traveled all over Germany for him, he should take a few days off and visit those who really counted. Varner declined to remind von Rundstedt that he'd already had one trip home in the last few months. The field marshal was giving these little bonuses to those on his staff who had served him well.

Varner had found it disconcerting to see his beautiful wife and only child carrying guns. He knew the reason, of course. The reports of attacks on refugee columns had been a topic of conversation at the OKW. If Germany could not protect its own civilians, just how could they resist the Americans?

Despite the presence of the war hanging over them, they did manage a festive Christmas Eve. Only a few presents were handed out and they were mainly symbolic, like cookies or sweets.

This time his young pilot, Lieutenant Hans Hart, sat with them at the main table. Everyone said that no one should be alone on Christmas. Both Ernst and Magda thought the way he stared at Margarete was hilarious, especially after she gave him a Christmas cookie as a present. Not quite as funny were the looks she returned. The young couple was growing up far too quickly.

"I'm too young to be a grandfather," he whispered to Magda.

"No, you're not," she replied sweetly.

Before they retired to bed, Varner stepped outside in his full uniform with his MP38 machine pistol slung over his shoulder and conspicuously visible as well as the Luger in its holster. The attacks on civilians had diminished. In part, he thought, because the Rhine bridges were down, which meant no more refugees were coming from the Rhineland, which was now occupied by the Americans. That didn't mean that the human vultures weren't out there. He'd read the reports and understood that while many of the attacks were by Germans, a number had been by foreigners. German criminals were bad enough, but the Reich had brought countless numbers of foreign workers, slaves, to work in factories and farms, and many of these had been uprooted by the bombings and were hiding wherever they could. Escaped POWs were another possibility. In particular, freed Russian prisoners wanted to wreak a terrible vengeance on their captors.

He stepped into the barn. The three foreign workers had finished their Christmas dinner and Bertha had given them a couple of bottles of the bad wine she made. Varner had mixed thoughts about giving them alcohol, but concluded that there wasn't enough to get them drunk and dangerous.

The three men shuffled to their feet, but did not look him in the face. Were they among the ones who'd attacked refugees? The two Latvians looked harmless enough—large, but harmless. However, the Czech or Frenchman or whatever he was, Mastny, looked positively feral. Varner wondered what he'd find if he searched the many recesses of the barn? Money? Jewelry? Nothing?

He stared at them, again making sure they saw his weapons. His look told them he could and would cut them down in an instant. The Latvians looked frightened, but Mastny didn't. He understood the game Varner was playing.

Varner wished them a good Christmas and a peaceful future and left them. He would tell Magda to keep a watch on Mastny and to push Bertha to send him back to the prison camp if he gave even a hint of trouble. He would give Margarete the same message.

He saw shadows on the porch. He almost stopped but smiled and kept on walking as if he had not seen his daughter and his pilot standing so close together.

It was after midnight when Margarete padded softly down the stairs. The wooden floor was cold on her bare feet, but she didn't mind. She thought she looked like an old lady. Her flannel nightgown was full and came down to her ankles. She thought she also resembled a very lovely ghost in the dim light. She found the door to the spare bedroom that had once housed a servant. Heart pounding, she opened it and slipped in.

Hans was awake in an instant. "I was beginning to think you wouldn't come."

"I had to wait until it was safe." He started to get up from the bed, but she pushed him back. She could see that he was wearing his underwear and thought it made him look cute. She pulled back the blanket and slid in beside him. His arms went around her and their bodies strained against each other as they kissed with an intensity that surprised them both.

Margarete felt his erection against her, gasped, and pushed her belly against it. "Do you know what you're doing?" Hans asked.

She giggled and licked his ear. "I am a silly little virgin, but not a stupid one. And be still, we only have a minute before my mother realizes I didn't go to the kitchen for a cookie."

He laughed and they kissed again, their tongues eagerly exploring. "We will not go all the way, Hansi, but I won't fall to pieces if you touch me."

Hans began to stroke her, feeling her body under the cloth. "This way," she said and shifted so her nightgown was above her bottom. His hands on her bare flesh excited her. He pushed the nightgown up to her shoulders. She sucked in her breath as he gently caressed her breasts and her nipples. He shifted so his lips were on her nipples and his hand was down her panties and between her thighs, which were suddenly moist and seemingly moving of their own volition. Margarete had never known such sensations and wanted them to continue forever. It was nothing like that idiot Detloff's pawing of her. This was the way it should be.

However, a rational corner of her mind said it had to stop and, with great regrets, she pushed him away.

Hans lay back gasping. "You are so beautiful."

"So are you, Hansi."

"Nobody's ever called me Hansi. I don't know if I like it. But if you say it, it must be all right."

She gazed at his erection stretching the fabric of his shorts and felt bolder than she'd ever been in her life. "This is to make sure you do come back," she said as she slid his shorts down. He sighed as she took his manhood in her hands and stroked it. She'd never done it before, but she'd talked with friends who had. Shortly, he gasped and climaxed.

Margarete stood and smiled down at the stunned young pilot. "Good night, Hansi dearest, and if I don't have a chance to talk to you in the morning, I very much want you to come back safely."

Hans smiled and said he would. When she was gone he thought how nice it was for her to want him to come back safely. What the devil was safe to a pilot in a war where the enemy ruled the skies? Even a man who flew something as innocuous as a Storch was at risk and, besides, he was sick of not pulling his weight in the war. He decided it was not the time to tell her he'd applied for a transfer to train as a jet fighter pilot.

Magda was waiting for her daughter at the top of the stairs. "Well? I gave you ten minutes with him and you took twelve," she said with a knowing smile.

"I lost track of time, but don't worry, my precious virtue is safe."

Magda gave her daughter a hug. "I never doubted for a minute. Now go to bed, and this time I mean yours."

Margarete walked towards her bedroom, turned and grinned wickedly. "I'm still a virgin, Mama, just a much more knowledgeable one."

Himmler paced his office. Never the most secure of persons, his doubts were getting the best of him and the presence of the stern field marshal commanding his armies was not comforting.

"I never should have agreed to let you pull our armies behind the Rhine."

Rundstedt almost yawned. They had basically the same discussion every time they met. "You didn't have a choice, Herr Himmler. If you had ordered the army to fight on the west bank it would have been defeated and destroyed, and the Rhine Wall would now be empty of troops. Then, regardless of the weather, the

Allies would have poured across, and all of us would be in hiding or running for our lives."

Himmler waved him off. "I know, I know. But I am being criticized for the loss of the lands and the cities. Think of it, Aachen, Cologne, Koblenz, and so many other places that have been German forever are gone."

"Once more, Reichsfuhrer, the lands were lost for nearly two decades after the Treaty of Versailles and were subsequently recovered. If we stick to our plan, they will be German again in a much shorter period of time. As to the plan, it is going well. Our armies are intact and safely on the east of the Rhine where they are continually building their strength."

This latter statement was a sop to the paranoid Himmler. There were serious problems in the military. Thanks to the moves he'd made, the army had large numbers of men, but many of them were either very young or very old, and so many were poorly trained. Also, the loss of the Rhineland had devastated the morale of the troops, many of whom had homes now occupied by the Yanks. Worse, many of the soldiers defending the Reich weren't even German, but conscripts from other conquered nations, and whose reliability was doubted.

In most cases, the German army had superior weapons compared with the Americans, but not enough of them. The infusion of two thousand Soviet tanks would help, but German armor would still be horribly outnumbered. Worse, the Americans had found one tank park and largely obliterated it. How many more tanks would be destroyed before they even got to the front?

It was much the same with the Luftwaffe. The ME262 jet was a marvelous machine, but would they have more than a few hundred of them when the decisive battles came? There were enough experienced and elite pilots to man the jets, but what about the rest of the Luftwaffe? Galland was distraught at the fact that so many pilots were getting little training because there just wasn't enough fuel, or air space in which to train as the Reich contracted. American pilots jumped on the trainees like vultures whenever they took off. As a result, the dispirited army suffered from almost daily bombings the Luftwaffe was powerless to prevent.

The German navy, the Kriegsmarine, was a fading memory. Only a handful of U-boats still operated and the surface fleet was being dismantled and the personnel transferred to duties on land and supporting the army.

Qualitatively, American artillery was at least on a par with Germany's and vastly outnumbered what Rundstedt could bring to battle. He foresaw his defenses being pounded by both bombs and guns and being essentially powerless to do anything about it. The field marshal was acutely aware that he would have only one chance to stop the Americans and it would not be at the Rhine. With seven hundred miles of river to defend, he could not stretch his forces too thin.

"Tell me truthfully, Field Marshal, can the Americans defeat us? Can they cross the Rhine after all we've done?"

"Yes," Rundstedt answered bluntly. He almost enjoyed the look of dismay on Himmler's face. "However, it will require them to pay a great blood price, and they may not wish to do that."

"What if that is wishful thinking?"

"Then we will emulate Churchill and fight them on the landing beaches, the hills, and everywhere else. We will counterattack them savagely with the armor we've stored for such a purpose."

Himmler took a deep breath and appeared to relax. "Ah yes, the reserve army. And who will you place in command? Rommel?"

Rundstedt shook his head. "Although Rommel's health has largely returned, there are questions regarding his, say, reliability and temperament following the injury. It's been decided that Dietrich will command the army while Rommel continues to mend."

Himmler nodded thoughtfully. There had been suspicions about Rommel's loyalty to Hitler and the Reich, and Rundstedt seemed to be taking them into consideration with the appointment of the fifty-three-year-old Lieutenant General Sepp Dietrich, a long-time and loyal member of the SS. The decision pleased him. The SS was finally getting its due as a military organization alongside and equivalent to the regular army.

Rundstedt smiled and continued. "There is also the fact that Rommel and I disagreed on how to defend against the Allies when they invaded at Normandy. In my opinion, the arguments confused the issue and delayed our response. This time we shall speak with one voice, mine, and we will react appropriately, and not in a piecemeal and confused manner."

Himmler winced. It was yet another criticism of the late Fuhrer. Someday, von Rundstedt and the rest of his arrogant coterie would be brought to justice for their actions and statements, but not this day. His and the skills of the others were needed.

"Reichsfuhrer, you must understand that we will get only one chance to make the Americans wish to stop. We have no margin for error and, therefore, cannot afford to make any mistakes."

"I do understand, Field Marshal," Himmler said.

"Now, I have a question for you, Reichsfuhrer. What the devil is the situation in America regarding Roosevelt?"

Himmler laughed. "As usual, the intelligence service under Admiral Canaris is awful. We are in large part relegated to reading two-week old American newspapers delivered via diplomatic pouch from the Swedish and Spanish embassies, or to listening to equally heavily censored broadcasts on American radio. The only thing that is certain is that the Jew Roosevelt is ill, perhaps deathly ill. Our Swedish, Swiss, and Spanish diplomatic contacts in Washington insist that America is concerned that FDR might be dying, or even dead. We may know for certain when their inauguration takes place on January 20. Idiotically, the Americans say they cannot postpone it."

Rundstedt actually smiled. "What if they give an inauguration and nobody shows up?"

Moments after Rundstedt left Himmler's office, Otto Skorzeny stalked in. As usual, he looked like a feral animal and Himmler suppressed a shudder.

"What is the latest on Heisenberg's bomb?"

Skorzeny smiled ghoulishly. "Apparently it is going surprisingly well and should be ready in a couple of months, which is good since it will have to be delivered by truck and the roads to Russia won't be passable until then."

"Excellent."

Russia was currently out of the war but could come back in at any time that Stalin decided was to Russia's advantage. Russia had to be permanently out of the war and soon.

"Reichsfuhrer, I understand you've been informed about the lingering effects of radiation. Does that change anything?"

Himmler shook his head vigorously. "Of course not. In fact, it makes things better. The more people who die and the longer and more agonizingly it takes for death to happen, they better off we are. No, lingering radiation is a wonderful secondary effect of the bomb."

Skorzeny was not surprised. Himmler had so much blood on his hands that a new way of killing would be a good idea to him. Of course, he thought, his own hands weren't clean either.

"Skorzeny, I'm puzzled. You say you are going to deliver the bomb by truck? What will the Russians do about that?"

Skorzeny grinned wolfishly. "Why, they will bend over backwards to help me."

There were times when Alfie and the two Jews thought they were going to die and other times when they were certain of it. They had found a small cave and lined it with brush and anything they thought would keep out the cold. They blocked the entrance and hunkered down to wait out the winter in a tiny underground room that afforded them no privacy and, as it turned out, damned little warmth. As the snows piled up and the temperature dropped, they knew they had to do something else.

Alfie had solved one problem—he had managed to

find some abandoned suitcases filled with clothing that had been discarded by refugees. Why they dropped the suitcases he didn't know and didn't care. The warm clothing was priceless and they wore it in bulky layers. Perhaps equally important, it enabled the Jews to discard their prison rags and Alfie to change out of a British Army uniform. The Jews gleefully abandoned their rags, but Alfie kept his uniform after hiding it. He hoped that someday he would be able to put it back on and wear it with pride. He did make sure that each man had at least one weapon. The Jews each got a Luger while Alfie kept the rifle.

Even more important than fighting the cold was finding food. Food would provide some of the energy needed to combat the brutal weather. Rosenberg and Blum had proven surprisingly resourceful when it came to catching small game, but how far could a rabbit stretch? And cooking it on a small fire outdoors took forever. They couldn't start a large fire for fear it would attract notice and usually wound up regularly eating nearly raw rabbit meat.

The two former concentration camp inmates were weakened already and required more food to regain their health. They didn't complain. Being free still made them euphoric and they worked harder than Alfie thought possible. They spent time teaching German to Alfie while improving their own English. Still, it wouldn't be long before they weakened and death overtook them.

Finally, good fortune found them. Deep in the woods they found a small wooden cabin piled with snow. It was in a gully and they almost missed it. Even though there was no sign of life, they approached it with their weapons at the ready.

They could not see through the windows which, while filthy, were intact. There was no fire and no sign of life. They tried the door and pushed it opened. Inside, they found a two-room cabin. The part they entered was a combination kitchen and living room while the second was a bedroom. They entered the bedroom and gasped. A mummified body lay on the floor by the bed.

"Jesus," said Alfie. "I wonder what the hell happened to him."

They took a close look at the corpse. The parchmentlike skin stretched over bones, and wisps of white hair showed through the scalp, indicating that the body was that of an older man. Incongruously, the remains of a Hitler style mustache remained on his lip.

Rosenberg smiled. "Probably a heart attack and that's good for us. Notice that he's wearing a nightshirt and he's alone. Also note that he's been lying there a very long time in order to turn into a mummy, which means that nobody comes here to check on him. He's probably a hermit or woodsman or a recluse that nobody misses, if they even knew he was here in the first place."

Alfie grinned. "And that means we can move in here without having to worry about nosy neighbors."

Blum found some newspapers that were more than two years old, which reinforced the idea that no one was likely to come to the cabin. It was well hidden and sheer chance, or divine intervention as Blum said, had led them to find it.

Blum started checking the closet and a pair of chests. They were filled with clothing. The dead man seemed about normal size and none of the three was exceptional, so they cheerfully added more layers to their clothing. Even though there was no fire in the cabin, they already felt warmer then they'd been in weeks. The cabin was sturdily built and kept out the wind. Rosenberg thought the snow piled up outside acted as insulation.

They also found a pair of shotguns and a couple of boxes of shells to add to their arsenal.

Shelves in the kitchen were stacked with canned food. Rosenberg almost broke down. "If we're careful, we can live for weeks on this, and I don't care if it isn't Kosher."

"Just so it isn't rotten," Alfie said.

"Who cares if it's rotten?" Blum laughed. "We've eaten worse, or have you forgotten?"

Alfie gestured towards the corpse. "What do we do with Adolf here?"

Blum frowned. "The ground's frozen, so a decent burial is out of the question. Too bad. Even if he is a Nazi, he deserves it for possibly saving our lives."

Rosenberg shook his head. "What we should do is dress him in his own clothing and drag his corpse several miles from here. When the spring thaw comes, someone may find him and bury him."

"So why the hell dress him up?" Alfie asked.

Rosenberg smiled. "If he's found in his nightshirt, people might get suspicious as to why he was wandering around the woods dressed like that. Clothed, they'll think he had an accident and then bury what's left after the animals are through with him."

Alfie shuddered at the thought of woodland creatures nibbling on his body. On the other hand, their chances of surviving the winter had just taken a big jump upwards. However, they knew that surviving the coming spring might be even more difficult than making it through the winter.

"Comes the thaw," Alfie said, "we are likely to be in the middle of the biggest fucking battle in the history of mankind."

"I won't mind," said Rosenberg and Blum nodded. "Just so long as we're on the right side and maybe, just maybe, we'll get a chance to do something about it."

Alfie looked over at the wide bed. "Three of us gonna sleep in that?"

Blum chuckled. "I hope so. Of course, you realize that if you sleep with us for more than a week, you'll become Jewish."

Alfie looked up, shocked. "You're joking."

Blum roared with laughter. It felt good. "Yes, Alfie, I am."

★ CHAPTER 19 ★

JESSICA'S SUPERVISOR WAS A PLEASANT AND PLUMP woman in her forties named Turnbull. She was a formal but friendly Brit and nobody knew her first name. Maybe she didn't have one, they joked. Another British girl said everything in England was rationed, so maybe first names were as well. They presumed she was married so they all called her Mrs. Turnbull. Turnbull neither commented nor corrected them, simply smiling contentedly.

When Jessica arrived, Mrs. Turnbull waved her into her small and tidy office. "Things are changing, Jessica, I need to ask you some questions regarding your future with us."

Jessica tried to keep from showing her surprise. Had she done something wrong? She did not want to be sent back in disgrace especially since she couldn't think of anything she might have done, or anyone she might have offended. Had the situation with Monique and her thieving boyfriend come to haunt her?

Turnbull continued. "Because of all the fighting in and around Paris, it's been decided that we're going to break up into smaller parts and get out of here. Tell me, do you have any problems dealing with Germans?"

"Not really," she said, relieved. "I guess we all knew the time would come when we would have German refugees. I'm just a little surprised that you're inferring that the time is now. I guess I should have realized it since we conquered the Rhineland."

"Correct. We are moving a group of our people into the suburbs of the occupied German city of Aachen. The city itself is pretty well ruined, but I've been informed that there are suitable places on the outskirts and in suburbs just outside the city. We believe it is far enough from the Rhine to be safe and, incredibly enough, its being in Germany might just render it safer than France. At least we won't have DeGaulle and the communists fighting each other to contend with."

"Indeed," Jessica said.

Turnbull grinned. "And you'll be several hundred miles closer to your paramour."

Jessica laughed. "He isn't my paramour, at least not yet."

"I realize this will cause some complications, so take the rest of the day off, pay your bills, and get packed. Inform your roommate, Monique, that I'll help her get situated once you leave, and I'd like you to leave as quickly as possible. By the way, you'll be heading up a section there, so take one of our cars. You'll need it in Aachen."

Jessica took the long way home, electing to visit her uncle, who was also glad she was leaving Paris and then informed her that much of SHAEF was also heading for Aachen instead of Rheims, France, as originally planned. A token office would remain in Paris to keep French honor satisfied, but again there was the irony that it was safer with former Nazi enemies than with French allies as the civil war raged. There had been no serious fighting in Paris for the past several days, but that didn't mean it couldn't flare up in an instant. Nor would her Red Cross uniform necessarily protect her. A number of innocent bystanders had been swept up in the fighting and several had been killed.

Tom Granville could tell her little about the progress of the war except the obvious—everything was on hold because of the winter weather. "Not exactly a military secret," he said.

Nor could he tell her anything about FDR's health since he didn't know, a question everyone wanted answered. FDR was alive and apparently improving, but how healthy was he? It was becoming as obvious as the bad weather that his health problems went far beyond his contracting a simple case of the flu.

Her uncle did say that it was possible that GI's would be given leave time. "Until then," he said, "I don't think we can pull that chewing out trick again to bring young Captain Morgan to you."

Jessica was in good spirits as she arrived at the apartment. Being in charge of a group would be better than just being a clerk. She was confident she could handle the job and the fact that it would bring her closer to Jack was a legitimate bonus. The only difficulty she foresaw was telling Monique that she'd have to find a new place to stay. She hoped Mrs. Turnbull really could help her out, but, if she couldn't, then there always was the women's barracks.

Jessica turned the knob and entered. A hand clamped down on her mouth and she was thrown to the floor, knocking the wind out of her. Strong arms grabbed her and tied her hands behind her back, and a cloth was stuffed into her mouth. She was dragged into her bedroom and thrown onto the bed.

Jessica blinked. She thought she might have blacked out for an instant. Her chest hurt from where she'd slammed into the floor, but the pain was receding. She looked around and saw Monique looking down on her. Standing beside her was Monique's former lover, Charley Boyle.

"You idiot," Monique said to her. "Why did you have to come home now? Promise you won't scream and I'll remove the gag."

Jessica nodded and her mouth was freed. Monique gave her a glass of water but did not untie her.

"I guess you two are back together again," Jessica said dryly. "But what about Charley's status with the army? He's still a thief and a deserter, isn't he?"

"Nothing's changed," Monique said, "except that I'm going with him."

"Why?"

Monique shrugged. "Because I love him, and he takes care of me. You should also know that I've been his banker regarding all the things he's taken and sold. We hid twenty thousand dollars in the attic of this building, and now the two of us will take it and disappear. That kind of money will last a long time and give us a good start on a new life."

Charley laughed harshly. "It's not like we have a choice. The French cops and the MP's are looking for me along with some of my associates. Seems that some of the penicillin I sold turned out to have gone bad and now they want their money back. I didn't know it had to be stored carefully."

Jessica was stunned. Had bad medicine killed GI's? She had another thought. "Monique, but what about your son?"

Charley roared. "What son? Did you ever see him? That was all made up by Monique get your sympathy. And don't worry about my fat wife and her dumb kids back home in the States. They can go screw themselves blind for all I care."

Jessica sadly admitted to herself that she had never seen Monique's son. She just assumed he existed because Monique said he did.

Even Monique laughed. "I used that story to make you feel sorry for me and give me a job. I never dreamed it would work out as well as it has. Before I found you and Charley, I was a prostitute, and, yes, I did sleep with Germans. This war has provided me with a lot of opportunities and I'm taking them."

Jessica sagged. She had been a complete fool. Monique had lied to her from the moment she first opened her mouth. But what would happen to her now? She was tied up and helpless. Were they planning to kill her? After all, she knew all about them. But did she? She had no idea where they were going and what identities they might use.

"Don't worry," Monique said. "We'll leave you here, unharmed. The police probably know more about us than you do, so there's really nothing you can tell them except the obvious, that we've gone away. We'll disappear, change our names, and move on, right, Charley?"

Charley grinned. She felt even more uncomfortable the way he was looking down at her. "That's right, baby."

Monique patted her on the cheek. "Killing you is not only unnecessary, but something neither of us wants to do. Stealing is one thing, murder another. Consider yourself lucky, though. By the way, thank you for bringing that car with the Red Cross on it. It'll solve a lot of problems. We'll load it up and drive off and then simply disappear. Nobody will stop a Red Cross car."

With that she took a suitcase and left Charley to watch her. For the first time, she noticed a .45 automatic in the back of his belt. His expression changed and he glared at her.

"Y'know, I've always hated people like you. Rich bitches, officer's kids, officer's pussy. People like you don't even notice enlisted men, no matter how many stripes I have or how much experience I have. We're just part of the furniture to you."

"Not true. I've always respected you."

"Bullshit. You tolerated me. You know what else I hate? Teenage lieutenants giving me orders, that's what. Some of those young pricks are still in diapers, yet they're in charge. Ain't right. Used to be the army was for men, not for little kids."

He stood over her and leered. "Here's something to remember me by."

He put the rag back in her mouth and then tore her blouse apart. He pulled her bra over her breasts and she whimpered from the pain.

"Not bad," he said, fondling them as she tried to pull away.

Charley laughed and pushed her slacks down and

pulled her thighs apart. His hand slid inside her panties and began pawing her, hurting her.

Monica returned and pushed him aside. "Damn you, Charley, we don't have time for that. Take these packages and get down to that car."

Boyle laughed and did as instructed. Monique took the gag partway from Jessica's mouth. "You'll be able to spit it out in a bit. Then you can scream your little heart out and someone will probably find you before dark. Either that or you can crawl out the door and someone's bound to see you. Sorry it had to end this way, but that's life."

Monique disappeared out the door. Jessica lay there, working the gag. A moment later, she heard screams and the sound of popping. What now?

The door opened and an American MP entered, his gun drawn. "Oh shit," he said on seeing her. He threw a blanket over her and checked the other room, finally holstering his weapon. He took a knife and cut her bonds.

"What is happening?" Jessica asked, anxiously as she rearranged her clothing under the blanket. Another man entered and she recognized him as Major Harmon, one of the Provost Marshal types who'd questioned her before. She heard the unique squeal of Parisian sirens coming from the street below.

"Sorry this had to happen, Miss Granville," said Harmon, "but we've been watching this place for several weeks and were about ready to rush in when we saw Boyle. But then we saw you go in and wondered what the hell was going on."

"You thought I was part of it?" she said, clutching the blanket closer.

"Yep. Not anymore, though."

Jessica stood and took a deep breath. She made it down the stairs without help, even though she thought she knew what she would find.

Monique lay on the floor by the door. A medic was treating her for gunshot wounds in her chest and leg. Monique's face was pale, her eyes unfocused and rolled back in her head.

Jessica felt unsteady and Major Harmon took her arm. "She actually pulled a pistol on us," he said. "If she lives, she'll spend a long time in a French jail, maybe forever. Not so for Boyle."

Charley Boyle lay on his back on the sidewalk. A cloth covered his face. Blood had poured from wounds in his skull and run down the sidewalk and into the gutter.

"He could have surrendered," said the OPMG officer. "But I guess he couldn't abide the thought of spending the rest of his life in a federal prison. Tough."

What a waste, she thought. Charley's family was destroyed and Monique would spend much, if not all, of her life in prison, assuming she recovered.

Harry Truman took the oath of office as Vice President in FDR's residence in the White House on Saturday, January 20, 1945. Eleanor was present, looking even more somber and gloomy than she usually did. Fewer than a dozen dignitaries were present at the low-key event. All plans for a gala were cancelled. The public was informed that the President was too ill to attend, although he was steadily improving. After the swearing in, Truman wondered if the poor man was alive enough to be cognizant of where he was and what was happening.

Chief Justice Stone administered the oath to the four-term President. FDR did not speak. He merely nodded to questions regarding whether he would preserve and protect the Constitution. His eyes were glassy and his breath was shallow. His cheeks were sunken and his skin was gray. This is a farce, Truman thought.

On the way out of the White House, Truman was intercepted by the departing Vice President, Henry Wallace.

"Best wishes, Harry, and I hope you are better prepared to step in than I was. At least Franklin lived long enough to prevent me from becoming President, which I think was one of his goals. I don't think he will accomplish that regarding you."

Nor do I, Truman thought.

"By the way, Harry, I understand there's a strategy meeting tomorrow morning at ten in the Executive Office Building. Have you been invited?"

Truman bristled. He had not. What the hell had happened to the idea that he would be informed and involved? He would see about that.

Promptly at ten the next morning, the uninvited Truman strode forcefully into the conference room. He loved the look of surprise on everyone's faces. "What is the problem, gentlemen? Or had you forgotten I existed and, more important, that I am the Vice President who will shortly become President and commander in chief?"

Jim Byrnes responded angrily. "That's presumptuous, Harry. Franklin's still alive."

"Is he?" Truman retorted. "Yesterday, a breathing corpse began his fourth term as President. He was barely present at the occasion. Was he conscious, or was somebody pulling his strings like he was a puppet? And since when did we use a Ouija Board to determine presidential responses?"

Byrnes stood and glared, his face was turning red as his Irish temper showed. "That is disgusting and I demand an apology."

Truman returned his glare. "And I demand one for being ignored. Who the hell decided not to include me, Franklin or you people?"

Truman looked at those assembled. Along with Byrnes were Marshall, Admiral King, and the secretaries of defense and navy. No one answered, although he thought he detected quiet amusement in the eyes of the unflappable Marshall.

"Gentlemen," Truman continued, "with the exception of me, no one in this room is elected to public office. Therefore, no one besides me is entitled to run this nation."

"You're forgetting that FDR still lives," Byrnes said softly. His choler was receding.

"Once again, does he? Gentlemen, I'll give you a most unpleasant choice. You immediately accept the fact that I am the surrogate President, or I will go to federal court tomorrow and file suit alleging that Roosevelt is mentally incompetent and unable to serve as President."

"Justice Stone will put a stop to that," Byrnes said, but he was clearly uneasy at the prospect. Just what would the Chief Justice really do? Chief Justice Stone was a law unto himself. Nobody knew for certain what he would decide. Besides, he thought, Truman had a point. Was FDR mentally competent or not? Why the devil was the Constitution so silent on the question of a disabled president?

"If Stone does try to stop me, I guarantee you that I will speak to the press. The *Chicago Daily Tribune* has always hated FDR and would be glad to assist me." The *Tribune* hated Roosevelt enough to have printed military secrets and almost been prosecuted for the fact.

Byrnes looked at Truman with growing respect. "You wouldn't dare. You would be jeopardizing the war effort."

"If you don't believe I'd dare, watch me. And as to the war effort, you are jeopardizing it by the coup you are pulling off, however inadvertent it might be. We are a democracy and that cannot ever be forgotten."

General Marshall quietly but firmly injected himself into the discussion. "Vice President Truman is totally correct. We have, ah, accidentally overreached ourselves in our desire to protect the President and our country. Presidents have died in office before and doubtless will again. The country will go on regardless of what happens if and when FDR actually does pass on."

"Then it's conceded that his death is imminent?" Truman asked.

Byrnes shrugged. Anguish was evident on his face. "Ten minutes, ten days, ten months, Harry. Who the hell knows? And you and the general are right. You have to be here. In fact, the sooner you get totally up to speed, the better off we'll all be. I suggest that you give us direction as if you were receiving it from Roosevelt. No one here will question it because, you're right, it's something we have to do."

Truman smiled wickedly. "Does this mean you're

finally going to tell me what the hell's going on in New Mexico?"

"Young Corporal Snyder, what the hell is this thing you've just shoved under my nose?" Morgan said in an attempt at humor. He knew exactly what it was. Rumors of their existence had been circulating for some time now.

Snyder was not intimidated, but kept the conversation formal. "Sir, it's a petition. We're trying to get everyone in the army to sign it and we're going to collect them and send them to the White House."

"And what do you hope will happen?"

"Pardon my French, sir, but we hope to get this fucking war over with. It's been going on for long enough and there's no end in sight, and there's no reason to invade Germany if we can get them to negotiate a peace, just like they did the last time."

"Snyder, are you aware that the last peace resulted in the next war, the one we're fighting?"

"Which means that we have to do a better job ending this one, sir, and hopefully we've learned something from the past. Look, if we don't do this, we'll be confronting the biggest and bloodiest battle in American history and for what? Hitler is dead, and so are a lot of the Nazis who started this thing. It's time to settle the score and move on."

"What about the Jews in the concentration camps?" Morgan asked. "All those people are being murdered. Doesn't that mean something?"

"Sir, I hate to sound cruel or bigoted, but aren't almost all of them dead already and won't the rest of them die before they can be liberated? Maybe the peace negotiations can result in those who are left being sent to a neutral country. And besides, sir, how many Americans should have to die to liberate a handful of Jews?"

Morgan didn't have an answer to Snyder's comments because he was right. It was very likely that all the Jews in German camps would be dead long before they could be liberated. American dead versus living Jews—it was a hell of an equation.

"Are you aware that what you are doing is against military regulations?"

"Captain, there are tens of thousands of us organizing and circulating petitions and hundreds of thousands signing them. Do you really think it's feasible for the army to punish American citizens for exercising their rights of assembly and free speech?"

Again Morgan admitted that the corporal had a point. Even though many constitutional rights were suspended in the military, they didn't totally disappear and there was safety in numbers. As long as the signers and organizers did nothing overt, like fomenting mutiny or assaulting officers, they were fairly safe. Word had come from the top that the petitions were to be tolerated, which had outraged some of the officers and noncoms. People like Snyder might never be promoted, but that meant nothing to them. They wanted to go home. Hell, so did he.

The petitions were nothing new. They'd been circulating for a couple of months, although the arrival of Christmas seemed to have accelerated the process. Jack had to admit that Christmas for him in snowy, cold, and lonely Germany was incredibly depressing. So too was the fact that Jessica was closer but so far away.

"You know I'm not going to sign it."

"Didn't think you would, sir, but I had to ask. Some officers have, in case you're curious."

Jack grinned. "Ike?"

Snyder's stern facade cracked. "We're working on him, sir."

"So what happens when you send these in, assuming the army will let you, and nothing happens. What will you do when the time comes to cross the Rhine?"

Snyder took a deep breath. "I hope it doesn't come to that, although I have to admit it will probably happen. If we have to fight, everybody I've talked to says they will. Nobody's going to let anybody else down."

Snyder took the unsigned petition and left Morgan alone in the tent. Jack poured himself a cup of the black tar that passed for coffee in the army. The quiet revolution in the army was yet another item for concern. He sympathized with Snyder and all the others who simply wanted to go home, and he also sympathized with those like Levin who had relatives who'd disappeared into the maniacally evil beast that was Nazi Germany. The thought of the monsters who did that going unpunished and allowed to continue in charge of Germany was repugnant. Jack smiled at the thought of Snyder asking Captain Levin to sign the petition. It wouldn't happen. Snyder wasn't that crazy.

To further complicate matters, he'd received another letter from Jessica. She and three others had made it to Aachen where they were setting up a refugee information center. She mentioned that the military police had arrested her friend Monique and that Monique's friend, Master Sergeant Boyle, had been killed. Reading in-between the lines, Jack had come to the conclusion that Jessica had been involved in the operation and it chilled him. Jessica should not have been in danger. What the hell was this world coming to when soldiers circulate peace petitions and women working for the Red Cross are put in danger?

How many thousand years ago was it when he played football for Michigan State and his primary concerns were wondering which hole to hit, which classes needed more study, and which coeds would go out with him?

Someday he might go back to civilian life, but neither he nor anyone else in the military would ever be the same, especially those who'd killed and seen their comrades killed or maimed.

Nor, he realized, would Jessica. Damn. The world was changing way too fast.

Carter got out of the Jeep and stared at the vast storage depot. Rows of vehicles of all kinds, tracked and wheeled, along with enormous stacks of materiel, seemed to stretch to the horizon. Out of sight but just as huge were stockpiles of gasoline, diesel and other material deemed flammable or explosive; thus requiring special storage facilities away from the other items.

Located a little more than twenty miles from the Rhine, the depot was considered out of the range of German artillery and it was protected by American fighters who maintained patrols overhead and were aided by radar that could usually pick up a German plane from far away.

The depot was surrounded by barbed wire, and grim-faced MP's patrolled the perimeter. The depot was in occupied Germany and the army was taking no chances with saboteurs. Germany was still hostile territory. Some

GI's had taken to referring to the Rhineland Germans as Apaches and the Rhineland as a reservation.

Carter, Morgan, and the others all had to show ID and their orders at several layers of security before gaining admission to the supply depot that was more of a city than a storage facility.

And it was only one of a number of similar sites filling up with materiel in anticipation of the dreaded Rhine crossing.

"This must've been what it was like in England just before D-Day," Carter said. "I heard jokes that the island almost sank under the weight of all the GI's and supplies. Now I believe it."

"You weren't in England?" Jack asked.

"Nah, most of us came straight over from New Jersey, which is why we didn't go into combat right away. They didn't think we were ready. As it turned out, they were right."

Morgan wondered if there were any landing craft in the depot. He couldn't see any, but that didn't mean a thing. The presence of landing craft would confirm the rumor that at least part of the assault on what the krauts called the Rhine Wall would come from their area. What joy, they all thought at the prospect.

"I wonder why the Germans don't lob their V-rockets at this site. It's not like they could miss it," Jeb asked.

"Why don't you go ask them?" Morgan teased.

Actually, he thought he knew why. The rockets were terribly inaccurate and might not find the depot. Also, the warheads weren't all that large, which meant any explosion, unless it was a direct hit on a large supply of ammo or fuel, wouldn't accomplish all that much. And, even if they did hit something that went boom, losses could be made up fairly quickly. The United States, as the Arsenal of Democracy, was going full bore, pouring out an incredible stream of supplies. The air force was also doing a marvelous job of making life miserable for the Germans who had to manufacture and then launch the abominable rockets.

A guide in a lead Jeep turned left and they followed, passing a long line of replacement Sherman tanks. Finally, they stopped and Jeb gazed in wonder.

"Look at that," he said. "Aren't they just too beautiful for words?"

Jack laughed. "Tanks are not beautiful. In fact most sane people would think they're kind of ugly."

"Okay, asshole, so they're not beautiful in a Betty Grable sort of way, but they are sinister and beautiful in a sexy life-saving sort of way."

All the officers and enlisted men left their Jeeps and trucks and gazed in combinations of wonder and delight at the metal behemoths lined up to greet them.

They were all Pershing M26 tanks. A Captain Powell from the depot checked their orders and officiously confirmed everything. He was slightly overweight like most supply soldiers, which this time was not resented by the men of the 74th.

Carter patted the hull of one of the tanks and grinned. "Not quite as big or as fast as a Panther, but, damn, there's that big, beautiful 90mm main gun that's badder than a Panther, even a T34 if the rumors that the Germans have some are true."

The tank also had a .50 caliber and two .30 caliber machine guns. It carried a crew of five and had a gas engine. Carter counted twelve of the tanks.

Carter continued to smile. "These are all ours, right?"

"Just be careful with them and don't scratch them up," Powell said, proving he had a sense of humor. "They don't have to be whitewashed or otherwise camouflaged since the krauts already know they're here. Probably every third German in the area is a spy and has seen them come in by train. After all, they are kind of hard to hide."

Sirens went off and Powell guided them to a trench, which they entered almost casually. All over the area, soldiers were doing the same thing.

"It's just a Jerry on a recon flight," Powell said as he lit a cigarette. "They do that almost every day. If they would be so kind as to make it a scheduled stop, we might be able to ambush the bastard. Otherwise they're just too damn fast."

A Nazi jet streaked across the sky and disappeared as quickly as it had arrived. A couple of American planes appeared to give chase, but they lost ground with each passing second. No bombs were dropped.

"What is he up to?" Carter asked.

"I assume he's taking pictures," Jack answered before Powell could respond.

They climbed out of the trench. "There's a school of thought," Powell said, "that we should let them take all the pictures they want just to show them what they're up against. However, I don't think they'll scare very easily."

Morgan didn't think so either. "So, the Seventy-Fourth gets twelve of these. Who gets the rest?"

Powell looked surprised. "What rest? This is it. Didn't you know?"

"Wait," said Carter. "You telling me that this is all the Seventy-Fourth gets?"

Powell laughed. "To the best of my knowledge, this

is all the entire First Army gets. For some reason, Patton's Third Army doesn't want any, and we aren't sharing with the frogs, of course. There will be more, but, for the time being, these are all the Pershings in Europe. Congratulations, Captains, but you are it when it comes to taking on German armor."

Heinrich Himmler did not like to leave Berlin and the perceived safety of the Chancellery building. Even though it had been the target of Allied bombers on several occasions, luck had held and damage was still minimal. Of course, if he wished to, he could retreat to Hitler's vast underground bunker system. Himmler had considered that option but dismissed it. The place was damp and depressing, and moving underground smacked of cowardice. He would not move there until and unless it became absolutely necessary.

Himmler and a small entourage traveled at night and in his private armored train, hiding on sidings during the day. They made it safely to the outskirts of Frankfurt. The city center had been badly bombed; thus, no suitable and secure facilities were available for him. Himmler needed no further reminders that Allied bombers and fighters ruled the skies.

They left the train and traveled by car to an estate once owned by a long ago disappeared Jewish family and now run by the SS as a rest area. Tomorrow, he would take a brief drive to the Rhine Wall. Himmler didn't want to, but Goebbels had convinced him that pictures of him with soldiers at the front would help with morale. Rundstedt added that viewing the defenses firsthand would help him understand just what the military was confronting.

Himmler was very nervous and worked hard to hide it. He didn't like being so close to the enemy. He felt that men who were very brave often wound up very dead. While he did not think of himself as a coward, he felt that his place was in Berlin, organizing and running the Third Reich and not anywhere near the front lines.

He met with von Rundstedt and his staff, along with the Luftwaffe's Galland and Canaris the spymaster. They assembled in a dining room that could have doubled as a medieval banquet hall. Himmler thought it was far too nice for a Jew to have ever owned.

"What happened to the people who lived here?" he whispered to an aide.

"Bought their way out before the war and went to Brazil."

Himmler smiled. They had paid dearly for their lives. Excellent. Their money had helped fund Hitler. Belatedly, Himmler had come to the realization that it would have been far better to have allowed all the Jews to buy their way out, rather than the politically messy results of the Final Solution in places like Auschwitz. Of course, many countries, including the falsely pious United States, had closed their doors to Jewish emigrés. Hypocrites all, he thought.

"I would like you to see some of these photos, Reichsfuhrer," Rundstedt said. "These were just taken by pilots flying over American lines."

Varner handed them over. Himmler nodded briefly as he tried to identify objects on the ground. "What am I looking at?"

"A number of things," said Rundstedt. "First, these are pictures of several incredibly vast supply depots that the Americans are building up in anticipation of the invasion of Germany. They are spread up and down the length of the Rhine, which gives us no clue as to their intended target. Still, look at the enormous number of tanks and other armored vehicles, which include a handful of a new and very large tank that we believe is their Pershing. It is designed to counter the Panther."

Himmler sniffed. "A handful? That is hardly a threat."

"At one point there were only a handful of their dreadful Shermans," Rundstedt said acidly, "and now there are tens of thousands, and that will be the case with this new tank within a year from now. And I'm certain it will be better than the Sherman since the Americans almost always learn from their mistakes."

Himmler nodded. "Then the war must be over sooner. Now, what is this?" he asked as he picked up other photos.

Varner pointed. "These are the American defenses along the Rhine. They aren't very deep and they aren't well hidden. They know we can do nothing about them and that we don't have the capability to counterattack across the river."

"Which brings us to a point, Herr Himmler," Rundstedt said, intentionally not using his rank. "There is one important thing missing from all these photos and that is landing craft. The Americans will require hundreds of them to cross the river in force. Either they aren't there yet, or they are very well hidden. It is also possible that the craft are still in France, or even in England, and will be moved to the Rhine at the last minute."

Himmler turned to Canaris. "Well?"

"Our sources in either country say nothing, although I will push them for more intelligence," the admiral answered. "However, please recall that on January 9 the Americans landed in the Philippines in force. This must have required a large number of the platoon-sized landing craft called LCVI's, many of which would have to be transported here if they are going to be used in a crossing."

"Could they do it without those craft?" Himmler inquired.

"With great difficulty," Rundstedt answered. "Their only other option would be to use hundreds, perhaps thousands, of truly small boats and we've scoured both sides of the Rhine for anything that could float and be used. During our withdrawal, we destroyed any craft we found along all of the rivers. While we can't totally discount the possibility of them making small craft locally, I don't think it's feasible. No, I think they will have to have landing craft."

"What about paratroops?" Himmler asked.

Rundstedt laughed. "We almost wish they would. Intelligence says they have five airborne divisions, four American and one British. The British division is being rebuilt after the disaster at the Seine. We are well prepared for a paratroop attack, although, again, they would have to have large numbers of transports and gliders to fly such a horde and there are no indications that they exist in such quantities."

Himmler walked to the stone fireplace where a pile of logs burned. The warmth felt good.

"Who took the pictures?"

Galland smiled. "Some of our brave pilots flying our jet fighters, which were configured to be photographic platforms."

"If our jets can cross American bases with such

impunity, why don't we drop bombs on them?" Himmler asked.

Galland flushed. "Our jet is not designed to carry bombs. Hitler originally wanted it used as a long-range bomber, but it would have been able to carry only a small bomb load, so the idea was scrapped. In the final analysis, it was not considered feasible or even useful."

Himmler understood. Once again the military had changed Hitler's directive after his death, and his field marshals and admirals had all said it was for the good. Still, it galled him to have the finest army in the world and no air force to protect it. Galland had insisted, and Rundstedt had concurred, that the Americans and British had such vast fleets of planes that what remained of the Luftwaffe would be overwhelmed. The respite caused by winter would allow for the production of what would have been a large number of planes just a few years earlier, but the Americans' ability to produce weapons of all kinds and in such huge quantities had been a staggering and unwelcome discovery. For every plane or tank Germany produced, America turned out a half dozen.

Himmler smiled at Galland. The situation wasn't his fault. "I am certain that all your pilots will do their best."

Galland accepted the gesture. Yes, they would do their best with too few planes and too few pilots. Now that there was a cease-fire on the Eastern Front, pilot training had commenced in German occupied areas of Poland. Hopefully, they were far enough away to keep the Americans from shooting down the trainees, and, as long as the Russians stayed back, the trainees would have time to learn their craft. The Luftwaffe would fly and die for the Reich. They had no other choice.

★ CHAPTER 20 ★

PRIVATES FEENEY AND GOMEZ WALKED SLOWLY through the 74th's motor pool. The ground was slushy and churned up from a multitude of trucks and tanks. Care had to be taken to not trip and fall into the mess. A light, wet snow was falling, barely covering the ground.

They were on guard duty, protecting the trucks and tanks of the 74th, but neither man was taking things all that seriously. It was, after all, the dead of winter and they were well away from the Rhine, which the krauts couldn't cross in the first place. Even so, their weapons were loaded and they kept an eye out. There might not be any krauts around, but there were officers who might try to catch them goofing off.

Captain Morgan had warned them to be on the lookout for saboteurs or spies, but neither man thought it was likely a Nazi could get this far. To keep themselves alert and pass the time, they teased each other.

"How many more rosaries, Feeney?"

"Maybe six hundred, damn it. Hey, don't you Mexies say one each day? Maybe you and your Mexican buddies could say some for me."

"Feeney, how many times I gotta tell you, we ain't Mexican any more than you're an Irishman. I'm from California and you're from Boston. In fact, my ancestors were in California long before your people came over from Ireland, and they were literate long before your people knew what writing was about."

"Screw you," Feeney said genially, happy that he'd gotten to his friend. If you had to walk around a lonely motor pool in the cold and snow, then it was good to be with a buddy.

Gomez grabbed Feeney's arm. "What the hell, tracks."

The only tracks they'd seen in the new snow while on their rounds were their own. This fresh set of tracks was clearly somebody new. It was either saboteurs or some prick of an officer trying to trap them. The two men looked at each other and began to follow the tracks. As one, they shifted their rifles off their shoulders so they could be fired.

They turned a corner and were confronted by a row of the new M26 tanks. The footprints disappeared in between them. They could hear muffled sounds of someone working on a tank. Maybe it was a mechanic with a job to do, or maybe it was something else, something sinister. They walked farther and saw a man on the hull and crouching behind a turret.

"Watcha doin' there, buddy," Feeney said. He was supposed to say "halt" and "who goes there," but that sounded dumb. After all, the guy wasn't moving.

"Maintenance," came the answer.

"Now?" said Gomez. "In the middle of the fucking night? Maybe you should come down here so we can see you."

"Hey, don't get your horses in an uproar."

Feeney stared at Gomez. Horses in an uproar? Fuck. They pointed their rifles at the shape. "Get your ass down now!" Feeney snarled.

"Coming," the man said, and then slipped and fell off the tank. He rolled and came to his feet, a pistol in his hand. He snapped off a couple of shots. Gomez screamed and grabbed his face. Blood was gushing over his hand and, just then, Feeney felt something smash into his leg.

The son of a bitch is going to kill me, Feeney realized. He swung his rifle and pulled the trigger again and again. The attacker stumbled backwards and fell to the ground just as waves of pain reached Feeney's brain. As the world turned black, he wondered if he was dead.

He came to in a tent with Captain Morgan standing over him. "Welcome back, Feeney."

"How's Gomez?" Feeney asked. It was difficult to talk. His mouth felt fuzzy.

"Not good. He took a bullet in the face. He'll probably live, but he lost part of his jaw and one eye."

"Aw, Christ," Feeney said, then brightened. "Hey, it does mean he'll go home, doesn't it? Helluva price to pay, though. Jesus, he'll be going home with half a face."

"The man you shot is dead. No surprise, he was a German, complete with an SS tattoo. We found it a little above the inside of his left elbow. It also said gave us his blood type, which was useless information since he was already dead. I guess the rumors are true. They are trying to infiltrate English-speaking people behind our lines. This guy's job was to sabotage our tanks. He damaged a couple before you nailed him, but the tanks can all be repaired. And don't worry about your leg. You took a ricochet and you're just badly bruised."

"Good to hear, sir. But how the hell is Gomez going to live with half a face? Who would want to look at him? And, yeah, sir, I can't help but think that it could have been me who got shot."

Morgan had no real answer. "Couple of days' rest and you'll be as good as you ever were, which, some days, wasn't much," he teased and Feeney laughed. "Seriously, you did well, Feeney, I'll tell Father Serra I've suspended the remainder of your sentence."

Admiral Canaris sat nervously in front of Himmler. "Reichsfuhrer, Harry Truman is a complete nonentity. Our files on him are limited to nothing more than his age, sixty-one, and the fact that he is a farmer and a failed businessman from Missouri who somehow wound up as a United States senator and, even more improbably, as Vice President of the United States."

"Incredible," Himmler said, staring at a picture of a bespectacled Truman smiling vapidly at the camera. "Yet this is the man who will be succeeding Roosevelt if he dies."

"When Roosevelt dies, Reichsfuhrer. We believe his death is imminent. A few more things about Truman. He is married to a frumpy woman named Bess and they have an equally frumpy daughter named Margaret.

On the other hand, this Truman did serve in the First World War with some distinction as an artillery captain."

"What type of business?"

"We think it was men's clothing."

Himmler laughed. "A two-paragraph resume. Well then, can you tell me what he will do as a war leader?"

Canaris shrugged. "So little is known about him that we have no idea how he will react under stressful circumstances. However, his rise in American politics indicates willingness to compromise and his experience in combat might show that he understands what it is like to send men out to die."

Himmler shook his head. "In short, Admiral, you know absolutely nothing about the man."

"Correct, Reichsfuhrer. It is as if the postmaster of Potsdam is about to suddenly become Fuhrer of Germany. The situation is incredible, preposterous."

"Then he will be too inexperienced to be his own man. Will he be led by Churchill or someone in the American government, Marshall, for instance? And what about his future relations with Stalin? We must know these things and much more."

Canaris picked up his briefcase. "We are working on all of these matters. It is entirely possible that Stalin is as puzzled as we are. Churchill, however, must be salivating at the thought of dominating Truman."

Canaris departed. Himmler sat behind his desk and rubbed his eyes. Only the Americans could make such a mess of their politics. They were almost as bad as the French. But what the devil did all this mean for the future of the Third Reich? How would this Harry Truman react when the Rhine ran red with the blood of American soldiers, and how would he react when Moscow was wiped off the face of the earth by Heisenberg's bomb and the world realized that Germany had the power to destroy anyone and everything? A rational man would crumble at the prospect. But was Harry Truman rational?

And where would the Americans attack? Luftwaffe reconnaissance flights had not found any landing craft, nor had there been evidence of extraordinary troop buildups. Von Rundstedt had to know these things and Himmler shared that sense of urgency. And now they were confronted with the likelihood that a gray cipher named Harry Truman would shortly lead the armed forces of the mighty United States of America.

Himmler stared at the bad photo that showed a thin little man with a silly grin and cheap wire-rimmed glasses. The Postmaster from Potsdam indeed, Himmler thought and allowed himself a rare laugh. After all, hadn't he been a chicken farmer?

Jessica was called to the scene of the outburst by the military police. By the time she got there, just a couple of miles from the Red Cross's new offices, the violence had ceased, at least for a moment. An angry group of German women and old men confronted an equally old man and woman in terribly worn clothing who were clearly refugees. The couple stood bruised and bloodied, while the others glared at them.

Jessica found an American sergeant named Haney who appeared to be in charge. A pair of German policemen glared sullenly at the battered couple. "What's happened and why was I called here?"

"What we have, ma'am, is a property dispute. Do you speak German?"

"Only a little."

"Okay, I do and here's what's going on as much as I can tell. These two people said they lived in this house and that the house was theirs up until just before the war started. This other group represents a kraut family that says they bought the house from the German government; therefore, they say it belongs to them, and they have a deed for it."

Jessica understood the house's current desirability. It was almost undamaged. A couple of bullet holes in the outer wall were all that showed that a war had passed it by.

The sergeant laughed and gestured towards a belligerent couple in the crowd of Germans. "They say they've been paying taxes to Hitler on it for years so we can't take it from them. Maybe they can apply for a refund."

With the sergeant translating what she couldn't pick up, Jessica was able to ascertain that the German government had forced the couple, Jews named Strauss, to sell at a very low price and that the new owners did indeed actually buy the property from the Nazis. They said they had no idea who the previous owners were and had never seen them before. Haney said the story was believable.

The Strausses said they'd been in hiding in France since Hitler invaded and now wanted their home back. They insisted that the Nazis had stolen it from them and had forced them, literally at gunpoint, to sell.

The couple did speak passable French, which made it easier for Jessica to understand them. They'd been living in a cubbyhole in a farmhouse outside Marseille and had avoided being swept up by the Gestapo, because the family that had harbored them was able to keep their presence a secret.

"We are realistic," the old Jewish man said. "Now we know we can never come back here and live safely and peacefully. No one could protect us. You Americans would have to provide around the clock protection for the rest of our lives. No, all we want is some of our possessions that we managed to hide. When the Nazis forced us to sell, they gave us only an hour to pack and then searched us to make sure we weren't taking anything we shouldn't. Perhaps we will someday get proper compensation from a new German government, but I am not confident."

"How long will it take you to search for your property?"

"An hour at most and we will have to crack open a wall."

When Sergeant Haney explained this to the current owners, they became irate and exclaimed that anything in the house was theirs since they'd bought it legally. Jessica then sweetly asked them what it was they had bought and they, puzzled, couldn't respond.

"If you don't know what it is, you can't claim it as yours," she said.

Jessica had no idea if that would hold up in any court, but it sounded good and the Germans bought it. After all, she was the representative of the United States of America, wasn't she?

Haney told the Jewish couple to go in and sent two of his men to protect them and watch them. He told the Strausses to take as much time as they needed. The German owners again complained loudly until Haney stuck a submachine gun under their noses and spoke harshly. Jessica turned and stifled a grin. She knew enough German words to know he'd told them to shut their fucking mouths. Haney then went inside the house.

The sound of smashing wood lasted only a couple of moments. The Jewish couple emerged smiling and carrying a suitcase.

Haney grinned. "They had it hidden inside a wall and plastered it over before they had to leave. Some furniture hid it while it dried. Amazing nobody found it."

Jessica laughed. "Nobody ever claimed the Nazis were very smart."

Haney thought it would be fair play to confiscate the house, but decided not to. It was too far away from American facilities to be useful. Then he suggested taking a bulldozer and destroying the place, but again decided against it. Jessica thought it would be decades before all the legal squabbles about forced purchases would be settled and, even then, doubtless to nobody's satisfaction.

The Germans who'd bought the house could keep it, the Jewish couple told her. It was part of a hateful past and all they wanted now was a new future and the contents of the suitcase would start them on that road. They took her aside and opened the suitcase. Jessica gasped. It was full of paintings. She was no expert but she could read the signatures and recognized the styles. The top two were by Van Gogh. The couple said the others were by older masters and were even more valuable. They said they'd hidden it months before the house was taken from them so the paintings couldn't be plundered by looters.

Mr. and Mrs. Strauss were put in a Jeep and would be taken to a safe place. "It's going to take the wisdom of Solomon to settle some of these disputes," Jessica said.

Haney chortled. "In that case, the krauts are truly screwed."

"Why?"

"Wasn't Solomon Jewish?"

The Episcopal minister carefully and gently closed the eyes of the gray-skinned man who lay on the bed. He was so frail that he barely made a dent in the mattress. Franklin Delano Roosevelt was dead. Finally. His once strong body had given up a struggle it couldn't win.

Harry Truman trembled but nobody noticed. All eyes were on the body of the man who'd been President since 1932.

"The stress was too much," Jim Byrnes said.

Yes, Truman thought, and he was only beginning to feel the start of it. He was finally starting to comprehend the complexity and enormity of the worldwide war operation that FDR was running. Had been running, he corrected.

Truman left the bedroom and the grieving widow. Roosevelt's other relations, including his sons, would be arriving shortly. After seeming to reach a physical plateau, FDR had suddenly taken a sharp turn for the worse. Truman thought it was a blessing for the family and the nation. How long could they and it have endured with FDR in a coma?

Truman stepped outside and walked briskly, the only way he knew how to walk, to the Oval Office.

In the past few weeks, he'd avoided using it lest it seem like he was grasping for power. Now he needed to be there to show everyone that he was the man in charge.

He was aware of the eyes that were on him, ranging from marine guards to secret service to White House staffers and servants. The news had spread like wildfire and news bulletins, already prepared, were going out. The waiting and wondering were over. Harry Truman was the President of the United States and, he thought, the hell with Churchill and Himmler and Hirohito and Stalin and all the others. He would be his own man. They knew nothing about him and he thought it would give him a leg up on the opposition, both foreign and domestic.

He didn't want the job, hadn't asked for it, but, damn it, he would do it to the best of his ability.

★ CHAPTER 21 ★

"JESUS CHRIST," MORGAN THOUGHT IN DISBELIEF
as he read the mimeographed memo.

His hopes were dashed. There would be no leave
for him or any of the other troops confronting the
Nazis on the Rhine. The word had just come down
from Eisenhower and SHAEF that the situation would
not permit large numbers of American soldiers to
leave their stations for a little vacation. Of course, he
thought bitterly, those guys who were working behind
the lines probably got as much time off as they wished.
Once again, the combat trooper was getting fucked.

Realistically, he knew giving everyone leave was
impossible. Where would literally hundreds of thousands of GI's go, even if they got leave? France was
still in a state of chaos, and violence was an ongoing
possibility as the remnants of the communist uprising
fought on. Large numbers of soldiers taking leave in
the occupied Rhineland was also not possible. The
United States was still at war with Germany and the

German people simply could not be trusted. Again, how would the Rhineland, or any other European country, absorb so many hungry, horny and alcohol-deprived young men?

The notice said that the army would endeavor to make life a little more comfortable at the front. Beer would be provided and it wouldn't be the low alcohol piss they had been getting. Better, the nonfraternization rule was being relaxed to permit such "social, commercial, and cultural interactions with the German people as would be considered reasonable and in the military's best interests."

Jack and the others thought whoever at Ike's HQ had thought up that phrase must be laughing all the way to the officers' club. Social, commercial, and cultural interactions would obviously translate into screwing and drinking and paying for it.

The big disappointment was that he could not have a chance to see Jessica and they were both saddened. On the plus side, limited telephone service was now available and he'd managed to make several calls to her. He felt like a teenager who couldn't get a car and could only talk to his girlfriend by phone. It was great, however, to hear her voice, her laugh. He just wanted to reach out and grab her through the phone. He said it once and she giggled like a school kid and said it sounded like a good idea.

Not getting leave wasn't fair, he thought and was reminded by Jeb and Roy that life wasn't fair. "If it was," Roy said, "everybody would be Jewish."

"Or Southern," Jeb added with equal solemnity.

Miles away and in the suburbs of Aachen, Jessica came to a conclusion. If the mountain wouldn't come to Mohammed, she would go to the mountain. There was an opportunity to get much, much closer to where the 74th was stationed in and around Remagen. A large refugee camp had been set up near the small town of Reinbach and the Red Cross had heard bad things about it. Rumors of starvation and brutality, even rape, were being heard in Washington. Rumors also had German soldiers guarding the camp and keeping the refugees as prisoners. Mrs. Turnbull had asked for volunteers to go with her and see what was actually happening.

It didn't seem likely that the American army would countenance the creation of a concentration camp for refugees, but it would be checked out. Now all she had to do was let Jack know her schedule.

"We have been looking for clues and finally found them," Admiral Canaris exulted. "Many of the German people left behind when the Americans took the Rhineland have maintained their loyalty to the party and, once again, have provided us with the information we need."

High resolution photographs were projected onto a screen set up in Himmler's Chancellery office. "These were taken by General Galland's jets to confirm the reports," Canaris continued, "and show a large number of landing craft in the area known to be under Patton's control. As a result, we are confident that the American attack will be farther south at Coblenz and not at Bonn as was first thought."

The photographs clearly showed what were called LCVP, which stood for Landing Craft Vehicle/Personnel. Unofficially, they were often referred to as Higgins boats, after their designer, and were being made in the thousands. They could carry a full platoon at nine knots, had a crew of three, and had two machine guns.

"I believe they weigh nine tons and are launched from a mother ship, as was done at Normandy," said von Rundstedt. "How many are there, how did they get there and how will the Americans get them to the river?"

Varner stifled a smile. He had earlier raised the question with Rundstedt. Himmler looked intrigued.

"By rail," Canaris answered and changed photos. "Our sources documented them as they traveled from French ports to this spot in Patton's area. By the way, they counted far more than the number we've found. We are looking for the others.

"A spur line was built to this field where the boats are, well, parked," he continued. "The Yanks are building additional spurs from the staging area to the river where they will be launched."

Rundstedt nodded. "And how many landing craft did you say you found?"

"At least a hundred. But, as I said, we are looking for the others."

"Then let's assume you don't find any others," the field marshal said. "Instead, let's do the math. One hundred craft times fifty men if you stuff them in for a short journey, and you have five thousand men in their first wave. Since they will doubtless suffer casualties, perhaps eighty boats will be available for a second wave and sixty for a third and so on. They would be hard-pressed to land a full division before they ran out of landing craft."

Canaris flushed. He was not used to having his

data mocked. "It is the first such park we have found. There will doubtless be others. Besides, Field Marshal, I believe the Americans' intent would be to make a lodgment on the east bank of the Rhine and then build pontoon bridges. Therefore, a large number of landing craft might not be needed. I must remind you that the situation is so much different than what occurred last June when the Americans and Brits invaded in large numbers and with massive naval support. At that time, they also required far more landing craft and attacked on a very broad front, neither of which is necessary to cross the Rhine. Please recall that the Allied landing craft had to travel several miles each way, while the Rhine crossing would be less than one mile."

Rundstedt was unconvinced. "But will they land in the south and not north near Bonn? Admiral, I find nothing wrong with your assumptions; however, we must have accurate data. General Dietrich's Reserve Army must be on the move before the Americans attempt to cross. Right now nearly three quarters of a million soldiers and eight thousand tanks are scattered and hidden from American planes. If they are to succeed, we must provide them with every advantage possible."

They all understood that the hundreds of thousands of German soldiers weren't the highest quality, since the best remaining German infantry were dug in on the Rhine. However, the armor was of high quality, consisting of almost all available Panthers, Tigers, King Tigers, and, of course, the newly acquired and refurbished T34's.

Rundstedt continued. "Once Dietrich's army begins to move and converge on the American landing site, they will be vulnerable and we will suffer heavy casualties even before they reach the battle. If they have to move a second time because we guessed wrong, the results could be catastrophic. Even now Dietrich's soldiers are suffering from American planes as the Yanks either get smarter or luckier."

Canaris was about to respond when an aide entered and handed him a slip of paper. He read it, smiled, and turned to Himmler, who'd been quiet throughout the discussion.

"Reichsfuhrer, Field Marshal, we now have our answer. We have located two additional fields in Patton's area with large numbers of these LCVP's camouflaged and parked in neat rows alongside railroad spurs."

Himmler turned to Rundstedt. "Are you satisfied?"

"No, I am not," he said grimly, "but it is the best information we have. I can only remind everyone that the Americans used Patton as a decoy to fool us regarding their intentions at Normandy and how well it worked. We spent weeks waiting for an attack at the Pas de Calais that never occurred and involving an army that didn't exist."

"Surely they wouldn't do that again?" Himmler said, looking pained. "Patton is their best and most aggressive general. Would they be so insane as to hold him out a second time?"

Himmler stood and began pacing nervously. He fully understood that a wrong decision would be catastrophic for both him and the Reich. "No, we have to make a decision. Even though we all have doubts, I believe that the crossing attempt will come from Patton's Third Army and not Hodges' First and that it will be near Coblenz and not Bonn. Therefore, von Rundstedt, you can begin planning to move Dietrich's army south and not north."

Later, as Varner and von Rundstedt walked to their staff car, the field marshal said, "You're not pleased, are you, Varner? And by the way, congratulations on your promotion. It is well earned and long overdue. However, you are out of uniform."

Varner flushed. He'd received notice of his promotion to brigadier general earlier that morning and hadn't had a chance to change his insignia.

"Thank you, Field Marshal, and no, I am not pleased. It seems to me that the Americans went to great effort to let us find those landing craft."

Rundstedt snorted but seemed amused, not angry. "Go on."

"American planes rule the skies, yet we were able to overfly those areas without too much interference. And, why then did they do such a poor job of hiding those landing craft? And they surely must know that many of the Germans remaining in the Rhineland are spies."

Rundstedt paused. "Are you hinting that the Yanks will again use Patton, their best general, as a decoy?"

"I simply don't know, Field Marshal. But finding the landing craft does seem too pat, too easy. I believe we've found what the Americans wish us to find."

Rundstedt smiled grimly and tapped Varner on the shoulder with his field marshal's baton. "That kind of thinking is why you got promoted. Go find what we're not supposed to find, Varner, but do it soon."

"This is utter insanity," said Truman, now the thirty-third President of the United States. "Our soldiers are petitioning for us to negotiate a peace with the Germans?"

The President had a report saying more than half a

million GI's had so far signed the petitions, and hundreds of thousands more were expected to. Word had reached the news media and columnists were raising the question: would the U.S. and the world be better off if a peace was negotiated with the new Nazi regime? More and more, popular opinion was shifting towards a negotiated end to the war, even if it meant that Himmler and other monsters went unpunished for their crimes and atrocities against humanity. Let God be their judge, some were saying.

Also, nobody had forgotten that the war with Japan continued to rage with the Japanese military getting more and more fanatical in their resistance. The war in the Pacific was developing into a bloodbath. Could the American public handle two such wars?

The soldiers' petition was his first domestic crisis, and he had to wonder whether there was merit to their proposal. He also had to wonder whether he had enough clout in Congress to continue with the war against Germany's new regime. Nobody said the job would be easy, he mused.

And then there were the Russians.

"What the hell are they doing? Now, months after the Soviets abandon us they attack Japan?" He turned to Acheson. "And what did your good commie friend Gromyko have to say about this?"

Acheson shrugged. He had concluded his usual unsatisfactory meeting with the Russian ambassador only an hour earlier. "I would rather have a viper as a friend than Gromyko. I believe it was the usual pack of lies. He tried to say that they were responding to our needs by attacking our enemy, Japan. When I tried to tell him that invading Manchuria would do nothing to help Eisenhower, he simply shrugged. In my opinion, the invasion of Manchuria is another land grab by Stalin. I believe he feels that the Japanese army is so weakened that Soviet armor will punch through without much difficulty and they will wind up owning Manchuria and perhaps northern China. They will also be in a position to aid the Chinese communists if they so desire and simply crush Chiang Kai-shek's corrupt and ripe-for-failure Nationalist armies."

Truman turned to Marshall. "Can they do that?"

"Without too much difficulty," Marshall said. "We believe the Japs have been pulling their best front line forces back to Japan in anticipation of our invading the Home Islands. Even though the weather at this time of year in Manchuria is terrible at best, the Soviets have already mauled Japanese armies in battles prior to this war's beginning. The Japs cannot stand up to Russian armor and their other weaponry is really second rate at best."

"On a marginally positive note," Acheson said, "Gromyko insisted that rumors of a Russian invasion of Turkey are untrue, and that they simply moved some of their forces to the Turkish border to let them rest."

"Do you believe him?" Truman asked.

"About as far as I can throw him," Acheson said grimly. "Before you became President, sir, we did make the point that we considered both Turkey and Greece in our sphere of influence. We did so unofficially and without FDR's knowledge. Given his state of health and his feelings that Stalin was an honest broker, we did not think he would concur with our initiatives."

Truman nodded. "And how many secrets are you keeping from me now, Mister Acheson?"

The other man was unfazed and simply smiled frostily. "Well, sir, if I told you then they wouldn't be secrets, now would they?"

Otto Skorzeny enjoyed the flicker of fear on the face of Werner Heisenberg as he entered the physicist's cluttered office. He did not consider himself to be a particularly cruel man, but it did give him a sense of power to see others cringe when he confronted them. Size, strength, and those wicked dueling scars on his face frequently came in useful.

"When can you move the bomb?" he asked.

"Not for a couple of months," Heisenberg stammered. The stress of producing a true super-weapon was overwhelming and was beginning to affect his health. The scientist was pale and his hair was turning gray.

"You have two weeks," Skorzeny said.

Heisenberg was shocked. "That's too soon. The components might be ready, but the people who will detonate the bomb need to be trained in its assembly and the steps needed to detonate it."

"You know what to do, don't you?"

"Of course," Heisenberg said and then his face fell. "Oh, no."

Skorzeny laughed. "Oh yes, Professor Heisenberg. You and a small staff will accompany the bomb on its journey to the heart of Russia. And it will do you no good to protest. It's been decided by Reichsfuhrer Himmler himself. If the bomb does as promised you will be a hero to the Reich. If it doesn't, you won't wish to be in or near Berlin."

"But why so soon?"

"Himmler is concerned that the Reds are beginning

to move their armies back into position and will attack Germany at the height of the battle for the Rhine. Your bomb is the only way we can prevent such a stab in the back from the Bolsheviks from happening. Oh yes, you will leave notes behind so that the weapon can be reconstructed should that prove desirable."

"I don't speak Russian," Heisenberg said, grasping at straws.

"You won't have to. Others will take part in any conversations necessary. If anybody does question your and the others' presence, they will be told that you are captured German scientists, which is true in a way, isn't it?"

"But if I am captured, the Russians will be able to extract all our nuclear secrets from me."

Skorzeny shook his head. The poor academic fool didn't understand. "Doctor, you will not be captured. I will be right there with you and, should that unhappy event seem likely, I will personally blow your brains out."

Heisenberg understood and nodded solemnly. A quick and merciful death would be better than an eternity in the hands of the Russians. Or the Gestapo, for that matter. "And what about my family, especially if I should fail?"

"They are of no interest to us. They will be left alone. I am a soldier and I kill Germany's enemies, Doctor, I am not a murderer."

Heisenberg managed a small smile. "And tell me, Colonel, where will you be when the bomb goes off in the heart of Moscow?"

"And just what the fuck is this?" Sergeant Tyree Walls asked. "It looks like an abortion on wheels."

Normally, Walls wouldn't have spoken like that to a white man, but this sergeant at a huge motor pool outside the channel city of Cherbourg seemed to be an okay kind of guy.

Sergeant Copland laughed. "What's the matter? You don't recognize a General Motors truck?"

Walls returned the laugh. "I recall seeing a picture of something called a platypus, Copland, and this is just like it, neither fish nor fowl."

Walls read the poop sheet he'd been given. It was called a DUKW and, surprise, pronounced Duck. It was built by the Yellow Truck Division of General Motors on top of a standard 6×6 cab-over chassis. It weighed six and a half tons and could go fifty miles an hour on the ground and, real surprise, six in water. The damn thing was a boat. Now he knew where he'd seen the thing—in newsreels of the Normandy landings.

So what the hell was he doing looking at an amphibious machine that could go both in water and on land?

Oh shit—The Rhine.

Copland read his mind. "That's right, Sergeant, you and a whole bunch of others are going to be driving these abortions across the Rhine and right into the heart of Germany."

"I thought the navy drove ships."

"Small things like this are called boats, not ships, and I understand the navy isn't at all interested in providing drivers for these."

"I see where these things can have machine guns mounted. Can I have one? Might not hit anything, but it'd feel good."

"I can almost guarantee it."

Walls shook his head. He knew when he'd been

fucked. "Just out of curiosity, Sergeant Copland, where the hell will you be when I'm cruising the Rhine?"

"Maybe right alongside you, Sergeant Walls. I'll be skippering one of these things as well."

Tyree thought that was better. He stuck out his hand, which the white sergeant took. "Sergeant Copland, I'm proud to be a member of the U.S. Army's navy."

Morgan could barely conceal his elation. Jessica would be in Rheinbach, only a dozen or so miles away. Now all he had to do was find a way to get to Rheinbach without getting court-martialed.

He nobly considered that he didn't want much time with her and quickly discarded that ridiculous notion. He wanted a lifetime with her. However, he would settle for even just a few minutes.

In the quick phone call she'd made, she said that she had volunteered to check out the possibly deplorable refugee situation at a camp outside Rheinbach and that she hoped that he would, somehow, manage to get there. Damn. What the hell to do now?

He walked to where Jeb's quarters were. Like a number of enterprising GI's of all ranks, Jeb had managed to get a tent all to himself, whereas Jack was still sharing with Levin.

A piece of wood by the flap served as a knocker. Jack knocked, announced himself, and walked in. "Oh, shit," he said.

A pretty young blonde sat up in Jeb's cot. "Hello," she said with a radiant smile. "It's a pleasure to meet you. Jeb has said a lot of nice things about you."

She was naked and Jeb was asleep beside her. The cot looked too small for two people, but neither seemed to mind. "I'm Hilda Brunner and I'll wake him for you," she continued in heavily accented English.

Hilda wrapped an army blanket around herself and, after a few not so gentle shoves, Jeb woke up and yawned. "I see you've met Hilda. Hilda, this is Jack."

Hilda beamed again. "Hello." The army blanket had opened and Jack was acutely aware that she was a true natural blonde with an incredibly lean and slender body.

"Jeb, I have to ask, how old is she?"

"Sixteen."

"Jesus, that would be illegal in some states."

"Yeah, but not in Germany. Now you're going to ask what essential service she provides to make it legal according to the new fraternization rules. It's simple, she raises my morale."

Hilda patted Jeb on the cheek. "That's not all I raise."

Jeb grinned and Jack couldn't help but laugh. "Jack, if you hadn't taken an oath of celibacy in order to impress my cousin, there are a number of wonderful German women who'd love to meet you, including some of Hilda's relatives. And, in case you haven't noticed, Hilda speaks English, which means our relationship isn't all carnal."

Hilda giggled. "It isn't?"

"Now, Jack, what the hell is so important that you have to interrupt my afternoon siesta? I am just totally exhausted. Hilda is one hell of an athlete."

Jack explained the situation with Jessica going to Rheinbach as part of a Red Cross investigation of the refugee camp.

Carter patted Hilda on her delightful rump. "Rheinbach. Isn't that near where you live?"

"Yes. It's just a little place and wasn't badly bombed. My family still owns businesses there."

"And isn't one of them a hotel?"

"Ah, yes," she said, catching on quickly. "It's a small but lovely place on the Hauptstrasse, which is the town's main street. You will give me dates and I will ensure that Captain Morgan and his lover get the best of rooms and service."

When Jack started to protest that they weren't lovers yet, Jeb turned on him. "Damn it, my lovely cousin invited you to meet her in the German town and you're not going to have a place to take her if she's willing? How dumb are you? No, wait, we already know that. She's going to Rheinbach to meet you, Hilda's getting the rooms, and all you and I have to do is figure out a way to get to Rheinbach at the right time."

"You mean you're okay with my getting intense with your cousin?"

"My cousin's free, white, and over twenty-one. She can do whatever she wants with whoever she wishes, and yes, I do wish she'd had an affair with me, but that didn't happen and it ain't gonna happen since she's met you and is settling for less than she should. Look, we're in a period of what was once called 'sitzkrieg' or phony war, but we all know it's not going to last forever. When the weather turns nice all goddamn hell is going to break loose and a lot of us won't be around for next Christmas. For God's sake, take life when and how you can."

Hilda sat back down on the cot and pulled Jeb's hand down to her breast. "Don't forget, you have me."

"Right," Jeb said, calming down. "Hilda will make the arrangements and, if nothing happens, so be it.

If it does work out then you'll have a night or two to remember for the rest of your lives. And, with the invasion coming on, that might not be all that long. Live while you can, Jacko."

Still naked, Hilda walked with Jeb and Jack to the tent flap. "He is joking with you. I'm twenty-one and not sixteen. My family has decided that it will be a long time before Germany again controls the Rhineland, so we are cooperating to the fullest."

"And they are indeed," Jeb said happily. Hilda said goodbye and led an unprotesting Jeb back to the cot. Elated, Jack walked back to his own quarters.

The trip across Poland was about as Skorzeny had expected—appalling and miserable.

Eleven vehicles made up the column. In addition to the warm and fairly comfortable staff car he shared with Heisenberg, there were nine trucks of varying sizes and makes. Although a couple were the crude but robust Russian made Zis three-ton vehicles with their absurd wooden cabs, the majority were General Motors two-and-a-half-ton trucks sent to Russia via lend-lease and captured by the Germans. A bus carrying extra men and scientists completed the motorized menagerie.

All the vehicles were painted with the dread red shield insignia of the NKVD and their crews were, with the exception of the handful of scientists accompanying them, all Russians who hated the Soviets because they either lost everything in the Revolution, or had been part of Vlasov's anti-Soviet army and wanted revenge for his capture. Skorzeny declined to tell any of them that it'd been he who had turned Vlasov and the others over to the Reds to be butchered. Let them believe the fairy tale that a Soviet raid had captured Vlasov.

Skorzeny's second in command was a young major named Ivan Davidov. He hated Stalin with a white-hot fury because his parents and brother had disappeared into the Siberian gulags for the crime of being intellectuals who asked questions. He didn't give a crap what had happened to Vlasov whom he considered a turncoat who couldn't be trusted. Davidov considered himself to be a true patriot.

None of this was a great concern to Skorzeny. He had his orders from Himmler and would carry them out. Of course, Himmler had tried to pin him down as to how long it would take to get to Moscow and detonate the bomb. Skorzeny first had to remind the Reichsfuhrer that no one knew for certain if the damn thing would explode or not, which obviously frustrated Himmler.

Nor was Himmler happy when Skorzeny said they'd arrive when they got there, that he had no idea what the conditions were in Poland and western Russia, and what kind of delays would ensue.

Now he knew. Poland was a study in desolation. It had been fought over and savaged several times by both Russia and Germany since 1939 and in wars prior to that. Few buildings were intact. Decomposing and dismembered corpses, animal and human, lay everywhere. Mounds of rubble gave off intolerable stenches because thousands of bodies were buried underneath, the result of more recent battles.

Few people were seen. Either they were all dead, or had fled somewhere, or were living like rats in the rubble. Skorzeny didn't blame them for hiding. Both the Germans and the Russians despised the Poles.

Men had been massacred while women and children were raped by both sides. Poland was well on its way to becoming a ghost land.

Before the war, Poland had not been noted for its efficient road system and now the situation was worse. Craters forced detours and many bridges were down. Spring was coming and creeks were becoming rivers. Several times the convoy had to wait for the floods to go down or Soviet engineers to repair bridges.

While the NKVD insignia gave them priority, it was often an empty honor. Nothing could solve the problem of a downed bridge or a blasted road except patience. Still, slowly and gradually, they made their way across Poland and to the Russian border, where they found things only marginally different. At least there were people, even though they were gaunt and in filthy rags, and there were few children or old ones. When they noticed the hated and feared NKVD symbol they scurried away and hid as quickly as they could.

Nor did they push their luck when it came to taking priority against westward traveling columns of trucks and tanks. It was not lost on Skorzeny that the Soviet Army was again building up against the Reich. Himmler had told them that the Americans would attack as soon as the Rhine was clear and that the Reds were rebuilding. Therefore, the bomb had to be detonated as soon as possible.

All of this forced Skorzeny's group to have more contact with local military and police units than he wished and to either buy or confiscate food for his people. This was Davidov's job. He relished taking food and supplies from hungry Russians in the name of Beria's dreaded secret police.

"We did this, didn't we?" asked Heisenberg. "I once read something about making a wasteland and calling it peace."

Skorzeny laughed harshly. Heisenberg had never seen the realities of the world outside his laboratory. "Of course we did this. It's called war and as some American once said, war is hell. Don't fret, there are many more parts of Europe that are just as bad, if not worse. Germany will look like Poland unless we stop the Russians."

"This is terrible. Something must be done."

"Then think about this, Doctor! If your bomb does what we wish, Russia will be eliminated as an enemy for the foreseeable future. This means we can concentrate on the Americans and possibly drive them to discussing an armistice that will actually result in a long-lasting peace."

"I will pray for that," Heisenberg said.

Fool, Skorzeny thought. If the bomb works, Himmler will want more and more of them and will unleash them against the United States and England, creating additional peaceful wastelands. Heisenberg was a genial little simpleton, just like so many of his scientific brethren, with not a rational cell in their brains.

Skorzeny slowed the car. "What?" asked Heisenberg.

"Take a look," Skorzeny said.

"I don't see a thing except dirty Russian buildings. We've been driving so long I'm not certain where we are."

"See those spires in the distance?"

"Yes." A sense of awe entered Heisenberg's voice.

"That's the Kremlin, you ass. We've done it."

★ CHAPTER 22 ★

THE REFUGEE CAMP OUTSIDE RHEINBACH WASN'T
that big but it made up for its small footprint by being
stuffed with large numbers of wretched humanity.

The camp commander, an American army major
named Diggs, greeted them at the main gate of the
barb wire enclosed facility. In addition to Jessica and
Florence Turnbull, Jessica's Uncle Tom Granville was
representing SHAEF.

"Please tell me you're here to relieve me," Diggs
said with a wan smile as they took seats in his office
by the heavily guarded main gate of the camp.

Florence Turnbull took the lead. "Is it that bad?"

"Worse. And with all respects to you and the others
in the Red Cross, the United Nations, and SHAEF, I'm
getting next to nothing in the way of help or supplies."

"Are people actually starving?" Jessica asked. She'd
seen the camp's wasted inhabitants through the barb
wire that kept them in. It angered her. Refugees from
Nazi Germany should not be prisoners.

"Close enough," Diggs said with a sigh. "Not only am I not getting enough food, but there aren't enough tents or blankets, and there's damn little in the way of medicine. I'm sure you've noticed that the refugees are in rags and it's still cold, so, to answer your next question, yeah, a lot of people are still dying. Oh yes, I don't have enough men to administer this place. I've got two hundred American soldiers and most of them are castoffs, the petty criminals, dregs and dunces nobody else wants."

"So you're using Germans to help out? Nazis?" Turnbull snapped.

"Yes, another hundred or so, but only former local cops and no SS or Gestapo."

"Are you sure?" asked Tom.

Diggs shrugged. "Not really, Colonel, but they are all I have. We checked them all out and nobody's got an SS tattoo. Get me some more people and I'll get rid of them. Otherwise, I'm not ashamed to use them and I feel they are necessary to maintain order."

"I'm confused," said Jessica. "If these people are refugees why are you treating them like prisoners?"

Diggs laughed mirthlessly. "Because, if I let them loose, they and the local Germans would be at each other's throats in a heartbeat. All the German refugees have been moved to local households and the French ones have been shipped back to France. The ones in this camp are the Czechs, the Poles, and God knows what else. They hate the Germans because they were kept as slaves and now a lot of them want revenge. A number of Germans have been murdered and the women raped by rampaging gangs of refugees and I can't let that happen."

"And you can't send them home until their home-lands have been liberated," Jessica said, understanding. "How many are Jews?"

"Out of the twenty-five thousand in this camp, maybe three thousand, and most of them want to go to Palestine. Of course, the Brits don't want them going there and upsetting things in that mess of a country, so we can't move them anywhere for the time being. I understand this new United Nations is trying to set up better camps in France, but I haven't gotten any direction regarding sending anybody anywhere."

"Nor will you anytime soon," said Tom. "The French are overwhelmed with problems themselves."

Tell me about it, Jessica thought, thinking of the chaos and fighting she'd seen. "In the meantime, can we get them more food and other supplies?" she asked of her uncle.

"Jessica, I will try, but you have to understand that our fighting men have absolute priority, and that includes those men in hospitals and the thousands of American prisoners who are being liberated as we advance. Like it or not, the refugees come last."

"It's my understanding, Colonel, that supplies for civilians and refugees are coming into Europe," said Turnbull.

"They are," answered Jessica's uncle. "However, much of it is being diverted by the French, Dutch, and Belgian governments to feed their own people who are starving as well. And that doesn't take into account what is being stolen by criminals and making its way into the black market."

Jessica winced at that comment. It reminded her too much of Monique and her sergeant. Monique was recovering from her wounds and would be tried in a French court. If found guilty, which was extremely likely, she would be lucky if she wasn't hanged.

Jessica shook her head. "The American public won't like it when they find out that refugees are starving."

Tom glared her down. "They'd like it less if they knew our boys lacked food and ammunition for the coming battle."

"You're right, of course," Jessica admitted. "But can we buy food and other supplies from the locals now that the rules have been eased?"

Major Diggs shook his head. "We could, but the local Germans don't have much food or supplies to share, and, assuming we could buy supplies, how would we pay for them? The Nazi Deutschmark can't be used, and Germans aren't allowed to have American money."

"Then how is any commerce being done?" Jessica asked.

"With illegal money exchanges or, at the very local level, with cigarettes," her uncle explained.

"And women are selling their bodies for food, aren't they, Major Diggs?" Jessica asked, wondering if the camp commandant was one of those in the trade.

"Wouldn't surprise me at all," he said, unfazed. "But don't paint everybody that dark. Our own men eat in the mess hall and have more than enough to eat, and some of the good guys are giving leftovers to kids and the sick, but there's just not enough of it to make a difference."

Outside, screaming was heard. Diggs swore and ran outside and into the camp. Several dozen people were fighting over the shredded and bloody pieces of what might have been a chicken. Camp guards,

American and German, waded into the throng with cudgels and clubs and quickly broke up the fight. A few refugees had bloody heads, but no wounds seemed serious. A woman sat on the ground and wailed in emotional pain. She'd been the first to grab the chicken and considered it hers. Now all she had left was feathers.

"Someone threw it over the fence," said a grim Diggs, "and not out of charity. Some of the locals think it's great fun to start a riot."

They left Diggs with a promise to do what they could to ease the situation. Diggs thanked them but said he wouldn't hold his breath. "No disrespect, but it'll be a long time before we get this under control, and a lot more people are going to die. Oh yeah." He laughed harshly. "If you think this is bad, check out the German prisoners of war. They get what food the refugees don't want."

They left Diggs with the understanding that there was no solution to his problem. Jessica was angry, perplexed and frustrated, but understood the helplessness of those like Diggs who were trying their best.

"Going back to Aachen?" her uncle asked. "I can give you a lift."

"No, but you can take Florence. I plan on staying here a few days and surveying the situation."

"Surveying?" he laughed. "Is that what you call it? I ain't stupid, Jess, I know where the Seventy-Fourth is stationed."

"Then wish me good luck."

Her uncle kissed her on the cheek. "Make your own damn luck, Jessica."

★   ★   ★

Margarete listlessly poked at the food on her plate. It was no longer as inviting as it had been, although she would ultimately eat it. She would need it to keep up her strength for whatever ordeals were coming.

They were reaching the end of what food had been stored up for winter and there were serious questions regarding planting crops in the spring. Simply put, would the war let them? The specter of starvation was beginning to haunt them. Her aunt and uncle scoffed at her doubts. The Reich would be victorious well before food became an issue. Neither Margarete nor her mother felt that confident and she suspected that her aunt and uncle had unspoken doubts of their own. Meal portions had been reduced, and would shrink again. Still, one must eat. Food could not be wasted. What little they now had was much more than the people in the cities had.

The stress of waiting for the inevitable conflagration to sweep over them was sapping everyone's emotional strength. The weather was definitely warming up and each day brought them that much closer to "Armageddon on the Rhine," as Margarete liked to call it. Her uncle referred to it as the final German victory. Margarete was too polite to laugh at him and, besides, she really did like the pompous old man. If he didn't love the memory of Hitler so much, he would be quite charming.

Uncle Eric spoke softly. A new problem had arisen and the police had sent a notice. "Once upon a time I liked to go for walks in the woods. The forest was and is still thick and, when spring comes, it will be lovely again. However, it is now a place of death. The police fear that a number of bandits, deserters, refugees, and escaped workers are hiding in its depths and, when the snow is gone, we will be sweeping the place to get them out before they can emerge and attack us."

"Who is 'we'?" Margarete asked.

"Every man who can walk and carry a gun," Eric said. "It will be a motley army consisting of the very old and the very young, but we must get the criminals out of the woods."

"Is it that bad?" Magda asked.

Eric nodded solemnly. "Just the other day a man's body was found. It was badly decomposed and eaten by animals, but bodies should not be found in the forest, and not our forest. Once upon a time it was such a friendly place."

Bertha sniffed. "And we should not talk of dead bodies at dinnertime."

"And why the devil not?" Eric said. "All we've had for all these years is war and death. Hitler's dead. The Allies should negotiate an end to this."

Margarete agreed that the war should end, but she doubted that the Allies would ever deal with Himmler. Still, the idea of the forest being so hostile was depressing. She remembered wonderfully scary tales of monsters and witches and goblins in the depths of the woods, and the tale of Hansel and Gretel always gave her chills as a child. But these were not imaginary trolls or bogeymen, these were people who would kill. No, she would not go anywhere near the woods.

Nor did it surprise her that people were hiding in them. On those occasions that she had to go near the tree line a mile or so from her uncle's property, she'd had the uncomfortable feeling that eyes were on her.

On a happier note, she'd gotten a letter from Hans

Hart, the young pilot she idealistically thought of as her beloved. His attempt to transfer to jet fighters had been, as he wrote tongue in cheek, shot down. He'd been informed that there were far more experienced pilots than there were jet planes. If he wished to transfer to the Luftwaffe and fly an ME109 or some other, older plane, he was more than welcome.

Hans wrote that he was willing to fight for the Reich, but not commit suicide. He was, after all, German and not Japanese. Realistically, other than the ME262, all the other German planes were either second rate, or outnumbered a hundred to one, or both.

As a courtesy to her father, General Galland had spoken to Hans and told him to stick with ferrying officers in his Storch. The Luftwaffe was kaput. Stay alive, Galland had said, and Margarete wiped away a tear as she thought of the Luftwaffe general's courtesy.

"We will have to move," Alfie said and his two companions nodded agreement. Most of the snow had melted and tender green shoots were poking up from the wet ground. For a long time they'd been aware that they weren't alone. As they patrolled their area, they'd seen footprints and, on one occasion, watched in hiding as a handful of wretched men in German army uniforms tried to eke out an existence in the woods.

The three men made no attempt to make contact with any of the others. Desperation could drive refugees to do terrible things. They did not go out without weapons and, since few Germans and even fewer foreign refugees had guns, they assumed that anyone who'd seen them would think twice before attacking. They assumed the German soldiers they'd seen were deserters, which meant they were criminals in the eyes of German law and would do anything to keep themselves alive.

As far as they knew, the cottage had gone unnoticed. No footprints had been seen anywhere near it, but perhaps others had hidden their tracks just as they had swept away their own.

"And where shall we go?" asked Rosenfeld. He had taught them what tender young roots were edible. Alfie thought he was crazy, but damned if they didn't satisfy a craving and actually tasted good if you were hungry enough.

"Alfie's right," said Blum. "We can't stay here forever. Sooner or later, someone's going to stumble on this place just like we did. I wouldn't be surprised if the police don't send patrols into the forest to look for people like those deserters we saw, and if they find us they'll kill us. You heard the Ami planes last night, didn't you? Well, the Nazis will doubtless feel that someone is tipping off the Americans and we'll be likely candidates."

"But how would we ever do that without a radio? Smoke signals?"

"They won't care," said Blum. "If they catch us we're guilty and the local Nazis would have done their job."

"Jesus," Alfie said. Last night, several American fighters had flown tantalizingly low over the forest before bombing and strafing a nearby target that had exploded with a tremendous roar. They'd argued whether it had been gasoline or ammunition.

But Blum was right. They would not be treated as prisoners. For one thing, Alfie had already escaped once and, for another, Blum and Rosenfeld were clearly Jews. The crudely drawn tattoos on their arms so testified.

"If the Americans make it," Rosenfeld said, "we stand a chance. If not we'll have to do something desperate."

Alfie laughed. "As if this isn't desperate enough? Whatever the hell do you mean?"

"We should consider either heading east in the general direction of Berlin to where the situation might not be so violent," Rosenfeld said, "or, God help me, we should be trying to cross the Rhine."

Blum snorted. "And how the hell do we do that? Should we disguise ourselves as logs and try to drift across? And your idea of heading towards Berlin is sheer insanity."

Rosenfeld shrugged. "Then somebody come up with a better idea."

No one did.

Jessica did as Jeb directed and found the small hotel in Rheinbach. He said it belonged to someone he knew and Jessica met Hilda almost immediately.

"You are probably wondering if your cousin and I are lovers instead of just sleeping together, and the answer is yes."

Jessica forced a smile. "I would have been surprised if you weren't."

Hilda laughed. "I suppose you are right. The next question you'd like to ask is whether I or my family were Nazis and the answer is also yes, and at one time I was proud of that fact. Before you judge too harshly, recall that Hitler was chancellor since I was nine and before that there was chaos, hunger, and civil war in Germany and abject poverty here in the

Rhineland. Please recall it was administered by the French who despised us and abused us because we were German and had killed so many of their soldiers in the first war. Hitler brought order out of chaos and returned the Rhineland to Germany."

"Wonderful, but he also brought a second world war and death to millions of innocents."

"Which no one suspected would happen and which no one will believe now. And yes, we initially supported the takeover of Austria and Czechoslovakia and the recovery of the Rhineland to return us to our place in the world. Contrary to what some believe, however, there was not cheering all over Germany when we invaded Poland and wound up at war again with France and England. For so many, it was as if a nightmare had returned."

Jessica had heard the same from others, that many Germans had been shocked, appalled when the 1939 attack occurred, evoking memories of the horrors of the First World War. However, she wondered just what was reality and what was self-serving fabrication.

"Yes," Hilda continued, "we did support expelling the Jews, but not their murder. But we laid down with the devil, didn't we? And now my family is trying to repair its fortunes by dealing with the American army and whatever government is installed in the Rhineland."

"And that includes sleeping with Jeb?"

Hilda actually giggled. "No, that is pleasure, not business."

The two women went to the third floor of the hotel. There were only a dozen rooms, but all were clean and neat, although impersonal, typically German. Jess was pleased to note that no pictures of Hitler or

Himmler adorned the walls, but there were a couple of spots where a frame had been removed.

The room given to Jess had a double bed and its own bathroom with tub and shower and a nice view of the street below. She could see no damage from bombing or fighting. Hilda made a point of mentioning that it was the only such room in the building and Jessica was properly grateful. Even if Jack couldn't make it, a weekend with her own private bath and bed would be heavenly.

She put her toiletries in the bathroom and a change of clothing in the dresser. She had a civilian dress, but had worn her Red Cross uniform with slacks instead of a dress. Turnbull had told her that a young woman in civilian clothes apparently waiting for someone could easily be mistaken for a prostitute and harassed by the MP's.

She went downstairs and outside. The sky was clouding over and a hint of rain was in the air. More important, there was no sign of Jack. The few German civilians walking about ignored her while the GI's gave her the once-over and walked on. She heard one of them say "officers only."

"Hello there, Red Cross lady." It was Levin. Could Jack be far behind? He answered for her. "Your friend is looking for the address. These street names and numbers are a mess. Don't worry, he's just going around the block, and I was trying to find the place, too."

"Wonderful. And what are you doing here?"

Levin's expression became grim. "I've gotten permission from Colonel Stoddard to interview some of the Jewish refugees at the camp you inspected. I don't suppose you had a chance to talk to any of them?"

"Nope. Never went inside the compound," she said and told him about the fight over the chicken.

"No surprise," Levin said, "but I want to talk to people who actually survived the death camps. I want to know what really went on in them and whether it was as awful as I'm hearing before I make a decision regarding the rest of my life."

"What do you mean?"

"Palestine. We Jews are going to need a place to have as a homeland. We can't trust any other country except, possibly, the United States, and even there I'm not so certain. Therefore, having Jews migrate to Palestine and set up their own government is the only alternative. I've spent too much time not quite denying my Jewishness, but not living it either, so Palestine it is."

She had just finished wishing him well when Jack spotted them and ran up. He kissed Jessica, who quickly responded. Levin laughed, took the Jeep, and drove off.

Jack laughed. "Hey, he took my chariot."

"You don't need one, dear Jack, you're not going anywhere."

She didn't mention that her Red Cross car was behind the hotel. She took him by the hand and led him across the hotel's small lobby and up the stairs to her third-floor room.

"Here we have everything we need," she said. "There's food, wine, and each other."

"Are you sure?"

Jessica smiled and began to undress. "Don't just stand there, help me."

In a moment they were naked and in each other's

arms. Another and they were on the bed, caressing and enjoying each other. She gasped when he entered her and then, as he filled her, grasped him more tightly, pulling him deeper inside her. He climaxed first and, to her astonishment, she did too, just a couple of seconds later.

After they'd made love a second time, they rested and drank some very decent Rhine wine. Jessica felt she was a little drunk in more ways than one.

"We should have done this a long time ago," she said, giggling.

"I wanted to in Paris, but I was afraid you'd slap me silly."

She sighed. "I probably would have."

"Jess, I've been thinking a lot about you and us. Where do you see us in the future?"

"Hopefully in a better hotel," she said as she poured some more wine.

"No, do you see us together a year from now?"

"God, I hope so."

Jack smiled and began again caressing her, marveling at the beauty of her body. Her breasts were small but full and firm, and her belly was flat. Her legs were slender and surprisingly muscular. She'd told him she liked hiking and it showed. He loved it all. He kissed every inch of her body and she groaned with pleasure, quickly returning his intimate kisses.

Later, she smiled impishly. "Did you learn that at Catholic school?" she asked and he laughed. They made love again and slept.

The next morning, they heard the sound of thunder. The sky, however, was clear. "It's starting, isn't it?" she asked softly.

"Yep. We got a briefing a couple of days ago. What you're hearing is bombing. It's going to be a couple of weeks, though, before much else happens."

They got dressed and picked up her car. They drove an hour to a hill from which they could barely see the Rhine and the enemy hills behind. Bombs were falling and flashes were visible seconds before the sound washed over them. Jessica was starkly aware that she was seeing war, although from a safe distance, and it was nothing like the buzz-bombs in London or the riots in Paris. What she was watching was man-made hell.

"Can anyone survive?"

"Very likely quite a few. No matter how hard we bomb, a lot of them will make it. They are dug in deep and well."

Jessica shuddered and grasped his hand. "Enough. I'm glad you showed me, but enough. We're going to go back to the hotel and make love all night and make up for the time we missed and the time we may never have again."

"The word Kremlin is nothing more than Russian for fortress," Skorzeny said to a totally disinterested Heisenberg. "There are several kremlins all over Russia."

Heisenberg ignored him. He was too busy supervising his men's efforts to assemble the atomic bomb. They were in a warehouse across the Moscow River from the red walls of the Kremlin, the real Kremlin. It was less than half a mile away. His scientists were dressed in lead-lined suits they hoped would keep radiation at bay. Skorzeny was nearly a hundred feet from the bomb's components and the radioactive material.

Davidov had found the place, and brutally using his

NKVD identity, imprisoned the handful of inhabitants in a back room. Inside the warehouse's double doors there was plenty of room for the entire caravan.

A pair of trucks had been backed up to each other and the bomb was now on them. Heisenberg had been assembling it for two days and he was getting even more nervous than usual. They were hiding in plain sight in the center of the Soviet Union, trusting that their NKVD badges would keep out the curious long enough for them to do their job, and that the three men locked in the store room wouldn't be missed.

Some other NKVD officers had stopped by, curious, and had been told that this was a special project for Laventri Beria himself and that if they had any question they should ask him. No one would, of course. Beria, a murdering child-molester, was the second most feared person in the Soviet Union.

"Done," Heisenberg said and stepped away from the trucks.

It was almost noon. Skorzeny nodded. "Set the timer and we leave immediately."

Davidov had seen cars that could only belong to Stalin and others entering the Kremlin an hour earlier. They had to detonate it before Stalin left.

"Half an hour?" Heisenberg asked and Skorzeny agreed. It would give them time to get clear. They hoped. Heisenberg had no idea how powerful the bomb would be.

A moment later the physicist said the timing was set and the clock was ticking. Skorzeny, Heisenberg and Davidov got into a car and drove out. The remaining Russians and physicists clambered into the bus and departed behind them, leaving the three warehouse workers to their fate. "Martyrs to the cause," Davidov said sarcastically. It was time to return to Germany.

They had only been gone about fifteen minutes, driving through maddeningly slow traffic, when the world was lit by a glare so bright that they screamed and tried to cover their eyes. Seconds later, a shock wave washed over them, toppling the bus and ramming the car into a wall.

Inside the Kremlin, Laventri Beria stood by a window and wondered at the report he'd been given about some damn project across the river being done in his name. He was just about to give an order to investigate when an unholy fire washed over him and reduced him to ashes.

The blast and shock wave evaporated part of the river and completely destroyed Lenin's Tomb along with the stone wall of the fortress that faced the river.

In his office but not facing the blast, Josef Stalin sat at his desk while Vacheslav Molotov and several high-ranking generals waited nervously. The glare startled them but their minds had only a second to register the fact when the shock wave hurled them against and through the building's outer shell.

Two miles away, Skorzeny crawled out of the car. Heisenberg was badly injured and Davidov's arm hung limply. "What just happened?" Skorzeny said as he looked in amazement at the rising plume of boiling and flaming smoke towering above them like a living and angry god from hell.

"It worked," Heisenberg said weakly. "An atomic bomb. I've done it."

Skorzeny lurched to his feet. In every direction, thousands of people were milling in panic, wondering which way to run. Bodies littered the street and hundreds showed injuries of all kinds, many with horribly blackened skin. People with burns and peeling skin were running away from the explosion and the malevolent cloud expanding in all directions. Many staggered and fell, screaming through lipless mouths.

"It went off early," Heisenberg said, providing utterly useless information. He wondered if he would get another Nobel for physics.

Skorzeny swore and ran into an apartment building, fighting his way against a human tide that wanted to leave it. His uniform was of no use against mindless panic and it took him several minutes to where he could see the Kremlin.

It wasn't there. In its place was fire and ruin and that plume of black smoke still churning skyward. "We did it," he chortled in German and then looked around. No one had heard him and it wouldn't have mattered if they had.

Skorzeny then ran to the overturned bus. Several of the occupants were dead and the others badly hurt. He hated this part, but no one could be left behind to provide information to the Soviets. He pulled out his pistol and shot the survivors in the head.

Davidov came up. He seemed to have gotten his arm working. His face showed shock but then calmed. "I understand."

"Good. Now let us get the damned car going and get us out of this town before somebody takes charge and closes the doors."

It did occur to Skorzeny that it might be some time before somebody was found to take over the reins of Mother Russia.

★ CHAPTER 23 ★

TRUMAN WAS LIVID. "HOW THE HELL DID THE God-damned Nazis pull off a stunt like this?" he said into the speaker that connected him with General Leslie Groves in Alamogordo, New Mexico. "Didn't all your scientists assure me that we were well ahead of the Nazis?"

Groves' normally powerful voice came through clear but tinny. "Our scientists were clearly wrong. Oppenheimer and his pals are working on that now."

"Wonderful. I assume everybody heard Goebbels' announcement?"

The Reich Propaganda Minister had broadcast on the radio, gloating that a German secret weapon, an atomic bomb, had worked and destroyed Moscow and wiped out the leadership of the Soviet Union. He went on to say that the Reich had a number of atomic bombs in its arsenal and would use them to destroy London, Paris, New York, Washington, and God knows where else. In a twist of humor,

Goebbels even said Germany would have an atomic bomb destroy Independence, Missouri, Truman's hometown.

Truman clenched and unclenched his fists. He was the President. He had to maintain at least a semblance of his poise. "First, was it an atomic bomb?"

Groves answered. "No doubt about it, and other reports from neutral embassies broadcasting shortwave are confirming the bomb's destructive power. It went off either in or by the Kremlin and totally destroyed it and very probably killed everyone in it."

"Finally," Truman said wryly, "some good news. Can you confirm that lying Uncle Joe Stalin is well and truly dead?"

"We can't confirm anything," interrupted Assistant Secretary of State Acheson. He had just entered the room. "Admittedly, no one's heard from him since the bomb, but he could be in hiding. God knows I would."

"All right. Now, what about the other part, the threats to Allied cities?"

There was a pause while Groves conversed with others in the background. "Sir, the consensus is that they don't have any other bombs."

"Ha!" Truman said, pounding the desk, "You fellas also said they didn't have any in the first place, and that we were way ahead of everyone in the development of the bomb."

Groves continued. "Sir, again, we were wrong. But we are virtually dead certain that they don't have enough fissionable material to make any other bombs."

"But you're not a hundred percent certain, are you?"

"Is ninety-nine percent enough, Mister President?" Groves responded.

Truman glowered and admitted it would have to do. "Now, how did they get that thing to Moscow? What kind of plane did they use?"

General Marshall had entered and took a seat across from the President. "It would be almost impossible for a German bomber to penetrate that far into Soviet air space and it would have been too big a risk to take. Sir, I think it was shipped in parts by either truck or train and assembled in Moscow by a very daring group of saboteurs and scientists. If I were to guess, I'd bet that Skorzeny had something to do with it."

"And why didn't we hear of this?" Truman asked. "We have Ultra decodings, don't we?"

"We didn't hear about it because the Germans didn't say much," Marshall said. "We had picked up something about an Operation Kremlin possibly involving Skorzeny, but that's all we knew."

"Did we warn the commies?"

Marshall shook his head. "We had nothing concrete to tell them and we were concerned about them realizing we were reading German codes. They might then get concerned about their own."

Truman took a deep breath. "Can't undo what's been done. Now for the million dollar question—who the hell's in charge over there in Mother Russia?"

Acheson smiled tightly. "Thanks to Stalin's iron control, pun intended, perhaps nobody is, at least until his body is found, and that could take a while. It's possible his body was obliterated completely, which will keep his fate unknown until someone with enough balls is willing to step forward and take up the reins. After all, whoever seizes power and then finds a resurrected Stalin confronting him would be a dead man. And, absent a body, that will be a possibility, however remote."

"Is anybody helping the people of Moscow?" Truman asked. He had caught Acheson's pun. Stalin meant steel in Russian.

Marshall replied. "Again, neutral sources say medical help from other districts is beginning to flow into the city. Much of Moscow is in flames. It's a firestorm like what happened to Hamburg and it's raging out of control. It could be days before it's out. Estimates of dead and injured will run into the hundreds of thousands."

Truman shook his head in disbelief at the scope of the bomb's power. "Christ," Truman said, "what about other countries developing a bomb? If the Nazis were first, who else is out there?"

Marshall answered. "First, the Brits merged their efforts with us, however reluctantly. Next, the Japs understand the theory but don't have the resources. The Germans obviously beat us, but, according to Groves, the scientists are convinced that they have no others for the foreseeable future. Although, obviously, if the genie is out of the bottle, other nations will accelerate their efforts and that does include Germany. Given enough time, they will make a second bomb.

"That only leaves the Soviets and we're convinced they've been working on it. We have no idea how well they're doing."

"Is it possible that some of our secrets were stolen by the Germans?" the President asked.

Groves laughed harshly. "We've got a horde of FBI down here wondering the same thing and another horde on the way. Some of our foreign born and left of center scientists are going to go through the wringer. If there's a traitor, Hoover's boys will find him. Or her," he added. Who said men had a monopoly on treason?

"All right," Truman said thoughtfully. "Let's assume Uncle Joe's dead along with the hierarchy; once again, who's in charge?"

Atcheson answered. "Until the dust settles, candidates behind Beria and Molotov would include senior politburo members such as Malenkov, Bulganin, Kosygin, Khruschev and a couple of others. Of course any or all of them might be under the rubble. If the Communist Party is fragmented I'll put my money on the military to take charge, at least for the short term. Whether it's going to be Zhukov or Konev or somebody else, I don't know. Once again, any or all of them might have been in Moscow at the time of the bomb and be either dead or injured."

"Makes sense," said Truman. "Now for the big question, in light of the fact that the Nazis just destroyed Moscow and threatened to destroy a number of our cities, with additional bombs they may or may not have, do we cancel or postpone the Rhine crossings?"

All eyes turned to Marshall. He hesitated for a moment, sadness etched in his face. The inexperienced Truman was looking to him for leadership and his answer would send millions of American boys into hell. But then, a delay would give the Nazis more time to make bombs and to kill off the remnants of humanity dying in their concentration camps.

"No."

Schurmer had moved his offices to a hidden base outside the devastation that used to be Frankfurt. He and his small staff were part of Field Marshal Model's headquarters. As he saw it, the Rhine Wall was as complete as it was ever going to be. The Amis were bombing heavily and attempting to cut off the Rhine area from the rest of Germany. It was a tactic they had used in Italy and in Normandy and came as no surprise.

However, the sheer number of bombers was a shock. Was there no end to the parade of American B17, B24, and B25's as they flew over the Rhine Valley? To the north, vast swarms of British Lancaster and Halifax bombers were doing their part to obliterate all that Schurmer had built. Worse, there were rumors that the Yanks were going to send over some of their monstrous B29 bombers.

Schurmer stood and gave an indifferent salute as Varner entered. "Heil Himmler, General."

Varner grinned. "Go to hell, Colonel."

"I think I'm already there, Ernst. The Americans and Brits are destroying all my handiwork and there's nothing I can do to stop them. It doesn't matter how well constructed my defenses are if they are pounded mercilessly. Sooner or later, something will have to give. Say, you wouldn't happen to have one of those nuclear bombs on you, would you?"

Varner helped himself to some of Schurmer's last bottle of scotch. "We had one and it's gone. Worse, Heisenberg and a few of his key scientists have disappeared as well. We've heard nothing from them or from Skorzeny for that matter.

"Heisenberg was kind enough to leave his notes, but we don't have the scientists who can decipher them and build a new bomb. A second bomb can be built over time, but we won't have the luxury of time."

"Does Himmler know this?"

Varner laughed bitterly. "Oh yes, but he and Goebbels are bluffing. We may have knocked Russia out of the war, but they'll be back and the Americans are still here."

"Ernst, aren't the Yanks working on a bomb of their own?"

"I can say yes without betraying any secrets."

"And would our bomb have fit in an American B29?"

"From what I know of the plane, yes."

"Then have you heard that the B29 is heading to Europe?"

"Jesus," Varner said, chilled at the thought of American bombers dropping nuclear weapons on a defenseless Germany. Photos of the devastation in Moscow were beginning to come from diplomatic and news sources and the effect was horrific, although not all that different from the flaming hell rained on Hamburg and other German cities.

"Thank you for making my day, Hans, but that's not why I'm here. I am convinced that the main American attack will not come in the south, but will be in the north near Bonn. Unfortunately, I cannot find any proof. All the landing craft are in Patton's area, and not in Simpson's."

Varner explained what pilots and spies had located. Schurmer's eyes narrowed. He rose and closed the office door. "Tell me, when you became a general did you leave your brains behind? Where were you when the Yanks landed in Normandy?"

"Getting out of the hospital, as you well know."

"Have you seen photos or newsreels of the landings?"

"A few. What are you driving at?"

Schurmer split the last of the scotch with his guest, unevenly as Varner noticed. What the hell, it was his bottle.

"Rundstedt and Himmler are transfixed by platoon-sized landing craft," Schurmer said. "Did you ever hear of a 'duck'? And no, I am not talking about a feathered creature that waddles on the ground and quacks; instead, I am talking about the creature that swims rather well. In this context, the word duck stands for an absurd abbreviation for a vehicle that is half boat and half truck."

He stepped over to a wall shelf and pulled out a folder filled with photographs. "Look at this, General Varner."

Varner paled. He saw scores of small landing craft heading for the Normandy shore in a photo taken by an incredibly brave German photographer.

"The Americans have thousands of these things and they hold a squad each," Schurmer said. "Nor do they have to be hidden since they run on wheels when on land and act like a boat in water. They worked marvelously."

"Dear God."

"Don't get religious, Ernst, it doesn't become you. Here's another picture. This is a Sherman tank attempting to swim to shore using flotation devices during the Normandy invasion. They didn't work very well and almost all the tanks sank because the seas were too rough and they were dropped off too far from shore. Tell me, O newly anointed General, how rough is the Rhine and how far would they have to travel?"

"The water is as smooth as glass," Varner said softly. "And the distance to cross will be relatively short. This means I'm right. The main attack won't be in the south."

Schurmer laughed harshly. "We've always said that we couldn't stand up to American numbers and firepower, and that we needed the Rhine Wall to protect us. This shows that they can and doubtless will attack wherever they want and simply overwhelm our defenses. Dietrich's reserve army, now heading south to confront Patton, will be ordered to reorient itself and head north to confront the true menace, which means it will be vulnerable to American planes."

"Does Rundstedt know about this?"

"Of course, and he's chosen to ignore it."

Varner was aghast. "But why?"

Schurmer shrugged and gazed longingly at the empty bottle of Scotch. "Why don't you ask him yourself?"

Colonel Tom Granville looked up in surprise at the thin young man who stood before him. "Phips, what the devil are you doing here and in my office? Aren't you supposed to be in New York or someplace selling war bonds?"

"I can't do that anymore, sir. Getting people to buy bonds might be a good idea for some, but I'm beginning to feel like a pimp. Also, I'm yesterday's hero. Hitler's been dead for a while now and the war's still going on. Hell, sir, I've had people tell me it's my fault that we're still fighting."

"Phips, does the Pentagon know you're here?"

"No, sir. I faked my way across by telling who I was and that I had verbal orders from Ike."

"Good God, that's a court-martial offense. Correction, that's several of them. Why the devil did you do it?"

"Because of Stover, sir. His mother wrote me that they got word through the Red Cross that he'd died in a prison camp hospital after being shot down. I've talked with some people at State and in the OSS and they're convinced that he was probably beaten to death after parachuting safely from his damaged plane. Maybe they even knew he was one of the guys who killed Hitler. I decided it wasn't fair that I would be screwing around in American cities while my crewmen were dealing with danger. Colonel, I applied through channels and they all thought I was crazy."

"Well, you are," Granville said. Perhaps the boy had more balls then he'd originally thought. Still, there were problems. "What do you hope I will do?"

"Sir, I'd like to get back in a bomber. I've tried to reach people in the Eighth Air Force and they basically said they didn't want to talk to me. Since I used Ike's name so liberally, I thought I'd see you."

Granville sat back in his chair and sighed. "Son, there's no way in hell you're going back in a bomber."

Phips' jaw dropped in dismay. "Why?"

"Because if the Nazi fanatics even got a hint you were up they'd make every effort to kill you and that would include your crew, just like what might have happened to Stover. Some Nazis are so fanatic they'd even make like a Jap and try to ram your plane. In fact, some German fools are doing that already. Now tell me, would that be fair to your new crewmen?"

Phips sagged visibly. "No, sir, it wouldn't. I've got enough on my plate what with feeling guilty about Stover. His mom wrote me that he'd wanted to go back up and prove he was good as I was. Hell, sir, all I did was bomb some damn building. How was I supposed to know Adolf the Shithead was in it?"

"First, Captain Phips, you are not responsible for other people's behavior and I know you've been told that. I suggest you start believing it. As to what to do with you, I've just decided that we need another liaison officer to check on how well we're coordinating with the army. I'll make up some retroactive orders to cover your ass and keep you out of the stockade."

There was a knock on the door and a young woman entered carrying some folders. She smiled happily. "My God, it's Phipsie!"

Phips grinned happily. "In the flesh, Margie."

Granville rolled his eyes. "Margie, Captain Phips is being assigned here. Why don't you take him around and get him settled in."

Margie took Phips by the arm and led him away. "I've missed you, you silly boy."

"I've missed you too," he said and meant it.

"And I'll bet you don't even know my last name, do you? It's Fletcher, by the way. Well, you're going to have plenty of time to learn that and a lot of other really, really important things."

Morgan and Levin watched from a bunker as the west bank of the Rhine was gradually pulverized by the hundreds of pieces of American artillery that had taken over from the waves of bombers. These included the relatively small 105mm howitzers that the 74th possessed. Heavier artillery from neighboring divisions provided the bigger guns utilizing a technique referred to as "time on target." This meant that every gun that could be brought to bear fired on the exact

same place for a set period of time. It generally devastated the target and raised havoc with the morale of
the persons under fire, or nearby waiting their turn.
American tanks held their fire. They would need their
ammunition on the other side.

"Once again," said Levin, "how can anybody be
alive after all this? Yet I know that a lot of them will
be. I don't know about you, but I'm damn glad we
won't be going in with the first waves."

Jack offered no argument. The night before it had
been announced that Patton's Third Army was crossing
to their south and was meeting stiff resistance. "Why
don't we make our own atomic bomb and drop it on
the Nazis?" Jack asked. Levin merely grunted.

All around them hundreds of ducks stuffed with
men from the 116th Infantry Division were rolling
to their take-off points. Close to fifty Sherman tanks
fitted with flotation devices moved with them. Still, the
Germans hadn't responded to the American barrages.

Carter slipped in beside them. His Pershing tanks
wouldn't move until a pontoon bridge had been built.
They were too heavy for the existing flotation equipment and Carter was not brokenhearted about missing
the initial fighting. Tanks, he'd pronounced, were not
meant to float on anything.

"Hey, did you two see the drivers on the ducks?"

Morgan grinned. He knew what was coming. "No,
Jeb, why don't you tell me?"

"The drivers are Negroes. They are actually sending colored boys into combat. And you know what's
worse? They've got rifles in those trucks."

"How else are they supposed to defend themselves?"
Levin asked.

"They aren't supposed to fight, especially not against white men. Or hadn't you noticed that the krauts are white?"

Further discussion was silenced when the ducks and tanks began to move towards the river. "Looks like a herd of large turtles," Carter mused.

The vehicles splashed into the water and began to plow forward. Now the German guns opened up and multitudes of splashes kicked up around the swarm of American craft. The German fire was so intense that it looked like giant raindrops from an immense storm were falling among the craft.

In order to fire, however, the German gunners had to expose themselves, if only for a moment. American counterfire began to hit around the newly exposed targets.

Carter swore and ran off. His tanks could hit the German guns and could be reloaded with additional ammo before any pontoon bridge was built.

A duck was hit and blew apart. Another was swamped by a nearby shell, sending men into the deep and still frigid water. The ducks and tanks surged on as still more were killed. When the attack force got to the middle of the river, German heavy artillery fired from sites dug in behind the hills. They could not be seen by American gunners who depended on spotters to find their targets, but the huge weapons could destroy with a near miss as waves and concussion took out still more ducks. Morgan longed to go up and spot for American gunners, but it was too dangerous with so much metal flying around in the air. His turn would come when the barrage lifted.

Behind the hills, American dive bombers bombed and strafed as the big German guns came out to fire.

Enormous splashes landed among the landing craft. "Go faster," someone near Jack yelled, but the ducks and tanks couldn't. A glacial six miles an hour was about it for them. Several hundred small craft were now visible in a tableau that reminded many of the Normandy landings.

The ducks reached the far shore, which meant that the enemy bombardment would be lifted. "Time for me to go," Jack said. He stood and trotted to the rear where his tiny air force awaited. His planes were ready to lift off and spot for the amphibious Sherman tanks that were also reaching the shore. Most of the tanks and ducks had made it, although a disconcerting number were either burning, sinking or had disappeared. As with the crossing of the Seine, heads could be seen bobbing in the dark waters of the Rhine. The tank flotation devices worked, and only a handful of the Shermans had been hit.

Tanks and ducks lumbered over the ground. About a hundred yards in, the ducks disgorged their human cargo and turned around for the next trip. The tanks, with infantry beside them, moved slowly into the heart of the Rhine Wall while German machine guns and antitank guns raked the advancing Americans.

Fingers of flame shot out from the Shermans that had been modified to work as armored flamethrowers. Fire hit the German bunkers and Levin felt he could hear the screams from those inside as they were turned into human torches. He had a hard time feeling any sympathy.

Above it all Jack's plane flew high above the Rhine and then swooped down behind the hills that hid the German artillery. A nervous Snyder sat behind him.

Jack pointed downward. A short rail line was visible behind a hill. The Germans had hidden a big gun inside the hill, trundling it out on the tracks to fire at American targets, and rolling it back in for safety. But the act of firing had blown away its camouflage and the tracks stood out starkly.

"Aw shit, not again," howled Snyder as Morgan dropped to below tree-top level and slowed the plane.

"Get ready, Snyder." They approached the tracks. "Now," yelled Morgan.

Snyder quickly dropped a couple of flares out the window. They burst into a bright and glaring light. Morgan quickly radioed his position and a pair of dive-bombers soon strafed the area and bombed it. Jack flew back over and confirmed that the tracks had been destroyed. The gun hadn't been killed, but it had been immobilized. He grinned and banked to look for more tracks.

On the ground by the river, Sergeant Tyree Wall turned and yelled. "Everybody get the hell out of my bus!"

Ranger First Lieutenant Stan Bakowski slapped him on the shoulder. "Knew you'd get us here safely, Sergeant, that's why I asked for you."

"Fuck you. I'll never do another favor for a white man again."

Bakowski laughed and gathered his Rangers. With such a short crossing, most of them were close around, although a full truckload was missing. Bakowski didn't have time to dwell on those implications. His men had to maneuver around the German lines and get into the rear where the big guns were hidden. Planes and bombs could only do so much. Sooner or later, someone wearing combat boots was going to have to go underground and root them out.

Wall's duck hit the water and headed west. Long lines of American soldiers were waiting for his ferry service. It appeared to him that German fire was slackening. It also seemed there were far fewer landing craft than had set off just a little while before. A mangled body floated face down in the water and he swerved to avoid it. Part of him said he should pull it in but that would have meant stopping and making him a stationary target. Sorry buddy, he muttered to himself. If you looked wounded, I'd take a chance, but you are clearly dead. He hoped somebody downstream would pull the dead GI out.

German fire was still lethal. A duck to his right took a direct hit and disappeared. Water from the geyser washed over him and something soft glanced off his shoulder. It was someone's foot. He groaned and then threw up. Like everyone witnessing death, he thought that it could've been him and wondered why he was still alive. If he survived this, he would have questions that maybe nobody could answer.

As he closed on the west bank, he saw that work was progressing on no less than three pontoon bridges. Even though shells from German guns splashed around them, the engineers kept on. Brave bastards, Wall thought.

He pulled onto the shore. Men ran to get in, prodded and yelled at by their sergeants. "Get in, sit down, and shut up," Wall yelled at their frightened faces. "Keep your heads down. If we start to take on water, bail with your helmets. Got that?"

One soldier glared at him. "Kind of uppity, aren't you?"

Wall was about to respond when the man's sergeant smashed him in the face, bloodying his nose. "Watch yourself or he'll dump your worthless ass in this fucking river."

What a wonderful idea, Tyree thought.

★ CHAPTER 24 ★

MARGARETE AND THE OTHERS HUDDLED IN THE bomb shelter that had become her uncle's pride and joy. The battle wasn't anywhere near them yet, but it was evident that the Americans were invading to their west and, if successful, would overrun the farm. Now all they had to contend with was the sound of bombs and artillery. Nothing had yet fallen near them. Their move to the shelter was prudence. The laborers weren't with them. They had their own shelter just outside the barn.

Magda looked at her daughter in the dim candlelight and smiled wanly. "I sure am glad we came here to be safe, aren't you?"

Before Margarete could respond, her uncle glared at them. "We should be at peace. That fool Himmler should have negotiated with the Allies."

Margarete was shocked. "I thought you believed in Hitler and ultimate victory."

Her Uncle Eric sniffed. "I worshiped the ground

Hitler walked on but he is dead and Himmler is a pale shadow of the man. I believed all this shit about super weapons and then we've used them—rockets and atomic bombs—and what has it gotten us? More death, that's what. The Americans and British are still coming and we have nothing to stop them with. Tell me, when was the last time you saw a German plane, other than the pissant one Ernst and that boy you like arrived in? No, we have no planes and soon will have no army. The Americans can stand off and destroy us piece by piece and Himmler is letting that happen. If he cannot end the war then he should step aside and let someone who can take over."

He coughed and spat on the ground. Bertha was about to scold him but saw the look on his face and changed her mind. "And I've had it up to here with super weapons," he continued. "The V1 and V2 rockets were supposed to win the war and they didn't. Then the atomic bomb was supposed to win it for us, and what has happened? Russia may be slowed down but the Americans are still coming. You know what that means? We don't have any more bombs. We had one bullet in our gun and we fired it. We may have wounded the wild animal we shot at, but not mortally. Russia will be back and the Americans are here."

Eric coughed again. The air in the shelter was stuffy. He was about to light his pipe when Bertha smacked his arm. He glared at her but put the pipe away.

"And tell me, little Margarete, what did you think of our army, the Volkssturm? Old men and young boys, wasn't it? I should be in it. I got a letter calling me up and I ignored it. One war was enough. Half the Volkssturm will be slaughtered while the other half will surrender. It's already happening," he said glumly. "Germany is doomed."

His rage out of his system, Uncle Eric looked fondly at his niece while Bertha remained stonily silent. "I may be an old fool, but I am not so foolish that I cannot learn."

Himmler and the German high command had retreated to the reinforced bunker complex built for Hitler under the Chancellery. There was fear that the attacks on the Rhine Wall would bring on new and more devastating bombings of Berlin that would cripple Germany like the atomic bomb had wounded Russia.

Von Rundstedt thought the reason for going underground was that Reichsfuhrer Himmler was afraid. In his opinion, the former chicken farmer was himself a chicken. Himmler was pale, thin, and nervous. His hands shook and there was a twitch in his eye. The next few days would determine whether he and the Reich endured or would become footnotes in history.

Rundstedt broke protocol and began. "Reichsfuhrer, we have to make a decision. It appears that our plan to reinforce our troops confronting Patton might have been a mistake based on insufficient information. The Americans to the north used landing vehicles that didn't need to be hidden. The sighting of American landing craft in the south was a ruse, a kind of Trojan Horse."

"Why didn't we see this?" Himmler said. His voice was barely a whisper.

Varner stood quietly against a wall. Because you didn't want to see, he thought. But what game was Rundstedt playing?

"I've spoken with Admiral Canaris," said Rundstedt, "and he is now of the opinion that most, if not all, of our observers in the north have either been killed by the Americans or turned by them. In short, we were blind but didn't know it."

Himmler nodded. "What do you propose?"

"The reserve army must be turned around to confront the American First Army under Hodges and not Patton's Third."

Fifty-three-year-old SS General Sepp Dietrich, who commanded the Reserve Army, stiffened as he realized what Rundstedt was proposing. He'd been recently promoted by Himmler to the rank of field marshal, which greatly annoyed Rundstedt, who felt that Dietrich simply lacked the experience and qualifications to have such a distinguished rank or command such a large force. Rundstedt had suggested Dietrich, a mediocre general at best, command the Reserve Army, but had not expected the man's promotion to field marshal. That Dietrich also looked pale and exhausted seemed to confirm Rundstedt's doubts. But Dietrich was an SS man through and through, which meant that his total loyalty was to Heimrich Himmler.

"Can you do that?" Himmler asked of Dietrich.

"It will cost us," he answered with surprising candor. "We are now moving our tanks and troops at night to hide from the Americans and are still taking serious casualties. In order to get to the northern targets we will have to move during the day and the Americans will hurt us even more."

"But can you do it?" Himmler insisted, his voice rising. "Can you get your army to the Bonn-Remagen area and attack through to the Rhine? Can your army isolate the Amis before they become too strong? Can you cut them off and defeat them and force them to surrender?"

Dietrich looked like a man who'd just been offered a cup of poison. His reserve army had several thousand superb tanks, but the infantry was suspect, even though Volkssturm units had been reinforced by the remnants of SS divisions culled from the Russian front when the Soviets had stood down.

Before Dietrich could answer, Rundstedt turned to Himmler. "You have three divisions of SS in Berlin doing little more than standing around with their thumbs up their asses. I submit that they should be attached to Field Marshal Dietrich's army to help make up for losses and to stiffen the spine of the Volkssturm."

"But those forces are to maintain security in Berlin," Himmler said in what was almost a lament. Varner was shocked by the pain in Himmler's voice.

"Reichsfuhrer," Rundstedt said coldly. "If the Reserve Army is defeated, then there will be no need for security in Berlin as the Reich will have been destroyed and we will all be fugitives. Berlin is not now directly threatened and won't be if we win. If we lose, it won't much matter. You have garrison troops, remnants of Luftwaffe units, Volkssturm, and even some naval units who can be used to secure the city. Three full divisions of SS troops could turn the tide of battle."

"I could use them," Dietrich said so softly that Varner almost felt sorry for the man.

"Then take them," Himmler snapped, "and for God's sake, win with them."

★   ★   ★

Jessica was slumped over her desk in near despair. The rumbling sounds of battle could be heard in the distance and all she could think of was Jack. Was he safe? Was he involved at all in the battle? She thought she would be ill. Occasionally, thoughts of Jeb and Levin and the others she'd met intruded. She'd never realized how awful it was to have loved ones in harm's way. She didn't think she had the strength to go on, but what choice did she have? How did wives and mothers do it back home while awaiting news? The answer was simple—they endured their agony because they had to. There was no other choice.

At least there were no people wanting news of loved ones waiting for her to tell them that there was nothing she could say. With the battle raging, everybody seemed to have other things to do. It was as if everyone understood that nothing was going to be done until the fighting ceased.

The door to her office opened and Hilda came in, smiled tentatively, and took a seat. She took a deep breath. "I'm pregnant."

"I assume you're going to tell me Jeb's the father."

"Yes, and I will also tell you we're married. A minister outside of Rheinbach performed the ceremony after I found out. The American army won't like it, but there's nothing they can do."

"I don't know what to say."

Hilda started to shake. "I hoped you would congratulate us. I know what you think, that I'm an opportunist whore who hunted for an American to get me out of here, and that's not true. Jeb and I love each other. And I didn't chase him. He came up to me on the street and introduced himself."

Hilda had started to cry. So much for Teutonic reserve, Jessica thought. She handed the young woman a Kleenex from the box on her desk.

"Jessica, once upon a time I was a devoted little Nazi. I told you that. We were so happy when Hitler stopped the civil war and the economic disasters, and brought pride to being a German. We were dismayed when he had us invade Poland and France, but we felt it was all right if Hitler said it was necessary. I had a good friend, a lover, who was killed in Poland. I had a brother who was killed in France. We grieved but thought Hitler would soon stop and all would be better, even though we would have paid a terrible price. But then he invaded Russia and later declared war on the United States and my family and I realized it would never stop until Hitler died. Now he's dead and the fighting still goes on. Will it ever stop?"

There was nothing Jessica could say. She stood up and walked around the desk. Hilda stood and the two women embraced.

Colonel Tom Granville took the slip of paper from the solemn-faced young lieutenant who saluted and left as quickly as he could. Jeez, thought Granville, do I have that nasty a reputation? Or is it Beetle Smith?

He read the message, smiled, and walked into Smith's office. The general looked up and grimaced. "Hitler still dead?"

"Yes."

"Then why the hell are you bothering me?"

"Take a look at this, sir," Granville said as he held out the note.

Smith read quickly. "How reliable is your source?"

"Very."

Granville reminded Smith that he had been operating his own intelligence service and getting information from behind the German lines from a number of sources. Some were individuals who were heartily sick of the war and the brutality of the Nazi system, while others were simply hoping to save their asses if the Americans won, all the while hoping their betrayals would go undiscovered by the Gestapo. They were walking a fine line and one stumble could mean a horrible death.

He didn't care about their motives, only that their information was accurate.

"Refresh me," said Smith. "Who the hell is he?"

"His code name is Crow, and he picked it out himself. Easier to remember that way. He's a field grade German officer whose information heretofore had been limited to tactical issues such as unit locations, defensive strengths and location, and similar stuff. This is the first time he's provided anything even remotely this big."

"Do you know his real name?"

"Yes."

"Will you tell me?"

Tom smiled tightly. "When the war's over, General."

"Prick," Smith said amiably. He fully understood that he didn't have a need to know. "So this Crow makes contact with someone else who is higher up in the Nazi hierarchy who decides to let Crow in on a very important secret right out of the blue."

"There may be more to it than that. I suspect a long-standing personal relationship, but we won't know until later, if at all."

The general stroked his chin. "So Crow is reliable and, therefore, you believe this new character he code-named Cardinal is on the up and up as well."

"Sir, I believe Crow and Crow believes Cardinal. Crow explains how Cardinal got the information and it seems plausible."

"A lot of people said the Japs wouldn't attack Pearl Harbor and everyone thought that was plausible, too. Tom, do you believe in this enough to forward it up to Ike and then across the water to Marshall and Truman?"

"Absolutely."

"Well then," said Smith, "let's do just that."

Truman entered the Map Room, took a seat and lit up a cigarette. "What is it this time, gentlemen, good news or bad news?"

"A little bit of both is in order," said General Marshall. "First, we have confirmed that the Nazis only had one bomb and do not have the resources to build another. This has come from Ultra intercepts as well as reports from people on the ground who have spoken to key members of Himmler's staff. They also say that neither Heisenberg nor Skorzeny has yet emerged from Russia and are probably dead."

"No loss," Truman said. "Too bad Himmler's not dead as well. Now, what about Russia?"

Secretary of State Stettinius responded. "It does appear that Marshal Zhukov has taken over, at least temporarily. He's announced that a new prime minister will be elected shortly. However, 'temporarily' under those circumstances could stretch out into decades. Some of my analysts think Zhukov could be nominated and thus become the permanent head of state."

"Would that be bad?" Truman asked. He wished someone other than Stettinius was present. Dean Acheson was vastly preferable to the current secretary of state who seemed to have his own agenda when it came to dealing with the Soviet Union.

"We don't know," Marshall answered. "He's a ruthless, capable and hard-driving general who doesn't seem to care how many casualties he takes as long as he wins, but we don't know what he would do as head of state."

Truman laughed harshly. He was familiar with the situation. "Maybe he doesn't know either."

"The Germans will counterattack shortly," Marshall said, abruptly changing the subject. "Dietrich's Reserve Army has been ordered to shift north and attack the Remagen bridgehead. We believe he will leave a covering force to keep Patton in check. As if," he laughed grimly, "anyone can keep Patton in check. As soon as Patton confirms this, he will cross the Rhine in force."

Marshall stepped to the map of the Remagen area. "We are hitting the German armies, bombing them, with everything we have. Its mission has changed so it has to come out in the day to move. Dietrich's army is huge and, despite our efforts, a goodly portion of it will still reach the point where it will attack our Rhine beachheads."

Truman paled. "Can we defend them? Can we defeat that son of a bitch?"

"Mister President, we still don't have our full forces across. That will take weeks. If we are fortunate and can truly reduce them through air power, we will prevail, especially as we don't think their infantry is anywhere near first rate."

"What about their jets?" Truman inquired.

"Here we are on more solid ground, sir. Our air force has been pasting anything that looks like a landing strip or a fuel depot. Ultra says that German pilots are complaining about lacking enough fuel to even take off, much less fight, and that many fields have been so badly cratered as to be unusable. The Luftwaffe will not be a major factor."

Truman sat back. Were things looking up? "Then what can go wrong?"

Marshall answered. "The weather. Long-range forecasts are for clouds and rain, just like those that delayed the attack at Normandy. If the Germans are able to attack us without hindrance from above, then all bets are off and the battle could disintegrate into a bloody brawl."

Stan Bakowski had lost fully a third of his Rangers trying to fight and sneak their way behind German lines.

While they crept forward, the infantry and armor slogged their way up the steep hills of the Rhine valley, taking on each pillbox, slit trench and bunker one at a time. Flamethrowers searched each opening in the German defenses, no matter how small. Black smoke billowed from ventilation shafts, indicating that anyone inside had been cremated. Bakowski shuddered when he saw that.

The Rangers' job was to find a fifteen-inch naval gun intelligence said was situated well behind the German lines. Its massive shells were exploding in the river, swamping and overturning landing craft and killing by the force of the shock. Other shells exploded in the masses of men and vehicles awaiting

their turn to cross the Rhine. Thus, the Rangers'
orders were to avoid fighting. They were to bypass
German defenders every chance they could and get
in their rear. Of course, it didn't work out that way.
It never did. German defenders didn't want to be
bypassed and shot at the Rangers every chance they
could. More than a score of Rangers fell dead and
wounded while Bakowski's men were forced to take
out places they should have bypassed.

Finally and after several hours, they reached a point
behind the German lines where they could move with
relative ease and quickness. Bakowski took out his map
and the overhead photos of the area. Of course, the
terrain resembled nothing on any of them. Constant
bombing and shelling had transformed this part of
the world into a moonscape.

The Rangers spread out and looked for clues. They'd
been told that the gun was likely that the opening in
the hill would be on its east side so the hill could
shield it from direct fire. Railroad tracks would be the
clue. The giant gun was part of a small train. The
gun was mounted on railroad tracks which enabled its
crew to run it in and out between shellings.

Bakowski was about to order a search in another
direction when, like magic, a massive door in the
hill slowly opened. The Rangers dropped and hid.
A moment later, a crew of German soldiers ran out
and lifted the planking that hid the railroad tracks.

Another moment and the giant gun moved pon-
derously out into the open. The crew was fixated on
prepping the gun and not looking for Rangers.

Bakowski grinned. "First platoon take the gun,
second and third follow me."

Close to a hundred Rangers rose up. The first platoon sprayed the gun crew with bullets, killing many Germans before they knew what happened. A few Germans raised their hands in surrender, but most were cut down before anybody realized what they were trying to do.

Bakowski and two platoons raced into the man-made cavern and confronted a score or more astonished and horrified Germans. Only a couple of them were able to fight back and they died quickly. This time, a handful were able to give themselves up.

Dynamite charges were placed around the big gun and the train. Other charges were placed inside the cavern to drop the walls of the cave as well as to explode the many remaining shells.

They left the cave with their prisoners and moved a half mile away. A German staff car was approaching and they raked it with gunfire. Nobody got out.

"Faster," Bakowski urged but his demolitions men ignored him. Move too fast and they'd blow themselves up and not the target.

Finally, everything was in order. The plunger was rammed home. First, the wheels on one side of the train blew off. A second later, explosions ripped through the cab. Then without the wheels on one side, the train was unbalanced and it slowly tipped over onto its side. The gun ripped away from its mountings and, like a giant toy, rolled a few yards away.

Next, everything in the cavern exploded and the mountain caved in on what the Germans had built so laboriously. The smoke and dust attracted attention from some American planes. They flew low and quickly determined what had happened. One wagged its wings and they all flew off.

A good day's work, Bakowski thought. If only he hadn't had to lose so many good men.

Varner found his good friend Schurmer in his office stuffing papers into a briefcase. "The rats are deserting the ship," Varner said.

"Rats usually survive"—Schurmer smiled—"for the simple reason that they don't go down with the damned ship. You've noticed, I'm sure, that so many OKW staffers are conspicuous by their absence."

Varner sat down. "I assume they don't believe that Dietrich's army will change the course of history."

"They will alter it but not change it. They may precipitate a bloodbath, but win the war? I think not. However, if the improbable should occur, everyone who is fleeing will return and pretend that nothing happened."

"Hans, I am worried sick about my family. I cannot get through to them. The farm is going to be inundated by the battle."

Schurmer looked at him coldly. "How well can I trust you?"

"Implicitly," he answered, surprised by the question.

"Easy to say, but we will see." He wrote a number on a scrap of paper and handed it to Varner. "Here."

"And what is this?"

"What the Americans refer to as a get out of jail card. That is my contact in American intelligence. When you are captured by the Americans, or surrender if you prefer, ask for military intelligence and tell them to contact this person on your behalf. He will not know you but will know me as an agent named Crow, and you are Cardinal."

Varner was stunned. "You are a traitor?"

"You could say Hitler and Himmler were the traitors and I'm just trying to save Germany. You could also say I'm simply trying to save my ass. I don't care. I've been channeling information about the Rhine Wall, unit dispositions, and other bon mots to the Americans for more than a year now."

"How?"

Shurmer laughed. "Simple. I have access to a good German army radio. I operate it at night when I have to. No clerk is going to deny me. Do you recall when I negotiated with the Americans regarding Paris? Well, it was then that I formalized the arrangement with their intelligence."

Varner was still stunned. He looked at the paper. "I can't take this," he said and returned it.

"Fine. Then look forward to spending the next few years in an American prison camp while they try to figure out if you really were a war criminal and how many Jews you either killed or had killed as a result of your orders, actions, or inactions. Or have you forgotten that you are a general on the OKW staff, and that you actually conspired to hide the fact of Hitler's death? Oh yes, and weren't you close to Heisenberg and his blasphemous bomb? Be careful or they might actually think you are a war criminal, in which case you'll never see the light of day or your family again."

Schurmer again held out the paper. "With this, you won't spend more than a couple of weeks in a POW camp. Besides, you did provide me with excellent information that aided the allies."

"I did?"

Schurmer laughed. "You are such a noble ninny,

Ernst. Don't you remember the day you told me out of the blue that there were no more atomic bombs? That cleared the way for the Americans to cross the Rhine with that little problem taken care of. Now, what is it—prison or freedom to find your family?"

"I thought you were my friend."

"Ernst, I'm the best friend you ever had."

Varner nodded and put the piece of paper in his pocket.

It was time, thought Mastny, enough hiding in a barn and skulking. The Allies were nearby. He could hear the bombing and the artillery. He and the two others had to make their move soon or the opportunity would be lost. Once the Allies overran the farm, they would be nothing more than nameless, faceless refugees. They had to get the wealth they knew was hidden in the Mullers' house ahead of their so-called liberation.

They stuffed oily, greasy rags into several buckets and placed them near the barn door. Mastny lit the fires and waited. Very quickly, black smoke began to billow and find its way out the door. Janis was the least stupid of the two Latvians. He understood the value of money. And pussy.

Janis ran from the barn screaming the obvious—

"Fire, fire!" He reached the bomb shelter's hatch, pounded on it and continued yelling. A second later, it opened and Eric Muller bounded out followed by his wife. He turned and told the others not to follow them to the barn.

From the barn, Mastny could see the two women were armed and that was part of his plan. As Eric

Muller ran towards the barn, Janis added that Victor was badly hurt. Muller's expression didn't change. He was concerned about the barn, not some damn workers.

Eric reached the door first and rushed in. Once inside and in the dark, he paused, puzzled. Mastny hit him in the side of the neck with a shovel, nearly decapitating him. His wife lurched in, out of breath, and Mastny dropped her with a blow to the side of her head.

Victor grabbed Eric's shotgun while the Latvians took their pistols. They looked towards the house. Both the younger women were standing just outside the shelter, wondering what they should do. They had pistols, but they were safely tucked in their holsters.

"We need more help!" Victor shouted and nearly laughed when the two women raced toward him. A few feet from the barn, the three men stepped out, weapons pointing at the astonished women, who were too stunned to even think of their own guns.

★ CHAPTER 25 ★

"BUSINESS BEFORE PLEASURE," VICTOR PROCLAIMED while the two Latvians laughed. Magda and Margarete lay on the ground by the house where they'd been overwhelmed before they could defend themselves. They were bound hand and foot by ropes from the barn. Their assailants did not bother with gags. Who would hear their screams? In fact, Victor and the others wanted to hear them scream.

Uncle Eric's body had been dragged from the barn. He was clearly dead, but Bertha was breathing and moaning. Mastny wondered how long that would last. He didn't care. The German bitch deserved to die. The other two women were guilty but less so. Still, their punishment would be severe.

First they put out the fires in the smoke pots in the barn. Even though fires were common, attracting unwanted attention made no sense. Then they ransacked the house. The sounds of furniture being smashed and walls being broken into carried down to

Magda and Margarete. Mother and daughter lay side by side on the ground, still not quite comprehending the terrible turn of events.

The two women wiggled close to each other and tried to undo each other's bonds to no avail. Margarete began to cry. "Will he kill us?"

Even though there were three men, it was Mastny who was clearly in charge. Magda had no idea what lay before them. Perhaps it would only be rape, which they could survive as so many thousands of German women were learning to their shame and agony.

"I don't know," she said to her daughter. They had discussed the terrible fate befalling German women who fell into the hands of the Russians, but they never believed it could happen in the gentle lands east of the Rhine. Magda, however, had told her daughter that she should endure an assault and not fight. One could recover from rape, at least physically, but not from death or mutilation.

Shots rang out from inside the house. The two women looked at each other in shock. A few moments later, Mastny walked out carrying a small bag. He held it up to them.

"I'm disappointed. This is all you people had in the way of jewelry and foreign money? Deutschmarks are going to be useless except to wipe your ass with when this war is over. Why didn't the Mullers have any English or American money, or even Swiss?" He cackled. "Of course. They were good little Nazis, weren't they? They put their faith in Hitler and look what it got them."

He set the sack on the ground. "At least I won't have to share this with those two fools."

Magda and Margarete stared at him in horror. The gunshots were Mastny executing his two companions.

Mastny took out a large kitchen knife. "Now, this is going to be very simple. If either of you resists, I will use this knife to cut off the nose of the other one. We are going to do it in the dirt because you are German swine and a fuck in the dirt is all you are good for."

With that, he carefully sliced Magda's clothes off. He stared at her hungrily for a long moment and then stroked her breasts and thighs. He ignored the fact that she didn't respond, merely stared at a point above him while Margarete sobbed and turned away so that she didn't have to watch her mother being violated.

Mastny's voice was husky with excitement. "Excellent. I'd fuck the old lady first, but she's unconscious and would probably never realize it." He knelt between Magda's thighs and pushed them apart. "You don't have to cooperate. Just lie there and do nothing like all German women do when they fuck."

He mounted her and thrust inside her. Magda bit back a scream from the suddenness and pain of the assault. She would give him no reason to hurt her daughter.

Finished with Magda, he went to the barn to get his other possessions, the stolen goods he and the others had buried. "Yes," he said to the women. "We took these from refugees and you were too stupid to realize what was happening underneath your noses."

He looked down on Margarete. Her eyes were closed and she was crying. He was aroused again. "Please take me again," pleaded Magda. "Just don't hurt my daughter. She's only a child."

"Shut up, cow," he said and slapped her several times across the face. Again the knife cut through clothing until Margarete was naked. Her eyes remained closed tightly as if willing this to go away. Mastny went a little slower with Margarete, caressing her and fondling her before finally pushing his way inside her. She screamed, and he laughed.

Gasping and grinning, he lurched to his feet and arranged his clothing. He was about to say something when his skull exploded in mist of gray and red. He fell backwards and lay still.

Two hundred yards away, Alfie Swann lowered the Mauser he'd taken so long ago. "Damn good shot if I do say so." He wouldn't admit that he'd aimed for the chest and the shot had ridden up to the skull. He'd been lucky. He could have missed altogether.

The others grunted. They had no sympathy for Germans, but the man Alfie'd just killed was obviously committing rape and was about to commit murder.

They walked slowly forward to where the two women lay huddled and crying. Their nakedness did not arouse the three men. The women were dirty and bleeding.

"We won't hurt you," Rosenfeld said in German. He took Mastny's knife and cut their bonds. It was pathetic the way they immediately tried to cover themselves with the remnants of their clothing.

Magda was the first to recover her wits. She staggered to her feet. "Who are you?" she gasped.

The three men looked at each other. Alfie nodded. It was time to take a chance. Did they have a choice? The women had seen them and the only alternative was to kill them as well.

"Do you speak English?" Alfie asked. When Magda said yes, he continued. "These two are Jewish escapees from the slaughter houses and I am an escaped British POW."

"Then you are in grave danger, aren't you?" Magda said. She was not surprised. There were so many stray people wandering about. "If the Gestapo or the army catch you, you'll be lucky to be shot."

"Yes."

Margarete had regained her feet as well as some of her emotional poise. Magda put her arms around the weeping girl. Margarete's lip was bleeding from where she had bitten down and there was blood on her thighs.

"Then you will stay with us," Magda said. "We had three laborers who tried to kill us and they are dead. Now we have three men who saved us. We will keep you here and pretend you are the other three. Slave laborers are faceless so one will notice. You can stay as long as you wish. Perhaps the Americans will be here soon, perhaps not. At any rate, you'll be safe. And so will we."

Alfie looked at his companions. Staying with the two women was perfect. Nobody would be looking for them and, as laborers, they would be invisible. The two Jews took off their jackets and handed them to Magda who wrapped them around herself and her daughter.

Alfie laughed grimly. "Well then, I suppose you had better find some clothing and clean up while my friends and I bury the dead."

"There are two bodies in the house," Magda said.

Alfie acknowledged the simple statement, and the other two men went inside to remove the corpses.

"The three who attacked you will be buried out in a field. Your family members we'll bury with dignity when you are ready, but please make it soon." He looked in the sky. The sky was clouding up and he could almost smell the rain.

A fine mist had begun to cover the ground and visibility was dropping. It was Nazi weather once again. Somewhere out in front of the American lines a German army had been rendered invisible. Morgan had read the reports and heard comments from both fighters and recon planes. A mighty host of German infantry and armor was heading their way.

The 74th Armored Regiment was across the Rhine and dug in a couple of miles east of the river. More men, tanks, and supplies continued to pour across the pontoon bridges that connected the two sides. Jeb's Pershing tanks had crossed with little difficulty, although it had been a little nerve-wracking to see the mighty tanks rumbling across the shaking and shifting pontoons. Only inches on either side kept the tanks from sliding off the unstable bridge and into the river. Jeb was annoyed that they hadn't seen any real action yet while the rest of the regiment had sustained serious casualties both in the crossing and climbing the hills where the Germans were dug in.

"They are out there and they are coming," Stoddard said grimly. "We are going to live up to my nickname and dig in and make stockades like we've never done before. God only knows when the weather will break and our planes can begin killing the krauts again. In the meantime, we're going to fight them all by our lonesomes."

Jeb Carter raised his hand like a kid wanting to go the bathroom. "What you're saying is that they could be on our asses before we even know it."

"Correct and astute as always, Captain," Stoddard replied. "Any way we can prevent it?"

"Obviously we've got to send out patrols and hope they don't get overrun before they can signal back."

"That's being done, Captain."

"Great, sir, but I'd like to take it a step farther. The krauts will doubtless come down the clear land south of that fairly large stand of woods to our left. I want to send my tanks through the woods and into a position where they can take the Germans in either the flank or the rear."

Jack and Carter had taken a Jeep through the clear ground as well as the woods to their front the day before and when the weather was better. There were dirt paths snaking through the trees and both were confident that the Pershings could make it, stay hidden, and hit the Germans hard. Nor did they think the Germans would try to bull their own way through the forest. There was no need for them to do that and it would only slow them down. Speed was of the essence for the Germans. The sky could clear at any moment.

"Sir," said Jack. "We have maybe forty Shermans and a dozen tank destroyers left and we are digging in to let the earth provide additional protection for their thin armor. The Shermans all have either the better guns or flamethrowers and could give German armor an unpleasant surprise, especially if Jeb attacks their rear."

"That and the tank destroyers and our one-oh-five-millimeter guns along with the infantry would help," Jeb added.

In addition to their own armor, the regiment had been reinforced by several battalions from the 116th Infantry Division. That unit had been badly mauled crossing the Rhine and would not be functioning as a division for a while.

Stoddard smiled grimly. "Then let's make it happen, gentlemen, and that includes you, Carter."

"Sir," said Morgan, "does that mean I get to fly and try to find them?"

"It does not. At this time you will be more useful helping with the defenses. We have other men who can fly those dinky little planes and besides, there ain't much to see right now. Former air force Captain, you just became an infantry officer. Congratulations."

Muddy, dirty, filthy, wet, hungry and discouraged. All these terms described Volkmar Detloff as he trudged eastward accompanied by thousands of other Volkssturm soldiers and a sprinkling of totally mad SS types who actually thought they could win the war.

He no longer had any illusions. He was a coward and his men hated him. His new platoon was as bad as his first. When Colonel Schurmer told him he'd never command troops again he hadn't taken into consideration the Reich's desperate need for officers of any kind. Ergo, Volkmar once again commanded a platoon of old men and boys far younger than he.

Rain and snot dribbled from his nose and he wiped them with his sleeve. Somewhere up front hundreds of German tanks were approaching the American defenses. The infantry was supposed to accompany the tanks, but no one had considered the fact that there were too few trucks to transport the infantry. Many of the trucks the army had possessed had been pulverized by the American planes. Tramping through the mud, the infantry were simply incapable of keeping up with the armor.

Thankfully, no planes were overhead this day. Volkmar had seen enough of burned trucks and charred pieces of bodies to last a lifetime. A lifetime, he giggled nearly hysterically. His own lifetime could end any second now.

The German army was a mob. Not only had so many been killed by the Americans before even reaching the front, but large numbers of older men had simply collapsed and refused to move on. At first he'd been inclined to call them cowards, but many were older than his father and they were simply too exhausted to move. When they found them, SS soldiers shot them in the back of the head and called them traitors.

No, Volkmar thought, they were not traitors. They were simply old men who were poorly fed, inadequately clothed, and so tired they were incapable of moving. Was this the Reich he'd been supporting? Something was wrong. Worse, in his opinion, so many soldiers in the so-called German army weren't German at all. Instead, they were conscripts from various nations and whose loyalty was dubious at best.

Any unit coherence had also disappeared. Instead of a platoon, Volkmar was now followed by more than a hundred dispirited Volkssturm who had no idea who he was, only that he was an officer and he was taking them in some direction.

In the distance to his front, Volkmar could hear the sounds of cannon firing. He shivered. In a while he and the others around him would close up on the tanks and attack the Americans. Volkmar was sure he would piss himself again. This time, he didn't care.

★　　　★　　　★

Joachim Pieper was a veteran of the war against the Soviets and, at thirty, commanded an ad hoc mixed corps of infantry and armor. His force was supposed to penetrate the American defenses, reach the Rhine, and then turn north, cutting off the enemy defenders. Other units had similar assignments. With luck and skill they would defeat the Amis and take many prisoners.

He initially commanded two hundred and fifty tanks and an infantry brigade. He now had only maybe half that many tanks thanks to the American planes. God only knew how many infantry still followed him. They were a mixed bag of SS, regular army, and Volkssturm, and he didn't think the Volkssturm were capable of fighting. His armor was first rate, but many of the crews were inexperienced and had never worked together. It was a recipe for disaster, but he was hell bent on avoiding that. While he preferred to maneuver and attack simultaneously from several sides, his men's lack of experience would not permit him that luxury. No, he had chosen the simplest way and would attack straight on and smash his way to the river. They would endure heavy casualties for victory, but that was a blood price that had to be paid if the Americans were to be driven to the negotiating table.

In an attempt to reach his goal as soon as possible, Pieper's tanks had outpaced his infantry. It was unorthodox, but he had to hit his target before the sky cleared and the bombs began to fall anew. He particularly dreaded napalm. Fire from the sky had turned so many of his Panthers and T34's into burning pyres. If the weather turned and cleared, he might quickly find himself without any tanks at all.

Pieper opened the turret hatch of his Panther. He'd been offered a repainted T34 but had rejected it contemptuously. He would command a German tank, not a fucking piece of Russian shit. He had named the tank *Sigurd* after his wife, who'd tersely informed him in a letter that she didn't necessarily consider it a compliment. Pieper thought it was funny.

His driver looked up from his own hatch. "Any idea where we are, General?"

Pieper grinned. The driver was a good man who had served with him before. "Heading right towards the enemy and that's all that matters."

"Wonderful," his driver muttered and Pieper laughed. Was there anything better than fighting a war?

Muffled by the rain, he heard the sound of heavy weapons followed by the chatter of machine guns. Somebody had already made contact. He closed the hatch. No sense being a fool and getting killed by a sniper or a piece of shrapnel. They would find the Americans soon enough, maybe in minutes.

Carter's twelve heavy Pershing tanks were lined up along the dirt road a couple of hundred yards inside the forest. They would have been invisible even on a sunny day. He'd sent out scouts with walkie-talkies but had heard nothing from them. In the distance, he could hear the rumblings of explosions. The fighting had begun.

"Damn it," he muttered. Finally, the scouts came running back with the info that the German army was passing them and that there was a very large number of tanks. How many, they couldn't be sure because of the crappy visibility.

"Time to earn our pay," Carter muttered. He gave the order to move out, and the column slowly snaked its way out of the woods along paths he and Morgan had marked out with white tape on stakes the day before.

In short order they were in an open field. Carter arrayed his tanks in a line and they rumbled forward very slowly. He did not want to rear end the German army.

Shapes began to appear in front of him. Men, and they were hunched over and moving in the same direction as his tanks. Jeb keyed his radio. "We're gonna hit the kraut infantry. Use machine guns if you have to, but not our main guns. We save those for their tanks."

The sound of the approaching American tanks awoke the German infantry to their peril and they turned to confront the apparitions emerging from the mist. Some were puzzled. Were these more German tanks? Others saw the strange shapes and the American markings and reacted by either running or shooting. An old man leveled a panzerfaust, but a burst from a machine gun killed him. Other Pershings cut loose with their machine guns and German infantry began to drop by the score. "Kill them and keep moving," Jeb ordered. "Don't take chances."

He thought he could hear screams from the outside and over the sound of his engines but wasn't sure. He felt his tank run over something. Christ, was that a person?

Large shapes were dimly visible. German tanks. But so damn many of them, Carter thought. *What the hell have I gotten myself into?*

"Hit them in the rear. Kill them quickly."

★   ★   ★

Pieper was confused. What the devil was the source of the automatic weapons fire from his rear? What Volkssturm asshole had begun shooting his own men? Ah well, it was inevitable in such crummy fighting conditions.

At the same time his mind registered the sound of cannon fire also coming from his rear, the Panther to his left exploded. A second burst into flames, and then a third.

"Turn, turn," he ordered into his radio. "The goddamned Americans have tanks in our rear."

He spun his tank on its own axis to face the new threat. There, he saw one. It was bigger than any American tank he'd seen before, and he quickly identified it as a Pershing. There'd been rumors that the Amis had some in the area and they'd just been confirmed.

Several more Panthers and T34's exploded or started belching smoke before his men could find targets and respond. The American main gun was a killer. The attack on the American defenses would have to wait until this new threat was taken care of.

Carter was appalled. What kind of hornet's nest had he disturbed? The weather seemed to be lifting slightly and he could see maybe a quarter of a mile. More than a dozen German tanks were burning, but what looked like every tank in the whole damned German army was turning and driving in his direction. They were already within almost point blank range and this was going to turn into a street fight.

Reports came in that several of his Pershings were destroyed and there seemed to be at least fifty Panthers or T34's headed in his direction.

"Fall back," he ordered. They had done their bit to hurt the Germans. Now they had to get the hell out of danger. Suicide was not on his agenda. If they got back into the woods, maybe they could hide out.

His tank lurched hard, slamming him against the turret. "Won't move, sir," said his driver. "I think something hit a tread."

"Everybody out," Jeb yelled just as a half dozen shells from German guns hit his tank and turned it and everyone inside into cinders.

They could hear the fighting but not see it. Morgan leaned on the wall of the trench and tried to will himself to see. Something was indeed coming, but it wasn't tanks. Infantry, and thanks to the mist, they were only about a hundred yards away.

"Open fire," he yelled redundantly as everyone in the line was already shooting. Morgan put his submachine gun on the dirt wall and fired into the crowd. It was difficult to miss and men fell, but still more came in behind them.

The few strands of barb wire did little to stop the German horde and they swarmed over it and towards the American trenches.

"Bayonets," someone yelled. Shit, thought Morgan, I don't even have a bayonet. A screaming German was right in front of him. Jack fired a burst and the man fell back only to be replaced by another kraut. This one too went down and another ran at him. Jack pulled the trigger. Empty. He fumbled frantically to change the clip. Something slammed into his shoulder and spun him around. He checked and found that he wasn't shot, but his bad shoulder had been hurt again. A German jumped into the trench and started clawing at him with his bare hands. Jack tried to fight him off but his left arm wouldn't respond.

Sergeant Major Rolfe pushed Jack aside and shot the German in the head only to be gunned down himself by another. Jack took Rolfe's rifle and tried to fire with one hand. He hit nothing and screamed as the pain overwhelmed him.

Feeney and Snyder appeared beside him, shooting and killing. Jack pulled his pistol and shot another German in the face. He pointed the .45 at another who threw down his rifle and raised his hands. "Kamerad," he screamed. Others began to scream the same thing and they too dropped their weapons and held up their arms.

All around them, German soldiers were surrendering. Not only that, the sun was coming out. He paled. There were scores of German tanks approaching his position.

Overhead, Phips dropped through the clouds in his Piper and saw the German tanks heading west. He radioed in his position and gave a rough estimate of their numbers, admitting that there were so many that a proper count was impossible. Finally, he exulted, he was doing something useful.

All the American planes in the world, or so it seemed, had earlier been arrayed on landing strips for this very moment. In anticipation of the clearing weather pushing in from the west, they'd taken off and had been circling overhead, hoping to God that they'd find targets before they ran out of gas.

Even as he watched, the clouds began to part. It

was like a curtain lifting on the set of an epic play with him as a front row audience of one.

Time to get out of the way, he thought, and climbed to ten thousand feet. He laughed as he saw literally hundreds of American fighter-bombers converging on his position. He whooped with glee as they began their drops through the fading curtain of fog.

Joachim Pieper could also see his shadow. More precisely he could see the shadow of his tank, *Sigurd*, on the ground. Overhead they could hear the growl and whine of vast numbers of American planes. In a moment they would be through the rising cloud level and rain hell on what was left of his Panzers.

While he was annihilating the American tanks in his rear, his infantry had gone ahead and tried to storm the American lines. He could see the ground covered with their dead. At least they'd died more bravely than he'd suspected they could. It appeared that they'd made some penetration in the American defenses, but he could hear enemy automatic weapons firing. No, the Volkssturm and the few SS troops would not carry the day. They needed his armor.

He opened his hatch and looked around. Fewer than a score of tanks remained in his command. He looked ahead and squinted at something reflecting in the distance. Was that the Rhine? Was he that close to success?

A plane screamed low overhead and dropped a bomb. Two of his remaining tanks were engulfed in a sea of napalm. He paled as reality sank in. His tanks could not go forward. He had too few of them, but still, he could not stand still or retreat. The American planes would kill them all.

Another tank burst into flames. "Goodbye, Sigurd," he said, hoping he was saying farewell to his tank and not to his wife.

Pieper gave the order and his men climbed out of their remaining tanks and began to run to the rear. Maybe, just maybe, the American planes would pleasure themselves by shooting up abandoned German armor.

He'd gone only a few yards when a napalm bomb detonated nearby and consumed him in a billowing cloud of flame.

★ CHAPTER 26 ★

THE MEN OUTSIDE HIMMLER'S CLOSED OFFICE door stared in shock and horror at the thing coming toward them. The man's hair was white and stood out in clumps on his head. His cheeks were gaunt and his eyes wide like a lunatic's.

Otto Skorzeny had returned from hell.

When a female secretary tried to halt him, Skorzeny pushed her aside with surprising strength and entered Himmler's inner sanctum. The Reichsfuhrer looked up. His face registered the same shock and horror. "Good God, you look awful."

Two OKW generals were in the office and Skorzeny waved them out. They scuttled away like frightened insects. Skorzeny closed the door behind them. "And so do you, my dear Reichsfuhrer."

Himmler had lost weight and his hands were twitching. His eyes were red from lack of sleep and stress. Skorzeny laughed. "You bet and you lost, didn't you, Himmler?"

Himmler was annoyed at the familiarity, but endured it. Word was arriving that the great and final assault against the Amis had failed disastrously. While a few units had indeed pushed through to the Rhine, they'd been small and few in number and the Americans had quickly annihilated them. Dietrich's Reserve Army had been destroyed. The carefully husbanded armored force had been smashed by American artillery, armor, and waves of planes from the skies. Dietrich himself was nowhere to be found and there were rumors he'd committed suicide. Von Rundstedt had also left Berlin, possibly before Himmler could have him shot. It was over.

"Where are you going to run to?" Skorzeny asked. "I hear Argentina's a good place. Me, I'd prefer Spain. We have a good friend in Franco." Francisco Franco was the fascist dictator of Spain and, although officially neutral, was deeply sympathetic to the Nazi cause.

Himmler blinked. Of course it would be Argentina. Perhaps a small-fry like Skorzeny could hide in Spain, but not him. He and the rest of the Nazi hierarchy would be welcome in Argentina where they could begin planning anew.

"Where's Heisenberg?"

"Dead of the same radiation poison that nearly killed me. I'm getting better, or haven't you noticed?"

Himmler sniffed. "Frankly, Otto, I've seen better looking corpses. A shame. I was hoping he would make us another bomb or two to use against the Americans."

"Before he died, Heisenberg said it would take a large team several years to construct another one, assuming we had the resources, which we don't."

"You're right, we don't. But there's always a chance

to succeed in another manner. We will use what resources we do have to at least make a radiation bomb. Explosives wrapped in what uranium we have will make a deadly concoction."

Skorzeny listened in disbelief. "But you would have to detonate it in Germany. And if you did, the Americans would drop some of their own atomic bombs on our heads, or had you forgotten what they are up to in New Mexico?"

Himmler snarled. "I forget nothing. Regardless, I have a task for you. Our beloved generals are planning a coup. They are going to try to overthrow me and place Rommel in my stead. Apparently that was von Rundstedt's plan all along, which is why Rommel didn't have a field command. Von Rundstedt and the other generals seem to think that Rommel is saintly enough to make him acceptable to the Allies. My intelligence says Rommel is on his way to Berlin with several thousand soldiers loyal to him. They are to arrest me, and doubtless you as well."

Himmler's hands shook as he lit a cigarette. "Your orders are simple, Skorzeny, you are to intercept Rommel and kill him. That will buy all of us time. My staff estimates we have two to three months before the Allies arrive here."

Skorzeny laughed. It came out as a cackle. "You have maybe three weeks, Reichsfuhrer. Yes, Dietrich did maul the American First Army before he and his men ceased to exist, but Patton's Third is beginning to run loose to the First's south. And, in case you've forgotten, Montgomery's entire army group is also starting to cross the Rhine to the north. Not even he will take two to three months to drive to Berlin.

The English want your head on a platter as much as the Americans do."

"We'll stop them at the Elbe," Himmler said.

Skorzeny scoffed. "Compared with the Rhine, the Elbe is a stream a man can piss across. The Elbe won't even slow down the Amis. They will ride up in their little ducks and simply drive across. Himmler, half the army is dead, wounded, or captured, while the other half is looking for a way to surrender or is burying their uniforms and trying to pretend they are civilians. Maybe a few of your fanatics will delay the Allies for a short while, but that is all."

"We must have time," Himmler said stubbornly, his voice breaking.

Skorzeny stood and paced, winding up beside Himmler. "Perhaps you have an eternity," he said.

In one fluid motion, he removed the knife he'd hidden in his sleeve, slipped it into his hand and drew it across Himmler's throat. The Reichsfuhrer's eyes widened in shock and he tried to speak. Copious amounts of blood poured out of the wide gash and onto his desk. A few seconds later he slumped forward, dead.

Skorzeny wiped the blade on Himmler's sleeve and replaced it. He'd been frisked but not carefully. For some reason, no one had wanted to touch him.

He opened the door a little and backed out. "Heil Himmler," he said and gave the Nazi salute to the dead man only he could see. He closed the door behind him.

Skorzeny stared at the people waiting to see Himmler. "The Reichsfuhrer had just been given information that he must study. He requires at least an hour of privacy, perhaps more. After that he will call you. On his orders, you are not to bother him."

Heads bobbed in understanding. Fools, Skorzeny thought. He went downstairs and outside to where Davidov awaited with a staff car. The Russian had also recovered from his radiation poison and other injuries.

On to Spain, Skorzeny thought. The warm sun would speed his recovery.

Truman tried to keep pace with the rapidly changing scenario. Himmler was dead and Rommel was in charge, although he hadn't given himself a title just yet. The use of the word "Fuhrer" was too distasteful thanks to Hitler and Himmler.

"Tell Rommel that unconditional surrender still applies," Truman said. "The German armies will lay down their arms."

"He will agree," said Marshall. "Rommel is in complete control." Himmler's second in command, another monster named Kaltenbrunner had tried to take over, but had been killed in a brief firefight with troops loyal to Rommel.

Marshal continued. "But he wants assurances that all the German military can surrender to either the U.S. or Britain and not the Soviets."

"Agreed. And tell Rommel that we will be moving our men through Germany and through what's left of Poland to the Vistula River, which is where the Soviets have stopped. We expect full cooperation."

"They wish to send von Papen to negotiate with us," Stettinius said.

"Fine," said Truman, "only have him meet with our people in Switzerland and then only to iron out any administrative details of a full and unconditional surrender to us and to England. I have no wish to speak to him at this time."

"The Russians will be angry," said Stettinius. "According to our Yalta agreement, they are entitled to Germany up to the Elbe River."

"Fuck the Russians," Truman said with a grim smile. "They bailed out and left us all alone out on that proverbial limb. Hell, they even sold tanks to the Nazis. We don't owe the commies a damn thing. You tell Prime Minister Zhukov he can't have any more of Poland than he's already seized."

"But that means he will keep eastern Poland," Marshall said.

"Can't win 'em all. Maybe the Soviets will choke on Poland and the other countries they've swiped. But we are not going to fight a war with the Reds." He grinned wickedly. "At least not right away. Now, is it true they've stopped looking for Stalin?"

"It is," said Marshall with the hint of a smile. "Apparently large numbers of workers excavating the Kremlin site have come down with radiation sickness and a lot of them have died. They can't even get prisoners to work there. They feel they have a better chance of living to old age in a gulag in Siberia."

Truman laughed. "If Stalin ever does come out, he'll be glowing in the dark. Well, since we now know for certain that an atomic bomb will work and we're so close to having one of our own, isn't it time we finished off the damned Japs?"

★ CHAPTER 27 ★

IT HAD BEEN YEARS SINCE VARNER HAD RIDDEN a bicycle and his legs hurt from the effort. However, it was the best way of finding his way to his family. Cars were few and gasoline in short supply.

Schurmer had been right. The code-names had been a magic wand, a real get out of jail card. Instead of years in a prison camp, like so many would be enduring, he'd only spent a couple of months and most of that simply waiting for the inevitable bureaucratic snarls to clear up. Finally, he'd been given a pass and an identity card which he'd had to show several times before clearing the prison area along with several more times since then. After all, he still wore a German uniform and carried the rank of general.

He'd managed to write to Magda and gotten notes from her. Again, his exalted status as a friend of the United States, however undeserved, helped him. Magda had told him frankly and candidly of the terrible times they'd endured. She said that the two Jewish refugees were still at the farm waiting for things to settle while the Brit had gone to find his unit. A good man, Varner thought. No, good men. They'd saved his wife and daughter from a terrible death.

He pedaled through a village. Where had all the swastikas gone, he wondered with intended irony. The history of the Third Reich was being whitewashed away. He sighed. A coat of paint would not be enough to erase the horrors. Many high ranking Nazis would pay with their lives for their sins and their arrogance.

The Allies had been wise to let Rommel continue on as a figurehead leader. Although once a dedicated Nazi, Rommel had turned on the war criminals who had nearly destroyed Europe with a vengeance. He was making plans with the Allies for new elections in Germany. The Nazi Party, of course, would be prohibited.

Himmler was dead, but scores of SS leaders and a number of other high ranking Nazis were in custody awaiting trial or were running for their lives. Included in the latter group were Volkmar Detloff's father, who was rumored to be in Switzerland. Volkmar, that fool, was in a hospital. A tank had run over his legs, smashing them. He would live as either a cripple or an amputee.

Von Rundstedt was in prison along with a number of high ranking generals and admirals, and their fate was uncertain.

There were many other uncertainties. He had written to Margarete that no word had come from her first love, the appropriately named Hart. Apparently the base where he'd been stationed had been heavily bombed and casualty reports said he was missing and probably dead. She would have to get over that just as she would have to somehow get over being raped. He wondered if he was strong enough to help her, and Magda, who seemed stronger than all of them.

Rommel was forming a state militia to work with the Americans in keeping order. Varner had been offered a place in it with the rank of general. He would accept it. The alternative was working the Mullers' farm and he was not a farmer. The militia position would keep them all in food and shelter.

The Mullers' farm finally came in view, as did two women and two men, who stood and stared as he pedaled down the road. He smiled at the thought of how he looked. His once proud uniform was in rags and tatters.

The main building had suffered damage and he could see several burned out tanks in the fields, graphic testimony to the fighting that had swept over his family. Magda said they'd all endured by cowering in a shelter built by Uncle Eric.

As before, Margarete shrieked and ran out to him, grabbing him and almost knocking him off his bicycle. Magda followed a few strides later, and he engulfed her and their daughter in his arms.

He looked at them. Their eyes were wide and clear. "Are you all right?"

They nodded and smiled. "Everything is healing," said Magda and they all hugged again.

The two Jews silently took in the tableau. Their plans had been to return to their homes, but anti-Jewish rioting had changed their minds. They would be heading to Palestine. Varner noted the pistols in their belts. Some college professors, he thought. He shook their hands and thanked them. Magda suggested they all go inside for dinner.

Morgan thought of the poem that said something about poppies growing among the rows of crosses in a vast cemetery. He never liked poetry and only dimly remembered that it had been a tribute to the dead of World War I.

There was a bumper crop of white wooden crosses and the occasional Star of David in this field, but no poppies just yet. It had been too soon. Mounds of raw dirt were in front of each cross or star. Thousands of Americans had died in the last epic battle that ended the Third Reich and most of them were buried in this field south of Reinbach.

They had a map of the cemetery and good directions. Colonel Tom Granville had used Ike's name to get all of them access to the field. It had only been three months since the battle and it was a long ways from being ready to receive visitors, but it would likely be a long time, perhaps forever, before they would be able to return.

Hilda found it first. She sobbed and fell to her knees in front of Jeb's grave. Jack wondered just how much of Jeb was actually buried there. He'd heard from Levin that Jeb's tank had been blown to pieces and doubtless too was Jeb Carter.

Hilda's pregnancy was becoming pronounced and she would leave by plane for the United States the next day. She would be staying with Jeb's parents who desperately wanted a grandchild. The child would be born on American soil and, therefore, be a United States citizen.

Jessica and Jack stood back. They held hands, but said nothing. Finally, Jessica took a deep breath. "I will miss him. I have a lot to thank him for. After all, he did find me you."

"He was crazy," Jack said, "but crazy in a good way. So he gets the Medal of Honor, but he won't be around for the honor."

Jeb's heroism in attacking the enemy armor resulted in the posthumous Medal of Honor, which was another reason why Hilda's move to the States was being expedited. After all, she was the widow of a hero.

As for the two of them, their return would be routine. Permission to marry had been granted and a chaplain had performed the service. Jessica and Jack would be going back on one of the ocean liners that had been converted to military use. Ironically, that meant they would be separated for the voyage. There were no accommodations for married couples and Jack would be stuffed in with a large number of officers.

Jack would be discharged since his shoulder injury meant he would be incapable of being a soldier for at least a year, while Jessica had resigned from the Red Cross and simply wanted to go home with Jack.

"Too many," Jack said as he looked over the vast field of death. "Far, far too many."

Sergeant Major Rolfe was buried out there somewhere, as was Feeney. Snyder was still in a hospital but would recover. Levin was also wounded and recovering. He had reiterated his desire to go to Palestine as soon as he was able.

Jessica squeezed Jack's arm. Hilda had stood up. She nodded and smiled wanly. Jessica agreed. "Let's go home."

The following is an excerpt from:

RISING SUN

ROBERT CONROY

Available from Baen Books
December 2012
hardcover

CHAPTER 1

Lieutenant Tim Dane, USNR, couldn't sleep. Going into war for the first time, will do that to a man, he thought. Maybe it would happen every time. Then he hoped there wouldn't be a second time. Jesus, what kind of a mess was he in?

Instead of tossing in his bunk, he gotten up and paced along the flight deck of the aircraft carrier *Enterprise* as she plowed her way through the Pacific swells towards her destiny near Midway Island.

Dane was a very junior member of Admiral Spruance's staff on the carrier, so he was privy to the basic strategy. By this time, of course, so was every one of the two thousand men on the four-year old, twenty-five thousand ton carrier. The *Enterprise* was like a small town in which there were few secrets. Nor was there any need to keep quiet. After all, who could you tell?

The *Enterprise* was accompanied by a second carrier, the *Hornet*. The two carriers were protected by six heavy cruisers, one light cruiser, and nine destroyers. These made up Task Force 16 under the command of Admiral Raymond Spruance. The six heavies were the *Atlanta*, *Minneapolis*, *New Orleans*, *Pensacola*, *Northhampton* and *Vincennes* and constituted a powerful force by themselves. The light cruiser was the *Atlanta*.

Waiting for the arrival of the two carriers was TF 17, now off Midway with a third carrier, the *Yorktown*, and her escorts. These ships constituted almost all that was left of the United States Navy in the Pacific after the catastrophe at Pearl Harbor. One more carrier, the *Saratoga*, was reported to be undergoing repairs, probably in San Diego.

Prior to the attack on Pearl Harbor, many naval officers had stubbornly held onto the dogma that the battleship was the navy's primary weapon, and that the carrier's role was that of reconnaissance rather than battle. The attack on Pearl Harbor, in which eight U.S. battleships were either sunk or damaged by enemy airplanes launched from carriers, had done much to change that perception, but it had not totally gone away.

Part of this sense of nostalgia was because carriers weren't lovely ships. Like all carriers, the *Enterprise* lacked the graceful, rakish silhouette of a cruiser or destroyer, or of the new battleships whose pictures Dane had seen on the wall of the wardroom. The *Enterprise* was frankly a floating block that carried about eighty planes.

Possibly because of a carrier's lack of glamor or tradition, a number of very senior officers still considered the disaster at Pearl Harbor an aberration caused by the incompetence of those in command of the fleet. Guns would sink enemy ships. Always had, always would.

Since Pearl Harbor, the *Enterprise* had undergone modifications to enhance her ability to fight airplanes. A number of 20mm Oerlikon anti-aircraft guns had been added to her arsenal.

TF 16 was on its way to Midway Island to rendezvous with the *Yorktown* in a desperate attempt to stop the

Japanese from attacking and taking Midway and using it as a base for operations against Hawaii. Dane knew that not only would the three carriers and their escorts be outnumbered and outgunned by the Japanese, but they had to evade a picket line of Japanese submarines that highly classified intelligence said was going to be established in front of their approach. The enemy subs could either ruin the ambush by announcing their presence, or attack the carriers and possibly do great damage. The men of the *Enterprise* and *Hornet* were as ready as they could be, although many, like Dane, were half scared to death.

Tim Dane, however, did not feel he was ready at all. Like everyone else, he'd tried his hand at looking through binoculars for enemy subs and seen nothing. Enough, he thought. He decided to once more try to squeeze his frame into the small navy bunk he'd been allotted, and maybe he'd get at least a little sleep. He hoped the fleet and Spruance would be lucky and the enemy subs would be elsewhere. But every moment brought them closer to Midway and the Japanese fleet.

None of the hundreds of pairs of searching eyes could pierce the night and notice the slight feather of water made by the emergence of a periscope less than a mile away. With cruel luck, the Japanese sub had emerged in the middle of TF 16. She was an older boat, a Kaidai class sub and had six torpedo tubes in her bow, loaded and ready to kill, and eleven other torpedoes ready to replace the ones fired. She weighed in at just under three thousand tons, and had a crew of ninety-four officers and men. The ocean-going sub had a cruising range of fourteen thousand knots. This meant she could cruise far away from Japan and stay in position, waiting for her prey.

The Japanese sub and two others had arrived a day earlier than American intelligence anticipated. There had been confusion, perhaps even incompetence, among Japanese commanders regarding when the subs would depart and only these three had left on time. With equally cruel luck, the subs had placed themselves directly in the path of the American carriers who were on their way to a rendezvous at what had been incongruously named Point Luck. This night, however, luck was on the Japanese side.

Lookouts on the *Enterprise* didn't notice the disturbances in the water made by the first of the six torpedoes until they were less than a quarter mile away and approaching at nearly fifty land miles an hour. Screams and alarms were almost useless. Four of the six Type 94 torpedoes fired from the sub hit the carrier. One after another they slammed into her hull and exploded, sending plumes of water and debris high above the flight deck, with much of it landing on the deck. Men were injured and a few swept overboard to their deaths by the sudden assault.

The mighty *Enterprise* shuddered like a large, wounded animal and immediately began to lose speed. Secondary explosions soon followed as fuel and ammo ignited, further damaging the ship and causing large numbers of casualties. Fires raged while valiant sailors braved the flames to contain them.

Dane had been in his skivvies and sitting on the edge of his bunk when the first torpedo slammed into the carrier, hurling him facefirst onto the deck. He lay there for a stunned second and then quickly checked himself out. His lip was split and there was something wrong with the top of his head. It was wet and sticky with blood. He was bruised and shaken, but otherwise he thought he was okay.

Dane's first reaction as he picked himself up was to run and hide, but he quickly calmed himself and tried to gauge what had just happened. And besides, where the hell do you hide on a ship? As a new and minor member of Admiral Spruance's staff, he really didn't have any set place to go in an emergency. He had to do something, he thought as he threw on some clothes. He would be damned if he would run up to the flight deck in his skivvies.

Cramped passageways were filled with men either hastening to their duty stations or fleeing the greasy black smoke that was beginning to clog everything. The smoke was burning eyes and choking throats. Dane grabbed a life jacket and put it on. He would go to the flight deck, then try to climb up to the flag bridge where Spruance would be, which was as close as he could come to having a duty station. He was also horribly conscious of the fact that the carrier had begun listing to port.

Dane had just made it to the flight deck when a series of explosions knocked him down again. This time, the fuel from the planes parked on the stern of the ship was exploding and detonating ammunition, sending more billowing clouds of smoke and debris over the terribly wounded great ship. A wave of searing heat blew over him. He screamed and covered his face with his hands. His hair and clothes began to smoke. He rolled across the deck to where an abandoned fire hose was thrashing like a snake and spewing water, and put out the fires by rolling in puddles.

Scores of men lay prone on the deck, either dead or wounded, while others were being brought up from below. A priest was going from one mangled body to another, administering last rites. To Tim, the carnage was a scene from hell. Dane's hands and clothes were covered with something sticky and saw that it was blood, and that rivulets of the stuff were flowing across the flight deck and over the side.

Sailors with fire hoses tried valiantly to stem the flames, but were in danger of becoming overwhelmed by the size and intensity of the conflagration. Tim saw one man hit by flying debris and fall, leaving a wildly bucking hose understaffed. He grabbed on to help the remaining men who were fighting to keep control of the wild beast.

A sailor glanced at his rank and grinned. "Thanks, sir, it's appreciated."

"Just tell me what to do."

"Hang on!"

Dane anchored the hose while the real firemen played water on the flames. After a few moments, a grimy lieutenant commander replaced him with another sailor. "Nothing personal and thanks anyway, Dane, but you don't know what the hell you're doing."

Dane didn't argue the point. He gratefully handed the hose to a grim-faced seaman and turned to the other officer. His name was Mickey Greene and he'd befriended the bewildered Dane when he'd first come aboard.

"We gonna make it, commander?"

Greene shook his head, "Beats the hell out of me, Tim. We took at least three torpedoes and water's still coming in. We've got the flooded areas pretty well sealed off, but a lot of things are burning, even though we're throwing tons of water on the fires. The bad news is that all that water coupled with the torpedo holes is causing us to list, and that means we're helpless if Jap planes show up because the list prevents us from launching our planes."

"Christ."

"Yeah, and if you haven't noticed, the *Hornet's* also been badly hit."

Stunned by that piece of news, Dane looked out across the ocean and saw that the other carrier was also burning furiously. The cruisers *Atlanta* and *Pensacola* were alongside her and using their hoses to pour water on her, while destroyers frantically searched for the enemy sub. The *New Orleans* and *Minneapolis* were cautiously approaching the *Enterprise*, and water from their hoses began arching over and on to the wounded carrier. Jesus, he thought, most of what remained of the American navy after the massacre at Pearl Harbor was being destroyed before his eyes. Two carriers with just under two hundred planes were probably going to sink along with God only knew how many pilots and crewmen. And maybe Tim Dane would be among them. Well, not if he could help it, he thought angrily.

Making things even worse, the smoke from the burning ships would be a beacon for the Japanese ships and planes that must surely be homing in on the carnage.

Jochi Shigata was the captain of the Japanese submarine whose torpedoes had hit the *Enterprise*. He knew that he and his sub were doomed and relished the fact as the culmination of his destiny. He would die as a warrior. He and his comrades had severely damaged two American carriers and, with a little luck, at least one of them would sink.

He had radioed his location and his successes and had received an acknowledgment. His life could now be measured in minutes as American destroyers were converging on him like sharks to blood. He laughed. "Sharks to blood" was a wonderful phrase considering all the American blood he'd spilled today. With each hit, his crew had shouted *banzai* until they were now hoarse. He could ask for no better companions to die with. Two American carriers were either dead or badly wounded thanks to his efforts and those of the other two subs who had also attacked. Planes from the Japanese carrier force would soon find the wounded carriers and kill the American ships if they hadn't already sunk by the time they arrived. By that time it would be too late for him.

Depth charges exploded nearby and the sub shook violently. Glass on dials broke and small leaks spouted high pressure darts of water. Crewmen tumbled and fell, sometimes unable to stifle the screams and groans caused by their broken bones. There was no way they could escape their fate.

"Surface," Shigata ordered. "I have no wish to die skulking underwater."

Once he'd had doubts about Emperor Hirohito, a man who seemed more interested in marine biology than the ways of the warrior, but the God-Emperor had proven himself. He had taken Japan on the road to victory. "Now we will die for our emperor!"

His ninety-odd men cheered as he said that. There was no greater honor for a Japanese warrior. The sub surged upward, broaching and exploding onto the surface. She slammed back onto the water, raising a huge wave.

Astonished sailors from American destroyers watched incredulously as the sub's deck gun was quickly crewed and opened fire on the surrounding ships. At the same time, the sub launched her fresh load of torpedoes in the general direction of the American ships.

The destroyers returned fire, killing the gunners and sweeping their bodies into the sea. More shells shredded the conning tower and pierced the sub's hull with multiple hits. Moments later, the sub exploded and broke in two as a shell from a destroyer hit a remaining torpedo. The pieces rolled over and sank. There were no survivors. None of the Japanese wished to survive. Therefore, none of the dying Japanese were able to see that one of the indiscriminately fired torpedoes had struck the badly damaged *Enterprise*, killing any chance of saving her.

Once again, Dane found himself prone and stunned on the gore covered flight deck. He lurched to his feet. There was something wrong with his left leg. It hurt like hell and it was difficult to stand. He looked for his friend Greene for guidance, but couldn't find him. Many of the men of the damage control parties who'd been trying to douse the flames were also strewn about. Unmanned hoses whipped and snapped, sometimes hitting and injuring sailors who were trying to grab them. A lot of sailors lying on the deck weren't moving, and some of the bodies were smoldering. He assumed one of the bodies was Greene's and others were the sailors he'd been working with just a moment before. He felt sick as he realized the flames were going to win.

Another violent shudder and the ship listed farther to port. We're going over, Dane thought. What do I do now? Men were hollering, "Abandon ship!" But was this an order or were the sailors panicking? Hell, he was panicking. Someone yelled that Captain Murray was dead and that it was every man for himself.

An older man with blood streaming down his face grabbed Tim's arm in a strong grip. "Help me," he said.

Dane was shocked. It was Admiral Spruance. He grabbed the admiral's arm to steady him. Spruance's eyes were glazed and he stared intently at Dane. "I know you," he said with a slurred voice. "You're on my staff."

Still another shudder rumbled from an explosion below the deck, and Dane had to hold up the admiral who was quite likely concussed. "Admiral, I think we've got to get out of here."

Spruance mumbled something, but didn't protest as Dane took charge and guided him. The list was so pronounced that people and planes were tumbling off the flight deck like so many toys, falling into the ocean that was, while still quite a drop, much closer than it had been.

"Hang on," Dane said as he half pushed Spruance off the deck and into the sea, hoping that they wouldn't land on anything or that nothing would fall on top of them.

Dane had been holding the admiral's arm, but the impact drove him underwater and separated them for a moment. He came up spluttering and choking from spilled oil, but only a few feet away from the now even more thoroughly shaken and confused Spruance. Oil was burning on the water and they had to get away before they were burned alive. Dane's leg hurt and the salt water stung the cuts and burns in his scalp, face, and hands.

Dane grabbed the admiral. He started to look around for a life-raft or even some debris. He flailed his arms frantically until he realized his life jacket would not let him sink, at least not for a while. Other swimmers were doing the same thing, as the *Enterprise*, now almost on her side, slowly and mindlessly plowed on, propelled by the energy produced from her dying engines, and escorted by the cruisers who were still pouring water on the fires. He was horribly aware that there were very few men swimming in the water, although a number floated lifelessly. He reminded himself that the carrier had a crew of more than two thousand. Where were they?

An hour later, the two men lay awkwardly and alone on a damaged liferaft that was half filled with water. Dane was afraid that the raft would disintegrate, leaving them with nothing but their life jackets. Getting on it had proven extremely difficult. Dane's leg wasn't responding and he wondered if it was broken, and the shocked and stunned admiral was little help. Still, they somehow managed.

Far in the distance, the *Enterprise* lay on her side, while the *Hornet* burned furiously and began to settle by the bow. American cruisers and destroyers raced around, plucking sailors from the water. As yet, they hadn't found Dane and his high-ranking companion even though he'd waved his arms in a fruitless attempt to get attention.

A shrieking sound and a plane flew low overhead, bullets spitting from its guns. It was a Japanese Zero and a host of other enemy fighters and bombers followed. The Japanese carriers had found them.

Bombs exploded on and about the helpless and ruined carrier hulks, while still more planes attacked the escorting destroyers and cruisers. It was a massacre. Some enemy pilots amused themselves by strafing sailors in the water. Bullets kicked up spray a few feet from Dane and Spruance, but none hit them.

"Do you have a gun?" Spruance's eyes were clearing, but his voice was still a little slurred.

"No sir."

Spruance shook his head in an attempt to focus his thoughts. "Of course not. Carrying a heavy sidearm into the ocean is a dumb idea. Forget I asked. However, do you have a weapon of any kind?"

"A pocket knife," Dane answered, wondering just what the hell Spruance had in mind.

"Don't lose it. If it becomes necessary, I want you to kill me with it."

"What?"

"You heard me and that's an order. If it looks like we're going to be taken prisoner, you must kill me. If it's a small knife, you'll have to slice my throat. I'll resist instinctively, but you are doubtless stronger and must prevail. I know too many things that would endanger our country's security. Whatever happens, you must kill me. Do you acknowledge that order?"

Dane gulped. This couldn't be happening. Was Spruance even sane or had the blow to his head made him crazy? "I understand and I will obey, but tell me sir, did you ever read *Ben Hur* or see the movie with Bushman and Navarro?"

"I've done both, lieutenant, but what the devil does that have to do with our predicament?" Spruance asked and then understood. "Of course, there was a scene where Ben Hur and the Roman admiral were adrift in the sea, and the admiral wanted to die because he was shamed by what he wrongfully believed was a defeat. Nice thought, Dane, but I am not suicidal because I'm ashamed of a defeat. No, I want to live to get another crack at them; I simply know too much to be taken prisoner. They would torture me until I told them everything I know and that would be terrible for the United States."

Spruance looked away. He didn't want the young lieutenant to see the anguish in his eyes. He was fifty-six years old and the Midway battle was his first major command, and he'd botched it horribly. His two carriers were destroyed and only God knew how many other ships damaged or sunk and, Jesus, how many young men were dead or wounded? Surely the butcher's bill would eclipse that of the attack on Pearl Harbor. On a purely personal and selfish note, he wondered if he would ever get another command even if he did survive.

He shook his head. He had to think clearly. A new command was the least of his worries. He could not be captured. He did not want to die, but he could not live as a prisoner of the Japanese. He understood full well just how brutal interrogations could ultimately break anyone. He had no illusions regarding his strength to resist torture. Sooner or later and after untold agonies, he would break.

Aside from the sound of the waves slapping against their raft, there was silence. The Japanese planes were gone. A couple of American destroyers and the light cruiser *Atlanta* were burning furiously on the horizon. Worse, all the surviving ships were moving farther away. Dane and Spruance were truly alone in the vast Pacific. There was no drinking water in their damaged raft and their enemy would now be thirst, which Dane was feeling already, thanks to the salt water he'd swallowed. Unless the Japanese fleet arrived and plucked them from the sea they were doomed to die an agonizing death from thirst.

❖   ❖   ❖

Dane understood what Spruance had said and realized that the admiral was both sane and correct. Word of Japanese atrocities towards prisoners was spreading. He didn't want to be taken alive either, but could he kill himself after killing Spruance? He doubted it. Not only did he consider suicide morally wrong, but he simply wanted to live. Could it get any worse, Dane wondered?

Spruance grabbed Tim's arm. "Dane, is that a periscope or am I losing what's left of my mind?"

Dane turned in the direction the admiral was staring. A submarine's periscope peered at them from a distance of maybe a hundred yards. It looked like a one-eyed sea monster, which, Dane decided, was exactly what it was, but whose? He pulled the pocket knife from his pant's pocket and opened it. Spruance looked at it sadly and nodded.

There was a rush of water and the submarine surfaced.

"I can't see too well, lieutenant. Whose is it, ours or theirs?"

Dane rubbed his eyes to clear his vision. Damned salt water made it difficult to see. He squinted and caught the name. She was the *Nautilus*. He smiled. "Ours."

—end excerpt—

from *Rising Sun*
available in hardcover,
December 2012, from Baen Books